WATERS OF THE SANJAN

Authentic historical novel of the Masai

by

DAVID READ

Waters of the Sanjan

First published 1982 by
David William Lister Read
P.O. Box 423, Usa River, Tanzania, East Africa
info@david-read.com
www.david-read.com

Revised Edition 2011

ISBN 10: 1466433965
ISBN 13: 9781466433960

Cover design by Birgit Hendry www.wildsightsafrica.com
Drawings and map by Wayne and Birgit Hendry

Printed by Executive Printers, Nairobi

Titles by the same author:
Barefoot Over the Serengeti
Beating About the Bush
Another Load of Bull
Die Wasser des Sanjan (the German translation of Waters of the Sanjan)

For more information visit
www.david-read.com

This 2011 version of Waters of the Sanjan is dedicated to
Kaiti Lemunga

Acknowledgements

The author is grateful to all those who have so kindly helped to prepare the new version of Waters of the Sanjan: Annabel Ross, Birgit Hendry, Wayne Hendry, Sir Robin Ross, Petra Meyr, Gerti Meyr, Sonja Bass

For the original version of this book, the author remains grateful to Leslie and Bobbie Hammond, Sean Kays, Dr Hugh Norris, John and Jane Officer, Colin and Neil O'Brien, Moijo Olekeiwa and the late George and Sally Prentice. Their interest and help in preparing this book is very much appreciated. Grateful thanks are due also to Vincent Ole Ntekerei Memusi for his foreword, to Caroline Woodall, Davina Dobie, Francesca Pelizzoli and Sue Stollberg for the drawings, to Pat Stagg for the original cover painting and to Dame Daphne Sheldrick for her constructive criticism.
Special thanks go to Pamela Chapman who was responsible for doing most of the typing and editing of the original version of this book.

Author's Note

This book is not claimed to be a history of the Masai tribe for the period in question, for the simple reason that no research, as such, has gone into this book; the Masai people having no way of recording their history other than by word of mouth being passed down from one generation to another. Each clan claimed for itself the more attractive attributes, accrediting those less desirable to the other clans. Although every incident has been confirmed on many different occasions, other stories with a slightly different slant, or the same version, but associated with different people, were also common, but less so.
The customs and manner of speech in the novel are those of the Masai people. All the events and characters were genuine. The story is as it was related to me whilst living among the Masai in my early teens, as described in my book Barefoot Over the Serengeti.

David Read

Biography

David Read was born in Kenya in 1922, and spent his formative years living amongst the Masai people. From the age of seven Masai was David's first language, and he ran wild with the tribes-people, learning and absorbing their culture, customs, ceremonies and ethos.

This idyllic life was interrupted by the need for a more formal period of education in Tanganyika, where he also qualified and worked as a metallurgist. His work was cut short by the Second World War, during which he served with a number of East African units, and had the privilege of commanding the Uganda contingent at the Victory Parade in London in 1945.

After the War he spent six years working for the Tanganyika Veterinary Department, which gave him the opportunity to renew his early associations with the Masai people. He owned a farm on the slopes of Kilimanjaro, but with the gaining of independence by the East African countries, life became more tenuous and difficult for him. Finally in 1979 he returned to Kenya as an Agricultural Consultant.

David has a unique quiver of qualifications: farmer, cattle dealer, hunter, aviator, fisherman and boat builder. His first love remains the Masai people, with whom he remains closely involved.

www.david-read.com

Foreword

The author of Waters of the Sanjan is surely a man whose life has been as unique as that of any storybook character. He and I have had only one thing in common and that is that we both grew up in the heart of Masailand, in a place known as Loliondo, now in present day Tanzania. But even in this one thing, there is a difference. He did so in the thirties and I in the sixties; he is white and I chocolate.

There are few who can remember what happened ten years ago, let alone fifty, and not only remember, but do so with such lucid clarity as though the events took place yesterday. David Read's ability to marshal such details with unerring accuracy testifies to his deep knowledge, understanding and love of my people, or perhaps he would like me to say "our people", for at heart he is as much as a Masai as I. He has told me that that period of his life stands out in his memory as the most enjoyable. To have been able to spend his boyhood years wandering free and wild, untrammelled by the restrictions of his own society and their civilisation, has left a deep and abiding impression on him and has influenced him more than anything else in life. It was indeed a unique experience and a privilege to be accepted so completely within a community who adopted him as though he were one of their own, oblivious to the difference in the colour of his skin.

Waters of the Sanjan is fiction based on fact, woven around the life of a known warrior who lived at the turn of the century. In fact, it is an historical novel and the events portrayed were not unusual in the life of a warrior of those times. The customs and traditions are accurate; the places where events took place are real places and to date still go by the same names. Waters of the Sanjan translated literally, Inkariak-oo-Sanjan, means "Waters of the Sweethearts", and in fact is a place that lies to the north of that famous treeless undulating savannah known the world over as The Serengeti, and to the Masai as Sirinket. Isirinket are the people that lived in the now unique Serengeti National Park in Tanzania.

Culturally, the Masai today are a very homogeneous group of people. They are conservative and proud and a wonderful community of people whose traditions are firm and whose 'legal' system is both fair and just. But the Masai traditionally are also a turbulent people. Violence is the deterrent to any would-be adversary both within their own society and without, but more ruthlessly applied to other tribes. Something of an enigma is the rarity of now common violent crimes such as murder or suicide found in other communities. Within the Masai the incidence of these violent crimes is very low, even within such a violent tribe, and this is because the Masai practice rigid mind control.

Waters of the Sanjan is an accurate and admirable historic record of my people, recording their way of life at another point in time, yet not so very long ago. And because not many truly authentic books have been written about us, it is, I think, a valuable record of a proud people that will enlighten the reader and allow him to glimpse another world. He may, perhaps, shudder at the horror of some of the more violent sections, but he will emerge the wiser for knowing and understanding a little of what our forefathers had to cope with, and what they suffered, not only at the hands of encroaching colonialism, but at the hand of nature; climatic disaster; diseases of man and beast and inter/intra tribal wars that were the norm and claimed with monotonous regularity the lives of many.

In conclusion, what do I think about the book and its author? Frankly, I am impressed by both: in the case of the book by its authenticity, and in the case of the author by his tremendous zest for life.

David's "Dangoya", in Masai, is "Ntankuya" and Ntankuya was a living Masai Chief in Loliondo. Whether David's Dangoya and Chief Ole Ntankuya are one and the same person, I do not know, but in any case, I would end by urging the reader to "Read on".

Ole Nterekei Memusi
(At the time of writing, Ole Nterekei Memusi was the headmaster of the Ngurumens School in Tanzania)

Contents

Map

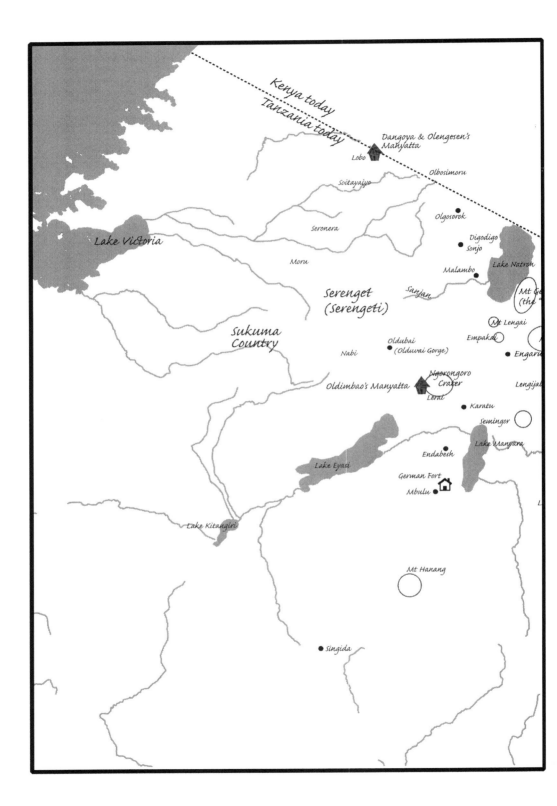

Kenya today
Tanzania today

Dangoya & Olengesen's
Manyatta

Lobo

Olbosimoru

Soitayaiyo

Olgosorok

Seronera

Digodigo
Sonjo

Lake Victoria

Moru

Malambo

Lake Natron

Serenget
(Serengeti)

Sanjan

Mt Ge
(the

Mt Lengai

Sukuma
Country

Empakai

Nabi

Oldubai
(Olduvai Gorge)

Engaru

Ngorongoro
Crater

Lengijal

Oldimbao's Manyatta

Lerai

Karatu

Semingor

Lake Manyara

Lake Eyasi

Endabesh

German Fort

Mbulu

Lake Kitangiri

Mt Hanang

Singida

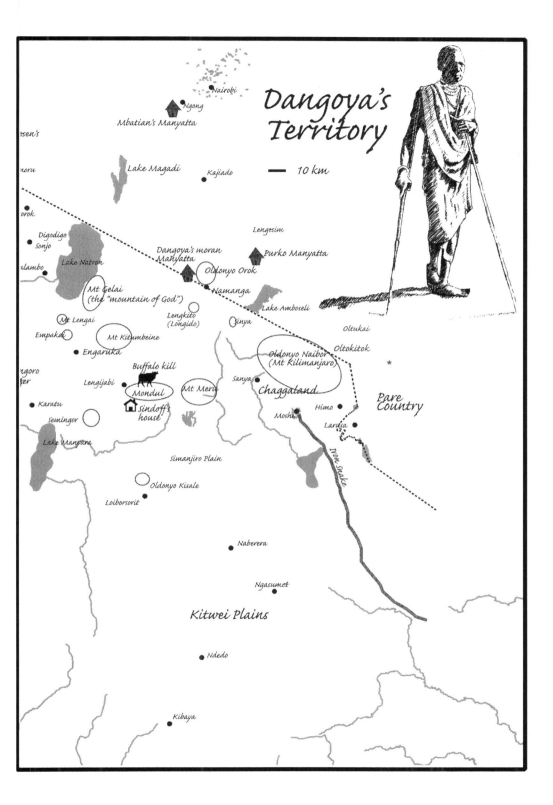

Dangoya's Territory

— 10 km

Nairobi
Ngong
Mbatian's Manyatta

~sen's

~noru

Lake Magadi   Kajiado

~orok

Digodigo
Sonjo   Lengesim

~zlambo   Lake Natron   Dangoya's moran   Purko Manyatta
                                     Manyatta
                                          Oldonyo Orok
Mt Gelai
(the "mountain of God")   Namanga

Mt Lengai   Lengkito   Sinya   Lake Amboseli
                   (Longido)
Empakai   Oltukai
          Mt Kitumbeine   Oltokitok
     Engaruka
                                        Oldonyo Naibor
~goro   Buffalo kill   (Mt Kilimanjaro)
~fer   Lengijabi   *
                   Mondul   Mt Meru   Sanya   Pare
     Karatu   Chaggaland   Country
                   Sindoff's
Semingor   house   Himo
                                        Moshi
Lake Manyara   Larusa

          Simanjiro Plain

          Oldonyo Kisale
     Loiborsorit

                         Naberera

                    Ngasumet

          Kitwei Plains

               Ndedo

          Kibaya

Glossary of Masai and other words

Abaya	a form of address used between male elders
Aish	expression of disapproval
Asanja	lover of the highest grade
Ashe	thank you
Bageteng	of my ox
Bagishu	of my cattle
Calabash	hollowed out gourd
Ebaye	yes
Eego	female reply to greeting
Gage engu	phew! it stinks
Gona moran mabe	you warriors let us go
Kiloriti	a stimulant bark which is added to soups
Kitoloswa	a stimulant bush which is added to soups
Knobkerrie	ball headed club (Afrikaans)
Laibon	witch doctor
Laigwanan	chief
Lameyu	disease or famine
Layoni	an uncircumcised boy
Lianas	thick tree-hanging vines
Lodwa	rinderpest
Lorien	wild olive tree
Magadi	soda / soda lake
Manyatta	village (enclosure containing both livestock and dwellings)
Mbarnoti	a newly circumcised warrior
Moran	a warrior
Nagaibara	turn white (a curse)
Naibor	white
Nairobi	cold
Na moruo	you elders (usually used by elders to elders)
Nanyuki	red
Narobong genteng ino	go screw your ox
Narabong gotonye	screw your mother / mother fucking
Ndaragwa	cedar tree
Ndawo	heifer

Ndelelia	part of foreskin not removed during circumcision
Ndereges	testicles
Ndito	girl (uncircumcised female)
Nena age	that is all
Ngai	God or rain
Ngalem ngiji	Masai broadsword
Ngare	water
Ngasa	shake hands
Ngelan	short cloak
Ngibot	milk drinking ceremony between lovers
Ngipataa	ceremony prior to male circumcision
Ngitati	cloak or clothing
Ngongu nabo	one eye
Njabo	penis
Oldigana	East Coast Fever
Oldonyo	the mountain
Oljore lai	my friend
Olkorom	buttocks
Olmeg	derogatory term for anyone not a Masai
Olmerega	Syphilis
Olpiron	the fire stick/also an age group relationship
Olpul	a meat feast
Orgesher	ceremony at which senior morans become elders
Rinderpest	cattle disease
Segenge	wire
Seki	a sacred bush
Sere (na moruo)	goodbye (you elders)
Serenget	Serengeti (famous national park today)
Siangiki	a young circumcised woman of breeding age
Silalei	chewing gum tree
Tagwenya	a greeting to a woman
Torgo	drink
Usho	a strong expression of disapproval

(There are no official plurals in Masai language so the author has used the English way to show a plural)

Chapter 1

The Girl

The dust whirled around the legs of the cattle and rose in thick clouds, suspended in the still evening air, the last rays of the sun illuminating the moving herds in pale yellow light, deepening the backdrop of mountain forest against which they passed. In the *manyatta* ahead, the penned calves caught the sounds of the nearing cattle, the shouts of the herders and the faint echo of wooden cowbells, and cried out in their eagerness to suckle, the cows answering and quickening their pace, udders full and straining after the day's good grazing. Outside the *manyatta* the elders waited, scanning their herds carefully as they came towards the high thorn enclosure, never counting the animals yet knowing and remembering each one as a father would know his children, and as the last slow old cows were driven in and the five gates were closed for the night.

A far-off yodelling announced the approach of the young warriors returning from their day's adventures, calling and singing to warn the women they were coming and for the little wicker gate to be left open. They called too to frighten off predators and for the sheer joy of making a noise.

The young girl Singira sat on her haunches and fiddled with the fire, hearing the distant cries of the *morans* but not the closer commands of her mother. The women, crouched among the cattle, sang to their cows to let down their milk, hungry wet calf muzzles nudging away the fingers for their share.

'Bring the guest *calabashes*!' Singira's mother called again, sharply.

The girl rose to her feet to run into her mother's hut, picking up a pair of *calabashes* and taking them to her where she squatted beside the cow.

'Have the visitors come?' Singira asked.

'You will have to open your eyes and wake up my girl! You will never have lovers among the *morans* like other *nditos* unless you stop dreaming and playing with young boys who are uncircumcised and dirty. Look at you! Already your breasts are swelling and soon your blood will flow, yet other girls your age have ten or more *morans* seeking their favours while you waste yours on *layonis*.' Singira's mother stood up with a full gourd of milk and nodded to the girl who held the guest *calabashes* ready to be filled. 'Hold them steady while I pour.'

The girl did as she was told, hoping her mother had forgotten her nagging, but she had not quite finished.

'It comes from your bad breeding!' and with that last stricture the woman walked ahead to her hut. In truth she was more fond of her adopted daughter than of her own, loving Singira since the day, as a small child not four rainy seasons old, she had been brought home as a prize captured in a raid on the Sukuma tribe.

Singira's father by adoption was of no great standing in the clan and she was therefore at a disadvantage when competing with the other girls and very conscious of her background. Inclined to shyness, but obedient and hard-working, she was growing into a beautiful girl although she had not as yet attracted the attention of anyone of importance, only the young uncircumcised boys paying her court away from the eyes of the elders.

Fast approaching puberty, Singira had lost her virginity and made love with a number of *layonis*, but she had not been noticed by any of the *morans* so it was a turning point in her life when that night one of the many visitors to her mother's house sent a message urging her to invite him to drink milk with her. He was a young *moran* from a neighbouring *manyatta*, tall and handsome, and Singira became very excited. As was the custom after drinking milk together, they spent the night making love and he became her *asanja*, lover of the first grade.

Singira had loved with such wild gratitude and passion that word soon spread, the young *moran* extolling her beauty and skill to all who would listen, and she was soon in great demand with *morans* competing for her favours, so much so that she became the most popular *ndito* in the nearby *moran manyatta*.

When one of her lovers, a young man called Lerionga, discovered she was not betrothed he asked her father to arrange a match with her family. This was done and the usual slaughter of an ox took place with the large quantities of honey beer being drunk by the elders in celebration, but Singira, although now betrothed, continued to see her lovers as and when she pleased.

One of her *asanjas* asked her to accompany him to the new warrior *manyatta* being built near Olbosimoru. It was quite unusual for girls to go to the *manyattas* with their favourite *morans*, sometimes alone but often with older women, perhaps aunts or grandmothers, who acted not as chaperones but rather as teachers, instructing the girls in house-building and looking after the *morans*, seeing they did not spend all their time making love and playing, although love-making and the arts involved were encouraged.

For nearly two years Singira enjoyed the happiest and most satisfying time of her life, blighted only when she found herself to be pregnant. She reported this fact to her mother who made arrangements for her immediate circumcision and marriage to her betrothed.

Lerionga's father tried extremely hard to reduce the bride price in view of Singira's pregnancy, but as her condition also proved her fertility beyond doubt her foster father was able to retain the agreed fee. With many tears shed for her lost happy life at the *moran manyatta* she was circumcised, married and carried off to live in her mother-in-law's house at a *manyatta* near Olgosorok. It was there while building her own hut under her mother-in-law's direction that she went into labour. Lerionga, being a warrior and away most of the time, was sent for at once as only he could give authority for his animals to be slaughtered for the celebration of the birth.

For three days Singira suffered the pain of protracted labour, calling often in her agony for her mother until at last a tiny crumpled boy was born, pathetic in his pre-maturity, too weak to cry. Going to the door of the hut the midwife called to a boy standing nearby to bring a steer which he quickly caught from amongst the milling mob about to go out grazing and pierced the jugular vein and took the blood to the hut for the exhausted mother to drink, his every action announcing to the people of the *manyatta* the birth of a son.

Although the women were ready to sing their songs of welcome to this newborn child of the Loitayo clan, the celebrations did not start immediately as it seemed that Singira and the baby would not live. Lerionga arrived to inspect his son, certainly not of his loins but which was nevertheless proudly accepted by him, then gave orders for a fat sheep to be killed for Singira and an ox for the people of the *manyatta* to feast on, an extravagance he could ill afford but expected of him. On the second day after the birth Singira began to recover, but the baby was weak and it was many days before the little infant showed signs of survival. He was named Dangoya.

Singira was widowed within four months of Dangoya's birth, her husband having returned to his warrior group and the tribal wars, and she according to custom, became the senior wife of Lerionga's young brother who at the time was still a child. Her father-in-law died shortly afterwards and her position in the *manyatta* became doubly tenuous as added to her lack of status was the constant battle she fought to protect her weakling son with no adult male in the family to give her assistance. When the children pestered him she rushed to his defence, sometimes becoming involved in actual fights with the other women when they made scathing remarks about him. It was a hard time for her, but her reward was in Dangoya's growing strength and bright intelligence. Some of the animosity aimed at her at this period may also have been due to jealousy on the part of the women because Singira was beautiful and found passionate respite from the abuse and scratchings of the day in the arms of her many lovers. She was a favourite with the men of the *manyatta* and their frequent visitors, and had a reputation for being active and knowledgeable in her lovemaking.

One day when Singira had had a particularly nasty skirmish with two women and had retired to her hut in angry tears, a former lover arrived at the *manyatta* and enquired after her. On seeing no spears outside her house he stuck his firmly in the ground beside the door and bending down entered the low-roofed hut. Dark and smoky, it was a few minutes before his eyes became accustomed to the dim light from the small wood fire and saw Singira sitting on the floor, her shaved head bent. She had recently wound wire stockings on her legs from her ankles to above the knees, a popular fashion amongst newly married women, and these with the bead necklaces resting on her breasts made the man catch his breath. She looked up in surprise.

'Lemomo! How good it is for you to be here!'

'I too am happy to be in your house,' he replied. 'I bring you news of your father and mother from your home *manyatta*. They miss you, and your mother weeps for not seeing you.'

Singira listened eagerly as he related in detail the news of her family and when all her questions had been answered he said, 'My spear is at your door and I have claimed your hospitality.' He waited, knowing this gave her the opportunity of refusing him if she wishes, but to his pleasure she replied, 'That is good,' and he knew he would be welcome in her bed.

In the dim hut the flickering fire gave off a scent of burning mutton fat and cow dung, and from the pen in the corner came the animal reek of calves' stale urine, to Lemomo's nostrils after days of sleeping in the open, the most welcoming of intimate smells.

'I have neglected you, my guest! May I give you fresh or sour milk?'

'Nothing,' he answered, 'I am alone and cannot drink milk without *moran* company.' He put out his hand to touch her, bending his head to the warmth of her breasts.

'How round and strong they have become since last I felt them. You must have mothered many warrior sons.'

'Only one very small boy,' she laughed. 'But he is growing fast. Already he sleeps in the children's house.'

Lemomo's fingers moved above the wires on her leg, touching her thigh, feeling the softness of her skin, his breath quickening.

'Do you like my new *segenge* stockings?' she whispered, and taking him by the hand led him to her bed. 'Come. The whole *manyatta* will hear me rattle my wires when you make love to me and those envious women will know that I am the best of all lovers!'

Later while Lemomo slept, Singira lay thinking of her home and family, tears of self-pity welling into her eyes as she thought of how good her life would be if she could take Dangoya back to her *manyatta*. Sitting up suddenly she shook Lemomo awake.

'You must go to my father and tell him to come and fetch me. This very day you must go for I cannot live here any longer!'

'You do not know what you say!' Lemomo looked at her in shock. 'Your place is here. Never could I carry such a message to your father.'

'Please, please help,' she sobbed. 'You do not understand my misery and what my child suffers with no man to teach and protect him. The husband they have given me is no more than a child himself.'

'I shall listen no more to you,' Lemomo said firmly. 'You must forget your bad thoughts and do the best you can for your son.'

All night Singira begged and entreated Lemomo to help her, but he remained deaf to her pleas. His sympathies were with her whole-heartedly, but he would not dare interfere and tired to comfort her with hopes of good years ahead when Dangoya was older and able to fend for himself.

Singira bore a healthy girl nine months after Lemomo's visit and although the father could have been one of half a dozen lovers, she hoped and was convinced in her own mind that the baby was his. Materially her position in the *manyatta* improved over the next few years with the herd of cattle and sheep left to Dangoya by her husband, thriving and increasing in size, but there remained the problem of Dangoya himself. The boy, small for his age, had often to call for help from elder *layonis* when ordered to carry out a difficult task and a great deal of bullying went on, particularly by Pushati, son of the head of the *manyatta*. If Singira was in earshot she would run to Dangoya's side and the women of the *manyatta* would reprimand her severely for interfering in the upbringing of the boy as this was considered man's work. It seemed to Singira that matters could only get worse as Dangoya grew to adolescence and once again her thoughts turned to her family. She weighed her present situation with care, for she realised the move she contemplated was a serious one with possible adverse consequences.

Singira was unfortunate in her choice of ally, yet the man behaved according to the tribal code. When asked to carry a message to her father to come and fetch her, he immediately reported her to the *laigwanan*, Pushati's father, who accused her of fomenting trouble between the clans and ordered her to be taken to the centre of the *manyatta*, stripped and beaten. With back raw and seeping blood, Singira made no sound and when the whipping was over walked as best she could to her house.

That night Dangoya went to his mother's hut and seeing she had no visitors called to her for permission to enter. Singira greeted him, surprised that he should be visiting her at that time of night.

'Have you come to see your baby sister?' she asked him, sitting very still on her bed, unable to lie on her back.

'I went to my grandmother's house to fetch medicine for you. If you turn over I shall put it on your back for you.'

Looking at her son, Singira almost wept. He was so small, so young, yet there was about him a firmness and resolve lacking in most children his age. Lying flat on her stomach while Dangoya smeared the mixture of herbs and mutton fat over her wounds, his small fingers soft and deft, she said, 'How you are growing my son. Soon you will not be able to stand upright in my house.'

He was silent for a moment then said, 'I saw what they did to you today and heard why they beat you. When I am big and become a *moran* the family of Pushati had better take care, and when I am a *laigwanan* I shall have my own *manyatta* and no will one will hurt you again.'

Singira could not help smiling at his serious words. 'And when you are a *laigwanan*, your old mother shall sit in the sun all day, with slave girls to fetch and carry for her!'

When he was about nine years old Dangoya was taken off herding the calves and sent with Pushati and one of the girls to look after the sheep. It was the dry season and good grazing near the *manyatta* was no longer available which meant having to take the flock far afield in search of grass, so the youngsters were out from early morning until dusk.

Dangoya had grown taller and stronger and Pushati found it expedient to bully him less, yet continually asked Dangoya to do him favours. He was a year or so older and it suited him to have a more amenable Dangoya to help with the sheep. He would ask Dangoya for instance to round up the flock while he tried unsuccessfully to make love to the girl, it being every boy's ambition to emulate the bigger *layonis* and Pushati was no exception. Dangoya knew quite well what was going on but realised his time would come.

One day Pushati called Dangoya to come and sit with him in the shade of an early flowering acacia, telling the girl to look after the sheep as they wished to talk man's talk together. The girl did not like being sent away but did as she was told, and when she was out of sight Pushati produced two strands of wildebeest tail hair which he laid on the ground. Taking his penis in one hand he pulled back the foreskin and Dangoya realised at once that Pushati expected his help in cutting the cord, a small operation performed among the boys long before the time of circumcision and if carried out successfully without showing pain the boys gained credit.

The wildebeest hair, cut at an angle and needle sharp, was used to pierce the cord then tied in a knot. However, each time Dangoya tried to do this Pushati pulled away and after the fifth attempt Dangoya said, 'Why do you make such a fuss about a little pain? Look!' and he quickly stuck the hair through his own cord and tied it. In vain he encouraged Pushati to let him try again, but to no avail. The girl in the meantime had crept back and heard the two boys, so it was not long before all the *layonis* in the *manyatta* knew of Pushati's failure.

A week later when Dangoya's slight wound had healed one of the older *layonis* called together the young boys and asked them to show him their genitals. Of the six boys present only Dangoya's cord was cut and the *layoni* ordered the others to hold Pushati down and pull back his foreskin. He cut the cord with a knife and warned the boys that that was the treatment given to cowards and that the same would happen to them unless they behaved with courage like Dangoya. This was a considerable compliment for Dangoya and from that day he began to be noticed and admired, not only by the *layonis* but also by the *morans* and elders of the *manyatta*. Singira was understandably filled with pride for her son and in small subtle ways her life in the community became easier.

The small girl who helped with the sheep refused one day to let Pushati try to pierce her maidenhead and offered herself to Dangoya instead. He was no more successful than Pushati had been, but the favour was appreciated for the recognition it showed him and he felt extremely pleased with himself, going about his chores with a new confidence.

Over the dry plains of Masailand the heat was almost visible and the people looked anxiously towards the mountains for the clouds which would bring the rain. Towards the end of October large thunderheads began to form and with the first rains the sheep moved off with a party of *morans* and older boys to follow the new green grass which sprang from the burnt earth. Dangoya yearned to be with the flocks, but he had to remain and help his mother with the migration to the wet-season's grazing beyond the Waso River near Lobo.

Singira had no adult male to assist her with the move. She now had two small daughters to care for and without Dangoya would have found it difficult to make the necessary preparations. The donkeys were caught and loaded, a strenuous task as each donkey carried two wicker frames which had to be strapped on with their wooden supports and tied down, one on each side. Loading the skins used for bedding was easy as they were soft, but the hides used as partitions in the hut were large, stiff and unwieldy. Often rained on when serving as temporary shelters, the hides dried in the sun into awkward shapes, and Dangoya found his arms neither long nor strong enough to get them rolled or folded with ease. He and Singira packed the hides first and tethered the three little donkeys to a post while they turned their attention to the remainder of their possessions. The earthenware cooking pots, breakable and heavy, were placed in saddle bags of skin and tied over the backs of a further two donkeys. Then the *calabashes*, a few empty but most full, had to be carefully placed in the wicker frames so they would not spill. All that morning's milk was in *calabashes* and also sour milk, and milk mixed with blood, with water too for the journey.

Singira had begun her day very early with the usual milking so that the herds of cattle could be started on their way to the new *manyatta*, and by midday she was exhausted. Her wire stockings made moving awkward and uncomfortable in the humid heat after the heavy rain of the night before, and added to this were the flies in their millions, attracted by the meat and still wet hide of cow which died a few days before. The other women had loaded their possessions and were ready to start when one of Singira's donkeys became skittish and tossed off its load. Dangoya ran to catch it and he and Singira spent a long time reloading which they both found more than frustrating. Meanwhile, the others had moved off and it was well past noon before they caught them up, urging the donkeys along at a fast trot. Dangoya had put his little sister Naidu on one of the donkeys and the baby was on Singira's hip, but even with that small weight he could see that his mother was not faring well.

As the afternoon wore on, so the weather deteriorated with a darkening sky and vivid flashes of lightning. With another three miles still to go before they reached the place for the first night's stop, the rain began to fall in almost a solid sheet. In a few moments the ground was a muddy, slippery morass and even the sure-footed donkeys had difficulty picking their way along, their heads hung low and ears flicking. At first the blessed cool and relief from the heat had raised everyone's spirit, but now their bowed figures, struggling against the falling rain and with feet slipping at every step, were metaphors of dejection. Singira moved in a dream of pain. The wire round her legs became shackles of agony and it was all she could do not to let Dangoya see her distress as her tears mingled with the rain on her face and went unnoticed.

Just before dark two *morans* came back to escort them to the temporary camp and the last mile was accomplished in better time. Even so, night was upon them when they arrived to the abuse of the elders, as all the cows were waiting to be milked and the calves crying and struggling to reach their mothers. One more job to be done, thought Singira, and then I can rest; and leaving Dangoya to see to the donkeys she took her *calabashes* and threaded her way amongst the cattle, singing for the first of her cows to come to be milked.

When all was quiet and the cattle settled for the night in a makeshift enclosure of thorn brush, Singira moved among the dark shapes sitting in groups around little fires and found Dangoya comforting the children before a cheerful blaze. She flopped down on the wet ground, pain and exhaustion overwhelming her at last, and when Dangoya persuaded her to try to eat a little she could not, asking only that he feed the children. She lay still for a long time, and then quietly asked Dangoya to remove the wire from her left leg.

It was slow work as the wire had to unwound from halfway up her thigh, and as the skin was exposed Dangoya saw the cause of Singira's pain. A large septic ulcer, probably several weeks in the making, had covered most of the front of her leg. Dangoya knew he would have trouble persuading one of the women to come and treat the wound at that time of night. He had often seen the method used for sores of this type so he went immediately among the cattle with an empty *calabash* and luckily caught an animal urinating. He poured the warm, strong-smelling urine over

Singira's leg, washing away the dirt and pus. Then rummaging amongst the saddle bags he found a small skin containing some mutton fat and this he smeared generously over the wound, believing implicitly – like all Masai – that there was nothing mutton fat could not cure, either by ingestion or topical application.

Singira was badly frightened by the ulcer on her leg and even though she felt very much better the next morning, she realised how close to danger she had come. She decided therefore to remove the other stocking too, but before doing so she had to request permission from her mother-in-law. The older woman, immured in the traditions of tribal life, at first forbade it, but when Singira threatened to abort the infant she was carrying she relented and herself unwound the wire from Singira's right leg. Singira recovered her health but never again wore stockings, and her strong legs bore the scars for the rest of her life.

Although nothing was ever said directly to Dangoya, his activities and behaviour began to be noticed by the bigger *layonis* and the *morans*, and even the elders of the clan became aware of this boy who had had such an unpromising start in life. Still small, he had nevertheless put on weight and was far stronger than other boys of his age. He was particularly good at wrestling and had often thrown *layonis* much older than himself. In some uncanny way which the majority of the boys could not understand, he seemed able to take advantage where no advantage appeared to exist. He used his brain and was bright enough to anticipate an opponent's next move.

Towards the end of Dangoya's tenth year preparations were being made for the elevation of the senior *morans* to elder status which meant that the warrior *morans* too would soon move up in the tribal hierarchy, making way for the newly circumcised youths. These countrywide changes took place every seven to ten years, but Dangoya's circumcision would not be for many years to come as he was still too young to be included in the coming round of initiation and circumcision, and would have to wait until the next.

Throughout Masailand the warrior *morans* were busy having their last fling for within the next few years they would have to play a more sedate role in the social system. They raided other tribes and held meat feasts, enjoying to the full their last carefree days, and Dangoya was occasionally asked to one of these *olpuls* to carry water, chop wood and run errands for the *morans*. Some of the bigger girls of eleven or more were also invited for the *morans'* pleasure and it amused Dangoya to hear these girls state that they would never, ever, make love with an unclean *layoni*. He would not dare to discuss this at an *olpul* in front of the *morans*, but afterwards he and his friends would take the girls to task and taunt them about the times they had lain in the bushes with them. It was all a great game although quite a few – Dangoya among them – had not yet succeeded in making love with anyone, let alone a girl of eleven.

Dangoya enjoyed the *olpuls* immensely. The smell of roasting meat and pots of herb soup, the big talk of the *morans*, their humour, the tales they told of men long dead and the brotherhood between them appealed to him very strongly. It was about this time that he first heard talk of strange people with white skins and hair like sansevera, wild sisal. Some said they worked with the Arab slave traders, that they were friendly and generous, or witches able to carry out amazing feats; that they were cannibals, eating whoever they could find. It was also rumoured that until recently these white men had not dared to face the Masai, but now unfortunately one of the clans in the north, probably the Purko, had befriended one and allowed him into their country. Dangoya found the talk fascinating, but could not presume to ask any question as he was a mere *layoni*. When he thought about the stories, he decided they could not be true as no one he knew had ever seen a white person, and he could not believe it possible for the one man with a small escorting group of *Olmeg* to enter Masai territory and leave it alive.

He thought often too of the *Olmeg*. He had never seen one himself, but knew the term was entirely derogatory and in Masai parlance embraced anyone of whatever tribe who was not a Masai. It was as simple as that. A man was born a Masai or an *Olmeg*, excepting only the Arabs who came from over the Big Water and now these new, pale people who carried with them an even more mysterious aura.

Singira teased him. 'I was born an *Olmeg*. My parents were of the Sukuma people.' Then seeing his startled face she quickly added, 'But of course I am now Masai, as you yourself are Masai.'

Other matters filled Dangoya's mind over the next few years including the birth of a third sister and a brother. The *olpiron* or Fire Stick was mended, marking the beginning of circumcisions throughout the country and Dangoya was recommended by the bigger youths for some of the duties they would be relinquishing, so by the time the *olpiron* was broken and all circumcisions ceased, his responsibilities were equal to those of any of the older *layonis* in the *manyatta*. He could wrestle with the best of them and his prowess in throwing the *ngalem ngiji* – the Masai broadsword, flat with sharpened edges and about two feet long – was on a par with some of the *morans*. His interest in his clan grew and he never missed an opportunity to learn more about it. Here his mother was a great help as she would question her lovers on tribal lore and pass on what she had heard to Dangoya.

His one regret at this time was that he had not as yet succeeded in making love to a girl, and when the girls began to whisper of his failing, his popularity waned; fortunately for him the rains came and it was time to move the sheep.

Chapter 2

The Boy

One of the *morans* who had shown an interest in Dangoya invited him and four other *layonis* to help herd the sheep. This was a great honour for the boys, although they knew only too well that their duties would be onerous. They would not only have to help guard and keep the sheep moving all day, but would also have to cook and fetch water and firewood.

The move this year was to be a very long one and would take a good six months, following the grazing which skirted the *Serenget* as far as Moru and back. This particular grazing area was considered to be one of the best in the country occupied by the Masai, but there were disadvantages, one of them being the length of absence from their main base and hence the accompanying discomfort and inconvenience. There would be predators to contend with and also the danger of raids by other clans, and the proximity to hostile tribes such as the Sukuma, the Wanyamwezi and the Barabaig. The *moran* protective force had therefore of necessity to be large, but the girls who were taken along for company were few in number and consequently very much in demand. There was no question of any of these girls daring to have contact with the *layonis* and this state of affairs suited Dangoya admirably as he knew he would not be pestered or even approached to demonstrate the sexual prowess he did not possess.

So for a while Dangoya was able to forget his main worry and concentrate on his work. His confidence returned and most of the *morans* liked him and would occasionally show him some consideration when others were not about. There was however a particular *moran* called Raien, elder brother to Pushati whom Dangoya had shown up so badly, who hated him and took every opportunity to abuse and thrash him for no apparent reason. No *moran* could spring to the defence of a *layoni* in an age-group conflict such as this, and even where the *layoni* was known to be in the right it was regarded improper to interfere. So the bullying was permitted to continue unhindered, until an event occurred which put Pushati's brother in an unfavourable light.

The flocks of sheep were so vast that the Masai had organised themselves into eight camps, each camp holding two, three or even four flocks of about five hundred sheep. They were now on the banks of the *Ngare Nanyuki* River, where it flowed down to the plains and the sheep had been taken out to graze. It was Dangoya's turn to stay in camp and attend to the cooking fires while the *moran* on camp guard sat under a tree and sharpened his weapons. Suddenly a *layoni* appeared running at full tilt to report that a leopard had taken a sheep and that the *moran* with the flock needed help. Dangoya and the other *moran* immediately picked up their spears and followed the *layoni* back to the sheep where they saw Pushati's brother Raien standing back from one of the few trees in the area.

As they approached Raien warned them that there was a leopard and her cubs up the tree with the dead sheep. The *moran* with Dangoya paid no heed to this warning and moved with speed towards the tree, his spear at the ready. As Raien appeared to be rooted to the spot, Dangoya followed the *moran* in order to cover his approach whereupon Raien yelled at him to keep his distance, but this Dangoya ignored. At that moment the leopard flung itself from the tree at the *moran* who just had time to raise his spear, but the spear was deflected by a branch and losing its thrust, entered the soft belly of the animal.

The weight of the leopard and the impact with which the *moran* fell dislodged the spear from his hand and before he could reach for his broadsword the leopard was upon him. Dangoya, seeing this, moved quickly to his aid and plunged his spear through the wounded animal's heart. The stricken leopard, in a last dying attempt at survival, turned on Dangoya who tried desperately to defend himself with his bare hands, no thought of running away in his mind. Suddenly the leopard went limp and collapsed, it claws drawing yet more blood from Dangoya's chest as it fell.

Slowly the boy got to his feet, and he and the *moran* surveyed one another, trembling with shock and excitement, their breath coming in great gulps. Nothing was said. Dangoya had saved the young man's life, but the *moran* could never acknowledge the fact to his face in the presence of other *morans*.

Raien approached, his orders to Dangoya to go immediately to the sheep, punctured with a stream of abuse. The boy had sustained many superficial wounds in his encounter and was bleeding profusely, but he obediently bent to the leopard, removed his spear and walked off without uttering a word, contempt for Raien obvious in his proud, straight-backed stride. When he had gone, Raien and the injured *moran* stared at one another.

Raien's eyes were the first to fall. 'I saw the *layoni* kill the leopard,' he said.

'Yes! And he saved my life in doing so. When he lost his spear he attacked it with his hands and did not run to his mother, yet a *moran* stood by and watched.' He spat in disgust. 'He has no fear and this incident I shall bring to the notice of the other *morans*.'

Raien looked at him, saying nothing, then pointed to the tree. 'Let us see how many cubs there are before you go back to the camp to have your wounds treated.'

'The *layoni* will come with me as he is also hurt. You must look after the sheep.'

They found two cubs in the tree and after clubbing them to death the *moran* called to Dangoya to go back to the camp with him. The news of the leopard kill had spread fast and several *morans* and young *layonis* came running. A few of the boys asked Dangoya what had happened, but he would say nothing and followed the *moran* to their camp.

That night with the sheep bedded down in rough enclosures, the *morans* gathered round their fire. The head *moran* pointedly enquired of the injured warrior if he had anything to say and the young man reported the happenings of the day adding: 'if it were not for the bravery of the *layoni* who cannot as yet lift his spear by its point, truly I would now be dead and a leopard and her cubs with a taste for sheep would be free to raid our stock.' His interference to Raien's lack of action had been made quite clear.

There were murmurs of approval from around the circle and one of the *morans* said he had noticed the good behaviour of Dangoya and the respect shown by him for his elders. Others concurred and the *laigwanan* sent for Dangoya who was told he had behaved well and that his action would be recognized by the slaughter of a fat sheep for his consumption to aid in his recovery. As a further reward all eight camps would give one ewe each to add to his flock which had been left him by his father.

This was heady talk for a boy not quite fourteen, but Dangoya's face showed nothing. He was running a temperature and the pain of his wounds made it difficult to stand upright. Eventually he was dismissed by the group round the fire and the talk turned to Raien's poor showing of the day.

For a few days both the mauled heroes were forced to lie low until the fevers of infection had run their course, but their recovery was remarkably quick. Both were left with scars they bore with pride, and Dangoya's popularity with the girls soared. All bullying stopped and he returned to his duties with renewed confidence.

While at Nabi word came of a small Barabaig raiding party in the area. The news brought the *morans* to their toes and a meeting was called to discuss the matter. This led to a consultation with the witchdoctor who, after two hours' meditation over his bones, came up with a plan of campaign. Their forces, he said should be split in to two, one to remain with the flocks of sheep and the other to confront the enemy. 'For success' he added, 'is assured.'

The chief *laigwanan* then took over, appointing a body of nineteen *morans*, thirty *layonis* and the girls to herd the stock while the remaining one hundred and twenty *morans* would operate in two files of sixty men each. These war parties were to advance in single file, two hundred paces apart. All *manyattas* and individuals encountered were to be investigated and on no account were their intentions to be made known or the size of the force revealed. Should they come across other Masai also intending to attack the Barabaig, or even lone *morans* willing to help, they should join forces. Scouts would be sent ahead and all high ground used for observation. In the event of the enemy being sighted great caution would be exercised and an attack made only after nightfall. If not diverted by the time they reached Dulen, a further meeting would be held. In the meantime, the herding party was to proceed along the grazing route as originally planned.

When the results of all these discussions filtered down to the *layonis* Dangoya viewed them with unease. His first thought was for the sheep. Here in their care they had almost twelve thousand sheep, a great portion of the wealth of the clan. To leave them exposed and vulnerable to the predations of not only the Barabaig, but also to the lion and leopard which were so common to the area, with a mere nineteen *morans* and a handful of boys and girls was, in his mind, madness. And he said so.

As a matter of course Dangoya was paraded before the *laigwanan* and berated for his remarks. Asked if he had dared to criticize the plan, he replied that he had not, but that if he were ever to find himself in a position of authority he would never leave the flocks so unprotected, particularly as there was nothing but prestige to be gained – or lost – by encountering a raiding party.

'And what is more,' he added, 'we could be walking into a trap!'

The *laigwanan* was astounded that this boy should sit before him discussing intelligently matters of such importance like a seasoned elder, and his anger grew as he asked Dangoya, 'We have consulted the witchdoctor and he, one of our greatest *laibons*, has advised this move. Do you not trust what he says?'

'I am but a *layoni* and have no say in the matter.'

'And yet you open your mouth!' And talk of not trusting the *laibon*'s judgement.'

'I do trust him! But other things can happen to change the *laibon*'s judgement.'

The *laigwanan* began to feel an inner anxiety and shouted, 'And what in your great wisdom do you think we should do? Speak up!'

'I think we should change the grazing plan now, without delay!'

Dangoya's words were received in hostile silence and he was abruptly dismissed. Later he was ordered to be thrashed, after which the *laigwanan* called a meeting of the *morans* and it was decided to move the sheep closer to another friendly herding force grazing along the central plains in the Fig Tree area. Those were Kisongo clansmen and the move to join them twenty miles away was started immediately.

It was late afternoon when the flocks turned west on their way to the

Kisongo grazing. The *moran* in charge told the herders they would stop to rest when it became dark as they had only a small force of *morans* to protect them, but they would move on later when the moon rose. Dangoya was glad to be walking again. He knew if he remained immobile his backside would be extra stiff and sore in the morning. Running along beside him, chattering like a little bird, was Masaiko, a girl who had often hinted that she would not be averse to making love, but he had always fobbed her off with a joke, unwilling to risk failure. Now he kept glancing at her, noting how pretty she was and wondering if he dared take a chance. He could not face the humiliation of being laughed at by this happy girl and the others who would soon know, but the more he became aware of her, seeing her small budding breasts, brown and pointed in the late afternoon sun, and the way her leather skirt moved over her rounded bottom with each hop and skip, the more excited he became and his fears receded with a growing ache in his groin and the longing for night to fall. Another hour, he thought, and I shall take this girl, and the more I think about it, the better it will be. Perhaps that is the secret. My head is always full of other things like sheep and weapons, and how far to the water, so that when a girl suddenly sits beside me, and demands I make love, I cannot because my head is so busy. Dangoya laughed out loud and the girl looked at him quickly.

'Has a feather tickled your *njabo*?' she teased, and giving his short skin cloak a quick flick she dodged away from him and ran on amongst the sheep.

The sun went down and the flocks were settled for a brief stop. No fires were lit and everyone took their rest as best they could, eating a little cold mutton and drinking from their *calabashes*. Dangoya was worried that one of the *morans* might call Masaiko away, but in the dark she went unnoticed and sat beside him.

'The *morans* are saying you were right about the dangers of the *laibon*'s plan,' she said. 'They only beat you so as not to lose face. Now you see, they are doing what you suggested.'

'I knew they would have to beat me and they have done it very well! I can hardly sit on my own *olkorom*, it bled like a speared Barabaig tribesman!'

'I think you are a very brave *layoni*, much braver than some of those *morans*.' She edged closer to him, her arm soft against his. 'You may take me if you like, and no one shall see us.'

Her hands reached out to touch him as she turned, and with a thudding heart and a roaring in his ears, Dangoya had his first girl. The wonder and warmth of her carried him away completely and he gave no thought to withdrawing, his innocence thrusting him headlong past the forgotten taboo. Bemused and enthralled he lay back, eyes wide at the stars, his hands on his heaving chest.

Later he reflected ruefully on what he had done, but Masaiko was unconcerned.

'I am to be circumcised when we reach Olgosorok and my marriage will take place soon after that. You shall not make love to me again for a long time, because I could never lie with a *layoni* once I am circumcised,' she said primly, 'but when you are a *moran* you will always be welcome in my house.'

Masaiko had long felt an affection for Dangoya and realised that she had been the means of breaking the spell for him. All the girls had discussed his sexual failings, now she could spread the good news and he would gain in popularity and prestige.

Just after midnight the moon rose and people stirred as they prepared to get the sheep moving. Dangoya got to his feet and looking down at the girl said one word, 'Ashe.' This 'thank you' was of the highest complimentary order amongst lovers and as Masaiko lowered her eyes in acknowledgement, she knew this boy would have a lasting hold on her heart.

At daybreak they were well away from the danger area and slowed down so the sheep could graze as they moved along. By midday the flocks of the Kisongo could be seen far across the plains and presently a group of Kisongo *morans* came over to meet them, asking why they had left their own grazing grounds.

'You can see that our grass is in very short supply,' the Kisongo spokesman's gesture embraced the wide rolling plains, lush with new grass.

The Loitayo *laigwanan* explained the situation.

'Why then do you not stand up and fight like true Masai?' asked the Kisongo.

'That is just what we are doing! Our main body has gone to defeat the Barabaig so that your sheep as well as ours may graze these plains without hindrance.'

'I hope for their sakes they do not meet up with the enemy. They are not women like the Sonjo and Olgogo. The Barabaig are skilled brave fighters and only the Kisongo can overthrow them.'

Negotiations were begun and the Kisongo reluctantly agreed to the newcomers remaining with them in the area until their warrior force returned. Hands were shaken and by dusk all the flocks were bedded down for the night. As there were no trees in the vicinity, enclosures could not be made, and the resting sheep were encircled by the Masai, each sitting at some distance from the next person.

Two incidents occurred during the following days which very nearly put a match to the tinder of the *morans'* discontent. In age-old custom the energy and restlessness of the young warriors had always to be manipulated by the *laibons*, and to a lesser extent by the *laigwanans*, in order to keep their positions of authority. The *laibons* knew that unless they could channel the vigour and drive of the *morans* into active participation in fighting, raiding and hunting, they would bring tribal turmoil upon their heads and the very structure of the social system would crumble.

The new arrivals to the Kisongo grazing area were made up mainly of Loitayo and Purko clansmen, the latter being the largest and strongest of all Masai clans whose territory lay in the north. The Kisongo were the biggest clan in the south and every year, while on their sheep run, took the opportunity of killing as many lion as they could to prove their manhood and for the making of ceremonial head-dresses. Lion abounded in the region and a Purko *moran* made a disparaging remark about 'this tame lion killing,' which was overheard. Immediately the Kisongo were up in arms, with much flourishing of spears and shouted abuse, and if it had not been for the intervention of the Loitayo *laigwanan*, blood would have been spilled. He simply asked for the protection of the *seki* branch which meant the cessation of all hostilities as from that moment.

Dangoya had often seen the *seki* bush with its small round leaves and edible berries, portions of which were carried into country where it did not grow. He knew that its name could be evoked in any inter-tribal disagreement or personal conflict to protect the weaker of the protagonists with no shame attached. Now for the first time Dangoya had actually been present when the *seki* was called on, and he was impressed with what alacrity the opposing sides backed down and went about their daily business.

The second incident occurred when the frustrated warrior force arrived having neither seen nor heard of any Barabaig raiders. Feelings ran high and dissatisfaction with the *laibon* and the chief *laigwanan* was openly expressed. These rumblings of discontent worried the witchdoctor exceedingly and to divert attention from his unwise advice sent for Dangoya. After questioning him about his earlier remarks, which had already stirred up trouble and caused alterations to the prearranged grazing plan, the *laibon* reprimanded Dangoya severely and commanded that he be beaten until his back was raw.

Now the recriminations became louder with Dangoya's Loitayo clansmen siding with him and insisting that he had been punished once. A meeting of all the *morans* was held and fierce arguments took place with the very leadership of the Purko and Loitayo clans being questioned. But the power of the *laibon* prevailed and sweeping aside all objections he ordered the clans to return to their previous grazing circuit and to make immediate plans for a raid into Sukumaland. Here the *laibon* played upon the *morans'* pride and their boiling desire to fulfil their warrior status and they knew his position, for the time being, was assured.

The huge flocks of sheep were taken eastwards and organisation for the Sukuma raid begun. These preparations of necessity now slowed down the movement of the stock and not a few of the *morans* began to worry about the situation. No rain had fallen for ten days and the return migration of game had started. Dangoya, inexperienced as he was, could see that nothing but trouble would result from this delay. While the *morans* sharpened their spears and practiced their battle tactics, the waterholes would slowly dry up leaving nothing but a crust of hardened mud. If they hoped to reach Soitayaiyo with their sheep in good health and without excessive losses amongst the lambs, they would have to move directly there without further ado. Dangoya was anxious too about his animals as a large part of his inheritance was tied up in the sheep, but he had learnt to keep his mouth shut and knew also that he had unintentionally caused animosity during the last disturbance between the clans.

The Masai at this stage were still in the Nabi area whereas by now they should have reached Malambo on the eastern edge of the plain where there was permanent water. Once again discussions started, with the hotheads shouted down, and it was agreed to consult a more powerful *laibon* from Moru.

This older and wiser man, more out of professional pique than good sense, advised strongly against a raid into Sukumaland and insisted that they move with all possible speed to the head-waters of the *Ngare Nanyuki* River, then go north to the end of the plains, cross over to Soitayaiya and return that way. This route would normally be avoided as they would have to face the returning tide of migrating plains game and their losses, particularly of lambs, would be heavy. Lion too would take their share, and with the need to travel at night, the sheep would lose the condition gained over the previous few months due to fatigue.

A large proportion of *morans* were not all that keen to hurry home to disgrace, as they thought, having no dead Barabaig to their credit or even captured stock. Therefore they did not overwork themselves on the journey back. In consequence, losses in their flocks were high. This was not the case in Dangoya's flock as the *morans* in charge were among those who felt enough damage had been done, and they encouraged and helped Dangoya to keep a good hold on the sheep during the move.

After crossing the plains to Soitayaiya the large flocks split up and slowed their pace to allow the worse affected sheep to regain some weight, but Dangoya's section, together with three others, chose to return home to Olgosorok by the traditional route.

Chapter 3

The Buffalo Kill

During the next year Dangoya regained his lost popularity with the girls and became a youth to be reckoned with among the *layonis*, so much so that he gradually took over their leadership. He had also been noticed by the *morans* and elders, although this recognition was not official because of his uncircumcised state. In a roundabout way he was listened to, and attention given to some of his ideas. He was now at an age when most of the work associated with the actual tending of the herds and flocks fell on his shoulders, and he was also called upon to discipline and train the younger *layonis*. It was a thankless, onerous and uninteresting time for him - in his particular case unusually long as he could not expect the next circumcisions to begin for another four years at the earliest.

The following few years were therefore most frustrating. Most of the boys of his age were no match for him, resulting in their admiration but not much liking. His leadership among the *layonis* was established and although he could not take the young girls openly as would a *moran*, he nevertheless had no need to press for their favours when the opportunity and the urge arose.

An outbreak of *rinderpest* had spread through the cattle with very heavy losses and this disaster was followed by famine after two years of scanty rain. A big *moran* meeting was called involving the Loitayo and a small section of the Purko and Kisongo clans from the areas most affected by the *rinderpest*, and after consultation with the witchdoctor, large raiding parties were sent out into the country of the tribes living to the west and northwest. Most families were thus able to restock their lost herds, but Dangoya's could do nothing as it had no warriors to serve in the raids, Singira's appointed husband having died before being circumcised, so it was forced to rely entirely on Dangoya's good management to increase its depleted herd.

During one of the raids, the young *moran* whom Dangoya had saved from the leopard, his only friend among the *morans*, was killed, and this depressed him particularly as some of the *morans* he disliked came back with great numbers of cattle and claims of bravery. The raids had taken a very serious toll of the two existing *moran* age groups and it was rumoured that the Purko in the north were about to repair the *olpiron* as a signal for circumcisions to begin, a move which would fill the reduced warrior ranks. So, too, in the Loitayo and other clans.

The senior *morans* who would become the *layoni's olpirons* and instructors called meetings for those boys whose fathers had approached them, Dangoya being put forward by the *laigwanan* of his *manyatta*, father of Pushati and Raien, who pronounced himself Dangoya's foster father. Overnight Dangoya and his contemporaries became people to be shown consideration and a genuine interest was taken in them and their activities. They were, after all, to be the protectors and wealth gatherers of the clan for the next fifteen to twenty years.

All the boys were taken before the *laibon* who gave his permission for the *ngipataa* ceremony to be held, forerunner to the circumcisions. Dangoya's foster father told him to choose eight others and that together they were to paint their bodies. This the youths did, stripped themselves and standing naked before daubing each other in stripes with white clay, red ochre and charcoal, emphasising their uncircumcised state for all to see. The remaining *layonis* due for circumcision were then painted too and all feasted on meat and milk. Each boy had given an ox, and honey to make beer for the elders and the instructors and after the celebratory meal, the circumcision candidates went to a nearby pond and danced throughout the night until they fell with exhaustion and slept until the sun was well up.

The fact that the *laigwanan* of the *manyatta* had selected Dangoya to choose the eight *layonis* for the initial painting was recognition of his leadership qualities, but all the instructors watched him very carefully for any trait which might go against him and prove him unsuitable. It was therefore most important that he make a good showing as he had no influence in the clan or blood ties to further his interests.

Dangoya's sponsor and instructor was a senior *moran* called Olengesen who had been *laigwanan* on one of the sheep grazing journeys and he had offered his services because, as he pointed out to Dangoya's foster father, the boy showed great potential as a leader.

News arrived that the 'Fire Stick' had been repaired and the day before their circumcision Dangoya and three others from his *manyatta* went with an elder of their fathers' age-group to the olive tree forest a good distance away where they each cut a sapling about ten feet high, removing all the branches except the top ones, and hurrying back as fast as possible in order to avoid sun wilting of the leaves. At the *manyatta* each *layoni* went to his own gate and dug a small hole in which he stood the olive sapling and watered it. Next to the sapling he placed a *calabash* with a wide mouth, filled it with water and put a ceremonial axe-head inside. This was the signal to all passers-by that a circumcision was to take place.

Early next day the four *layonis* set off once again with an instructor up into the mountains and on their way they cut long *lianas* which they carried to protect them from evil spirits. On reaching one of the many little pools fed by a spring they stepped in and sat down in the cold water, chilling their genitals in preparation for the operation.

By the time Dangoya and the others got back to the *manyatta* all was in readiness for the celebrations and the elders were seated on hides drinking honey beer and eating meat from a nearby *olpul*. Dangoya sat down on the hide placed near his gate and bent his knees, splaying them apart as he had been told to do. An elder of this father's age group sat close behind, legs stretched out on either side of Dangoya's body, while his arms clasped the boy firmly round the waist.

'Remember,' he said, 'to watch every move of the Ndorobo's knife, and you must neither flinch not cry out.'

Dangoya grunted impatiently. He had waited so long for this day and had no intention of sullying his reputation by showing any signs of weakness.

The Ndorobo circumciser squatted down in front of Dangoya and without much ado pushed his foreskin as far back as possible and made a quick cut round the inner layer. He then parted the outer from the inner layer and making a hole in the top of the outer layer, pushed the head of the penis through. All that remained to be done was to pare away the inner layer, leaving a piece about two inches long of the outer layer to hang below. This was the *ndelelia* which would ward off evil spirits from the vagina of any woman he had intercourse with, and protect him too from venereal disease. It was said to give a woman more pleasure when it had healed and contracted to about an inch in length, giving rise to the theory that women therefore preferred *morans* to be uncircumcised males.

The operation had taken barely two minutes to perform and Dangoya had watched the entire process with a smile on his face. The two elders who stood behind him, ready to pounce if he had shown any sign of cowardice, looked on in amazement and one remarked that he had never seen anyone behave in such an unconcerned manner or show such courage.

Olengesen too observed Dangoya's steady fortitude and when he carried the bleeding boy to this mother's house and laid him on her bed he could not help but say, 'You have a brave and true *moran* here of good blood.'

Outside in the burning light of the African day the Ndorobo continued with his work, going from gate to gate and from one *manyatta* to another, and by evening he had earned between twenty and thirty goats which he would collect when he had finished his delicate tasks in the area. Next season he would be back, harvesting his new crop of goats as more boys became eligible until at last the *olpiron* was once again broken.

In Dangoya's *manyatta* the celebrations continued, with huge amounts of meat consumed and much beer drunk by the elders until most were incapacitated, urinating where they sat or lay about in drunken abandon.

The *morans* drank in moderation as they had to be in a fit state to supervise the *olpul* and to perform with the girls. For two days the festivities carried on, gradually coming to an end when supplies of beer and meat were exhausted.

It was a happy time for Singira. She was excessively proud of Dangoya and tended him with the most loving consideration, appreciating every moment of having him to herself. The day after the operation she bathed him with hot water and anointed him with oil rendered down from the fat of the ox donated by him for the celebration. Dangoya himself was more than happy. He seemed well and lively and at last felt he could begin to implement the many plans he had been forming in his mind for a long time. His days of subservience and not being able to pass an opinion were over, and he could not wait to be on his feet again.

On the second night infection set in. The wound swelled and his temperature soared. He felt a harsh throbbing pain which by morning was almost impossible to bear, although he kept silent and said nothing to his mother. But Singira noticed the swelling when she tended him and felt his hot skin, and by the fourth day she was extremely worried about Dangoya's condition. He would neither drink nor eat and Singira went to tell Olengesen who, after seeing Dangoya, reported immediately to the *laibon*. Further anointing was advised, but to no effect, and Olengesen himself told Singira to wash the wound with hot water and bleed the area with small cuts and the use of a suction horn. When this was done warm cows' urine was liberally applied, followed by a smearing of mildewed dung. The treatment was repeated three days later and gradually Dangoya's fever subsided and the pain eased. He had eaten nothing for more than a week, but now drank a little curdled milk followed later in the day by a mixture of blood and milk.

Two of the other new *morans* came to visit Dangoya, but instead of cheering him up, he became depressed at the sight of them on their feet walking about. They soon left, because he greeted them coldly and would not talk. Their good health was an affront and a reflection on his recuperative powers, and he was angry with himself for not recovering as fast as the others. Shortly after they left he called for blood and milk with mutton fat, and Singira sent a *layoni* hurrying off to find a steer. The boy took a long time and Dangoya has dozed off and was half asleep when he returned with a big *calabash* of uncongealed blood taken from the jugular of a steer. The *layoni* was about to hand it to Singira when Dangoya opened his eyes.

'You *layoni*! What have you got in the *calabash*?'

'Fresh blood,' the boy replied.

'Well, bring it here,' Dangoya said, and taking the *calabash* from the *layoni* he removed the swizzle stick with which the boy had agitated the blood to stop congealment and drank a good amount, handing the remainder to his mother with instructions to mix it well with milk and mutton fat for him to drink later.

This, thought Singira, was a sure sign that her son was on the mend, and for the first time in many days she was able to sit near him on her bed and chat.

'You were too sick the other day to hear the excitement in the house next to this where one of the other new *morans* has been lying. Shall I tell you?' She knew it was a piece of information not only to raise his morale but also to amuse him.

'Tell me,' he said, 'because now I feel stronger.'

Singira then related how the young *moran*, lying on his bed recovering from his circumcision and nearly healed, had been visited by a married woman to whom he had once as a *layoni* made improper suggestions. There were several people in the hut at the same time so the story was quite true, Singira added. The woman sat down beside the young man, removed her skirt and began to caress him. All the while she spoke softly to him, telling him how she had often wanted him, but had been too frightened to take him as he was still a *layoni*. It was different now as he was a *moran* and nothing could stop them making love. Her hand moved gently in his pubic area and he started to have and erection whereupon she lay down at his side and invited him to move nearer.

'*Aish*! I cannot!' he said, 'and you know it.'

'We do not have to do anything until you are properly better,' she said, 'but there is nothing to stop us touching each other.'

With that the young *moran*'s erection split open his wound and he began to bleed. He begged the woman to leave him alone and she suddenly stood up, saying, 'You have paid for your insult as custom required and I shall hurt you no more. I have truly been fond of you and now that you are a *moran* and my husband's *olpiron*, you will be welcome in my house.'

Dangoya laughed out loud when he heard the story, for he knew that the other boy would have been set back considerably and it made him feel a good deal better to know he was not alone in his long recovery.

Day by day Dangoya grew in strength, his sheer determination and the will to live pulling him through. An infection such as he had developed was rare in a newly circumcised youth, and usually the recovery rate was astonishingly quick with no complications, but it was twenty-four days before Dangoya was able to get off his bed. He was still very weak and thin and had to be helped, but from then on his good health was assured.

When Dangoya was fully recovered he made preparations to set off in search of birds with which to fill his headdress. This was a customary activity for all new *morans*, or *mbarnoti* as they were now called, each vying with the next in the number and variety of birds caught. With great care Dangoya repaired and adjusted his long-dead father's bow, determined to have the biggest and most varied headdress of them all. He removed the iron heads from the arrows and on each fixed small balls of beeswax with which to stun the birds without damaging either the feathers or the skin.

The other three *mbarnoti* from his *manyatta*, circumcised at the same time, had already departed, so after informing Olengesen of his intended route, Dangoya set off on his own. That same day he met a group of four young *morans* from Sanjan who were bound for the north, all in high spirits and enjoying their new-found freedom as *morans*, and he decided to join them.

Each day they hunted for birds, pulling out the innards with all the flesh and stuffing the bodies with grass before attaching them to their halo-like headdresses. At night they slept at whatever *manyatta* they happened to be near, but the hospitality shown them at this stage in their lives was of a limited kind as they were considered untouchable with their unshaven, oiled bodies and long leather cloaks made from bare sheepskin. However, they were permitted to whip any young girls who came too near to spray the *mbarnotis* with water, milk and honey; an occasion for much shouting and laughter.

For nearly five months Dangoya wandered the country with various groups, spending perhaps a few weeks with one band before joining another; and in each instance, after a couple of days in new company, he would assume the leadership. From Olbosimoru to *Magadi*, to Lengkito, he made the long walk; and it was at Lengkito that he heard of the big Purko *moran manyatta* to be built north east of Namanga, and that behind

Namanga mountain to the west would be a Loitayo *manyatta*. Both these were of interest to him as he could attend either, but he had to consider very carefully where he should go for his warrior training and he knew, in fact, that it might be far more to his advantage, with the best chance of attaining leadership, to attend a smaller *manyatta* nearer home at Olgosorok. He had an important reputation as a *layoni* in his own area and this, bearing in mind his lack of family influence and the fact that there were many new *morans* with abilities equal to his own, might be the deciding factor. He could only wait until he saw Olengesen again at Mondul and there ask his instructor's advice.

Not long after leaving Lengkito, Dangoya and a companion came across Pushati whom Dangoya had not seen for some time as he had been circumcised at an uncle's *manyatta*. These three were later joined by a couple of full-fledged *morans* who set a fast pace and they arrived at the northern slopes of Mondul in two days. Here the *morans* said they were going over the top of the range through thick forest renowned for its herds of aggressive buffalo, a route which was less than a quarter of the distance by the usual track via the *Oldonyo* Sambu plains and through the northern end of *Ngare* Olmotonyi bordering Larusa country.

Dangoya pricked up his ears at this and suggested that he and the two youngsters with him be allowed to follow the *morans*. The *morans* agreed, but warned them of the dangers. They, as full *morans*, were armed whereas the *mbarnoti* carried only their bird hunting bows and a broadsword each. Dangoya was determined to go and the others with him could only agree and not show any nervousness, especially in front of him who they realised would probably be one of their *laigwanans* when they reached full warrior status.

The party set off, the *morans* in front and the three novices trailing two hundred yards behind, their headdresses a mass of fluttering feathers. The day was warm and close, the mountain incline fairly steep, and a waist-high grass slowed their progress and almost covered the seldom-used path. After several hours they came to the first trees and here the *morans* stopped to drink at a little stream while the *mbarnoti* kept their distance. Moving on, the *morans* shouted to the youngsters that they would wait for them while they too drank. Dangoya had never before been shown such consideration by *morans* and the change in attitude made him feel very superior as he grinned to himself in anticipation of the good times ahead.

At that instant the buffalo charged. Dangoya's body froze as he attempted to take in the situation, lightning impressions flashing across his vision. First the leading *moran* flinging his spear then shinning up a tree as fast as a cat; the others leaping to safety too, all making sure their legs were well out of reach of a buffalo's abrasive tongue. And like all good Masai they made a great deal of noise in their excitement.

Dangoya remained rigid, his only action to tweak off a small leaf from the bush beside him and to let it fall in the slowly moving air. He was downwind. Breathing more easily, he began to edge forward to a huge fallen tree, at least six feet in diameter. The *morans* saw then his predicament and yelled louder to distract the buffalo. He signalled his approval and one of the *morans* began to report on every move the animals made.

There were three buffalo, one with the *moran*'s spear trailing from its side, and they milled about from tree to tree unsure of what their enemy was or where it lay. The second *moran*, either out of guilt or in an attempt to attract the buffalo towards him, started to climb down his tree, but at that moment the wind changed and the animals caught Dangoya's scent.

In a wild run he reached the tree trunk and leapt up on to it, his feet finding purchase in the broken stumps of branches. He was just out of reach. The enraged buffalo added to the rising noise with their bellows, as the wounded one urinated on to its tail and swished it up at Dangoya, an old buffalo trick. He had heard too many stories about the irritating, burning effect of buffalo urine, so he moved along the trunk with alacrity to howls of laughter from the others. The injured animal then gave up the fight and wandered off to lie down some distance away, knocking the spear from its flank as it turned to go.

Once again the wind changed and the two remaining buffalo charged the *moran* who had almost touched ground. He shot back up the tree and leaned down to shout curses at them. Dangoya was making agitated signals and the *moran* quickly understood he wanted to get the fallen spear, so pointing to where it lay at the base of a young sapling, he added to his incentive in order to keep the animals' attention. Dangoya plunged down into the undergrowth, grabbed the spear and just regained the safety of his tree trunk before the pair of very angry buffalo made a maddened charge in his direction.

He knew he must keep his head and await the right opportunity otherwise he would lose his only weapon and achieve nothing, so he teased the buffalo and shouted oaths at them and all the while his sharp eyes watched and waited for the chance he knew would come.

Again and again the buffalo charged and butted the tree and the *morans* urged Dangoya on to do something. Encouraged by their shouts, Pushati, who could not see what was going on, remarked in a loud voice that perhaps Dangoya was scared. Through the hubbub Dangoya took note of what had been said, but showed no sign of having heard. He completely ignored the *morans'* impatient calls for action and then, when a louder taunt from his left distracted one of the buffalo, making it turn its head, he struck.

Like a flash the spear went deep into the great body between the brisket and the shoulder, into the animal's heart. Quickly Dangoya withdrew the spear.

'*Narobong gotonye!*' he roared, 'Fuck your mother!'

So sudden and swift was his attack that the onlookers did not realise what had happened until they heard Dangoya's words. The stricken buffalo too seemed as surprised as the Masai and stood stock-still for a few seconds before lumbering off and collapsing. The others could see, from their perches in the trees, where the beast died, but Dangoya's one remaining interest was in the surviving buffalo.

'If *Ngai* would make it come nearer, I could spear it,' he thought. But God was not listening. When the buffalo was distracted by the first wounded animal and moved off to go to it, Dangoya could wait no longer, nor stand the strain, so he leapt from the tree trunk and ran after it.

Instead of turning on him, the buffalo barged on through the forest with Dangoya in swift pursuit. The others watched his retreating form with astonishment for it was something they could barely credit. However, in five minutes or so he was back. The going had been heavy and he was tired, nor could he see any point in chasing an animal that would not turn and fight.

The first *moran* gave Dangoya his hand saying, '*Bageteng!* I give you an ox!' and this was repeated by the others, but when Pushati, maker of the derogatory remark, approached him and held out his hand, Dangoya told him to take his offering of an ox up a tree and screw it. '*Narabong geteng ino!*' he said, and turned away from the discomfited youth.

'What should we do next?' asked one *moran* of the other. 'This is perhaps the *mbarnoti*'s first buffalo and he will want the hide for his shield.'

His friend agreed and the night was spent in the forest, the young men eating their fill of the buffalo meat and cutting up the hide. Dangoya had not inherited his father's shield as it had been lost with him in battle, so he was elated at the thought of obtaining one from an animal he had killed himself. It would add enormously to his prestige and from the start, he had had no intention of leaving the scene of the killing without a part of the hide, whatever the others may have decided.

On reaching the Kisongo *manyatta* at Mondul the next day, their reception at first was cool as the Kisongo were inclined towards insularity and intolerance towards other clans. However, once the account of the buffalo kill was related, Dangoya and the two *morans* were hailed as heroes. Dangoya was no different from countless Masai and loved to have words of praise showered on him, and to boast and show off. He revelled in the adoration and spent ten days visiting the *manyattas* in the vicinity, enjoying every moment of his new fame.

With Olengesen's arrival however, Dangoya was brought back down to earth and had to give his instructor a detailed account of himself and put forward his plans for the immediate future. When he came to describe these intentions his entire form of address changed and he adopted the customary manner of speech which he had heard and seen so many of his seniors use when putting certain facts to a listener. Each point was enumerated, repeated and emphasised with long pauses, and he used his fingers and gestures of the whole hand to stress these, together with punctuating beats of his *knobkerrie* on the ground.

Olengesen listened politely then asked Dangoya why he did not want to go to the *olpul* and feed on meat with the others who had been circumcised at the same time. Dangoya knew then that Olengesen had turned down his plans and was ordering him to go home for the next stage of his initiation, and with no argument on his part, accompanied his instructor to Malambo the next day.

Dangoya was greeted effusively by the females in his *manyatta* with much ululating and chatter, the girls in particular pressing forward to examine his headdress and hear more about his glorious battle with the buffalo. Singira had great difficulty getting near him at all to whisper her love and pride, and to touch her son and know he was safe. The men were more restrained in their admiration, but it showed in their eyes nevertheless and when the three *mbarnoti* whom he had not seen since the time of his slow convalescence, boys he had known all his life, came to him and pressed his hand and asked that he should be their leader, Dangoya's reserve almost broke. Calmly, however, he turned then to accept greetings from *mbarnoti* from nearby *manyattas* and these youths too indicated that he was their choice as leader by calling him '*Laigwanan*'.

On the morning of the *olpul* the young *morans* were shaved, every hair on their bodies being removed, and then they covered themselves in red ochre, using their fingernails to pattern their arms and legs. With the help of the girls, designs were also drawn on their hands and bodies, pressing close to stroke their thighs and buttocks, moving their fingers enticingly over the most sensitive areas until the *mbarnotis* could bear it no longer and pushed the girls away and smacked their little round bottoms.

Dangoya's circumcision had caused heavy scarring and this the girls thought hilarious.

'What put the twist there?' one of them asked, taking his *njabo* in her hand and laughing up into his face. 'Was it that big buffalo or was it the leopard on the *Serenget*?'

'You just wait until after it's twisted you mad with pleasure, then I shall tell you the secret!' Dangoya grinned down at her, excitement running high in his blood.

A large crowd stood watching the boys being decorated and this last exchange amused them enormously. One of the older women called out to him, 'These silly girls don't know what's good for them. You punish her hard tonight!'

'That I will,' and Dangoya slipped on his new cloak made for him by his mother. Of supple brown and white calfskin, the *ngelan* barely covered his chest and was caught on one shoulder, leaving his buttocks exposed.

In his new position as leader, Dangoya chose three small *layonis* to go with the girls to help at the *olpul* and told them to take the soup pots and go to prepare the site, with water and firewood at the ready.

Turning to the cattle still enclosed in the *manyatta*, Dangoya selected the first of the four animals they would consume at their *olpul* over the next six weeks. He chose a fine black steer from his own herd and without difficulty slipped a hide rope around one of its back legs. Dangoya had spent much time with his stock and this ox and as a consequence was quiet and showed no objection to being handled. It was another matter, however, when they attempted to drive it away from the *manyatta*. It refused to budge and they had to resort to moving a bunch of animals along with it as far as the place of the *olpul* which was deep in a forest gorge with an overhang of rock giving shelter from the rain and a stream not fifty yards away. It was a popular spot and had been used by generations of *morans* for their feasts.

The *layonis* had a good fire going and the soup pots were already on the boil, waiting only for fat and pieces of meat and offal from the steer.

'What have you put in the soup?' one of the *morans* called.

'*Kiloriti*,' replied a *layoni*.

'And have you put in *kitoloswa*?'

'No,' answered the boy, 'we do not know where it grows.'

When cooked in a soup the bark from the *kiloriti* tree, a type of acacia, turned the liquid a pale mauve. Always drunk in large quantities by *morans* who believed it made them not only fearless but also aroused them sexually, it could cause an excitable and highly strung man to froth at the mouth and fall into a fit. *Kitoloswa* had the same effect, only stronger, but the bush was not available in every area.

Leading the steer into the *olpul*, the young *morans* tied its legs together and threw it to the ground. A broadsword was rammed down hard into the spinal cord at the base of the head and immediately withdrawn, then a stick was thrust into the surrounding skin and twisted as a tourniquet to stop any blood escaping.

As the animal was being skinned, Dangoya and another cut off chunks of body fat which everyone ate raw; and when the gut was opened, the entire spleen, a large proportion of the various stomachs, bits of liver and all the blood lying in the abdominal cavity were consumed raw. The carcass was then cut up and certain portions were selected and put to one side for eating later, such as the legs and most of the lean meat with fat was eaten in the first few days. Each cut was grilled over the fire, skewered on sticks, according to where the particular cut came from and with regard to the individual tastes of the *morans*. Cuts could be over-charred or underdone, suspended on a smoky part of the fire or not.

The smell was unbelievable and the new *morans* ate their fill, giving pieces to the girls and allowing the *layonis* to stuff themselves with leftover scraps. After eating came the love-play, and thus the days and weeks passed and ran into months, with many visits too to other *olpuls* in the surrounding country.

It was an idyllic time for the young men, yet a time for learning too. Most of the daylight hours while the girls attended to their usual chores in the *manyattas*, were spent with their instructors absorbing the legends and history of their people, battle tactics, weapon making and social behaviour. When the first meeting of the elders was held to choose leaders from amongst the *mbarnoti morans*, Dangoya was well equipped for a position of authority and was unanimously appointed a junior *laigwanan*.

The only cloud on Dangoya's horizon at this time was when his foster-father informed him that arrangements had been made for his betrothal and a steer was summarily taken from Dangoya's herd for meat for the entertainment of the girl's father. Two sheep in exchange for honey for making beer were also removed, the animals all part of the bride price.

Dangoya did not approve at all, especially as his herd was a small one, and he did not care for the distribution of his meagre property by others. However, he had no say in the matter as it was the custom, and he consoled himself with the thought that as a junior leader of a warrior group he would soon be in a position to increase his herd and obtain wives of his choosing – with no price attached – on raids against other tribes.

He was well content with his rapidly increasing *asanja* relationships and the very day his foster-father spoke to him about his betrothal he had been asked by a friend to 'drink milk' with a girl he fancied. The second-hand invitation meant the girl wished to go through the *ngibot* ceremony and become his *asanja*. She had already arranged with her mother to provide fresh milk in a *calabash* reserved for this purpose so Dangoya agreed to go to her *manyatta*. When he arrived, an older girl, in the presence of others of both sexes, placed the cowrie-beaded *calabash* at his feet. He picked it up and drank, then led his new sweetheart to a special hut, followed by other girls and *morans*, where they all spent the night together on the one large bed.

It seemed to Dangoya that with his many *asanjas* – at least one in each of the *manyattas* in the region – he in no way required the burden of an expensive wife and a completely unknown quantity at that. His thoughts towards his foster-father were resultingly bitter. The marriage had been arranged, as far as he could see, entirely to satisfy the older man's pretensions, as the girl came from a very wealthy and important family. Needless to say, Dangoya avoided that *manyatta* and when the girl died of pneumonia he was delighted, although he had never seen her.

Chapter 4

The Great White Mountain

It was the presence of the white man which decided Dangoya to choose the Loitayo warrior *manyatta* to the west of Namanga for his *moran* training.

Talk of Europeans to the north and to the south of *Oldonyo Naibor* – Kilimanjaro, the Great White Mountain – and along the northern Usambara mountains increased, and the young *morans'* conversations at the *olpuls* centred on these intriguing people. Dangoya was fascinated and although a man of few words, his questions to anyone coming from those areas were endless.

Speculations as to their appearance and behaviour were discussed at length, and the wonder of their weapons which made so much noise and which could kill from a great distance without touching the animal slain, was beyond belief, although the Arab slave buyers were reported to possess the same magic sticks.

For some reason which Dangoya could not have explained to anyone, let alone himself, he found his mind constantly occupied with thoughts of the white men to the point where the urge to see them became almost an obsession, overlying his ambitions of one day being a senior *laigwanan*. He was determined to see them and could think of nothing else. His curiosity about their every physical aspect and origin was intense, and he would wonder whether their bodies could be the same as his: they were so wrapped up that no one had reported seeing if they were made of flesh and bone with the same number of fingers and toes. They seemed too to be all of the same sex and there were no children in evidence.

Dangoya's plans began to formulate. He would have to go to these people as they had not as yet ventured to his part of Masai country; and the best way would be to get as near to them as possible. If he went to the Loitayo *manyatta* at Namanga, bigger than that at Olgosorok, he would be less well known, and his chances therefore of being chosen by the majority as a senior *laigwanan* with all the restrictive responsibilities would be reduced. Then, he reasoned, he would be free to take a raiding party deep into the areas frequented by the white men, round *Oldonyo Naibor*, south to the Pare mountains and also to the Taita Hills.

The Namanga *manyatta* would be rewarding in other ways too as it was close to the Mbulu who had plenty of cattle and very fine women, and a *moran* need not return empty-handed from forays into that territory.

Singira was opposed to these plans. Being close to her son, she made it quite clear that she thought he was foolish not to go to the warrior *manyatta* nearer home where his qualities would be recognised. Singira's was a happy, easy-going disposition while Dangoya was quieter, more serious; yet the ties between them were strong and, most unusually for a Masai woman and her son, each played confidant to the other. They spent hours talking together and discussing what Dangoya's next plans were to be and usually he would give in to her as she did not approve, but on the question of going to Namanga he would not back down.

Of the many *mbarnoti* who came to him and asked if they could accompany him Dangoya accepted twenty from his own and various other *manyattas* in the vicinity. They were without exception looking for excitement and quick recognition, and resolved that to follow a *moran* of Dangoya's calibre would be the best way of achieving their objectives.

Each young *moran* took a few cows, perhaps five for milking, a steer or two for meat, and a couple of donkeys to carry the hides and skins and cooking utensils. Some took their mothers and most took a girl to build the huts and see to their comfort and pleasure. Singira told Dangoya she would follow later, and also that she had found a girl for him. This was Ngenia of the Ildaresero clan.

Ngenia was an orphan from a poor family who had been taken under Singira's wing some years previously. Only about fourteen years old, she would one day be a beautiful woman with her exceptional height, long fine bones and warm bronze skin. Although slim almost to the point of being thin, her breasts were surprisingly large and round, a very recent development which Dangoya had noticed only since his return. She was quiet and withdrawn, and because of this and her lack of background, was not much sought after by the *morans*. She seldom lost her temper, but it was said of her that when she did she would be capable of killing someone. When the girl was persuaded by Singira to invite Dangoya to drink milk with her, he accepted willingly and became her *asanja* before they set off for Namanga.

Ngenia proved her worth very quickly at the *moran manyatta* and her house was built and ready long before those of other girls who had been their twice the time. Ngenia's success was largely due to her determination and the encouragement Dangoya gave her, having in his turn been admonished by Singira to treat the girl with care and consideration.

Dangoya, without realising it, was falling in love with Ngenia, but because of his popularity with the other girls and the demands made upon him by them, found he was spending fewer and fewer nights with her. Making love with some girl he would suddenly find himself thinking of Ngenia and wondering who was with her.

On warm dry evenings the young people would dance out in the open in front of the huts. During the dancing, the *morans* would throw their *knobkerries* into a pile on the ground, and when the dancing finished, the girls would rush to pick up the kerries belonging to the men they wished to spend the night with. Ngenia, being rather shy, never seemed to get the man of her choice until one night she actually had Dangoya's kerrie in her hand when suddenly another girl snatched it away.

'That is mine, you daughter of a workman!'

At that Ngenia pounced on her and stripped her of beads and clothing in seconds. The screaming girl fought back but was no match for Ngenia who had already drawn blood before being pulled away by Dangoya who led her back to their hut.

'Until tonight,' Dangoya said, 'I was thinking that you no longer liked me.'

'Well I do,' the still furious Ngenia replied. 'And if that *ndito* dares to pick up your kerrie again, I shall kill her! Child of a female jackal!'

'She will not try to pick it up again, not after tonight. But if you want a certain *moran*'s kerrie, you must be quicker than the others.'

Ngenia looked at him in silence then lifting her chin high said, 'But I only want yours, and so many others want it too.'

Stretching out his hands to the girl, Dangoya touched her beautiful body and found his arousal so intense that he was upon her and loving her before she was ready, his emotions at such high pitch that he remained sleepless most of the night.

It was a full and happy time for the *morans*, the days spent sometimes at neighbouring *olpuls*, or competing with one another in spear throwing or wrestling, putting into practice the lessons of their instructors. Control by the *manyatta laigwanan* was loose and everyone did more or less as they pleased.

Dangoya waited until he sensed boredom amongst his own followers, when they itched to be doing something more exciting. Then he casually announced that he was off on a raid to Chagga country, the other side of *Oldonyo Naibor*. Immediately there was a clamour from *morans* wanting to go with him, but he chose only eight and planned to make a quick raid, if possible catching a glimpse of the white men.

On the flat plain called Engasurai which lay below the south western bastions of the Great White Mountain they came by chance on a big herd of good cattle guarded by three Kisongo clansmen. Relations between the Kisongo and the other Masai clans were at the time strained, and being within one day's fast walk of the *manyatta* at Namanga, Dangoya would never have considered raiding the herd for fear of reprisals. It was not his country, nor would he put a *manyatta* which was not his own at risk.

He was, however, overruled. The ebullient and mercurial temperament of his own people was a fact of life he was fast learning to live with, and the excitable *morans* swept through the herd and drove off seven fat steers.

Four days after leaving the *manyatta* the raiding party was back with their prize. This was the first success so they were greeted with great acclaim and Dangoya, in particular, was feted. The expected reprisal from the Kisongo, for some strange reason, never materialised. Emboldened by this, a large group of *morans* set off a few days later in Dangoya's tracks, but were soundly thrashed and routed, leaving three dead behind and trailing seven wounded. They returned empty-handed and their enthusiasm for the time being was dampened.

Another party had gone east towards Kamba country and they too were beaten off with several casualties and nothing to show for their efforts. A number of very small raids brought back odd animals for slaughter at the *olpuls*, but never more than two head at a time.

Therefore when Dangoya let it be known that he was to go on another raid, other *laigwanans* and individual *morans* tried to join his party, but he declined the honour of leading such a large body and preferred to select a small band from amongst his own followers – men on whom he believed he could rely and, he hoped, of undivided loyalty.

On his first raid, he had been unable to fulfil his aim which was somehow to see the white men in Chaggaland. He intended now to achieve this and not be deflected as he had been on the Engasurai by a herd of fat steers. He would go to *Oldonyo Naibor* and perhaps south-east from there, and only on his return journey would he consider carrying out a raid. He would not discuss his plans with anyone. This secretive behaviour was considered most unusual and when he eventually departed with only fifteen men, the people of the *manyatta* thought he must be mad and the whole raid doomed to fail.

However, before they left, the chosen group of warriors went to an *olpul*, slaughtered and ox and drank their fill of soups containing as much *kitoloswa* and *kiloriti* as their bodies would stand. Dangoya had ordered the men to travel light which meant no festive regalia and no shields, but Ngenia had made him a pretty beaded belt with lucky charms sewn into two ornamental triangles at the back, and although the belt was stiff and uncomfortable he had not the heart to leave it behind.

Before leaving the *olpul* Dangoya held a short meeting with his warriors and told them of his plans. Bareto, also a junior *laigwanan* and because of this appointed by Dangoya to be his second in command (about which Dangoya had misgivings as Bareto was related to Pushati), began to remonstrate and argue, but when Dangoya challenged him to a duel and accused him of being a coward like the rest of his family, the young man agreed to obey orders.

Among other instructions Dangoya warned the men that secrecy was to be maintained throughout. This would mean no contact whatsoever with other Masai unless absolutely necessary, and they would have to keep away from the usual routes. Movement at that time of the year would in any event be slow and tiring as the grass was very long and the areas through which they would travel teemed with game, so Dangoya's orders were received with some surprise and much unspoken criticism.

Nothing unforeseen occurred the first day and they reached Sinya just before dark. Here they saw several flocks of sheep, but Dangoya would not allow his party to visit the camps and they spent the night on the high ground above Sinya on the lower slopes of the northern end of *Oldonyo Naibor*. Early in the morning before it grew light, Dangoya and a band of four quietly raided one of the camps and removed a sheep without any alarm being raised. They moved on up the mountain a short way before suffocating the animal and cutting it into pieces for easy carrying, and when they reached the forest east of Ol Molog they stopped to make a fire and cooked the meat.

By nightfall the *morans* were halfway between Ol Molog and Loitokitok. It had rained unceasingly since midday and spirits were low, aggravated when they had difficulty starting a fire. The wood was so wet that the friction stick could produce no sparks and when eventually a feeble flame licked at the sodden kindling, it provided poor comfort.

Bareto, who could contain himself no longer, leapt to his feet with a curse and said, 'You are a fool and a coward! Why do we have to hide in the forest like Ndorobo when there are *manyattas* aplenty down below on the plains, with milk and *nditos* begging for us?' Turning to the others he continued, 'I say leave this madman to perish in the forest and come with me! We shall spend the rest of the night in comfort and tomorrow can be on our way back to Namanga with as many cattle as we can handle.'

'Yes!' replied Dangoya, 'and with the whole force of the great Purko clan on your tail! You and the *manyatta* at Namanga will be wiped out before the rain stops. Go home to your girls and comforts if you wish, and take anyone with you who cannot keep away from the thighs of a woman even for one change of the moon. But remember, when I return to the *manyatta*, if you are still alive, you will account for your actions to me!'

'If Bareto wishes to leave our *laigwanan*, he'll do so a dead man,' one of the *morans* said angrily, 'or if he is a better man than I, I shall remain here for the hyena to feast on my flesh!'

Bareto said no more and the wet and miserable men settled down for sleep.

That night they were charged twice by rhino, but no one was hurt, and at least the diversion caused some excitement, with the result that their morale was higher in the morning and the rain too had stopped.

In the panic of the night one of the young men had a received a nasty splinter in his foot, and as the day wore on he sickened. By evening it became obvious that he would not be able to travel any further and it was decided to leave him behind at Loitokitok, to make his way to one of the *manyattas* there and eventually to return to Namanga when he had recovered. Bareto was given the opportunity of accompanying the sick man if he wished, but he refused and the *morans* continued to move east.

Most of the high country around the mountain was an *oldigana* (East Coast Fever) area grazed by the Masai only in a dry year, and then only during the dry season before the rains if no other grazing with accessible water was available. Herds with known resistance to the disease alone were risked. Bareto well knew Dangoya's reasons for moving along that route, but it irked him to think of the fat cattle they might now be acquiring down in the lower land. To him it seemed madness to waste their time in unoccupied territory; nor would they be able to bring susceptible cattle back through the *oldigana* region, should they be lucky enough to capture some near Chaggaland.

Bareto dared not contest Dangoya's leadership any further at this stage. As it was, he had not made much of an impression on the other *morans*, and he would have to try to make a better showing in the future or hope that Dangoya would be killed or badly injured so that he could then take over and lead the party to success.

After moving along the seven thousand feet contour for a day and a half, Dangoya led his men in a gradual descent towards three *manyattas* lying on the lower slopes of the mountain. The rain had stopped and in the clear air they could see, far below and to the east, tiny Lake Chala with its still, dark blue waters. Further to the east were the Taita Hills. Lengerebe who had once lived in the area pointed them out and showed them too the Pare mountains in the south.

61

When they were within a couple of miles of the first *manyatta*, Dangoya called a halt, and selecting Lengerebe and another to go with him, sent Bareto and the rest to wait on a hill about five miles away to the north east where he would join them the next day. The *morans* were extremely hungry as they had eaten the last sheep the day before, but Dangoya warned them not to attempt any sort of raid and thereby draw attention to themselves. Their bellies would have to be patient, and in the meantime he would find out what he could at one of the *manyattas*.

Swinging round to the north, Dangoya and the two men passed the first two *manyattas* and approached the third from the north east, yodelling from some distance away as it was fast becoming dark. On reaching the small main gate they found it closed, which was unusual as they had announced their arrival loudly and well in advance. While they looked around the thorn enclosure, thinking that perhaps they had missed an open gate, six heavily armed *morans* appeared from behind them and asked for identification.

As a *moran* would not announce his own name, Lengerebe stepped forward. 'He is Dangoya, *laigwanan* of the Malambo Loitayo *morans* now at the Namanga *manyatta*.'

'Open the gate!' the senior *moran* called to his clansmen inside. Turning to the visitors he said, 'You are welcome. We have heard of you. We are the last *manyatta* at the edge of Masailand and have to be careful with so many *Olmeg* of various tribes on our borders. Also some of our *morans* raided an *Olmeg* camp and captured a young boy who tells us that the white men may be coming this way.'

Dangoya's attention quickened, but he tried not to show any interest. They were taken inside the *manyatta* where Lengerebe was recognised by one of the women, and this dispersed any last reservations held by their hosts. Given milk in one of the huts, they sat and talked with the local *morans* for a while; and when they got up to go to visit another house, Dangoya turned to the young woman whose milk they had drunk and said, 'May I come back?'

'Yes!' she replied immediately which meant he would be made especially welcome. Had she said he could please himself, it would have signified that he was free to feed and sleep in her house, but no personal hospitality would have been extended to him, and her bed would be out of bounds. As he left he stuck his spear upright in the ground outside her door to indicate that the house was committed to a guest.

After visiting several huts his men separated and took themselves off to sleep while Dangoya returned to the first house where he found the young woman waiting for him.

Although she was short and plump, with rounded hips and thighs much admired no doubt by many men, Dangoya found the woman unattractive, but he smiled and talked to her pleasantly and learnt that she was a widow with a small child. Since her husband's death from a Taita arrow she had lived here in her father-in-law's *manyatta*.

She had heard of Dangoya, she said, and of his buffalo kill at Mondul, and she was happy to show him hospitality. When Dangoya asked her to sit beside him so they would not have to talk so loudly, she invited him to her bed, and he rose to follow her to the small bed behind the partition.

Dangoya had no desire to make love to this woman, but he knew it was the only way to obtain information from her. No doubt too the *laigwanan* of the *manyatta* had enlisted her aid in finding out more about him and his men, but she could not conceive where his interest lay and it should not be too difficult to lead her conversation to matters relating to the white men.

He thought he and his two companions would not arouse suspicion – three men could hardly pose a threat. He was however a *laigwanan*, and it must seem unusual for a man of his rank, and at his age, to waste time visiting so far from home. He did not want to give any cause for distrust as he might at some stage in the future wish to return to the area with a large raiding party. So he told her a story of how a *moran* called Bareto had led a group of warriors on a raid into Chagga country. They were to return this way but nothing had been seen or heard of them for many moons and it was Dangoya's task to discover what had happened to them.

The woman was taken in by his tale, and not a little by his person. Soon she relaxed and began to answer his questions. She told him that at Larusa where the Masai had established a settlement for their slave tobacco growers, there were a number of Chagga slaves who returned often to their home regions selling tobacco. One of these was a well-known informer called Sawati, whose Chagga name was Mshiu, and this man was in contact with the white men. In fact it was he who brought the news that the Europeans intended visiting this very *manyatta*.

'Has the *laigwanan* agreed to see them?' asked Dangoya.

'Yes!' she replied, 'But I do not know any more than that,' and thereafter she refused to answer further questions, saying, 'I do not know,' each time he made a query.

He concentrated on love-making, hoping that by morning he would have regained her confidence – which was the case – for she invited him to return should he pass that way again.

The next day on their way to join Bareto and the others, Dangoya questioned Lengerebe who had much the same story to tell, except that he had heard the white men were to be ambushed before they reached the rendezvous with the *manyatta laigwanan*. The other *moran* had nothing to report, and Dangoya guessed he had not tried very hard and that some giggling girl had driven all thoughts of intrigue from his head.

As they approached Bareto's hiding place, a strong smell of roasting meat in the air angered Dangoya as he had given strict instructions to the men to take nothing. Telling Lengerebe and the other to wait, he crept forward and was met by a lookout.

'Where did the meat come from?' he snapped.

'It is not raided meat, *laigwanan*! We have not moved from here. It was just lucky that some Purko were returning from a raid in Chaggaland and one of the cows slipped and broke its leg. When they moved on, they said we could have what remained.'

Slightly mollified by the explanation, Dangoya sent him back to fetch the others and stalked into what had now become an *olpul*.

Holding a big piece of meat on a skewer, Bareto lifted it to his mouth, held the end of the meat in his teeth and with his razor-sharp broadsword sliced off a mouthful flush with his lips. As he chewed, his strong white teeth showed in a grin, and he gestured to Dangoya to help himself. Again the skewer went to his mouth, and he cut off another portion.

Relieved, Dangoya commended him, and taking his broadsword out of its scabbard prepared to eat.

Once more they climbed the foothills of the mountain and crossed the great shoulder under the jagged peak of *Oldonyo Naibor*'s little brother, Mawenzi. When they halted for the night they had already begun their descent to the plains, and the following morning reached the flat land and moved south with ease. Towards evening they made contact with some *layonis* herding cattle who gave them directions to Larusa, and when they spotted the smoke from the cooking fires of the settlement they selected a concealed place beside a river and made camp.

Early the next morning Dangoya sent off three *morans* to try to contact Sawati and a further three to investigate Masai *manyattas* towards the south. He told the latter party not to return until they had made reasonably sure which *manyatta* would welcome them without their having to divulge their intentions.

Oleserya, one of the *morans* who had gone to Larusa, returned with his party later that day and reported that they had seen Sawati who said there would be no difficulty in arranging for the white men to come down to meet them. Sawati would go into Chaggaland the following day to talk to the foreigners, but he would expect payment from both sides for negotiating the meeting.

'What have you agreed for payment, and how is Sawati to let us know the outcome of his visit to the white men?' asked Dangoya.

'I shall go to see him again in three days, when he will tell me the plans and state his fee,' said Oleserya. 'The man is a hyena,' he added.

For two days the men kept to their hiding place, not only bored but hungry too as they had eaten the remains of the Purkos' cow. All were impatient for action. Dangoya had to keep a tight hold on discipline and would not allow them out of the hideout, even to raid an animal to stave off their hunger.

On the third day the other group of *morans* returned from their investigations with the news that there were several *manyattas* to the south, all of which were friendly. They had heard too that the Chagga people were no problem as they could not stand and fight, and that the Europeans only wanted to talk and had no designs on the Masai herds.

It was now the day on which Sawati was due to return from his meeting with the white men up on the mountain, so Dangoya and Oleserya went to Larusa to see him. Sawati, however told them he had been far too busy picking his tobacco to go visiting, but he would perhaps go in the next day or two – after he had received payment.

Truly, thought Dangoya, this man is a hyena. 'What is your price?' he asked.

'One fully grown heifer now, and another when I get back from seeing the white men.'

'I agree to your price, although it is high, but I will not pay you until after I have seen these people.'

'Well,' said Sawati, 'if you think you can find the price by stealing heifers from them, you are mistaken. They have no cattle, only cloth, beads, blankets and knives. And if you had something good to offer in exchange, you could get a magic spear, but you could not use it for long as they would give you only a little of the medicine that goes into it to make it work.'

'Have you any of these things?'

'Yes, I have!' Sawati went into his house and came out carrying a knife and a blanket which he had been given, he said, by the white men.

The *morans* spent some time admiring these, and they marvelled particularly over the blanket of bright red and blue. Then Dangoya asked if Sawati had ever seen a magic spear. Without a word the Chagga went back into his hut and reappeared holding a rifle, the working of which he tried to explain to the *morans*.

'What happens,' Dangoya asked, 'when you have thrown the stone out?'

'Then you reload with another stone.'

Dangoya laughed. 'And what does the enemy do while you are doing that? No wonder these people have never dared to come to Masailand! How many cattle did you give for this?'

'I took it from a dead Arab, but I cannot use it as I have no medicine stones for it!'

'What can it kill?'

'Anything! Even a fully grown elephant, if you get close enough.'

'My spear can do that!'

'That is true,' Sawati conceded, 'but if you spear an elephant through the heart it can still turn and kill you, even with ten spears in it. But if you hit it with the stone of the gun in the head, even from twenty paces, it will fall. If you cannot get it in the head, you can aim for and break its front leg so it cannot move and will die of thirst where it falls, or you can finish it off with your spear or another stone from the gun.'

Dangoya set the rifle down with a grunt of disbelief and picked up the blanket, feeling again its softness, holding it close to his nose to sniff the strange smell. He nudged Oleserya and exclaimed, 'This thing is very nice!'

'I agree. It is nice,' and Oleserya stroked the blanket too.

Wrapping it around himself Dangoya said to Sawati, 'Give me this blanket!'

'No!' retorted Sawati.

'Are you not my friend?' Dangoya asked, but Sawati quickly brought this conversation to an end by enquiring when he could expect the heifer.

'I have no heifers here,' Dangoya said, 'but I promise on my oath that I will not leave this place after meeting with the white men without first paying you the agreed price.'

'For what reason do you want to see these men? All you Masai are so inquisitive!' And without waiting for a reply Sawati added, 'Go away, and come back in two days' time. I want to think about whether I will do your work before receiving payment.

Oleserya moved closer to the Chagga, and bending over him said, 'You think good or I will come and kill you!' And the two Masai strode off to their camp.

Dangoya thought there was little point in lying up any longer and dispersed his men to different *manyattas* where they could be sure of a welcome. All were to return to the hideout in three days when Dangoya would once again visit Larusa and the wily Sawati. The arrangement was greeted with pleasure and the *morans* went off happily in their various groups.

The procedure of meeting up and separating every few days went on for two full changes of the moon. Each time Dangoya saw Sawati he had some fresh excuse why he had been unable to arrange a meeting with the Europeans, until one day the Chagga told him the white men would not come to see him, but they would be happy to have Dangoya visit them on the mountain if he was prepared to face the Chagga tribe. Alternatively he could wait until they went to meet the *laigwanan* at Loitokitok and see them there.

Dangoya was angry. When Sawati asked for payment he refused, saying he would pay only when the meeting had taken place.

'Then go and see them,' the Chagga said viciously, 'but remember my curse is upon you until you have paid me the two heifers!'

Dangoya turned on his heel and left Sawati for the last time.

Two days later Dangoya's entire force ventured into the wooded country of Chaggaland on the slopes of *Oldonyo Naibor*, but met with fierce resistance from the Chagga who had been warned of their approach by Sawati. The Masai were very nearly surrounded and Dangoya gave the order to retreat. Even then they had to fight their way out, but fortunately for the *morans* the Chagga were only too pleased to see them go, for they had often suffered at the hands of the Masai when engaged in close combat and preferred to keep their distance leasing off a shower of arrows, none of which found its mark.

That night in a new bivouac just outside Chagga territory, the *morans* sat round the fire roasting a goat they had picked up on their way down the mountain. They were in low spirits and conversation was desultory except where Bareto sat with his henchmen, talking urgently to them in a soft voice. Dangoya had walked away down to the nearby stream to drink, and now as he returned to the camp he approached slowly and quietly, standing hidden in the dark of the trees.

There was a sudden lull in the talk around the fire and Bareto's voice rose distinctly as he struck the ground with his *knobkerrie* and said, 'Are we to continue to be ordered about by this imbecile? Who wants to see, or, for that matter, have anything to do with the white men? Certainly not I!'

At that point Dangoya stepped into the firelight. Walking deliberately and calmly, taking his broadsword from its scabbard, he picked up a big piece of meat on its skewer, bit into the hot dripping meat and sliced off a mouthful at his lips. Chewing a few times, he repeated his action. There was complete silence. Dangoya looked around, saying nothing, then he wiped his broadsword clean and slid it back into the scabbard.

'Has no one any ideas other than Bareto?'

The *morans* did not move and nobody replied.

Then Dangoya turned to Bareto and said, 'Have you finished speaking?'

The man looked at Dangoya in silence.

Facing the others Dangoya said, 'That *moran* has very good ideas, so ask him to tell us what we are to do next. My plans have failed and I shall hand over the leadership to him.' He went back to the fire and sat down, once again pulling out his broadsword to eat.

Gradually the others followed suit and after a while began to talk amongst themselves. When they had finished eating, one of the young *morans* called out to Dangoya, asking if he had a plan.

'Yes!' Dangoya shouted back. 'I have! But first let us hear our new leader, and what he has in mind for us!'

With every eye fixed upon him, Bareto got to his feet and stalked out of the camp. In a few seconds he was back, and striding over to Dangoya stretched out his arm and handed him a *seki* branch.

Not a sound was made. The *morans* sat motionless and watched Dangoya. Presently he stood up, spat into the fire and walked to the edge of the clearing where he urinated. Going back to the fire he sat down, belched a couple of times and ordered one of the men to go and relieve the lookout.

Striking the ground with his *knobkerrie*, Dangoya spoke in a strong clear voice. 'Listen, you *morans*! Am I your leader?'

'*Ebaye*! Yes!' they shouted.

'Did I not tell you we would bring back riches?'

'*Ebaye*!'

'Have we gone home yet?'

'*Usho*! Not likely!' and the *morans* laughed as they answered.

'Then why are some of you crying like women about our failure? We have not seen the white men yet it is true, but that was only part of our plan and tomorrow I start on the second and most important part – with those who wish to accompany me. Anyone who prefers the red flesh between an *ndito*'s thighs to the true work of a *moran*, which is making battle, can leave and choose his own leader, but do not ever come back to our *moran manyatta*!'

Here Lengerebe lifted his kerrie, struck the ground, and jumping to his feet said, 'You are our *laigwanan* and if anyone wants to challenge me on this, let him do so – or bring his *seki*!' He looked around the company and when no one replied, continued, 'We have our *laigwanan* and we go with only him!'

There was a hum of agreement from all present, including Bareto. Dangoya, his position once more secure, thumped his kerrie on the earth and declared, 'Tomorrow we go to observe the herds grazing the slopes to the north. And remember, when the time comes we have to find two heifers to pay that *Olmeg* Sawati, who deserves nothing.'

Bareto interjected here, also striking the ground. 'Why pay Sawati? You yourself have said he deserves nothing. We should put a spear through his chest, not give him our cattle!'

Immediately Oleserya joined the argument, banging his *knobkerrie* twice and shouting at Bareto. 'Remember Sawati's curse! You go and spear him if you wish and take the consequences, but I shall not start on the move home until Sawati has received his full payment, whether he is dead or alive!'

There was loud agreement from the *morans* at this, and Oleserya carried on with his speech. 'When this *laigwanan* of ours chose us from amongst all the *morans* who wished to accompany him on his journey, we were very pleased to join him because he is a leader of renown. Yet we had barely started on our way before some of you complained like women.' Here he looked directly at Bareto. 'Our *laigwanan* has offered you the opportunity to go home. He has also offered you the leadership, but I doubt if anyone would be willing to be led by anyone other than our *laigwanan*. I say let those who wish to leave this group stand up and do so now!'

Opinion amongst the men was undivided and all murmured their approval, looking at Bareto to see what he would do next.

There was silence for a moment and then Bareto picked up his *knobkerrie* and beat the earth with it saying, 'I have wronged you, my *laigwanan*, and I am willing to be replaced by one of the others as your deputy, if you so wish.'

Dangoya ignored Bareto's statement and proceeded to outline the plans for the following day.

Chapter 5

The Raid

The country lying between what is now called Himo and the mass of *Oldonyo Naibor* swept down from the mountain to the plains in long bare shoulders or ridges, with thickly forested ravines running alongside each through which the many rivers ran, carrying water from the snow-capped summit to the dry land below. Here on the slopes of the mountain the Chagga grazed their herds of cattle and goats, no longer true pastoralists but forced by the Masai to remain hemmed in, tending their crops and never venturing far with their stock.

Dangoya assigned his men to small groups, each to go out in different directions to observe the habits of the Chagga herds. As they had not eaten for two days, Bareto was to take two *morans* in search of food and afterwards to find a suitable hideout, sending one man back to wait at the spot where they stood in order to lead the others to camp at nightfall.

Bareto eventually set up camp further away than planned, at a place where he had been lucky enough to kill a young buffalo whose carcass was too heavy to move. Each day the *morans* went out spying on the Chagga herds, and each night they gathered in their camp and exchanged information. On the third day Dangoya took Bareto and his two men to see the area for themselves, telling the others to lie up and rest.

Dangoya was now fairly satisfied in his own mind what the next move should be and which Chagga herd would be attacked. All his men apart from Bareto's party were well acquainted with the lie of the land, and for this reason he led these three *morans* up through thick forest beside a fast flowing river, climbing the steep banks until they were clear of the gorge. Here they scaled an old olive tree, its gnarled trunk and branches affording easy footholds and its profusion of leaves complete cover. Across the glade in front of them they saw four herds, three grazing slowly towards them and the fourth, consisting of nearly a hundred head, moving away.

'The cattle coming towards us,' Dangoya said, 'will water at midday at the ford we crossed a short while ago, returning across the glade and over the far side of the ridge by dusk. Those with their backs to us will turn and water much later. After drinking they will cross the river and disappear over the ridge behind us. From that herd, we will take our pick.'

The *morans* listened keenly as Dangoya detailed the observations he had made over the past few days. The herd was guarded by four men with bows and arrows and two younger men carrying spears. These latter, Dangoya explained, stood with the cattle as they watered, while the bowmen took up positions on each side of the ford - two going ahead through the water to watch the front and two remaining on the slope behind to protect the rear.

All afternoon the *morans* sat in the tree and waited for the herd to return. Stealthily they followed the cattle to the river and from a distance saw them drink, the Chagga standing guard just as Dangoya had described it. When the last animal had disappeared from sight Dangoya took his men back to their camp, moving fast and silently through the darkening trees of the gorge.

As they slipped into the hideout Lengerebe said, 'I hope we decide to make the raid soon because the vultures have discovered our buffalo and it will be too dangerous to stay here another day.'

'We move tonight,' Dangoya replied, 'when the moon is well up. But first we eat, then I shall tell you my plan.'

Sitting around the glowing embers of the fire, the young men ate with gusto, filling their bellies with the succulent meat. Belching loudly, one of the *morans* said he thought they should stay until the buffalo was finished. It was too good, he said, to waste. All agreed it was the best meat they had tasted, but it would have to be left for the hyena and vultures to enjoy.

When everyone had finished eating Dangoya called for attention.

'Na *moran*! You *morans*! Listen to me carefully,' and Dangoya struck the ground with his *knobkerrie* and spat into the fire. 'When the moon is there' - he pointed above his head – 'we leave this place in silence. No one is to speak. We will go to the ford which you all know, and every man will hide in the position I tell him to go to. Bareto and one man will lie in wait and attack the leading bowmen as they cross the river before they have time to fit their arrows to their bows. No one will move until they have been attacked. Then Lengerebe and I shall take the rear bowmen and the rest of you will strike the young Chagga carrying spears and split the herd in two, driving off the leading cattle as those will be the strongest and fastest moving. Do not take too many animals and try to scatter the remainder as much as possible so that it will take the *narobong gotonye* Chagga some time to round them up. The delay will give us a chance to get away before they start following, by which time it should be dark.

'The cattle are to be kept close to the river until you reach the next ford. There you will re-cross and head for that hill.' Dangoya pointed to the south. 'Bareto will join me at the second ford where we will lie in ambush until dark. If the Chagga do not follow, we shall hurry to join you.'

The *morans* digested all Dangoya had said, then one of them asked, 'Why do we not just take the cattle and fight it out with the Chagga?'

'Because we have come this long way. By the time we get back to Namanga the moon will have gone through each change at least twice. We came to gather wealth, not to feed the hyena!'

'*Ebaye!*' several of the *morans* called out.

'Now you will sleep,' Dangoya ordered, and the *morans* slept in their usual fashion - sitting up with heads lowered between their bent legs, their spears stuck in the ground either in front or to one side, hands clasping the shafts.

When the moon was well over the top of the trees, Dangoya stood up and turning away from the remains of the fire, spat and relieved himself. The others stirred and began to move about, some talking loudly until Dangoya told them to be quiet. When all were fully alert he spoke again. '*Gona moran mabe*! Let us go!' and led the way out of the camp.

Silently the young *morans* moved through the night, the moon catching a glint from a spear, or the white of an upturned eye. They breathed easily, their long straight legs moving with an animal rhythm, their agile feet finding always the right place so no ankle twisted or knee wrenched in unsure step. Like the spirits of their forebears they passed beneath the trees of the gorge, excitement rampant in their blood at the thought of the dangers to come and the wealth and renown that would be theirs when tales of this day's work were told round the fires of the *manyattas* of Masailand.

It was almost dawn when they reached the lower ford and Dangoya called a halt to show Bareto and Lengerebe where they would join him in ambush after the cattle had re-crossed the river. Moving on upstream, they walked faster as the sky lightened in the east. With dawn it grew colder and the dew lay wet on the grass, brushing their legs with chilling drops.

Arriving at the next ford, each man took up his position after Dangoya explained again what he wanted done. Their wait would be a long one, until late afternoon, so they made themselves as comfortable as possible, some in trees, others in thick bush and several tucked away amongst the rocky crevices of the riverbank.

Soon after sunrise they observed the herd which they were to attack come to the river and cross over on its way to the grazing grounds, all eyes taking immediate note of the extra bowman. Dangoya knew this need not cause concern - his men outnumbered the Chagga by double - but it worried him nevertheless, and all morning the nagging doubt disturbed him until he slipped from his hiding place to find Oleserya.

'You must be responsible for the extra man. You will keep a good watch on him when they come to drink and place yourself suitably.'

At midday the first of the herds came to water and an incident occurred which reduced Bareto's confidence and caused him genuine fear. One of the cows smelled the Masai and lifted its head. Then without pausing to drink, it splashed its way through the water and up the slope towards Bareto and his companion. The cow looked them straight in the eye and having satisfied its curiosity turned and went back to the river.

Bareto found himself trembling with fright, barely able to contain the urge to run. When the herd left and went back to the grazing in the glade, he and the other *moran* changed their positions, going deeper into the bush. Bareto knew that had they been discovered it would have meant abandoning the raid, and he, for one, would have been thrown out by Dangoya or else forced to fight him. The outcome would have been certain defeat as he was no match for Dangoya.

Dangoya had watched the incident with foreboding and could only hope that Bareto would gain from the experience, and carry out his instructions as laid down by Dangoya when the time came to strike. Added to the worry of the extra guard was Dangoya's inner feeling of doubt concerning Bareto. He was now more than ever certain of the *moran*'s unreliability, and any trust he might have had in him faded.

The next two herds came to the river to drink and departed with no more alarms, and when the last bunch of cattle appeared excitement among the Masai rose to fever pitch. For most, it was their first important raid and among not a few were thoughts of how they would acquit themselves when the attack began.

In front of the herd strolled the two leading bowmen, oblivious to danger, with their poison arrow quivered and only large-headed clean arrows in their hands. Tucked in their waist-belts were big *knobkerries*, longer and thicker than those made by the Masai. Both men stopped in midstream, bending down to cup water in their free hands and talking to each other as they drank. Then they crossed to the opposite bank and moved up the slope towards Bareto's cover, turning their backs on the hidden *morans* as they watched their cattle drink.

With a yell that turned Dangoya's blood cold, Bareto fell on the first of the guards, killing him with one lunge of his spear, while the other *moran* dealt with the second man. Bareto continued to shout at the top of his voice, cursing the Chagga as he speared the corpses time and again. Pandemonium swept the scene. The cattle took fright, plunging in every direction, but the Masai moved in swiftly, knocking down the two young Chagga and driving off the greater part of the herd.

At the top of the slope leading to the ford, Dangoya, Lengerebe and Oleserya raced towards the three rear guards, one of whom raised his bow and sent an arrow flying. It lodged in Lengerebe's arm, but did not halt his headlong run. At that instant Dangoya threw his broadsword, cleaving the bowman's chest. The man pivoted to run and as Dangoya reached him he fell, one leg kicking up incongruously so that it tripped Dangoya who dropped hard beside the dying Chagga.

As Dangoya rose, one of the other bowmen struck him in the left eye with his *knobkerrie*, knocking him almost senseless. Staggering forward, knowing nothing but the stars in his head, Dangoya collapsed and lost consciousness, rolling as he fell into a vine-covered gully.

How long he lay hidden - blind, deaf and with no feeling – Dangoya never knew. He seemed to surface through mists of pain, only vaguely aware of voices nearby, which, as his head cleared, he realised were those of the Chagga calling to one another, perhaps turning over their dead and certainly searching for wounded Masai to finish off. He lay still, scarcely breathing, sure that soon they would find him, but gradually silence fell upon the scene and he sank once more into the peace of unconsciousness; only the tumble and splash of the river remained.

Dangoya was jolted back to wakefulness by shooting thrusts of pain, not in the agony-filled area of his head, but in his crotch and on his legs and thighs, and his first thought was of the Chagga enemy. Sweeping in and out of oblivion, the jabbing hurt grew worse and brought him at last to full alert. Like a man released from paralysis, he moved his hand down to his genitals and felt there the hard, brittle body of a safari ant, and another and another. Feverishly he began to pick them off, squashing the voracious wire-like insects in his fingers as he sat up and with swimming head prepared to move away.

The light was failing as Dangoya crawled from his hiding place and staggered down to the river, washing his injured and swollen eye as best he could, and removing the last of the ants from his flesh. Gulping handfuls of water, he knew he must get away and not stay exposed at the ford. The trail of the raiding party was not hard to follow and he made good progress as far as the approaches to the lower ford, but as the sky darkened he climbed out of the gorge and made tracks across the open country towards the hill he knew his *morans* would head for.

At first the going was easy, but as the pain in his eye grew worse, becoming almost unbearable, he found he had to stop to sit a while, resting his aching head on his arms. With moonrise he struggled on, his rests more frequent, and at one stage he fell into a delirium lasting several hours, for when he roused himself the moon had begun to slide from its zenith and he knew it would soon be morning.

With daybreak he was able to pick up the tracks of his party with ease and his spirits rose. Even the agony of his eye seemed to recede, but this respite was short-lived, and as the morning wore on he became weaker, halting more often and for longer periods, so that by midday he truly felt he was going to die. Now his only thought was to hide again, for if the Chagga found his body they would lay an eternal curse upon it. Stumbling away from the track he had been following, he found a low thorn tree and crawled in under its blessed shade, unconsciousness washing over him like the tide of death as his outstretched hands scrabbled a little in the dust and fell still.

Far to the south the *morans* ran with the raided cattle, dust rising in clouds about them, masking their faces with grey; sweat streaking from foreheads to chins, as they urged the thirsty animals on with shouts. By the middle of the day, they were safely in Masai country - at least safe from the Chagga – and on reaching a fast flowing river, Bareto called a halt.

Lengerebe was exhausted and weak from loss of blood, the arrow deeply embedded in the flesh of his upper arm. He sat for a moment to recover his breath. He, Bareto and another *moran* had successfully ambushed the Chagga at the lower ford while still light the evening before. Moving downstream they had laid a second ambush, but the Chagga had been so severely thrashed, losing five men, that no one had appeared and the three *morans* were able to follow on and catch up with the main body moving the cattle.

Now in relative safety men and cattle drank greedily after which two men stood guard while the stock grazed. At last Lengerebe could have his wound attended to, something he could not do for himself. One man held the arrow steady while another broke the shaft as close to the head as possible, then using considerable force the arrow was pushed through to the other side and removed.

Lengerebe sat stoically throughout, beads of perspiration breaking out on his top lip, but he showed no other signs of distress.

'Now wash it,' he said, and one of the *morans* urinated over his arm while Lengerebe turned it from side to side, the hot liquid comforting on the open wound.

'Are we sending anyone back to look for our *laigwanan*?' he called out to Bareto.

'That son of a dog is in the belly of a hyena by now!' Bareto replied.

'I saw him hit,' Lengerebe said, 'and he was not killed. Unless the Chagga killed him after we left, he is still alive!'

'Yes!' shouted one of the *morans*, 'and we cannot now go on and forget about our *laigwanan*!'

Bareto retorted angrily, 'I want to hear no more about Dangoya. *Nagaibara*! I curse him - burn his arm till he turns white. He is dead, the dog!'

Suddenly Oleserya jumped up, striking the ground with his *knobkerrie* and spitting at Bareto's feet. 'I have just three things to say.' He made the sign for three. 'Say three,' and answered himself, 'Three. One: we have forty-seven head of cattle,' and using both hands he made the sign for that number. 'How many? Forty-seven, and after paying our debt to the Chagga Sawati they will be shared amongst us, as though Dangoya was here and still our *laigwanan*. Two. Say two.' He answered himself again, holding up his fingers for two. 'Two. One or more of us has to go to find Dangoya, dead or alive. Three. Say three.' Once more his hand went up to show the number. 'Three. We ourselves shall appoint a *laigwanan* to act in Dangoya's place. I will not be led by him,' and Oleserya pointed at Bareto, spitting on the ground. 'That is all I have to say.'

Bareto could not take up this challenge as there was an immediate chorus of '*Ebaye*! Yes!' and one of the *morans* lifted his kerrie and thumped the ground hard. 'Good words have been said. I too am of the same feelings.'

Now Lengerebe also used his kerrie to attract attention. 'This *moran*,' he said, pointing to Oleserya, 'has the respect of us all, and he is experienced. I am happy that he should be our *laigwanan* until Dangoya returns.'

'*Ebaye*!' the *morans* shouted.

Lengerebe continued, 'We are a small group with many cattle which may draw attention. We therefore need as many *morans* as possible to guard them. For this reason I shall return alone to look for Dangoya.'

'We shall cross the river now,' Oleserya said, 'and move to the west. If you go with speed we should be on the far side of *Oldonyo Naibor* by the time you return.'

Lengerebe set off, ignoring the pain in his arm and trying not to think of when last he had eaten. It was not unusual for a *moran* to go three or even four days without food, but he was sure he would find some berries once he reached the forest. Through the long hot afternoon he strode, the mountain looming above him, the snow on the rounded summit gleaming in the bright sun and later changing from white, to pink, and then to an icy mauve as the day ended.

At dusk he halted, sitting beneath an old fig tree while he fed on its dry, sweetish fruit, the flesh sticking to his lips and teeth. The faintness he had felt earlier receded and he fell into a deep sleep, waking only when the moon rode high. Then getting to his feet he continued his journey. As the forest thickened the going became harder, but at first light he was at the ford where they had attacked the Chagga and it was easy for him to find the place where Dangoya had fallen, then to follow the marks of his dragging feet to where he had lain hidden in the little gully.

There was no mistaking the flattened undergrowth, but with relief he could find no blood. As the sun rose and washed the gorge in light, other little signs of Dangoya's progress became visible to Lengerebe's sharp eyes, but down beside the water the tracks were confused, so reasoning that Dangoya would have attempted to follow the cattle, he did likewise. Aware throughout that he was in Chagga country, he moved circumspectly down the gorge and came once more upon the scene of the second ambush. It was impossible here to pick out individual tracks, such a welter of men and animals had passed, but he searched all thick bush in case Dangoya was lying hidden and unable to move, making bird calls which he knew Dangoya would recognise and reply to if he could.

Lengerebe was slightly heartened at not finding Dangoya there as it must mean his injuries were not serious, and the further he had progressed away from the gorge the better would be his chances of escape. Travelling fairly fast Lengerebe left the gorge behind and made good time across the open country towards the hill they had used as their direction guide. Signs of the cattle they had taken were very evident, but still he kept his eyes pinned for any digression by one pair of feet away from the trail. This was the area he had traversed in the dark the night before and he might easily have passed Dangoya if he had been lying up resting.

As the day wore on Lengerebe's pace slowed while his spirits sank. He was very tired and at times felt faint. His wound throbbed and the flies pestered him, sucking maddeningly at the open flesh. He found a large pat of manure and scraping away the crust, dug out the moist inside and smeared it on his arm. Hope of finding Dangoya faded and Lengerebe could only guess that either the Chagga had discovered him or that hyena had dragged his body away and eaten him.

Despondently he picked a few berries from a nearby *seki* bush, being careful of the thorns, and as he moved around the bush to reach for a succulent cluster of fruit, his eye was caught by a movement in the top branches of a tree about five hundred yards away to his left. Again a movement, and he saw first one vulture then another as they dropped from the tree down to the ground. High up in the hot blue sky more birds circled to join the others.

Lengerebe could see no smoke which would have meant an *olpul*, but he decided to go and investigate before finally moving off on his long journey to rejoin the others of his party. He approached cautiously, the thought of a lion kill uppermost in his mind, but as he neared the tree it became evident that the birds were feeding on something small lying tucked under a bush at the base of the tree.

The vultures suddenly noticed Lengerebe and some lifted off the ground and perched in the branches above his head. Others flopped away insolently, not bothering to take flight. He was now quite close to the bush and could see one lone vulture feeding in the deep shadow. He shouted at the bird. It came out glaring at him, its obscene head covered in blood. Then to his horror he realised that he was looking at Dangoya's body.

There was no mistaking it. The beaded belt Ngenia had made, the red scabbard with its distinctive design, and the short *ngelan* were undoubtedly Dangoya's. Scrabbling through the bush on his hands and knees, Lengerebe reached the body and his heart thumped as he saw the damage the vultures had done.

Dangoya's left eye had been completely torn from its socket, leaving a bloody, oozing mess. Lengerebe saw pus too and the entire area was so swollen that he guessed it must have been the site of Dangoya's injury in the fight with the Chagga.

Feeling sick with shock and despair, Lengerebe moved away and sat down under the tree, waves of nausea sweeping over him as he thought of the quiet, determined *moran* whom he had come to admire and even love in so short a time. He looked over at the waiting vultures, bile rising thickly in his throat, and resolved that before he left his friend to them and the hyena that would certainly come, he would take Dangoya's scabbard with the pretty belt.

Crawling once more through the bush, he touched the body for the first time as he tried to unloosen the belt, and his heart gave a great leap at the warmth and softness under his trembling fingers. Spreading his hands over Dangoya's chest he could feel now the feeble breathing, and with joy surging through him he called Dangoya's name, over and over again.

Tearing soft green leaves from the bush about him, Lengerebe began to wipe away the blood and pus from the face of the unconscious *moran*.

Tenderly he pressed the swollen wound, smoothing and wiping away the pus until only blood seeped out. Then kneeling beside Dangoya he urinated, washing the gaping hole in the fine-boned face while covering the nose and mouth with one hand.

Lengerebe was parched with thirst and knew he must get water for Dangoya too, to help revive him, but it was some way to the last stream he had crossed earlier that afternoon and there was no question of leaving Dangoya where he was at the mercy of the vultures. Some men, he knew, would simply go on alone, but if it killed him in the attempt, he would carry Dangoya to water if necessary.

Thin and wiry, Lengerebe could walk for days on end and his stamina was that of an ox, but he had never done a day's manual work in his life. Nevertheless, he dragged the inert body out from under the bush and somehow hefted the far heavier Dangoya over his shoulder, grunting at the pain in his injured arm. For a hundred yards Lengerebe staggered with his burden, then had to stop to rest, lowering Dangoya to the ground. Panting and dry-mouthed, he stumbled to a fallen tree trunk and sat a while, resting his head on his knees and drawing deep breaths in an effort to regain his strength.

Glancing over at Dangoya he noticed a slight movement, the merest twitching, before the lips in the tortured face opened in a faint groan. Hurrying to him, Lengerebe knelt beside him, seeing Dangoya's one remaining eye open then close sharply against the glare of the sun. Gradually Dangoya regained consciousness and life came back to his limbs. He seemed aware too of Lengerebe's presence and when he tried to rise, Lengerebe helped him to a sitting position, supporting him with his good arm.

'I must bring you water, but I cannot leave you lying flat where the birds can reach you,' Lengerebe said. 'Let me try to get you as far as the log over there, so you can lean against it.'

With one of Dangoya's arms around his shoulders, Lengerebe raised him to his feet and slowly, half carrying him, assisted him to the fallen tree.

Ruefully examining his own *ngelan* which was badly torn, Lengerebe removed Dangoya's and saw with satisfaction that the cloak would hold water. Placing his *knobkerrie* in Dangoya's right hand, he told him to try to keep alert in case the birds appeared while he was at the stream.

'Go fetch the water, *moran*! Neither the vultures nor the hyena will get me this time!' whispered Dangoya, barely able to speak.

Hurrying off with the short calfskin *ngelan*, Lengerebe felt reasonably confident that Dangoya would be safe while he was away. Nevertheless, he ran the entire distance, drank and splashed himself, and filled the *ngelan* with as much water as it would hold. Speeding back to Dangoya he was relieved to find him standing unsteadily clutching the trunk of a tree. He led Dangoya back to the log and holding the water to his lips, let him drink his fill, then emptied the rest of the water over his head.

By nightfall Dangoya's mind had cleared and he was able to talk, although he was still very weak and his head ached.

'That mother-fucking Chagga hit me in the eye, the *narobong gotonye*,' he said, 'and it hurts.'

'Your eye has gone.' Lengerebe looked with concern at Dangoya. 'The vultures took it before I reached you.'

There was a small shocked silence. Sitting dead still Dangoya gazed unseeingly at the sinking sun. Then, picking up a stone, he flung it from him.

'Well,' he said, 'Have I not one eye left, and can I not see with that?'

Both young men sat in silence for a while, then Dangoya asked about the cattle and how many they had taken. With relief Lengerebe began to talk, telling Dangoya how they had fared and about the altercations with Bareto. Dangoya was in no fit state to say much, sitting hunched up against the log, but he listened and after a time dropped off to sleep.

Lengerebe used his friction stick to make a fire and the warmth helped allay the pangs of hunger. For several hours he kept watch over the sleeping Dangoya and when the moon rose he woke him.

'We must move on, and get as far as we can before daybreak.'

Dangoya shook his head, but the pain caught him sharply and he put a hand up to his eyeless socket. 'Leave me here and you go on. You cannot carry me.'

'Never will I leave you!' Lengerebe grunted in reply. 'I came all this way to get you, and I am not going back without you. Come on, *laigwanan*!'

Hauling Dangoya to his feet, Lengerebe put an arm around his waist and together they shuffled off through the cold night. Hour after hour Lengerebe endured the agony of the extra weight, seeming he thought, to push him into the ground. Delirious at times, Dangoya somehow kept his legs moving – one foot forward, then the other - and in his lucid moments he desired death with a longing Lengerebe so staunchly denied him.

'Come on!' Lengerebe would urge, 'By morning we shall be far from here and then you can rest!'

So the night wore on and as the sky imperceptibly lightened a chill wind sprang up and Lengerebe decided it was time to rest. Leading Dangoya under a big acacia tree, he lowered the exhausted *moran* to the ground and sat himself, looking towards the east.

Like a gift from *Ngai* he saw a small herd of eland grazing slowly away from them, heads bent as they cropped the short grass. The breeze blew in his face as he carefully rose to his feet and advanced on the herd. Cover was scarce as the country was open with scattered acacias, but he made headway towards the eland and after stalking them for more than half an hour was able to approach within a few yards of a lagging cow.

Suddenly the animal sensed danger, turning her head and spotting him as he raised his spear and threw it with all the power he could muster. In an instant the cow was gone, his spear fixed firmly in her side. He cursed loudly as he saw both his meal and his precious weapon disappear in a cloud of dust as the whole herd took to its heels.

Dejectedly, he began his return to Dangoya, when he unexpectedly found himself in the midst of a leaping herd of impala, frightened by the sudden stampede of the eland. Without thinking he drew his broadsword from its scabbard and, more in rage than with thought to kill, flung it at a well-grown male. The animal dashed away at speed, tumbling to the ground about a hundred yards from him. He ran after it to retrieve his sword which had entered the shoulder and cut through to the heart. Pulling it free, he wiped the blade on the glossy rufous hide and slid it back into his scabbard.'

'*Gage engu!*' he said, spitting on the impala, 'It stinks!' and walked back to Dangoya to tell him what had happened.

'Good,' said Dangoya. 'We must now find water, then eat and rest.'

'We cannot eat that filthy meat!' Lengerebe was appalled.

'Why then did you kill it? The *Olmeg* eat it, and like it. What must we do? Sit here and die of starvation while there is meat enough to feed us for a few days? No one will know we have eaten it, so go and skin it. I think we shall find water near those trees at the bottom of the slope. If you do not wish to stay, you must go on. But I am so weak and hungry, and cannot continue until I have my strength back.'

Dangoya tried to get to his feet, but could not on his own; so, helped by Lengerebe, he rose and stood swaying, then they walked together to the impala. Again Dangoya sank down and watched while Lengerebe skinned the animal. Suddenly the sight of fresh, bloody meat was too much for them and like animals they tore off the flesh and stuffed their mouths with the raw meat. Then cutting off what he could carry, remembering he had to assist Dangoya too, Lengerebe rose and once more helped Dangoya to stand.

'You were right,' Lengerebe grinned, 'when you are hungry it does not matter what you eat.'

Under the trees they found a spring and Dangoya fell to the long dry grass with a sigh. Lengerebe put down the meat and returned to the kill to fetch the remainder. He slept then for a while, and on seeing Dangoya sleeping peacefully, set off to see if he could recover his spear. He knew his chances of retrieving it were good; that he would either come across the eland lying dead or would find where it had fallen from the animal's body.

Within an hour Lengerebe came upon his bent spear and after straightening it, wiped off the dried blood with sand and a handful of grass. He was now close to the slave settlement at Larusa so decided to go to Sawati's house to see if their debt had been paid, throwing his *ngelan* over his left shoulder to hide his wound.

The Chagga was at home, laying out tobacco leaves to dry in the shade, and he greeted Lengerebe with civility, telling him he had received the two heifers and that he was pleased with them. Lengerebe was relieved to hear this news as it meant the Chagga who had lost the cattle had not got as far as Larusa in search of them. He learnt too that Sawati had lifted the curse and this, to Lengerebe's mind, could only mean that Dangoya would recover from his injury.

'I hear,' said the wily Sawati, 'that a band of strange Masai have raided a Chagga herd. These warriors killed many Chagga and left one of their own for dead, and took one hundred cattle with them.'

'That is a very great number.' Lengerebe waited expectantly for more news.

'I hear too that the Chagga have offered the white men land if they will help fight the Masai. The foreigners have not replied yet to the suggestion.'

Sawati's eyes narrowed as he watched the *moran*'s face, then he continued. 'I am told that the Masai on the plains surrounding all this part are very angry about the raid as they consider this to be their hunting ground.'

'Indeed, you have much news to tell me. I shall come another day to hear more.'

'Yes, and perhaps for a small fee I could still arrange for you to meet the white men. Things have changed since you were last here, and it might be easier.'

Lengerebe looked with contempt at the Chagga slave and said, 'I must go now, and leave you to your brothers on the mountain.'

Dangoya had made a fire and appeared to be much stronger, walking about unaided. Suspended over the embers to cook were pieces of the impala on long sticks, and the two *morans* ate with relish while Lengerebe reported on his meeting with Sawati, his hands busy as he scraped out the *calabash* he had picked up at Larusa.

Later they left by starlight, not waiting for the waning moon to rise, picking their way carefully through the unknown terrain, carrying as much of the cooked meat as they could manage plus the *calabash* filled with water. On passing Larusa they turned north-west, the Great White Mountain forever on their right and a guide to them through this new, strange country.

As they plodded on through the night, the enormity of their predicament came to Dangoya with full force. They could not possibly now catch up with their main body, and would have to fend for themselves - two injured, debilitated *morans* in strange, if not hostile, Masai territory.

By morning they were very tired, but Dangoya would not stop to rest.

'We will continue until the sun is above us in the centre of the sky before we sleep. Then when it grows cool we shall move on, stopping only when it is dark, and waiting for the moon to rise.'

Lengerebe's arm was healing fast and although the pain in Dangoya's head had eased, the wound was tender to the touch and suppurating. Every day he washed it with urine and kept it covered with cow dung to hasten the healing, feeling with his fingers the gradual decrease in swelling.

Hunger once again became a problem, but at least half the water in the *calabash* remained. They drank sparingly for they had heard there was no water before the *Ngare Nairobi*, the river of Cold Water, on the western side of the mountain.

For two days they walked in virtual silence, stopping in the heat of midday to rest before moving on again. Dangoya, always inclined to reticence unless he had something worthwhile to say, occupied his mind with many thoughts, and one day called out to Lengerebe.

'*Oljore*! Friend!'

Lengerebe stopped in his tracks and turned to look at Dangoya in happy surprise at being thus accepted as a tribal friend. It meant that from that day forward they would address each other as '*Oljore*' and Dangoya would, when they arrived back at their *manyatta*, present Lengerebe with a goat, sheep, ox or even a heifer from his own herd, depending on how the friendship grew.

'*Oljore lai*! My friend!' Lengerebe called back, and the two young men grinned at each other. The excitement of the raid, the deprivations they had suffered, and the horror of the vultures - all their mutual experiences sealed forever their friendship.

On the third day they approached a small hill and planned to rest on its summit, to gain a good view of their surroundings. Lengerebe was first to reach the top, his wiry legs taking him over the rocks on the steep incline with goat-like ease.

'*Oljore*!' he shouted down to Dangoya, 'Look there to the north! Is that not Lengkito?'

Hurrying up the hill Dangoya gazed across the wide plains to the horizon. There, with the cap of white cloud which always covered its peak at that time of the year, rose the bastion of blue Lengkito mountain.

'That's him!' shouted Dangoya happily. 'Two days at our slow pace and we shall be on the Engasurai.'

Encouraged by the thought that soon they would be in known territory, the *morans* ran down the hillside, laughing excitedly and slapping each other on the back.

Suddenly Lengerebe froze, his eyes widening at the sight before him. Quickly Dangoya swung round and his heart leapt into his throat as he saw a lion with two females not forty yards away. As he looked one of the lionesses charged, her tail up, eyes fixed and moving at speed.

Without hesitation Lengerebe stepped in front of the unarmed Dangoya, his spear raised, ready for the attack. Incredibly, sensing that the men were standing firm, the lioness stopped her charge a mere ten paces from them and turned back to the other lion. Then with great unconcern all three animals padded off, leaving the *morans* breathless and trembling.

Dangoya held out his hand to Lengerebe. '*Ngasa*, shake hands. I have a *moran* for a friend,' and he spat at his feet to emphasise the compliment.

Anxious to be as far from the lion as possible, the *morans* hurried on and knowing they were within reach of water abandoned the idea of any rest at all. Throughout the night they stumbled on until they could go no further, so a stop was forced on them and they sank into an exhausted sleep. Partly revived they continued the next day, their spirits lifting when they saw a *manyatta* within an hour's walk.

Weak with hunger and thirst, it was a very long hour before they entered the enclosure of the *manyatta*. Their arrival excited no reaction from the residents until they learned who the two *morans* were, and then the questions and answers flew back and forth.

The raiding party had reached Namanga with a large herd of cattle, so much the people knew; but Dangoya, they had heard, was dead - killed in the battle with the Chagga.

'That is what we have been told,' said an elder, 'and now we hear there is to be conflict in your *manyatta* over who is to be *laigwanan* after your death, because of the distribution of the cattle taken in the raid.'

For two days Dangoya and Lengerebe rested and filled themselves with blood and milk, regaining their strength and sleeping for hours at a time. The head of the *manyatta* had despatched two of his men to Namanga to carry news of Dangoya's imminent arrival there, in the hope of preventing any further rumblings of battle; and the men had travelled fast, for on the third day all of Dangoya's *morans*, except for Bareto and one other, arrived to escort him to Namanga in triumph.

Dangoya and Lengerebe were filled with pride and satisfaction at the honour shown them, and when Dangoya related to the others how Lengerebe had stood up to the lioness, that young man's prestige was further enhanced, especially as the story came from the lips of Dangoya himself.

At Namanga they received a welcome befitting their new status as heroes, with the girls crowding around them, and the other *morans* eager to hear about their adventures.

Dangoya searched the crowd for Ngenia and suddenly she was before him, her eyes lowered. Tenderly he placed his hand on her head in greeting.

'My *asanja*,' he said softly.

'My *asanja*,' the girl replied. Then looking up into his face, she cried, 'Oh! How badly you have been hurt! I shall find medicines for you at once!'

That night Dangoya lay with Ngenia beside him. She had pampered him with food and dressed his wound with little exclamations of pity and endearment, her fingers gentle about his face, and eventually he fell into the deepest sleep he had known in months, the warm smell of the hides and the slow burning olive-wood fire comforting in his nostrils.

When a meeting was held the next day, it was learned that Bareto, after consulting a witchdoctor, had left on his advice for another *manyatta*. The *morans* were unanimous in their choice of Dangoya as the premier junior leader of the *manyatta*, but despite their clamour and persuasion he declined the honour, feeling that in his present health he could not accept the responsibility. He had other plans for the future.

Over the past few months he had given a lot of thought to the question of his position in his foster-father's *manyatta*, and fretted at the bonds which tied him. He would never, he told himself, live in amity with the family. His previous troubles with Pushati and his brother Raien, the clashes with Bareto, the insidious methods of his foster-father to try to gain control over him, persuaded him the time had come to make a break and start his own *manyatta* – and before any more marriage contracts were made and his herd depleted by bride price. The sooner he could go home and set his plans in motion the better.

His eye too needed more experienced treatment than the loving Ngenia could provide. He had made up his mind to marry her. She was hard working, loyal, strong and healthy, and being an orphan very cheap. The fact that he loved her did not come into the matter and was of secondary importance. She would have to be taken home and circumcised first and Dangoya knew his mother would be only too pleased to assist with the arrangements.

Dangoya announced that he would be leaving Namanga immediately as he had urgent business to attend to at home. He was not well, he told the *morans*, and only when he was fully recovered would he return to the warrior *manyatta*. Some of the *morans* wanted to go with him, but he refused to take anyone other than Lengerebe who was to join him in his new *manyatta*.

Chapter 6

The Adoption

Naidu, second sister to Dangoya, was married to the witchdoctor at Gelai and it was to this *manyatta* that Dangoya and Lengerebe headed, driving their stock before them, their new acquisitions from the raid on the Chagga, a source of great pride. Ngenia brought up the rear with the loaded donkeys, excited about going home and her coming circumcision and marriage.

Gelai Mountain stood in their path to Malambo and Dangoya looked forward to seeing his sister again, but their arrival was not a happy one and Dangoya found Naidu in a state of extreme anguish, scarcely able to speak for tears. Her husband, the *laibon*, she told him, on hearing that Dangoya and his favourite nephew Bareto had fallen out, and later that Dangoya had been killed, had begun to treat the girl abominably, demanding the return of the bride price, accusing her of infidelity, and removing from her care their small son. He had stated for all to hear that the child she was about to bear was not his, and that when it was born it would be laid in one of the gateways of the *manyatta* for the Test, carried out only when a *laibon* disputed the paternity of his wife's child. This news filled Dangoya with horror, but there was nothing he could do except wait for the birth and hope to see justice done.

The infant, a healthy girl of medium size, was born on the second change of the moon, as the gates were closed after the cattle came in. On hearing of the birth, Dangoya went to the *laibon*'s house and informed his brother-in-law that he would be at his sister's gate in the morning when the stock went through. The *laibon* told him the child would be trampled to death as there was no question of it being his.

The next morning, when the milking had been completed and all the calves returned to their pens, no move was made to open the gates.

'Brother-in-law,' shouted Dangoya, 'why are the gates not being opened?'

'The child has not yet been brought,' the *laibon* replied, knowing the cattle would grow impatient.

'She is here waiting at her mother's gate and you should be here also! But let me warn you that if only this one gate is opened, causing the cattle to mass together, or if any other evil action is taken today, you and the culprits will answer me with your spears, and no *seki* shall be brought. I say this with respect, my *laibon*, but I mean it!' This was a grave challenge to a *laibon*, but Dangoya was too angry and distressed to be cowed by the eminence of the man.

The tiny infant was laid in the gateway and the people told to stand back.

'This child is not of my seed,' shouted the witchdoctor, 'and when the cattle go through the gate it will be stamped to death as you will all see. And this woman,' he pointed at Naidu, 'shall go from here leaving my son behind. From her brother, who is head of his house, I shall claim half of what I gave for her. Have you all heard?'

Dangoya's voice rang out in reply. 'You elders of this *manyatta*, I beg of you to hear me! First, all the gates must be opened. Second, my sister and I have listened to what the *laibon* has said, but I must state that if the child survives these many hooves the *laibon* will have admitted his lie, and my sister and the baby will go with me to my *manyatta*. The *laibon* may keep his son, but he will have nothing further from me.'

The *laibon* looked about him at the expectant faces then gave the order for all the gates to be opened, affording Dangoya some small relief and hope, and the cattle began to surge forward, eager for their grazing after the long night's fast. Naidu screamed and tried to run to her baby, but the women with her held her back.

With dread Dangoya watched as the leading animal, a huge brown steer with a bell round its neck, reached the child. Surprised, it saw the tiny naked form at its feet and in a frozen instant of time stood poised on the threshold of destruction, then digging its hooves in the soft dust, it leapt over the baby and was out and away from the *manyatta*. The rest of the cattle followed suit, jumping or sidestepping, dust rising in clouds about their legs, the baby invisible in the confusion.

For minute after long minute the cattle ran past, Naidu weeping dementedly, and with the passage of the last old cow the watchers saw a little heap lying on the ground, the faint wails of near suffocation from dust and dry cow dung pitiful in their ears.

Now the restraining women let Naidu go, and she and Dangoya ran forward to reach down for the child, the mother wiping and blowing away the dust from its face, cries of relief wracking her body as she held her baby close. One of the older women, clucking softly, came to Naidu and took the child from her, examining the tiny limbs carefully and finding it quite unscathed.

The witchdoctor gathered the elders about him and left the *manyatta* for a large tree outside where they all sat down in arrogant silence. Dangoya, still angry, was summoned. He obeyed the call out of respect, but as he approached the tree he was told to remain at a distance until their meeting was completed.

For a long time he was left to kick his heels in impatience, while the murmurs of their discussion rose and fell in the early morning air. Eventually they were ready for him and he was told to join the meeting and sit down.

From the folds of his *ngelan*, longer and made from heavier skin than those worn by the *morans*, one of the elders took out his bamboo tobacco tube which hung from his neck on a piece of thin hide. With long, slow deliberation he opened one end, shaking out a little tobacco into the palm of his hand. Carefully he replaced the small leather lid and opened the other end of the tube. Very delicately he shook out a pinch of soda, capping that end of the tube too before stirring the mixture with his forefinger. Letting the tube fall about his neck, he picked up the concoction and inserted it in his mouth between the lower lip and gum. Only then did he give his attention to the assembly of elders, a stream of saliva shooting out into the dust as he lifted his long herding stick to strike the ground.

'*Abaya*! Elders! We have here before us today a young *laigwanan* of exceptional fame and ability.' He paused to give himself time to spit again and to urinate where he sat. 'He is related to us, for is his sister not married to our *laibon*? And did we not prove that her newly born child is truly conceived from our *laibon*'s own testicles?' Another pause while he spat. 'Why then does this *moran* threaten to take the mother and the child away? Tell me!' A long pause, giving the elders time to reflect. 'Someone tell our son he must not listen to the woman's lies about being cruelly treated. Do we not all know how badly his sister has behaved and how well our *laibon* has cared for her?

'Someone tell this, our respected son, to go on his way to the wars and let his wise and experienced elders deal with the complaints of women! *Nena age*. That is all.'

Another elder struck the ground, spat and said, 'I say let the *laibon* tell us what happened.'

With aggravating slowness the witchdoctor looked at the elders surrounding him and then with insolence let his gaze fall upon Dangoya. Spitting precisely at Dangoya's feet he thumped the ground with his ebony *knobkerrie*.

'Brother of my wife,' he said. 'Did I not do everything according to custom? And did I not prove without any doubt that your sister's child comes from my *nderege* which hang here between my legs? How else can I prove with more certainty that the child of your sister is also my child whom I placed inside her?'

The elders murmured agreement, and each in turn had his say. All the while Dangoya sat silent out of respect, biding his time and undaunted by the flow of words, waiting to be invited to speak. When at last the senior elder asked if he wished to say anything Dangoya straightened and faced the company.

'*Na moruo*' he said, 'You elders. With respect I wish to speak. You saw what happened this morning and you were all a party to it, accepting the terms as custom dictates. But if I had not been here you would have killed my sister's child.' There were a few angry rumblings from the elders but Dangoya ignored them, blowing his nose with his fingers, wiping them clean on the shaft of his spear. 'Tomorrow before the dust of the cattle leaving the *manyatta* has settled, I go from here with my sister and her newborn child. If this *laibon* wishes to have her and the baby back he can do one of three things.' He made the sign for three. 'One, he can go to my sister's mother's house and talk with the women. I shall not interfere. Two, he can take the matter to a meeting of the senior elders of our two clans. Or three, he can send the *morans* of this clan to take my sister forcibly from her mother's house!'

They were strong words from so young a *moran*, but before any of the elders could reply he was striding away calling, '*Sere na moruo*! Goodbye you elders!' over his shoulder.

As Dangoya had promised, they left the *manyatta* early the next morning, Ngenia helping Naidu with her donkeys and comforting her as she said goodbye, with many tears, to the little son she had borne the *laibon* three years before.

Travelling slowly over the next few days as Naidu was weak and bleeding heavily, the party neared Malambo. They had heard on route that Dangoya's people had not yet moved to their new grazing grounds and Dangoya was pleased with this news as he wanted now to set up his own *manyatta* in the Jaegarsumet - Engaruka area close to that of Olengesen his instructor.

Dangoya's wound continued to give trouble and a deep-seated infection set in, so that by the time they arrived at Malambo he was ill with fever. Filled with concern and desperately worried about her son, Singira sent for a female witchdoctor from Olalaa who performed an operation of sorts and cauterized the wound with a red-hot knife. Although Dangoya made a rapid recovery, he was severely scarred and the flesh puckered around the empty eye socket in grotesque contrast to the smooth planes of the right side of his face.

'But at least you are alive and strong,' said Singira, ever comforting.

Ngenia was circumcised and married to Dangoya, and according to custom lived not with him but with his mother. The marriage annoyed the elders as they considered Ngenia beneath him, and had intended linking their own families to that of the fast-rising *Ngongu Nabo*, One Eye, as he became known.

With time to think, Dangoya discussed with Singira his plans to break away from their present *manyatta*, but she was opposed to his proposition. Although a junior *laigwanan* of some standing amongst the *mbarnoti* age-group, he would still have to carry out more raids to increase his wealth and go to war to establish firmly his present position. It was not until he pointed out that he would build his *manyatta* beside that of Olengesen where he could continue to be guided by that great man, that Singira was finally persuaded and agreed to fall in with his plans.

With Lengerebe and a young *moran* called Loito, who begged to go with them, Dangoya went in search of Olengesen. They were a happy group, full of good humour and rested after their trials of the past few months. Dangoya had presented Lengerebe with a heifer to seal their friendship, so now they called each other *Ndawo*, 'heifer', and Lengerebe, having discovered that Dangoya's youngest sister Nairasha was not spoken for, said he would ask his father to make the necessary approach.

They found Olengesen at Engaruka and he welcomed Dangoya with genuine affection; and when he learned the reason for the visit, showed his pleasure by presenting the young men with an ox for slaughter. They took the animal into the forest and made an *olpul* where they were joined by other *morans*, one of them producing yet a second ox, when the first had been eaten.

There were girls aplenty too, and several days stretched into ten, then twenty before Dangoya decided they must go back to Malambo to arrange the removal of his stock to Engaruka, but on passing a *manyatta* at Jaegarsumet they were again waylaid for Dangoya found his sweetheart Masaiko living there. For two days he dallied, enjoying her company and her bed, loath to leave the girl who, more than any other, could make him laugh. She was now married with several children, but in her maturity was as teasing as ever and her astonishing vigour when making love left him gasping. With reluctance he dragged himself away.

A day's fast walk from home, the sky darkened with heavy cloud ahead, lit with flashes of lightning, and thunder rumbled with ever-increasing tempo until it cracked and boomed above their heads. With no sheltering *manyatta* in sight, all the *morans* could do was keep moving.

As they passed a low ridge bearing a couple of large flat-topped thorn trees, the new green growth strangely pale in the peculiar light of the coming storm, Lengerebe called out.

'Look, *Ndawo*, over there! Smoke under that tree.'

Dangoya and Loito turned to look and without a word being said, all three changed direction and walked towards the ridge.

Suddenly the heavens opened and they were deluged in solid sheets of rain and hail. Still some distance from the thorn trees, their only protection their short *ngelan*, which they pulled hastily from their shoulders to cover their heads, they had to halt. The hailstones were so big and damaging, they had to raise the skins well above their heads to lessen the impact, and huddled together with arms up-stretched they called out curses to the sky, waiting for the storm to pass.

As the torrent eased to a gentle drizzle, they made their way up the incline of the ridge to the first of the trees where they found the remains of a small fire, and slightly to one side the skinned carcass of a huge male lion. With exclamations at its size they examined the body, poking it with their spears and spitting on it.

On the edge of his limited vision - before he could shout in warning - Dangoya saw a swift blurred movement as they were charged by a lioness. Then he yelled, and with the speed of a great cat himself, Lengerebe lunged forward, his weight transferred smoothly from his right to his left leg as his sinewy, supple arm drove home the spear cleanly into the animal's heart. It was a perfect kill, the *moran*'s action like liquid, flowing steel: no hesitation, no interruption in the command from brain to muscle.

Dangoya too was prepared, and as the lioness fell towards him, knocking him over, his spear pierced her side, and she was dead before she touched the ground. Taking no chances, Lengerebe struck her between the eyes with his kerrie with a resounding crack, grunting himself with the effort. Breathing hard, the *morans* had barely time to straighten up before seeing yet a second lioness coming in fast, but she thought better of it and veered off, Loito hot on her heels and eager to emulate the others.

With wild shouts all three chased the lioness, but when it became obvious she was not going to turn and do battle, they gave up and went back to the carcasses. The *morans* were in a highly excited state and when Lengerebe began to throw a fit, jumping up and down and frothing at the mouth, Dangoya restrained him, pulling him down to the ground until he recovered.

'*Ndawo*! The *kiloriti* is working well on you today,' he said, watching his friend gradually return to normal.

Dangoya had not had a fit himself, but had seen others in that condition, the build-up of the drug in their blood causing convulsions after excitement and great exertion.

When Lengerebe sat up and saw them skinning the lioness he said, 'You both have better head-dresses than that will make.'

'This is yours, and I am skinning it for you,' Loito replied.

'I will only wear male lion skin.' Lengerebe pointed to the first carcass. 'Like that one. He surely had a beautiful mane.'

'There must be a camp or a *manyatta* close, or the people who skinned that one could not have carried the whole skin a long way. Let us go and find them.'

They walked to the top of the ridge and looking down on the flat country beneath them, saw three sheep camps set in the midst of green, new grass, the flocks grazing as they moved closer to the night enclosures.

'The rains have been early here.' Dangoya took in the scene, surface water glinting in the sunlight which pierced its way through the hurrying storm clouds. 'It will be dark soon and you saw how that lioness nearly flattened me in the daylight! Let us hurry.'

Yodelling to warn the camp of their arrival, they walked quickly over the wet ground, darkness falling fast.

'Who are you?' a voice called.

'*Laigwanan* Dangoya of the One Eye!' Lengerebe answered for him.

'This camp is yours,' the voice replied.

There was an abrupt change in the wind and wafting into their nostrils came the welcoming smell of sodden sheep's wool and dung, the slightly acrid smoke of the fire and the aroma of roasting mutton. It set the saliva flowing in their mouths and they smacked their lips, bellies rumbling with the joyful pain of hunger soon to be assuaged.

They were led before the fire where a number of *morans* sat with several girls, boasting of the lion they had killed. When they heard Dangoya's name they turned to greet the newcomers, the men shaking hands and the girls bending their shaven heads for the guests to lay their hands on.

An older *moran*, an instructor, told them they were celebrating as the young *mbarnotis* of the camp had killed their first lion that day.

'A beautiful specimen.' he boasted.

96

'We know,' Dangoya said.

'How do you know?' the man asked in surprise.

'Because Lengerebe killed its mate when it charged us, and Loito here chased away the other one.'

'Did you really kill the lioness?' asked one of the *morans*. 'If so, where is the skin?'

'Go and see for yourself,' Lengerebe flung out an arm. 'It is lying under the tree next to the male you killed, and its skin is on its back.'

'But you have no headdress! Why did you not take the skin?'

With scorn in his voice Lengerebe said, 'I do not wear female skin!'

Suitably impressed the *mbarnotis* fell silent, and the senior *moran* told them that the lioness they claimed to have killed had chased away twelve *morans* from the dead male. 'She was the fiercest female I have ever seen.'

One of the young men called out, 'Let us go now to fetch her skin before she is eaten in the night.'

The instructor turned quickly on the hothead and reproached him. 'What are you? A hyena also, picking up other people's leftovers? You should all be ashamed that you left a fierce lioness for someone else to kill!'

The young men grinned and continued with their meal, while their talk turned to real and imagined feats. Dangoya refused to be drawn about his own achievements, preferring to tell of how Lengerebe had twice saved his life from lion. The girls, who had heard of Dangoya, tried to cajole him into talking as they were eager to hear about the Chagga and how he had lost his eye, but he remained reticent.

Long after they had finished eating the *morans* sat round the fire talking and sleeping. Occasionally one would get up to join a girl in the small hide shelters on the edge of the camp, then return to the fire to sleep with head on drawn-up knees, a hand on the shaft of his spear.

At dawn when the *layonis* took the sheep out to graze on the wide plain, Dangoya and his party left the camp on the last day of their journey back to Malambo. They moved north on the edge of the *Serenget*, always an area abounding in lion, so they were not surprised to see a large black-maned lion lying under a tree, alone and unattended by females.

'Would either of you like that fine head-dress?' Dangoya asked the others.

'I have my father's,' said Loito, 'but I am willing to help if anyone wants it.'

'Yes! I want it!' Lengerebe's reply was quick. 'But only if I get the first spear in it.'

'It's yours! So take the lead,' and Dangoya fell back, following Lengerebe towards the lion, he and Loito at intervals of about three paces behind.

Lengerebe gave his instructions. 'We advance, talking as usual. *Ndawo*, when we get near, you will go in front at two spear lengths out to my right. Loito, you will move out the same distance but behind me.'

The lion took no notice of them as they got nearer.

'He looks very quiet,' Lengerebe eyed him. 'When I draw level with him at about five spear lengths, I shall move in and spear him in the shoulder, then retreat to a position between you both. He should then be facing you, Loito, but hold your spear unless he charges. As soon as I have given him my spear, *Ndawo*, help him on his way with yours. We must then both be ready to protect Loito. If the lion moves off, then let him go. With two spears in him he cannot go far. Another thing may happen: he may turn with us as we walk past. In that case you two must reverse your roles.'

The plan complete, the three *morans* advanced on the lion which watched their casual approach with indifference. It looked at each in turn, then when Dangoya was past, Lengerebe struck, throwing his spear at the sitting lion. It rose in an instant and began to run off, and Dangoya had to move fast after it to fling his spear at it. Immediately it turned on him, but Dangoya was already putting ground between the lion and himself.

All this was too much for Loito, and he too had to let the animal have his spear. Once again the lion turned, but the shaft of one of the spears embedded in its shoulder dug into the ground, making its move clumsy and giving Loito just enough time to side-step a mighty slap from its paw which would surely have killed him outright. Lengerebe won the day again as he struck the back of the animal's head with his *knobkerrie* and it collapsed in a heap.

Panting hard and full of excitement, the *morans* pulled their spears from the body and roughly straightened them, congratulating each other with slaps on the back, still trembling with the thrill of the kill. When they had quietened down they began to remove the shoulder skin with its fine black mane. Certain bones and the claws were cut out for decoration and the fat taken for medicine.

'Now we must hurry or we shall be hit on the head again as we were yesterday.' Dangoya looked up at the threatening sky, not relishing another soaking or battering with hailstones.

They did not linger, loping along fast with some distance still to cover before they arrived at Malambo. On the way Lengerebe cut some thin sticks to make a drying frame for his new headdress. It was customary for this type of work to be done at an *olpul*, and knowing that Lengerebe had no small stock at the *manyatta* and that being the rainy season it was not the proper time for an *olpul*, Dangoya arranged for Loito to go with him when they neared the grazing flocks and take one of his own goats for slaughter. It would be a makeshift *olpul* and they would have to find a place with an overhanging rock on one of the hillsides where they would have some protection from the rain, but it would suffice.

At the *manyatta*, where they were met with much acclaim, everyone wanting to inspect the lion skin and hear about what had happened, Dangoya told Lengerebe that if he had no one to do the sewing for him, he would ask his mother. If Lengerebe took advantage of the offer, it would mean inviting Nairasha, Dangoya's youngest sister, to help him. Being uncircumcised, she would be allowed to visit the *olpul* for measurements and fittings which would give Lengerebe a chance to get to know her.

A wide grin spread over his face as he thanked Dangoya. '*Ndawo*, my friend.'

While Dangoya was at the *olpul* his foster-father, *laigwanan* of the *manyatta*, announced that they would be moving to their wet-season grazing at the next change of the moon. On hearing this news Dangoya went directly to him and told him of his intention to break away to start his own *manyatta*. He told him too which cattle he would be leaving for the old man's use and offered to take certain of his animals in return. This was customary, and Loito, having expressed a wish to accompany Dangoya and being a grandson to the *laigwanan*, would be able to keep a watch over his interests.

Dangoya's herd was fast becoming one of the largest in the area. With good husbandry he had taken care of the animals inherited from his father and the natural increase over the past years together with the bride price received for his two married sisters had swelled the numbers. Likewise with his sheep and goats, and he was well on the way to being a wealthy man.

With the close members of his clan about him, responsibility weighed heavily on him for he realised that all these people were from that day forward dependent on his good judgement, and his strength, for their food, their shelter and their happiness. Dangoya led the founding stock of his new *manyatta* out on the plains, setting their faces to the wind from the south.

Scampering along and ostensibly in charge of the goats, was Dangoya's young brother, excited to be going somewhere new, and Naidu with her child, recovered from her ordeal at the hands of her former husband. Nairasha, all eyes and longing looks at Lengerebe, helped her mother with the laden donkeys, as did Ngenia, always calm and capable; and Singira herself, her carriage and beauty undiminished by the years and a person of importance in the tribe, walked in pride behind the dust raised by her son's herd. Having borne more than four children, she had been given the freedom of the *manyatta* they had just left, with the title 'Mother Dangoya', and been presented with a full-length female *ngelan* made from shaved, white sheep skins with a border of wool around its edges. She had more than earned the honours bestowed upon her, having had five children all of whom were still alive, and enjoyed her new status which was that of an elder of the *manyatta*.

Loito accompanied the family, together with his mother, his brother and a small sister. He, Lengerebe and Dangoya flanked the cattle - over three hundred head - well-grown, strong animals for the most part, with numerous calves of varying ages. Dangoya's flocks of five hundred sheep were on the annual grazing round of the *Serenget* and these he would collect during the next dry season.

Dangoya would have preferred to wait for the rains to ease before making the move, but his impatience had not allowed for any delay. The rain slowed their progress and the season's new crop of calves which were born along the way, also prevented any rapid drive towards Engaruka. They were short too of manpower which meant a constant alert for everyone save the smallest children, as predators were rife in the area.

There was no danger of a major raid being launched on them as they were in Masai occupied country, but this would not have precluded a band of youthful *morans*, full of bravado, from stealing a few head of cattle for an *olpul*, especially as it was obvious for all to see that Dangoya's party was undermanned, with only three *morans* to protect it. Dangoya's reputation, however, probably kept such hotheads in check and they suffered no losses.

For two full changes of the moon, the length of the journey, no one had very much sleep, although on several occasions they were able to stay within *manyattas* on the route, and once or twice occupied empty *manyattas* which gave the men some rest as they were able to shut the cattle in for the night.

When the weary travellers eventually arrived at Olengesen's *manyatta*, they found he had demarcated the site for Dangoya's new *manyatta*, close to his two, with a light surround of thorn bush, and the first house was almost ready.

There was rejoicing on both sides, and on the following day the building of the *manyatta* and the huts began in earnest. When the thorn enclosure was strong and complete, its five gates in place, Dangoya called Lengerebe and said, 'Only women's work remains. Loito will stay in charge and tomorrow you and I leave for Naberera.'

During the long march from Malambo, the serious lack of grown males in his group had been brought home to Dangoya, who looked with objectivity at the load he was now to bear. The only solution would be to employ a family of poor, working Masai with grown sons to help herd the cattle and sheep, a gap which could not be filled by either Lengerebe or Loito, neither of whom were poor nor of the working class. He would have to be careful in his selection as whoever he chose would be brought into his family and become a part of it, being given stock for their own use which would still belong to Dangoya or other cattle owners, but progeny of that stock would from time to time be given outright to them.

Lengerebe knew of a family at Naberera, descendants of the Ngasumet well-digger slaves and the Lumbwa clan of Masai blacksmiths, whom he thought would fill their requirements. The family consisted of Kilimben, a working elder, and his wife and three sons, two of whom would be circumcised before the *olpiron* was broken - one almost immediately and the other by the time the next rains were due - while the third boy was still a child. There was also a grandfather, Lengerebe reported, very old and very blind but much loved by his family.

'No matter,' Dangoya said, 'how old and blind he is. If the family agrees to come, he shall come too.'

On the way to Naberera they called in at a warrior *manyatta* at *Oldonyo* Kisale and there Dangoya again met Olembere, one of the Kisongo *morans* who had been with him at Mondul when he killed the buffalo.

Over the fire that night the story was retold with many embellishments, but Dangoya in turn advanced Lengerebe's reputation with the accounts of how he had saved his life. Both young men grew in stature in the eyes of the Kisongo *morans* and when the dancing in the *manyatta* came to an end with the usual scramble by the girls for the *morans' knobkerries*, those belonging to Dangoya and Lengerebe were among the first to be snatched up.

The *ndito* with whom Lengerebe spent the night was an expert plaiter and twister of hair, and she had no difficulty persuading the two young men to stay on for a few days to have their hair done.

With deft fingers and amid much laughter and teasing, she joined and twisted bits of sheep wool to their hair, increasing the length and forming numerous strings of it, while the *morans* carved sticks like wishbones on to which the mass of twisted strands were joined in one pigtail.

The other girls, in between their chores, crowded around the *morans*, teasing and arousing them, begging them not to leave - a suggestion endorsed by the senior *laigwanan* in person, who invited Dangoya to join their *manyatta*, Dangoya would not commit himself, explaining the business he had to attend to at Naberera but promising that when the time came for him to rejoin a *moran manyatta* he would consider the offer.

On the morning of the third day they were able to depart with Olembere accompanying them, their new hair styles evoking much admiration from the girls, their heads adorned with trinkets given in remembrance and their bodies sated with too much love-making.

For some distance they walked in silence then Lengerebe said, 'Those Kisongo girls are worse than bitches on heat!'

'What else can you expect,' Olembere laughed, 'if you go about with a leader with the reputation of One Eye!'

Dangoya was glad of Olembere's company in an area populated by Kisongo clansmen. Although not at war with the other clans at the time, the Kisongo, being the largest and most dominant in that part of Masailand, were intolerant of the lesser clans and Dangoya found Olembere's presence a leavening factor in their movement through the region.

When they reached Naberera they were told where they could find the family of Kilimben.

'The old man is very sick and not expected to live,' their informant said, news which Dangoya was not really sorry to hear as the removal of the old man all the way to Engaruka had been a worry, although he had been willing to take him.

There were three *manyattas* in a close semi-circle and they were directed to the last of these which was small and dilapidated, containing only five huts. The enclosure looked abandoned, but as they approached people could be seen outside one of the houses. A young girl poked her head out of a door and they called her over, the flies descending in their hundreds on her face, obliterating her vision until she put up a hand to brush them away. Then, bending her head to each *moran* in greeting, they briefly laid their hands on the shaven skull.

'Where is the house of Kilimben?' enquired Olembere.

The girl turned to point at one of the houses outside which stood a middle aged woman who greeted them as they walked up to her.

'Kilimben has gone with his sons to layout his father for the hyena, but he will soon return,' she said.

'When did the old man die?'

'He is not yet dead.' The woman began to cry softly. 'But he will die tonight when the hyena eat him.'

'Is he very sick?' Lengerebe knew how poor this family was, unable to afford the death of the old man in his house and the subsequent fee to the corpse carriers.

'Never could he have lived another two days.' She pulled herself together, asking their business and where they had come from. They told her only that they had important matters to discuss with her husband, and on hearing this she offered them the hospitality of the little *manyatta*.

'You may go for a little milk to each of the houses as we have few cattle and little to give to guests.'

They drank sparingly from the woman's *calabash*, then Dangoya said to Olembere, 'Tell her we will come in the morning to state our business with Kilimben.'

Olembere passed this information on, saying, '*Laigwanan* Dangoya of the One Eye will return tomorrow morning.'

Dangoya addressed the woman himself then, asking after her eldest son.

'He was circumcised at the last full moon,' she said, 'and in a day or two he leaves to hunt for his headdress. He cannot be away for long as he is needed here to help with the cattle.' She smoothed her hands together, feeling a slight apprehension before the *morans*, and a tiny crease appeared between her eyes.

'Your son must not leave until I have talked with his father.' It was not an order from Dangoya but a request, and the woman was quick to catch the implication that her young *mbarnoti*'s participation in the talk with her husband would be required, and that the talk would be of great importance.

'Both my husband and my son will be here when you return.'

As they left the *manyatta* by the western gate, the afternoon sun strong in their eyes and the air humid with impending rain, they passed close by a flat-topped acacia, the delicate branches giving perch to marabou storks and vultures, their rapacious eyes unblinking as they waited impatiently for the old man lying beneath to die. Like a gnarled tree trunk, pitted and twisted with age, the worn body lay; a piece of hide suspended from a branch fluttered in the soft wind about his face - poor protection from the wicked beaks which would soon pluck out the eyes. Sightless for many years, the fragile paper-thin lids opened every now and then when the birds jostled too noisily for position, a reflex action for the eyelids covered only blind, milky blue pupils. The ancient brown hands, once strong and dexterous as they dug the hard clay deep into the flat land of Ngasumet, shaping the circular ramps that led to the water below, scarcely moved as they lay on the thin sunken chest. Soon the birds would become emboldened by his stillness, first one then another flopping down from the branches above to strut forward and tear the forlorn flesh. Before nightfall other scavengers too would converge, bigger fiercer jaws that would rip and savage - one bite only to snap the tenuous thread between life and death.

The next day Lengerebe and Olembere sought Kilimben, and found him sitting beside a fire with an elder under a tree outside his *manyatta*. The *morans* greeted the older men as 'Father', and they in turn were addressed by Kilimben as 'my sons'.

The formalities over, Kilimben said, 'What is the nature of your business?'

Respectfully Olembere replied, 'I have no business with you, my father, but we have with us *Laigwanan* Dangoya of the One Eye who has matters to discuss with you.'

'This Dangoya you speak of, is he not the Dangoya who killed the buffalo at Mondul? And who slew the leopard when still a *layoni*? What could a *moran* of his achievements want with a man of no standing like me?'

'That he will tell you himself, if you will allow him the honour of addressing you.'

'Go fetch him, my son.' Then pointing out a youth to Lengerebe he said, 'and tell my eldest son to come here.'

When Dangoya came he greeted both older men with deference then sat silent waiting for Kilimben's invitation to speak.

'You have words for my ears?' Kilimben asked.

'I have, my father, and I shall explain all to you.' Slowly and in detail Dangoya told Kilimben of his difficulties and that he was prepared to offer the family adoption. 'You would all be as of my family: you, your wife and your sons.' He glanced up as Kilimben's newly circumcised son walked over to join them beneath the tree. He was a good-looking youth, strong and exceptionally well built.

Kilimben looked thoughtfully at Dangoya, his eyes shrewd, liking the honesty in his approach. 'I too have difficulties,' he said. 'Fourteen head of cattle are all I possess, with seven goats and three donkeys. Soon I must slaughter an ox for my son's first *olpul*, then next rainy season my second son must be circumcised. That will be a further drain on my meagre stock. Turning to his son he told him to fetch his mother and brothers and sat silent; waiting until his family were all present before speaking again. 'When would you want us to go with you?'

'In the next few days,' Dangoya said. 'We shall go with you as far as Lolkisale. There I shall find some *morans* to escort you to Semingor and probably further.'

'I will be the escort,' Olembere spoke up. 'I shall find two or three *morans* to come with me and we will take them all the way to Engaruka.'

'But what will my eldest son Lesirwa do? He cannot come with us and start work before he has spent some time hunting and learning how a *moran* should behave. Would you, a *laigwanan* of your standing, have your new brother - my son - be like an *Olmeg*? And what is my second son to do? Am I to leave him a *layoni* for the remainder of his life? You ask too much of a poor man!' Kilimben had become quite agitated, rising to his feet.

Quickly Dangoya reassured him. 'My father, I have asked your family to be part of mine, and am I not head of my family? Am I not proud? What would the *morans* of our tribe say of me if I treated my own brothers as *Olmeg*?'

There was a long silence before Kilimben replied. 'The cattle will soon be coming in for the night. Go, my son, find yourself food and comfort and meet me here tomorrow when the herd has gone out to graze.'

Not speaking, Kilimben and his family walked to their *manyatta*, and as they entered the enclosure he motioned to his eldest son to stay beside him. With the others out of earshot he said, 'You heard what *Laigwanan* Dangoya had to say. What now have you to say?'

'All has been said for the present.' Lesirwa looked steadily at his father. 'After I have been shaved I shall seek to be admitted to his warrior *manyatta*.' He paused, thinking. 'Good words have been spoken today and I look forward to taking my place beside my new *laigwanan* and brother.'

Meeting the next morning with Kilimben, Lesirwa and a few elders, the filigree maze of the thorn tree branches above casting fine shadows across their faces, Dangoya and the *morans* greeted them with respect.

Sitting very straight, and with great dignity, Kilimben addressed Dangoya. 'As from this day I and my family are of your family, for you to do with as you wish: feed us or starve us, work us or play with us, hurt us or laugh with us, take away from us or give to us, abuse or encourage us.' He struck the ground with his *knobkerrie* and spat, then looking briefly at his wife and sons added, '*Nena age*. That is all.'

Dangoya jumped up, eager to have the business over and done with, yet knowing the formalities were necessary. 'Hear me, my respected elders and brothers! Remember what I say! From this day your family, my father, is of my family, and whatever the future brings, it brings to us all. We are one family,' and he held up his little finger, the others folded to his palm. Then shaking hands with Kilimben, their left hands clasping each other's shoulders, he called out to Lesirwa. 'My brother! Are you ready to go bird hunting?'

A wide smile spread over the *mbarnoti*'s face. 'I have been - these last two days!'

'Then go! And when you are ready to be shaved, come to your *manyatta* at Engaruka!'

Seeing the smiling faces about him, Kilimben's wife looking a trifle anxious, but no doubts shown by the boys of the family, Dangoya said to Kilimben, 'My father, we leave tomorrow. At first light we shall be here to help you.'

Because of the dangers and the small number of animals to be moved, they travelled in one group, the speed of the cattle reduced to that of the slow walking, laden donkeys, so it was four days before they reached Lolkisale.

Dangoya and Lengerebe walked beside Kilimben, discussing their plans and telling of their family histories, and of how Lengerebe's family too would soon join the *manyatta*. Olembere had gone on ahead to arrange the escort from Lolkisale, and when they arrived there he greeted Dangoya with the news that the girls of the *moran manyatta* were asking after him and Lengerebe.

'A big party of Kisongo warriors has gone on a raid to the Ufiomi country, so the girls have not enough *morans* and are lonely.'

This was sufficient to persuade them to say their farewells to Kilimben and go immediately to the *moran manyatta* where they were received with excited cries of welcome.

One night of uninhibited lovemaking left the *morans* drained and weary, but very happy too.

'Never have I known such hungry girls!' Lengerebe said with amazement.

'And they will be hungrier still because two of their *morans* wish to come with us to Lengkito.' Dangoya smiled. 'Come *Ndawo*! We shall go now to settle your family affairs. When that is done we can return to the *moran manyatta* at Namanga.'

Chapter 7

Muriet's Dream

Across the great flat plain the *morans* walked, their strides long and easy, spears resting lightly on one shoulder, *ngelan* flapping above their buttocks with bellies lean and muscled, the red of their scabbards bright against the smooth brown of their loose-moving thighs. Scattered flat-topped thorns punctuated the level vastness of the savannah, the grass short and green with the benison of the rains, the sky wide and free. It was good country to cross, with no fear of sudden attack from man or beast, and the warriors walked with unconcern through the myriad creatures of the plain, fellow nomads, sojourners of short duration feeding and watering and moving on when the goodness was gone.

In their thousands grazed the fat garish zebra, close companions to the bearded wildebeest whose doleful bearing could change in an instant to clowning absurdity; gazelles fed in constant motion, tails flicking without stop, the young rams prinking before stately, cow-like eland; and kongoni, awkward-gaited, rocking as they ran when startled. Well-fed prides of lion lay indolently at rest or padded with purpose about their daily business, the herbivorous animals of the plain knowing always whether the lion were hungry or not, either taking to their heels or continuing to crop the grass.

A dry-season waterhole overflowed, its marshy boundaries extending further with each shower of rain, two old buffalo standing with wet hocks in daydreaming oblivion, chewing endlessly on the cud, flicking an ear at the flies, their escorting egrets dazzling in their whiteness. To the water came spurwing, knob nose and Egyptian geese, annoying the fast moving coots; a family of warthog, noisy in their drinking, tails pointed stiffly at the sky; in a nearby tree marabou storks perched untidily, too big for the thin branches. Above the chatterings, squawks and low chucklings of the birds on the water, came the call of a fish eagle: loud, clear and liquid, its mate answering the haunting cry.

A flurry as a herd of elephant advanced, their great bodies making so little noise, ears flapping and trunks waving this way and that, catching the scent, testing the air, the birds retreating reluctantly from the water to sit at one side while the monsters drank and bathed.

Giraffe picked at the topmost green shoots of the thorn trees, and two silver-backed jackal darted about, finding scraps at the site of a kill now several days old. Some distance from the water a small rocky outcrop teemed with soft furry hyrax, worshipping the morning sun, while two elegant cheetah sat side by side gazing into space, communication between them fine-tuned, for as one they rose and stalked off together.

'If I were an Ndorobo,' said one of the Kisongo *morans*, 'I should come here to live and hunt.' Exceptionally thin and tall, he towered over his companions.

'And what would you do when the rains were over?' Dangoya, ever pragmatic, asked. 'You cannot have been here in the dry season or you would know this place is no different from *Magadi* at that time of the year.'

'He would eat from the tops of the trees - his mother was mated with a giraffe!' Lengerebe laughed and jumped away quickly to avoid the Kisongo's *knobkerrie*.

Just then they spotted a male ostrich and not far from him a female on guard over her nest of eggs. As telepathic as animals, the four *morans* without a word advanced on the big birds, in their minds the common thought of plucking feathers from the male for headdresses and spear shafts.

Over-confident, their past successes contributing to their conceit, they made no plan and with only kerries at the ready, moved too close to the female ostrich - which was more than the male was prepared to allow. With the unleashed fury of a tornado the bird whirled in at Legetonyi, the leading *moran*, knocking him flat and kicking at his chest with its huge horny feet before the others realised the seriousness of the attack and in unison set to with spears and *knobkerries*, reducing the enraged bird to a fluttering, heaving mass of blood and feathers.

The female ostrich showed signs of great agitation and Dangoya yelled to the others to get the hurt man and the dead male away. Awkwardly, the enforced physical labour to which they were unaccustomed making their movements clumsy and slow, the three *morans* dragged the unconscious Legetonyi and the carcass to the shade of a tree a hundred yards away.

Breathing hard, they flung themselves to the ground, the tall Kisongo settling beside his clansman to examine the contusions on his head and the fast-swelling area around the broken ribs. Gradually the injured man recovered consciousness and, allowing him time to rest, the others plucked the feathers they wanted from the dead ostrich.

Chastened by their foolish action, Dangoya felt shame that he had indulged in such an impetuous and thoughtless attack on an extremely dangerous creature.

'We were like stupid girls stealing the ornaments from a *moran*'s hair in play.'

'It went well in the end,' one of the others said, and they all laughed, still full of excitement.

'And I can walk!' Legetonyi got to his feet, gasping as the pain in his chest killed his laughter.

'You were very nearly dead!' retorted Dangoya, contempt in his voice for his reckless comrades. 'Come, let us go.'

As the day advanced they made slower time, with frequent stops to allow the injured *moran* to sit and rest; and by late afternoon it became clear that he would be unable to continue much further. Helped along by the gangling Kisongo, he complained of an agonising pain in his chest, and it was with relief that they saw a herd of home-going cattle which they followed to its *manyatta*.

An Ndorobo medicine-man was sent for and that evening the *moran* was bled, three small cuts being made to one side of the swelling on his chest and an ox horn placed over the cuts. Sucking steadily on the hole at the thin end, the medicine man repeated the operation until the swollen area was ringed with cuts. However, after two days the *moran* was no better and Dangoya and Lengerebe continued their journey to Lengkito, leaving both the Kisongo *morans* behind at the *manyatta*.

Dangoya himself by-passed Lengerebe's *manyatta*, making straight for the warrior *manyatta* at Namanga. For one thing he did not wish to be involved in the discussions at which Lengerebe would have to persuade his *laigwanan* father to let him, his mother and his young brother leave to join Dangoya at Engaruka. This he thought would not prove too difficult for Lengerebe, as his father's *manyatta* was full to overflowing with related families and numerous males capable of caring for the stock. Lengerebe's mother was the second of six wives and should not, having only two sons, be sorely missed.

Dangoya's second reason for giving the *manyatta* a wide berth at this stage was that Lengerebe would also have to approach his father with regard to speaking for Dangoya's sister and for appearances sake, this, by custom, could not be done in Dangoya's presence.

He therefore walked on to Namanga where he was well received, the girls wishing to know how long he would stay and the *morans* begging him to remain as their *laigwanan*. Oleserya, now a junior *laigwanan* himself with most of Dangoya's previous followers and several new recruits of his own, greeted Dangoya with noisy affection, and when he heard his friend was seeking help to move Lengerebe's cattle to Engaruka, he immediately offered his services, but Dangoya declined the gesture.

'You must stay here and keep your warriors in training. When my personal business is finished I shall return and make many raids with you. Then we shall grow rich together!'

Selecting three men who had been to Chaggaland with him, Dangoya returned to the *manyatta* at Lengkito, and after visiting several houses he was summoned before Lengerebe's father who sat in the company of another elder. Greetings were exchanged, followed by a long pause after which Lengerebe's father asked Dangoya what he was looking for at his *manyatta*, and why was he not with the warriors at Namanga.

'You have come here to steal my children and their herds in order to swell your own *manyatta*.'

'That is true,' Dangoya replied, not put off by the customary rudeness. More insults would follow, he knew, but they would mean nothing to either side.

The older man narrowed his eyes, looking intently at Dangoya, then he handed him a gourd of honey beer.

'*Torgo*! Drink!' he ordered.

Dangoya took a sip and gave the gourd back.

'I hear you have a good-for-nothing young sister who will soon be going with the *morans*, yet has not been spoken for.' The *laigwanan* ejected a stream of spittle into the dust and belched loudly before he continued the business at hand.

'She will grow old at your expense unless I take her for one of my worthless sons! And with what shall I pay the bride price? A donkey? And even that is too much!'

Dangoya could not suppress a smile and found himself liking this tough, battle-worn man.

'If Lengerebe is truly a son of your loins, then I say the branch is as strong as the root, but its leaves are prettier!' He wondered if perhaps he had gone too far, but the older man threw back his head and laughed, digging the other elder in the ribs.

'This mother-fucking lion cub has not only bravery in his heart but a tongue in his head too!'

So the negotiations continued for some time, Lengerebe's father increasingly impressed with Dangoya and privately pleased that his family should become a close-knit part with that of Dangoya. Finally dismissing the young man, he told him to attend him in his house that evening after the cattle had come home, and Dangoya left to find Lengerebe.

All the elders had congregated in the *laigwanan*'s house, drinking beer that had been prepared in advance for the occasion. The singing was raucous and all competed in boastful tales about their herds, and about particular animals in their herds, down to the smallest calves.

When Dangoya was invited to enter together with his *morans*, the young men had to bend double under the low roof, finding somewhere to sit in the already overcrowded hut, the stench of beer, the smell of smoke, dung and sweat thick in the air. They were handed a huge round *calabash*, bigger than a man's head, with a long thin neck ending in a small swollen top, and this was full of honey beer. Dangoya took the first sip and passed it on to the *morans*. Back and forth the *calabash* went, being refilled when it was empty, and the young men's heads began to swim with the unaccustomed drinking.

In the midst of the congenial hubbub, Lengerebe's father announced that he had that day asked Dangoya for his youngest sister to be reserved for the elder son of his second wife, and went on to extol Dangoya's wealth, his position in his clan, his connections, and his achievements to date. The lengthy speech drew noisy approval from the elders and *morans* alike, and the *laigwanan* had to wait for the clamour to subside before going on to say that a certain heifer from his herd would be presented to Dangoya as the first payment of the bride price, which had yet to be discussed in full. A fat steer, he said, would be slaughtered the next day for an *olpul* to entertain Dangoya, who would be given the prescribed choice cuts as he acted in place of his dead father.

When the *morans* had drunk two full *calabashes* of beer they excused themselves and left the elders, most of whom were well on the way to becoming speechless, to the serious business of drinking which continued for two days and nights.

The drunken party was interrupted at intervals when the *morans* brought the elders meat from the *olpul*, taking a few sips of beer themselves, but always careful not to take too much for fear of decreasing their sexual prowess and losing face with the girls.

Lengerebe's father could either hold his drink better than the others or else he drank less, but of all the elders in the house he was the only man not to become incapable, and this impressed Dangoya who took the opportunity of discussing a variety of subjects with him. They had great respect for each other, liking too, which spanned the gulf of their age-groups.

On completion of the *olpul*, Dangoya and Lengerebe made ready to leave for Engaruka, assembling over two hundred head of cattle, eight donkeys and twenty seven sheep. Less than half the stock belonged to Lengerebe, his mother and young brother; the greater part of the herd being owned by other members of the family, and loaned to Lengerebe for safe-keeping.

A new addition to the party was a young slave girl, adopted by Lengerebe's mother some years before, whom she refused to leave behind at Lengkito.

'She has no family but ours, and if she cannot go, I shall not go either!'

The woman was adamant and Dangoya marvelled at the strong wills bred in Lengerebe's family.

'Of course she may come,' he said. 'I have not said that she could not.'

'But I saw in your face that you were about to refuse!'

'You did not see refusal,' Dangoya smiled, 'only surprise. Surprise at how quickly my new *manyatta* is to grow with so many people.'

The rains were almost over and the cattle, including the brown and white heifer - first instalment of the bride price for Nairasha - were in good fettle for travelling. Water still ran in the small streams and the larger waterholes had not yet dried up. Even in the sand rivers there were pools, although these could not last long. Grazing was plentiful, but *manyattas* on their route were far and few between, so most nights they slept in the open with the *morans* taking turns to guard the stock. Although the country through which they moved was friendly, on two occasions in broad daylight they experienced unsuccessful raids by small bands of *morans* who were swiftly sent packing by Dangoya's belligerent team.

Four days from their destination, while crossing swampy land between Kitumbeine and Lengai, the *morans* saw movement in a clump of reed grass and on going to investigate discovered a warthog caught fast in the coils of a big python which was too occupied in its efforts to crush and kill to take any notice of the people watching. When the warthog was dead the python uncoiled itself, opened its jaws wide and ingested the animal whole. This took some time to accomplish and when at last the *morans'* curiosity was satisfied they found the cattle were nearly out of sight so they had to run to catch up with them.

Lengerebe's mother was very cutting in her remarks to her son, 'Call yourself a *moran*! The only blood you will ever see will be that of an ox at an *olpul*, or a *calabash*-full collected by an elder or a *layoni*!'

She had barely closed her mouth with a snap when a lioness attacked the herd from the left, stampeding the animals in all directions. Everyone was taken completely unawares and in the resulting pandemonium the lioness efficiently dropped a cow, but was chased off by Lengerebe who shouted to all the *morans* to leave the lioness and concentrate on rounding up the stock. Dangoya was already on his way after the cattle, followed by Lengerebe's young brother who ran wide-eyed behind the scattering sheep, but the three *morans* from Namanga, wild and headstrong, took no notice of Lengerebe's orders and rushed after the lioness, eager to prove their manhood, their yells of excitement filling the late afternoon air as they disappeared behind a thicket.

Frustration rising like gall in his throat, Lengerebe ran to help Dangoya with the girl Muriet hot on his heels, leaving his mother to follow with the donkeys which had remained huddled together, their heavy loads making flight impossible.

It was almost dark and a long way from where the cow had been killed before the herd was safely rounded up and sufficiently calmed so the cows could be milked. While the women attended to this, Dangoya and Lengerebe discussed their predicament.

The three lion-hungry *morans* were nowhere to be seen and Dangoya knew that neither he nor Lengerebe dare leave the stock unprotected, although Lengerebe suggested that he go in search of the others. Up to this point Lengerebe had been in command, the family stock being his responsibility, but with a curt refusal to allow him to leave, Dangoya took control.

Since leaving Lengkito, Dangoya guessed it was his reputation alone which had saved them from the depredations of a large well-organised raid. Now, should word get about that a mere two *morans* were left to guard the herd, they would be fair game for any marauding band of *morans* intent on plunder.

An anxious, sleepless night behind them, it was long before dawn when they prodded and cajoled the stock into moving, their destination a *manyatta* half a day's journey away to the north. It was off their track, but at least the herd would be safe while they sought reinforcements to help them complete the move to Engaruka. Lengerebe agreed to the diversion, but once again suggested that he should go back to look for the others. Dangoya objected vehemently.

'*Ndawo*! You heard what your wise mother said yesterday, and you have seen the situation our behaviour has brought us! Are we to continue to act like children? If the *morans* are in trouble, it is of their own doing. There are three of them with no encumbrances. They have all been well-blooded and are not fools - although after what I saw yesterday I doubt they have any sense left! They can take care of themselves and would not expect us to help them. If they have not been hurt, they will follow our tracks; if wounded, they will make for the nearest *manyatta* which is what we are doing. By now they may be in the comfort of a *manyatta*, and there will be raiding parties out looking for us to swell their herds, so let us stop talking and start moving!'

'What if they have all been killed?'

'Then the hyena will be laughing.'

Picking his way through the dark, Dangoya walked ahead of the cattle while Lengerebe and the women brought up the rear, with Lengerebe's brother taking care of any straying animal to left or right. They had travelled about a mile when suddenly far to their left half the night sky was lit with a bright, quick-dying blaze followed by a low fearful rumble. In shock everyone stood still, the ensuing darkness so black and intense that they rubbed their eyes until their night vision returned. Lengerebe ran forward to ask Dangoya what he thought the phenomenon could be.

'Truly that was never lightning!'

They continued to gaze to the left and again the bright flaring light erupted - longer this time - illuminating their faces and all the cattle about them, the accompanying low grumble like the roar of ten thousand lion in a rage. Now they could see a tremendous fire sweeping out from the top of Lengai Mountain, great balls of burning rock flying through the air and rolling down the steep sides, doused quickly as they cooled in the sharp cold before dawn.

Dangoya found his knees trembling, the fear of this awesome, flaming mountain sweeping over him, and it was all he could do not to run. As the burning died down and the noise subsided to a murmur, he walked back past the cattle to check the rear when Lengerebe's mother called out to him.

'What is this thing?' She was frightened, but her voice was firm.

'I do not know, but I think it is *Ngai* telling us something.'

She caught her breath and was about to speak when again the mountain erupted, but less fiercely than before, so her courage returned.

'Tell the *laigwanan*,' she said urgently to the slave girl, 'Tell him of your dream!'

For the first time Muriet spoke, her eyes fixed on Lengai. 'In the dream I was told there would be a killing disease in our cattle, and many animals would be lost. We would suffer then from a terrible famine which would leave the Masai poor. But not only this!' Her eyes flicked over Dangoya. 'I was told also that there would come an unknown sickness to strike our people and leave many dead, and that the *morans* who survived would go to war against the other clans and tribes - for the last time - to build up the numbers of their herds. Then when the fighting was over a new tribe of *laigwanans* would rule the Masai. I also dreamed that a great fire would come out of *Oldonyo* Lengai and that this would be a warning of things to come.'

'She lies!' shouted Dangoya. 'When did she tell you of this dream?'

'Two days ago.' Lengerebe's mother looked anxiously at the girl then took her in her arms as she began to tremble and weep.

Bewildered, Dangoya turned away and walked to the front of the herd.

The eruptions had almost ceased and with daylight the fears of the night receded. With Dangoya once more in the lead and the cattle moving briskly, everyone began to feel more cheerful as they pressed on towards the *manyatta*, even the donkeys trotting along under their unwieldy loads, a spanking pace for them, as though they knew the urgency of the moment.

A fine grey ash began to settle softly over the country, covering the backs of the animals and dusting the heads of the people, their eyelashes pale and furred, their nostrils tickling so they sneezed continually.

Dangoya's tension eased, feeling the worst of their present troubles were nearly over, although the girl's prophecies worried him; but his guard was never down as his eye moved constantly from left to right, seeking any movement however slight, turning occasionally to examine the country behind them, every sense alert to danger.

From the rear he caught the call of a honeybird followed by a sound so faint his keen ears almost missed it: the tap tap of two sticks beaten together, then the unmistakable whistle of a man replying to the honeybird. Quietly he called the boy to run and tell Lengerebe to carry on while he investigated. Slipping off to one side, he worked his way back towards the noises, moving silently in the sparse cover. It could only be *morans*, he thought, and not his three missing *morans* as they would have made their presence known.

With stealth he stalked the strangers, freezing into immobility behind a bush as he saw five Kisongo *morans* bent over the spoor of Lengerebe's cattle, their intentions absolutely clear. With a sinking heart he knew he and Lengerebe were in for trouble: a fight against five unencumbered men was a battle lost before it started, and the only recourse was to reduce their numbers at the outset - and quickly - before Lengerebe appeared on the scene and gave the game away.

Two of the Kisongo had straightened and were approaching Dangoya's hiding place fast, well in front of the others and oblivious to the danger. As they passed him he launched an attack so furious in its intensity and surprise that they never knew what hit them. Their skulls cracked with two well aimed blows of Dangoya's *knobkerrie* that smote them to the ground, killing them before they fell.

Shouting for Lengerebe to watch out for the others, Dangoya ran again into cover, almost falling over Lengerebe who was on his way to the rescue and keen to attack the remaining Kisongo, but Dangoya managed to restrain him.

The Kisongo, having seen what had befallen their comrades, took to their heels, falling, unfortunately for them, into the arms of Dangoya's missing lion hunters. Surprised by this assault, they very nearly came to grief and only just escaped, running away to the shouts of *'Narobong gotonye*, you Kisongo cowards! You'd better learn to steal from the *Olmeg* who are women like yourselves!'

The shouting and abuse followed them long after they were out of sight and hearing, and Dangoya used considerable persuasion to stop his entire party from continuing the chase.

As they walked quickly to catch up with the herd the three *morans* explained their absence. They had killed the lioness, they said, and disposed of her cubs and were busy skinning the dead cow when the five Kisongo clansmen stumbled on them as they followed the tracks of the cattle.

'It was clear they had been tracking us,' the spokesman said. 'One asked where we had got the cow, as if he did not know! And I replied a lion had killed it. Then he asked where the lion was, and I told him to look behind a bush, so they walked over and looked at the dead lioness and the cubs. We realised what they were up to so decided to tell them we were going to have an *olpul* and eat the cow.

'We could hear them making plans too, no doubt discussing the fact that the herd now had only two *morans* on guard and that they must attack it before we could join you. Then they came back from looking at the lioness and asked us what we were going to do with all the meat. 'Eat it,' we told them, and 'why didn't they stay to eat it with us?'

'So they stayed and helped us skin the cow. We made a fire and sat as friends, eating our fill and talking of everything except our true plans. When they thought we were asleep they crept off, but we followed at a distance and they did not know we were behind them.'

Although still angry at their impetuous departure after the lioness, Dangoya had to concede that for the first time *morans* had used their heads, conceiving a plan and carrying it through, rather than rushing blindly into action without thought of the outcome. It was, he thought, a predominant trait in their character, his own too at times, their bravery so often brought to nought by reckless, foolhardy lust for acclaim.

The herd was lost from sight in the light bush and Lengerebe urged them to hurry.

'My mother and the girl do not know what has happened and will be anxious, although my mother would never admit her worry!' Calling back over his shoulder as he hurried on he added, '*Ndawo*! You have used your *knobkerrie* to good effect against the blind Kisongo, and I shall tell all when we get back to the *manyatta*!'

Lengerebe reached the herd before the others and found the women and the boy frightened but tight-lipped as they pressed forward gamely. They had feared the worst, expecting at any moment to be assailed, and their relief on seeing Lengerebe was great.

Muriet burst into tears, but Lengerebe's mother, exhausted after the strain and anxiety of the past day, coupled with a sleepless night before and the terrifying eruption of Lengai, simply sat down and looked her son over, her back straight and her gaze steady as she listened to what he had to say.

She had liked Dangoya, thinking him a quiet, respectful young *laigwanan*, but had not understood the reasons for her son's over-enthusiastic admiration. Now, as she heard how Dangoya had killed the Kisongo *morans*, her own regard for him grew and she remembered the stories she had been told of his achievements and knew them to be true.

The others soon joined them and Dangoya announced that they would once again change direction, to follow their original route, and that all occupied *manyattas* would be avoided, moving as quickly as they could towards Engaruka.

As she got to her feet Lengerebe's mother addressed the girl, but her voice carried loud and clear to the rest. 'I like a *moran* who knows what he wants and can make a decision without having to discuss it for half a day!' and she stalked off to see to her donkeys.

Two matters were foremost in Dangoya's mind when he made his decision. First he felt he must consult with the *laibons* and elders about the Lengai phenomenon, and secondly he would have to bring up the problem of the Kisongo. Of late, relations between the Kisongo and other clans had been less antagonistic, with the Kisongo on their part showing far more tolerance to lesser members of the tribe. Unless the correct version of what had occurred that morning was reported immediately to the elders on both sides, the old feuds would flare up, fuelled by mistrust and a natural animosity.

For three days they travelled fast, resting only in the darkest hours of the night. The first evening they stopped at a disused *manyatta* and Lengerebe ordered a sheep killed, the girl and his brother taking choice, juicy pieces of the roasted meat to his mother where she rested. After this one night when they could all relax for a few hours, there would be no respite, for Dangoya was determined to thrust on relentlessly, his fear of reprisal by the Kisongo overridden by his anxiety of punitive action on a much larger scale in the near future.

When at last the *manyattas* at Engaruka came in sight, Dangoya left the herd and hurried on ahead, eager to find Olengesen and discuss with him the serious situation.

Olengesen was supervising the cauterisation of a wound on a frisky young steer. Two *layonis* had thrown the animal successfully, but its threshing legs gave Olengesen no opportunity to move in with his hot iron. Without a word, Dangoya stepped in, and with the free end of the hide rope tied round its front legs, quickly immobilised the wildly kicking back feet. In a few minutes the wound was cleansed and burnt, and the steer leapt to its feet with a bellow.

'I have much to tell you, my *olpiron*,' Dangoya said, and the two men went into Olengesen's house where Dangoya reported the happenings on their journey to Engaruka. Olengesen listened intently, occasionally asking a question or pressing for more details. When Dangoya fell silent, his story complete, the older man sat thoughtfully for a long time before speaking.

'For two days the *laibons* have been discussing the spitting of fire from Lengai. You, my pupil, may have found the reason for this strange thing. Whenever *Ngai*'s children are about to act foolishly he spits in fury to warn them. I shall go to the *laibons* to tell them everything you have related to me. I shall also tell them of the girl Muriet's dream. Now go and find rest and comfort.' He picked up his ebony stick and prepared to leave his hut. 'It was necessary for you to kill the two Kisongo *morans*, so be proud of the way you struck them down. One day when you are a senior *moran* and *laigwanan*, you shall lead the Loitayo clan into battle.'

'Your words do me great honour.'

'And I do not utter them lightly.' Olengesen grasped his hand for a moment and strode from the hut.

A noisy welcome was in progress at Dangoya's *manyatta* when he arrived and he went first to greet Kilimben and hear his news.

'All is well here,' the elder reported. 'We had a safe journey and Olembere and the others who escorted us have returned to Lolkisale. The cattle are in good condition, with several new calves which you shall see at milking time. Most of the huts are complete and we have brought in sufficient building material to start on those for Lengerebe and his family.'

Dangoya was extremely pleased as he listened to the long and efficient report from this new member of his family. He was also secretly amused at the proprietary way in which Kilimben surveyed the *manyatta*. My choice was good, he thought, Kilimben is truly of my family and would die for me and mine as surely would a father.

Leaving Kilimben, Dangoya made his way through the *manyatta* to his mother's house. In her new status equal to that of an elder, Mother Dangoya warranted great respect and could no longer mix with the welcoming throng at the *manyatta* gates, and for this reason Dangoya had despatched his sister to tell Singira he was coming. As he neared her house and saw her at the door, her cry of 'My son!' filled him with delight, and she flung herself into his arms, kissing his mouth, her fingers fluttering over his shoulders and chest.

'My mother! You are too young for the honours bestowed upon you by the clan! More are you like an *ndito*! I am happy to see you safe and well.'

'Have you come to boast of how you killed two Kisongo single-handed?' she teased, 'or have you come to make excuses about how one ostrich beat off four *morans* including the Great One Eye?'

'None of these things,' he laughed. 'How fast you have heard the news.'

'Olembere told us, and that Legetonyi is recovering slowly. They call him "Ostrich" now, and he and his friend - the tall one - await your call to go to the *moran manyatta*. But tell me first your news.'

'Well,' Dangoya said, 'I have found a worthy husband for that ill-begotten Ndorobo daughter of yours.' He watched Singira's eyes fly open in mock anger.

'Let me tell you, my feeble son, Nairasha was sired by one of the greatest warriors of his day, unlike you! You were the son of a *moran* whose seed was so weak, you could barely wriggle out of my body alive!' She threw back her head and laughed, Dangoya finding her good humour so infectious that his preoccupation with weightier and more important matters receded to the back of his mind, and he was able to laugh with her.

When he told her Lengerebe's father had spoken for Nairasha, she seemed very pleased but made no comment, and he went on to tell her about the arrangements made for the marriage.

They discussed Kilimben and his family at length, and this too pleased Singira. 'They are good people and work hard. Our family and cattle will grow in strength under Kilimben's hand.' Then she said, 'Are you going to the *olpul* tomorrow?'

'Yes, why do you ask?'

'Have you chosen any *layonis* yet to work at the *olpul*?'

'No.' He was surprised at her interest.

'I would like you to take Sinyok, Kilimben's youngest boy, with you. He is clever and hardworking, but is bullied by the bigger boys and has never been to an *olpul*. It is time he was given a chance to learn.'

'I shall do as you ask.' Dangoya touched her hand in affection and rose to go. 'But first I must see Ngenia.'

Going out into the bright sunlight Dangoya walked to his wife's house, quickening his step in anticipation. In his brief meeting with her at the gate he had observed her growing belly and how her face had become rounder and softer. Now, as he bent to enter the hut, she gave a little cry and was in his arms before he was through the door.

Although married to him, Ngenia continued to be treated as Dangoya's *asanja*, and not until he became an elder would this change. Then his opportunities for intimacy would be less frequent, with Ngenia showing hospitality to his guests and to those of her choosing.

'I thought I would not see you again, so long have you been gone!' Ngenia cried.

'I see you are with child and you have grown sleek and fat like my best brown heifer.' That it was perhaps not his own child never entered his head; all the children she bore would be considered his. 'Tonight, if you have no guests, I shall come to visit you. Now I go to see the cattle come in and attend to my other business.'

Feeling light-hearted for the first time in many days, he went to stand beside Kilimben outside the *manyatta*, a cloud of dust not far off signalling the approach of the stock. As they discussed the weather and the state of the grazing, Dangoya found his thoughts straying continually to Ngenia.

Brought back to earth by the lead animals lumbering past, he gave his full attention to the cattle, examining them with care and noting with pleasure how good they looked. He observed too, young Sinyok, running about the *manyatta* on his last chores of the day, putting the calves in their pens after suckling, fetching and carrying for the women, a busy time after a long day's herding. Dangoya called the boy to him and Sinyok came running, presenting his head for the *moran*'s greeting.

'My brother,' Dangoya placed his hand on the child's head. 'You will warn the *layonis* that you will not be herding tomorrow, and they must arrange for someone else to go out with the bigger calves. You shall come to work in the *olpul*.'

The boy smiled excitedly and listened carefully as Dangoya told him to collect the soup pots from his house and that Nairasha would tell him where to go and what to do.

'Have you ever been to an *olpul* before?'

'No.'

'You have much to learn, and there will be another *layoni* to help you.'

Dangoya went in search of Lengerebe whom he found in a house surrounded by girls, and called him outside to talk. He told him what arrangements had been made for the *olpul*.

'Could you take your young brother Tebelit? He has been to *olpuls* and could show Sinyok what to do.'

Lengerebe was a little surprised at Dangoya's behaviour as it was most unusual for a *moran* to be concerned about a *layoni*, but after Dangoya had explained the situation he agreed, then burst out laughing.

'Why do you laugh?' Dangoya felt self-conscious.

'Three days ago I saw you kill two *morans* of the Kisongo clan as a lioness would kill a dikdik, the smallest of all the antelope, and here you are today worrying over a *layoni*, with no connections to you, who might be teased and laughed at.'

'He is now my adopted brother,' Dangoya said in excuse, and grinned at his friend as they entered the hut.

Inside a party was in progress with the *morans* vying with each other as they boasted of their feats, egged on by the girls. They sat on two large beds, a small flickering fire on the floor in the middle. The *morans* from Namanga were re-telling the story of the lioness and how they had trailed the Kisongo.

When Dangoya's turn came, he told of how four *morans* had been very nearly defeated by a lone male ostrich, and the girls laughed at his description of the furious flapping bird, but Dangoya had told the tale with a purpose, hoping his version of the story would soon spread, showing Legetonyi in a better light.

Remembering he was to sleep in Ngenia's house that night, he rose to go, but the *ndito* beside whom he had been sitting on the bed caught his hand and begged him not to leave.

'You I shall see tomorrow at the *olpul*. Tonight I visit my *asanja*,' and he walked out into the night, bored with the trivialities of the past hour and eager to be with Ngenia.

Chapter 8

The Meat Feast

A fat steer chosen from Dangoya's herd was led to the place of the *olpul* and after slaughtering it, Dangoya left the others to skin and open it up, telling the *morans* to be careful with the main stomach as he wished to make a hood for his hair. Then calling to the two small *layonis*, he picked up an axe and led them up into the forest.

'Do either of you know what a *kiloriti* bush looks like?'

The boys replied that they did and pointed to the numerous *kiloritis* growing about them.

'We have already taken some bark to the *olpul*.'

'And have you ever seen a swizzle stick?'

They said they had seen their mothers use swizzle sticks made from sheep's vertebrae.

'Ah, but that is a different sort,' Dangoya said. 'You would never get the *kiloriti* soup to froth up unless you used a proper one. I shall show you how it is made. Look carefully and remember well as I shall only show you once.'

Dangoya cut a long thin branch from a bush, about a thumb width wide at the base with long thorns growing in opposite pairs at intervals of six inches or so. He cut off all the thorns but for the two at the base, cutting the branch neatly about half an inch below these and trimming the top, leaving the stick about two feet long. Removing the bark he tidied the thorns so they were the same length.

'That is a swizzle stick. Now each take a branch back with you to finish at the *olpul*. The stick can be straightened later by heating it over the fire.'

Next Dangoya cut off a young branch from an olive tree, again about an inch wide at the base and two feet long. This, he explained to the boys, must have no side shoots over its entire length otherwise it would be impossible to shave it properly.

'I shall cut one the correct size for you both and back at the *olpul* I will show you how to make a soup strainer.'

When they returned, the *olpul* was well in progress, with meat roasting over the fire and two *morans* staking out the ox hide. Instructing the *layonis* to bring the big earthenware pot, Dangoya placed three stones in the hot coals and half-filled the pot with water. Next he added pieces of meat, offal and fat, dropping bits of *kiloriti* bark into the soup and leaving it to boil until the next day. The *layonis* would see that the pot was topped up with water and not allowed to boil dry.

The main stomach of the steer lay to one side and Dangoya cut away the spleen, giving half to the boys to eat and eating some himself, handing out pieces of the raw meat to others as they passed by. He then cut the stomach in half and removed the partly digested food from inside with his hands, wiping his fingers on the dry grass growing at his feet. When the stomach was sufficiently clean he parted the thin layer from the fleshy tripe, trimming it as he went along and eating the bits he cut off. On a little frame of staked twigs like an inverted boat he stretched the skin to dry.

'In this warm weather it will take half a day to dry,' he told the *layonis*.

'Now cut up the rest of the stomach and put it in the soup.'

The *morans* ate through most of the day and Dangoya straightened the swizzle stick he had made, watching the boys' progress with theirs. He put the olive branches into the hot ash, checking occasionally to see if they were ready, and when they were charred and black he took one from the fire and removed the bark. Then with a sharp knife he scraped the stick carefully, working from each end to the middle, not cutting off the parings but leaving them white and curly at the centre to form a large ball of fibre about nine inches in diameter. One end was cut off at the ball and the other left long as a handle.

Placing the strainer in a cleft stick, Dangoya left it to dry and turned his attention to the hood which was dry enough to finish off. Taking it from its frame he trimmed it again, trying it on for size several times until it was just right, then finding some gut he tied it to his necklace and let it hang down his back, ready for a rainy day.

'When the big rain falls I shall wear this and the water will not wet my hair,' he told the *layonis*. 'Now make your strainers as I have done and tomorrow you can use them for the soup.'

Several girls arrived at the *olpul* and prepared little bowers to one side using soft branches and leaves, their love-nests ready and inviting for the *morans* who outnumbered them, but all would share the favours of the *nditos* without jealousy or rancour.

Two unexpected arrivals were the young men of the ostrich fight, Legetonyi and his tall thin friend. Legetonyi's ribs had mended and he was now eager to go hunting buffalo for shields. Dangoya could not be persuaded to leave, but Lengerebe set off with the two *morans* several days later.

The first time Dangoya was called away from the *olpul* was in answer to a summons from Olengesen, and he found his instructor with Singira in her house.

'I have brought news from the *laibons* and also from the Kisongo *laigwanans* at Ngorongoro.'

'Tell me, my *olpiron*, for I have waited anxiously for your return.' Dangoya sat, his attention fixed on Olengesen.

'The deaths of the two *morans* at your hand will not affect in any way the good relations existing at present between the Kisongo and the other clans.' Olengesen paused, a faint smile creasing his face. 'I think the spitting of the mountain has put fear into many strong hearts and they do not understand the reasons. More meetings will have to be held before they can interpret the voice of *Ngai*, but in the meantime I am told that a great number of Kisongo *morans* would willingly join you at whichever warrior *manyatta* you choose.'

'You have brought me good news,' Dangoya said, preparing to leave, but Olengesen gestured to him to sit.

'Do not go. I have something further to say to you and your mother shall hear it too.' He fiddled with his tube of tobacco, mixing it with his big fingers and putting a pinch in his mouth. 'Your choice of a family to help you with your growing herds is a good one. Now I would like to see you complete the adoption by formally bringing Kilimben's family into yours, with the proper ceremony held here in your *manyatta*. This would give you the opportunity to go away and continue with your instruction at the *moran manyatta*, and Kilimben in turn would hold the power to act on your behalf.'

'This matter has been very much in my head,' Dangoya replied, 'and I am only waiting for his eldest son Lesirwa to return from his bird hunting. Lesirwa can then be shaved and sent to his first *olpul*. After that will be time enough to arrange the adoption ceremony and the circumcision of the second son, probably with Loito's brother.'

'And the youngest boy Sinyok is already helping at the *olpul* here, with Dangoya teaching him,' Singira interrupted, smiling at her son.

'I am pleased with what I hear,' Olengesen said, 'And that you are thinking of these things, unlike most of the *morans* who think only of females and the honour they can achieve. Go back now to the *olpul* and find an *ndito* to warm your blood.'

The buffalo hunters returned in triumph with two dead bulls to their credit and the still-wet hides for making shields. They also brought some *kitoloswa* for the soup and started a new brew, removing the larger pieces of meat with a skewer and straining the soup into another pot. The *morans* took it in turns to whisk the pale mauve liquid, the froth rising to the lip of the pot before being poured into a bowl-like *calabash* with a handle and passed around, the stringent taste bitter in their mouths as they waited for the drug to take effect.

They had not long to wait, and began to dance and shake in ecstasies of abandon, Lengerebe as usual being particularly susceptible and the first to fall to the ground in convulsions. The girls joined in the dancing, but the soup was denied them as it was to the small *layonis*, who watched in wonder the doings of the *morans*.

The shield-making was started in earnest the next day as a young calf had died in the night at one of the *manyattas* and its skin, cut into strips, would be ideal for binding the outer edges of the buffalo hides to the frames, and for attaching the strong handles to the shields. Two of the *morans* set off to find light, pliant wood for the frames and pieces of stronger wood for the grips, while another went to skin the calf and bury its soft new hide in mud to make removal of the hair easier.

The *morans* were now on their second ox, contributed by Loito, and all that day while they worked on shaping the frames for their shields, they sustained their hearty appetites with choice pieces of roasted meat. When the frames were ready and tied with bark they were laid on the ground, anchored in the sun with heavy rocks to prevent warping. The hand-grips were carefully carved and hidden under leaves in the shade to stop complete drying out of the wood as the handles would dry and take their final shape best when fixed permanently to the shields. The edges of the buffalo hides, already cut to shape, were packed with softening mud and the *morans* sat back for four days and waited until the smell of the putrefying calfskin signalled that all was ready.

Scraping away the hair on the calfskin, it was cut into one long, thin strip and the buffalo hides were pierced at one inch intervals all round their softened edges, with another line of fine holes down the centre of each. The well-wetted frames were laid on the shaped hides and tied firmly with the calfskin strips, and the handles too bound to the shields which were almost ready except for drying out and painting. The insides would have to be buffed with sandstone later to enhance the appearance and for comfort's sake.

Dangoya observed Sinyok covertly throughout the period of the *olpul* and was impressed at the quick way in which the boy gained in confidence. He showed resourcefulness too and was eager to learn, and Dangoya was reminded of himself at the same age. They were about to slaughter a third steer and should, Dangoya thought, change the *layonis*, giving a couple of the others a chance to attend the *olpul* otherwise it might be noticed that he was taking an unusual interest in Sinyok. He therefore gave the two boys orders to return to their herding duties and although Sinyok looked crestfallen, Dangoya dared not show any understanding of his disappointment and looked pointedly in the opposite direction.

Nairasha, who had been absent for a few days, arrived in a flurry to tell her brother that Mother Dangoya wished to see him on an urgent matter. She added excitedly that Lesirwa was back from his bird hunting with the most beautiful head-dress she had ever seen.

'Truly, my brother, he has caught every bird in the world with the prettiest colours, like rainbows!'

'Come with me,' Dangoya said to Loito. 'I have business to attend to and you can see to the *layoni* replacements.'

The two *morans* walked in silence, Dangoya knowing his mother would only send for him if something serious had occurred. He listened with half an ear when Loito spoke and eventually Loito asked if he were ill.

'No, I was wondering when Lesirwa should be shaved and go to his first *olpul*.'

'Why not have him shaved tomorrow and bring him to ours? He can kill his ox the next after mine.'

'That would be good,' Dangoya said, 'if the other *morans* do not object.'

'Why should they object? Is he not one of us?'

'You are right in what you say. If you will tell the others, I shall make the arrangements for him to be shaved.'

They parted at the gate of the *manyatta* and Dangoya went directly to his mother's house, calling at the door for permission to enter. Singira invited him in and they greeted each other with affection.

'Why have you sent for me?'

Singira motioned him to sit. 'I do not wish to trouble you with the problems of women, but this is a serious matter to do with your sister Naidu's child. She is pregnant again and I fear that unless something is done she will drop her unborn child, which might quite well be a son. I have sent her to a *laibon*, but he can do nothing for her until he finds out if a curse has been laid on the little girl.'

'But what is wrong with the child?'

'You do not know?' Singira's voice rose in astonishment. The child's teeth are now growing, but not in the normal way. They are growing into her lower lip and one has broken through the skin - showing on the outside below her mouth! With the second one coming through the same way! It is too terrible and Naidu is beside herself with worry.'

'Has the child been spoken for?' Dangoya tried to take the news calmly.

'She has, but will look like a warthog unless the curse is removed! Go now and see her, then come back here.'

Dangoya went to his sister's house to inspect the child, and to his horror it was as his mother had said. Naidu sat in deep depression, her eyes dull and unseeing as she rocked the little girl in her arms.

'Do you know who has laid this curse upon your child?' Dangoya's compassion for his sister was mixed with a wild anger.

'Who else but my *laibon* husband, who tried to kill her when she was born.'

'If I can persuade him to lift the curse, would you go back to him?'

'Dead, yes!' she replied. 'But never alive!' For the first time she showed some animation, her hate a palpable force in the dark of the hut.

Dangoya looked at her with shock, then threw off the feeling of evil which seemed to surround the mother and her deformed child. 'When do you expect to have the baby you are at present carrying?'

'*Ngai* knows. I do not care.' Her head dropped forward, her lips on the child's fat cheek.

'Rest well.' Dangoya left hurriedly and returned to his mother.

As soon as Singira saw his face she knew he was distressed - and angry too - and that he would act. She could only hope he would not make a wrong move.

'I shall go now to discuss the matter with Olengesen and obtain his advice,' he said.

'You are wise, child of my belly, but take no hasty decisions.'

Singira could not expect to hear more from Dangoya regarding Naidu's daughter, but she knew if he wanted to consult her he would. In the meantime Olengesen would keep her informed and she in turn would tell Naidu.

On leaving his mother's hut Dangoya went first to find Lesirwa and his father, to tell them of his intention of having Lesirwa shaved the next day so he could join the *olpul*, an honour more than acceptable to them both. Dangoya also told Kilimben that the ceremony for joining the families would be held soon, and that he could proceed with arrangements for the second son's circumcision before the rains came. 'Loito's young brother will be circumcised at the same time. The sooner we can have full *morans* in the *manyatta*, the better,' and Dangoya moved on to see Olengesen.

His instructor sat patiently while Dangoya told him of the arrangements made for Lesirwa. They then discussed Naidu's child and Olengesen pondered the matter for some time before asking Dangoya whether he would be prepared to return his sister and the child to her husband.

'Never!' Dangoya said vehemently. 'But I would be prepared to return the bride price once the child had recovered!'

'You would not give back the mother and child, yet you would let the *laibon* have the bride price? What is so good about this sister of yours that you prefer her happiness to the possession of cattle?'

'She is my sister,' replied Dangoya simply, 'and her daughter is as my daughter.'

'Go back to your *olpul*. I shall talk to Mother Dangoya and send for you when I want you.' Olengesen studied the younger man thoughtfully for a minute. 'You must soon return to the warrior *manyatta* and your duties as a leader of our *morans* otherwise those less capable will take over as great *laigwanans*, leaving you as a mere senior *moran*.'

Dangoya considered Olengesen's remarks then said, 'I respect you greatly and will do anything you ask. It is you who have taught me all I know, and it is you to whom I come when I wish to learn more. To me you are like the *ndaragwa*, the cedar. You start small with all the thick bush and trees around you. You do not run. You do not even walk. You crawl, and in your own time you leave the *seki* bush, then the *lorien*, the olive, and you continue going up and up until you have left all the trees of the forest behind and never can they catch you.

'But I am like the flood in the rains, taking all before it and then disappearing as nothing into the dry earth.' Dangoya paused, taking time to find his next words. 'I cannot go to war with large groups of *morans* who run blindly into battle, acting as individuals with no plan, heeding no leader. I would sooner have twenty *morans* of my own choosing, who will hear what I say.'

Olengesen listened intently, his eyes never leaving Dangoya's face. 'Go on, my *olpiron*.'

'The lion of the *Serenget* has a plan. He sends off his females to hide and lie quietly hidden in the bush or long grass as they are lighter and more agile than he. Then he goes upwind of the stupid zebra and makes a great noise, chasing the herd into the claws and mouths of the waiting lionesses.

'The hyena also has a head which he uses, which is more than we *morans* do. He has a jaw stronger than any other animal, but he has no speed. So what does he do? He waits outside a *manyatta* and when an ox or cow is sick, or a cow is giving birth, he attacks when they cannot move fast, or he waits until the foolish Masai dies and is laid out for him to eat at his leisure.'

'What then do you intend to do?' asked Olengesen. 'Sit and wait around the *manyatta* like the hyena, selling off your sisters and their fatherless children?'

'I shall return to the warrior *manyatta* in good time when I have selected enough of my own *morans* to join those of my men who are already there, but I shall never lead or go to battle with a large party that I have not chosen myself. I was offered the junior leadership of the *moran manyatta*, but I did not accept. It has been said, but not in my hearing, that I became a coward after I lost my eye.'

'Have you denied such allegations?'

'Why should I throw away my time, to have the *seki* handed to me? Have I not proved my courage on many occasions, and have not those who said these words lost the comfort of many *nditos* and been laughed at by the *morans* and elders?'

When Dangoya got back to the *olpul* he noticed three new faces amongst the girls, and the girl he had invited himself had returned after an absence of some days. As the meat was finished and it would soon be dark, there was nothing to do but sit by the fire and talk or play with the *nditos*.

Dangoya asked each girl in turn who had invited her to the *olpul*, and all replied except the girl who was there at his invitation.'

'And you,' he asked. 'Who did you come with?'

'*Laigwanan* Dangoya of the One Eye,' she said coyly, sitting down beside him.

'Why then did you leave the *olpul* without telling me?'

'Because I find I am with child and my mother made me stay at home until arrangements for my circumcision and marriage had been made.' The girl lowered her eyes, the picture of demureness.

'Who is the father?' one of the *morans* called out, teasing her.

'How should I know?' she snapped back. 'If it is born with one eye and a twisted *njabo* I shall know it is his!' and she pressed close to Dangoya, her fingers entwined beneath his left knee and her head and breast resting on his thigh between her arms.

'You seem to like them twisted,' Dangoya replied, the softness of her breast warm on his leg and her restless fingers light against his skin.

'*Ebaye!*' she said a little breathlessly as she felt his manhood rise firmly to her elbow. Turning her head slightly she gave him a knowing look, a laugh on her lips as she let her arm drop lower, feeling more of him. Her eyes grew large and unseeing, her voice husky. 'Let us go to my bower,' and they moved away together to the little shelter she had made of leaves and soft branches.

At dawn the *morans* began to move about, preparing to fetch the next ox for slaughter, but the *olpul* could not be left unguarded as the new *layonis* had not yet arrived and hyena would make short work of the drying hides, so Dangoya volunteered to remain until he went to escort the new *moran* back to the *olpul*. The girls set off for the *manyatta*, eager to be present when Lesirwa was shaved, and to paint him in red ochre, and their enthusiasm showed that he was already popular, a fact which pleased Dangoya immensely as the young man would gain in confidence and prestige.

Down by the river the *nditos* had finished painting Lesirwa, teasing and challenging him for an invitation to the *olpul*, when he noticed Dangoya and the other *morans* waiting for him. Turning quickly to Nairasha he asked her to be his first guest and all the girls burst into friendly laughter, calling 'Aririri, aririri' as they led him to the *morans* who all greeted him as '*Moran!*'

Although he was the newest of the *morans*, Lesirwa was older than most and far bigger in physique, his height well balanced by his wide chest and strong legs. He was blessed too with a quiet, easy-going nature and this, together with his constant cheerfulness, made him a welcome addition to the *moran* ranks and he very soon settled in amongst his peers, learning much from his new brother Dangoya.

The ceremony for adoption was held over the period of the full moon, differing only from that held for a new born child in that an elder and a circumcised woman drew blood from a steer for all the members of Kilimben's family to drink. The elders retired to Mother Dangoya's hut to drink honey beer, but Dangoya himself made only a brief appearance to sip a little beer as Olengesen, being head of the three *manyattas* at Engaruka, acted throughout on his behalf.

Walking back to the *olpul* with Lesirwa at his side, Dangoya looked north towards the stark sentinel of Lengai. 'Do you see that *magadi* dust which darkens the sky from Sonjo beyond? It means at last the rains are nearly here, and in the next few days you will hear the people talking about getting the *laibon* to attend meetings to bring rain. They will pay the witch doctor five or ten head of cattle, because the rain is late; and when it rains - as it will – the *laibon* will claim to have brought it.'

'Shall we not give cattle for the rain?' asked Lesirwa.

'We shall, but only because if it does not rain the elders will blame us and the *laibon* will curse us.' Dangoya glanced at his companion, measuring his reaction to his words.

'We should not say such things about the *laibons*,' Lesirwa frowned, 'but I must admit I have never seen them bring rain from a clear sky. The clouds have been there first and a child could see it was due.'

Dangoya walked on, knowing his thoughts bordered on the seditious, but he could not be less than honest with himself. 'I have true belief and trust in the great *laibons* such as Mbatian, and for healing the sick I think some of the lesser *laibons* are very clever, but when it comes to making rain and war only the great *laibons* can be relied upon.' Dangoya stopped and faced Lesirwa. 'After your brother Suyanga has been circumcised I shall be going to the *manyatta* at Namanga, and if you wish to join me there, we shall go together one day to see whom I believe to be the true *laibons*.'

'The true *laibons*?' Lesirwa looked puzzled. 'Where do they live?'

'They can be found on *Oldonyo Naibor*, but have come from far away. I am told they have hair as straight as sansevera, with skin as white as milk. They have the spitting fire which can kill an elephant from here to there,' he said, pointing to a tree two hundred paces away. 'I was once shown a magic spear stolen from a dead Arab, but it could only throw one fire arrow, then it had to be fed with more medicine and pieces of metal before it could throw another. It is said these things of the white men can go on killing without pause.'

'Yes!' Lesirwa was very excited. 'I have heard of these people too. I met two *mbarnotis* from a place called Loitokitok who said when they were *layonis* they witnessed from a distance a big meeting between two white men with some *Olmeg* and the elders from five *manyattas*. There were many *morans* dressed for battle flanking the elders and the white men carried magic spears that they call guns, and wore strange skins on their heads with skins of different colours on their bodies, only their faces and arms showing.

The *Olmeg* carried gifts for the *laigwanans* of the *manyattas*, and they came towards the *morans* who lifted their spears in battle and it looked as though the white men and their *Olmeg* friends would all be killed. Then suddenly one of the *Olmeg* lifted his gun and made a loud bang with it and shouted, 'The white *laibons* have come here in peace to talk and bring gifts. Tell the *morans* to keep their distance and make way for the white men to come and meet you!'"

'What happened then? What did the *laigwanans* say?' Dangoya listened avidly as Lesirwa told the story.

'One of the *moran* leaders shouted back to put their gifts on the ground where they could be seen, then they would be allowed to talk to the *laigwanans*, but the *Olmeg* spokesman got very angry and said the white *laibons* had matters to discuss which did not concern the *morans*. At that moment a Purko elder who was the senior *laigwanan* in the area stepped forward to speak to the white men, one of whom had two large eyes, extra ones, on top of his others and carried a little gun in his belt. Just then a marabou stork settled in a tree nearby and the white man with the four eyes pointed his little gun at it. It made a great noise and the bird fell to the ground. One of the *morans* ran to the dead bird and he said its body was in pieces and there was no sign of the spirit which hit it. After that the *morans* showed the white men great respect!'

'Did the *mbarnotis* say what was discussed?'

'Only that arrangements were to be made for another meeting at which *morans* would be selected to escort the white men further into Masai country.'

'But what did the white men come for?' Dangoya wondered.

'No one seems to know,' Lesirwa shrugged. 'They do not want cattle or slaves, or the big teeth of the elephant. They do not seem to be like the Arabs at all.'

Dangoya mulled over his conversation with Lesirwa, his thoughts turning at last to the young man himself. Dangoya liked him more and more; his behaviour, his bearing and his general attitude pleased Dangoya, and he felt they would have much in common.

'You have a very good spear,' said Dangoya. 'I lost my best *moran* spear in Chaggaland and have another being made for me at Gelai which I shall fetch one day. Have you a shield?'

'No, but Lengerebe has told me where I can get the hide to make one from the last buffalo hunt. And he gave me some ostrich feathers which are being made into a headdress for me. But I would prefer to kill my own shield!'

'Good!' Dangoya grinned. 'I shall arrange a buffalo hunt soon.'

At the *olpul* Dangoya called Lengerebe aside and the two strolled up the river together. As they had now exchanged more than one beast as gifts, their mode of address had changed again. '*Bagishu*, Dangoya said to Lengerebe, 'I like that *moran* Lesirwa. What do you think of him?'

'I too like him. He talks good talk and is strong, but no one here knows what he was like as a *layoni*.'

'I heard he behaved well at his circumcision.' Dangoya picked up a pebble to throw in the river, noting how quickly the water was dropping in the hot dry days. 'I think we shall keep a watch on him and give him many chances to prove himself.'

'The girls like him too, but say he does not talk much about what he has done.'

'That too is good.' Dangoya looked up at the sky. 'The rains are late and although the signs of rain are there, no cloud is forming as it should, and I do not like it at all. Yesterday I was not worried, but today I am anxious about the weather.' He glanced again at the water, then again up at the sky, coming quickly to a decision. 'We must end the *olpul* and give up thoughts of buffalo hunts. Come, there is much to do!'

Dangoya stood outside his mother's gate and watched the cattle coming through, the early morning cool giving way to heat as the sun climbed higher above the trees. Kilimben stood inside the enclosure, ready to follow the herd out on its long day's grazing, knowing the cattle would have to walk far today as the grazing nearby was so poor. As the older man came out behind the last animal he greeted Dangoya.

'Where,' Dangoya said, 'is the brown steer with the white spot on its head?'

Kilimben pointed to the hut beside Singira's where the steer stood while a boy drew blood from its neck, young Sinyok waiting beside it with a *calabash*.

So, thought Dangoya, Naidu has given birth to a boy. He would have liked to have seen the child immediately, forebodings of yet another curse filling his mind, but he knew he could not, as a male, enter his sister's house until the next day when the afterbirth had been removed during the hours of darkness. He would have to ask Nairasha for news in the meantime.

Kilimben was quick to see his concern, and nodding his head in the direction of the hut said, 'The child must be strong! It woke the *manyatta* before dawn with its cries.'

With that Dangoya had to be content.

Kilimben turned his attention to the state of the weather. 'We should think now of moving the herds to new grazing, before the rain. Olengesen's dry cattle are moving soon, and the only good grazing left in this part is up in the *oldigana* area.' He shook his head, the idea of taking cattle into East Coast Fever country perturbed him. 'If all the cattle remain here much longer, there will be nothing left for the milking herds, and even when the rains do fall the grazing here will need time to recover.'

Dangoya replied, 'You are responsible for the herds, my father, and when you are ready give us our instructions.'

Kilimben laughed dryly. 'You have taken all my *moran* helpers to the *olpuls*, and soon my second son Suyanga is to be circumcised so I shall lose him too. I have not had time to search for good grazing.'

Sinyok appeared just then at the gate, driving the blooded ox before him and the two men followed in the tracks of the cattle.

'I shall come a short way with you,' Dangoya said, 'so we can talk.'

The boy trotted behind the steer and caught up with the main herd, his cries and whistles clear across the country as he urged the cattle down the slope to the plains below.

'I shall find out where Olengesen's dry herds are going and will leave tomorrow myself to seek new grazing,' said Dangoya. 'The *morans* and I will relieve you then of all the dry animals, but I shall see that someone is here to attend Suyanga's circumcision.'

That evening Dangoya called a meeting of all the *morans*, not only from their *olpul* but also from other *olpuls* in the area, ordering the girls and *layonis* to leave.

When everyone was seated around the fire he stood up and called in a loud, clear voice. 'Na *moran*! When we are short of cattle and the women and children and the old people have insufficient milk to drink, what happens? The senior *moran laigwanan* takes us on raids to build up the numbers of our herds. In these *manyattas* of ours we have no senior *morans* available. So what do we do? Close our eyes and pretend nothing is wrong? I say we must act!'

At this the excitement among the *morans* rose as they leaned forward eagerly to hear his next words, sure that he would announce an impending raid.

One of the young men jumped to his feet, striking the ground with his stick and interrupting Dangoya. 'We do not need a senior *moran laigwanan!* We have you!'

'*Ebaye!*' the *morans* shouted, bored with long days at the *olpuls*, avid for adventure.

'Wait until I have told you all.' Dangoya was silent until their excitement had subsided. 'We have many cattle, but where good grazing can be found for them near these *manyattas* they will die from *oldigana* and we shall be poor. There are *layonis* of our age-group ready for circumcision, but they will not be circumcised before the *olpiron* is broken unless,' and he stressed the word as he struck the ground with his kerrie, 'unless they are relieved from their duties with the herds.' Some of the *morans* shifted restlessly, not liking this mundane talk but Dangoya ignored them. 'There are not enough elders to take the dry herds away to graze, and our sheep flocks are already under-protected.' He paused, his glance sweeping over the faces of the *morans*, seeing some dissatisfaction and impatience, but allegiance and interest too in the expressions of others. 'We can prove ourselves as well, and better, herding our stock than we can raiding cattle from old men and boys or frightened *Olmeg*, and we have more to gain by doing so.

'You have been very quick to suggest that I am your *laigwanan*. Now listen to me until I have finished, then choose your *laigwanan*. You see that *moran* there?' and he pointed at Lengerebe. 'We went on a raid which took three whole changes of the moon, and it was said to be one of the greatest and most successful raids of the present *olpiron*.' Addressing Lengerebe directly, he called, '*Bagishu!* How many head of cattle did you get on that raid?'

'Two! And an *Olmeg* arrow in my arm.'

'You heard him - two head of cattle only! If we do not forget about raiding and *olpuls* for the next three changes of the moon and do some work, there will not be one of us here who will not lose ten times that number of cattle from starvation alone, and if our stock is raided in our absence, there may be nothing left!' Dangoya felt the mood of the *morans* wavering, and he ended forcefully, 'Now decide on your *laigwanan*, but be warned! Tomorrow I go to find grazing for my *manyatta* and when

I have found it I shall remain with my herds until I am satisfied there are enough able people to take proper care of them before I return to the *moran manyatta. Nena age*, that is all!' Dangoya sat down and spat into the fire.

Lengerebe stood up. '*Bagishu*, you have spoken well. I go with you tomorrow.' He faced the others saying, 'This is our *laigwanan*, do you all agree?' and the company shouted and called their approval, with few dissensions.

So the arrangements were made and the duties allotted. The *morans* from other *manyattas* went back to their *olpuls*, and the girls and *layonis* drifted into the clearing to resume the routine activities of the evening.

Dangoya was not in a flirting mood and brushed aside all advances, even those of Muriet the slave girl. He was extremely worried about the cattle and the weather, and about Naidu's new-born son, wondering if it too had had a curse laid upon its tiny head. If the child had indeed been born with a deformity he would have to swallow his pride and beg the *laibon*'s forgiveness; but Naidu would kill herself, of that he was sure. His sister was a good girl and hardworking, and did not deserve to be treated by her husband in this cruel way because of Dangoya's quarrel with Bareto. That afternoon he had tried to see Nairasha or his mother in an effort to learn something about the new baby, but was not permitted near the hut.

Dangoya slept fitfully, vivid dreams jolting him awake so that he sat cold and sweating until the first light of morning touched the trees above his head. He had convinced himself that a curse had been put on Naidu's child and that if the *laibon* did not reverse his witchcraft, he would have to kill Bareto. He called softly to Lengerebe that he was going to the *manyatta* and would wait there for him.

'I'll come with you,' Lengerebe replied and together they walked up from the river to stand before Singira's gate, waiting for it to be opened. Slowly the *manyatta* awakened and people began to move about, the women calling to their cows. Slipping through as a *layoni* opened the gate, Dangoya went straight to his mother's house, but found only his young brother who bowed his head in greeting.

Placing his hand on the boy's head, Dangoya asked, 'Where is our mother?'

'There she comes,' the little boy said. 'She saw you walking in.'

Singira approached, her skin in the bright morning light as smooth and clear as a young girl's, her teeth strong and white as she smiled in welcome.

'What brings you here so early in the day?'

From behind him Lengerebe spoke. 'We are on our way to find grazing for the cattle, but have come first to enquire after the health of your daughter and her new-born son.'

Then you may go in peace, my children,' Singira said, the happiness in her voice unmistakable. 'Your sister has given birth to a boy who will put you both to shame when he grows to manhood!'

'You have given us good news, our mother,' Lengerebe replied. 'And how is Naidu?'

'She is full of joy and will be milking her cows when the sun goes down.'

Singira moved to enter her hut. 'Come, you will both drink milk before you leave. Olengesen has gone to see the *laibon* about the other child,' she added.

Dangoya's relief on hearing that the child was normal was overwhelming and later he told Lengerebe of his fears.

'I thought you were troubled,' his friend said, 'when you did not respond to Muriet's attentions. I have never known her to fail with you before.'

Dangoya laughed, then fell serious. 'Tell me, *Bagishu*, have you ever thought again about the dream she had? It is strange that the *laibons* Olengesen saw should have said nothing about it.'

'I have thought of it many times, and I say we should consult one of the great *laibons* like Mbatian. And I meant to speak to you about Muriet. My mother has told me since that she predicted other happenings, such as I finding my *laigwanan* dead after a battle, with his eye missing, and how I brought him back to life.'

'Is that the truth?' Dangoya was amazed. 'I must ask Olengesen's advice when he returns from seeing Naidu's husband at Gelai.'

The two *morans* walked fast, leaving the *manyattas* at Engaruka behind them and traversing the high country towards the north, heading for the plains beyond Jaegarsumet, the hot blue sky holding back the promise of rain.

141

Chapter 9

In the Dust of the Herd

By midday Dangoya and Lengerebe had reached the country which sloped down from Jaegarsumet to the plains below, and they approached one of the herds of grazing cattle to enquire about their sheep. These, they were told, were half a day's walk around the shoulder of the mountain at Olbalbal. They asked the herdsman if there was sufficient water for extra herds in the vicinity, should they decide to bring cattle there.

'Water yes, but no grazing. The herds you see here are 'wet' herds, all milking cows, with the dry cattle grazing up in the forest where only *oldigana*-immune stock can survive.' The man squinted in the glare of the sun, brushing the flies from his face. His recognition of Dangoya had been immediate and he was prepared to be helpful. 'If you can get your cattle down to the Sanjan there is good grazing and water there, but there is much game and you will need many *morans* to protect them until the rains come and the game moves away into the *Serenget*.'

'Are there any herds there now?'

'I do not know,' the man replied, 'but I do not think so as the year has been a good one for grass. Because of the game, the Sanjan area is used only in a very dry year.'

'How long would it take a herd to reach this place called Sanjan?'

'Ours are mountain cattle and would not survive the distance at this time of year, but if yours come from the plains and are in good condition they could travel the two full days without water. Also if you had enough *morans* so that you could move at night, you would leave very few animals behind.'

The *morans* journeyed on to the sheep, stopping to talk to other herdsmen, and they heard very much the same story from all. Fame and courage being rated above all else, Dangoya was recognised and accorded help by everyone they met, but for all the friendly assistance they had received he was despondent by the time they reached their own flocks.

Along their entire route grazing had been poor and even at Olbalbal where a few out-of-season showers had fallen, raising short green grass, the outlook was not good. Too many cattle and sheep were concentrated in a small area with more animals arriving daily and the feed could not possibly last – giving rise to a situation, in Dangoya's opinion, that was far more serious than it appeared. Before the next change of the moon the water would dry up with the present demands being made on it - more than double the usual numbers slaking their thirst from the fast-decreasing flow in the rivers and streams. Between them the *manyattas* of Olengesen and Dangoya possessed well over two thousand sheep and a large proportion of these were carrying lambs. The position was therefore critical and remedial action would have to be taken.

Although a *laigwanan* in his own age-group Dangoya was nevertheless still an *mbarnoti moran*, while the man in charge of the sheep was a senior *moran* and brother to Olengesen so could not be dictated to. Dangoya could pull out his own sheep, but that would mean breaking his ties with Olengesen which was out of the question, and he dismissed the thought from his mind. For a long while he stood silent considering the matter, his gaze sweeping the country before him as the sun went down, taking in the darkening, rainless sky, and the sparse green cover of the land being cropped away to dust by the feeding stock.

'*Bagishu!*' he said at last, 'let us go and talk with this *moran*,' and they walked forward to the little temporary camp where Olengesen's brother greeted them with courtesy.

Dangoya said, 'I have come to bring you news of our people and to arrange for our two *layonis* to be relieved so they can go to their homes to be circumcised.' He knew he would have to be as tactful as possible, not giving the older man cause to feel offended. 'Then we are going on to search for grazing for my dry herds in the Sanjan. Conditions there are good I am told, if we can get our cattle there and can protect them from the game.'

'Have you sufficient *morans* to take the herds?'

'I shall get as many *morans* as I wish.'

'Why then do you not send more *morans* to help with the sheep?' the man asked.

Dangoya hesitated for a moment then looked towards Lengerebe as he did not wish to appear boastful before a senior *moran*.

'My *laigwanan* here,' Lengerebe spoke on his behalf, 'as is well known, has a very strong reputation among the *morans* of our age-group. Many believe he has supernatural powers and wish to accompany him to the *moran manyatta*, but when they learn that he is going with the herds they will beg to go with him.'

Olengesen's brother received his statement in silence, then said, pointing to the roasting mutton on the fire, 'Eat,' and they took out their broadswords and began to cut off pieces of meat, relishing the good taste after their long day's walk. The older man talked as they ate, explaining how the Kisongo flocks and herds had moved in, adding to the deteriorating state of the grazing.

'The Sanjan is good sheep country when the grass is there,' he said, 'but it is difficult to get to the Sanjan at this time unless you have numbers of *morans* to protect the stock.' A note of despair crept into his voice as he added, 'We cannot stay here with all these *narobong gotonye* Kisongo.'

Dangoya was delighted with the way the man's thoughts were running, but said nothing, waiting for him to speak again.

'Which way do you intend to move your cattle?' he asked.

'Until we have been there and seen the Sanjan with our own eyes, which is what we will do when we leave here before daylight comes, we cannot say,' Dangoya replied, choosing his words with care.

'I can give you a *moran* who knows the area well, and if the water and the grass is good send me at least six *morans* to help. Together with those I have here, we can move with the moon when the ground is cool.' He leaned forward in his eagerness, anxious to impress upon Dangoya the severity of the situation. 'We have water here for five days only, then the sheep will start to suffer. You have a long way to go, so hurry. You are to look for water and grazing, and not for tame lions to prove yourselves,' and here Olengesen's brother included a sly dig at their reputations saying, 'you will have my *moran* to protect you on your journey!'

Dangoya grinned, more than pleased at the outcome of their conversation, and Lengerebe laughed out loud.

'We leave as soon as the stars are bright,' Dangoya said, eating with gusto. 'Call your *moran* now to be ready.'

By midday the three *morans* were well past the last water and *manyattas*. The sun was hot, the ground bare and dusty, and they sweated and thirsted in their fatigue. The few thorn trees dotted about showed new green leaves, a sure sign of the coming rains, and as they sat resting in the meagre shade of one of these, Dangoya remarked that it was so dry even the game had left. Since leaving the sheep they had not seen a single living creature except for two lesser bustards and a few vultures circling high above them. The going was heavy as the ground was loose and a strong wind blew stinging sand in their faces, so they had to screw up their eyes and peer at the world about them through partly closed fingers.

As night fell, the wind, if anything, blew more viciously, bringing with it a chill that depressed their lowered spirits still further. When it became too dark to find their way, they stopped beside an anthill for protection, a gnarled and withered little thorn tree growing up through the hard clay of the man-high peak. The *morans* were exhausted and very thirsty, and they rested for a long time, too weary to move, too dry-mouthed to speak.

After a while the wind eased and to the east they saw vivid flashes of lightning which gradually advanced until all about them the sky was lit, and thunder clapped and rolled across the heavens, sending at last the precious rain which fell in great drops to begin with, and the *morans* laughed and opened wide their mouths to feel the blessed cool of the rain on their tongues.

Throughout the night the rain fell and the *morans'* exhilaration turned to damp discomfort as they huddled together in the wet, and the sky lightened to a continuing drizzle, the cloud cover low and sodden. Pools lay everywhere and when at last feeble rays of sun broke through, the sheets of water shone and sparkled, cheering the tired, cold men and restoring their good humour.

It was decided that the *moran* from the sheep flocks should return immediately with the good news of the rain, but that Dangoya and Lengerebe should carry on to the Sanjan. There was no grazing at all where they stood, but if the rain continued for a day or two, there would at least be surface water for the sheep as they passed through the area.

Moving on north, they tramped through rain-soaked country for several hours, but soon found themselves once again on arid ground, while the sky cleared to a hot burning sun. This was disappointing as it showed the storm of the night before to be an isolated one, although spread over a fair distance. With no rain to follow, the ground would soak up the moisture, leaving nothing on the surface, nor would the grass grow unless rain fell over several days.

Not far from the Sanjan river conditions improved, with grazing suitable for dry herds. Dangoya found this most encouraging, especially as the area was unoccupied by cattle or sheep as far as he could see, but as they moved further north game began to be in evidence. This however was a sure indication that water flowed in the river.

The herds of game increased in size as the *morans* drew closer to the Sanjan, the animals facing the direction of the rainfall as they fed. If the rain were to continue, this would be the start of the migration to the wet-season grazing on the *Serenget*, relieving the already over-taxed plains of the Sanjan and the region would be free for the Masai herds. Here the cattle and sheep would survive until new growth appeared and the need for large contingents of warrior *morans* would be reduced as most of the predators would follow the game to *Serenget*. The river held sufficient water - more than enough if the game moved away within the next few days - and while the grazing was not all that good, it was certainly better than that at Engaruka. If they moved fast they could take advantage of the pools lying in the dry river beds and in the natural hollows to water their stock on route, even should no further showers fall.

The decision to return to Engaruka at once was made with a view to persuading Olengesen to move his cattle too. After drinking at the river and a short rest, Dangoya and Lengerebe made for home by a shorter and more direct route, and it was not long before they were on damp ground with pools appearing at more frequent intervals, and even the normally dry 'sand rivers' contained running water.

They were further to the east and it became apparent that the rain of the night before had been far heavier in this part. By noon the sun was hot and the atmosphere sticky and humid, with a great build-up of cumulus cloud to the east which looked most promising.

Again they walked through dry country and their weariness and hunger, not having eaten since leaving the sheep at Olbalbal, slowed their steps, but they found sustenance of a sort from the *silalei* trees, removing the resin from the scarred trunks where game had browsed and chewing it, then spitting out the unpleasant juice until the gum was clean. Chewing kept their thoughts off hunger, and when the sun went down they kept on walking in the cool of the evening, watching the lightning, hearing the thunder, stopping only to rest when the last light had faded from the sky.

Lying on their sides in a small gully out of the wind they heard the plains game on the move: zebra yelping like young dogs, wildebeest with their strange gruff calls, and now and then the crazy voice of a lone hyena, but the gazelle were mute as they passed by, not even the clip of a hoof against a stone as they joined in the great migration to *Serenget*.

At dawn the *morans* rose and travelled on fast to reach the *manyattas* at Engaruka by the middle of the day.

After drinking their fill of a mixture of blood and milk, Lengerebe went to arrange escorts for the flocks of sheep, despatching eight *morans* with orders to hurry, while Dangoya visited Olengesen who had seen Naidu's husband at Gelai.

'You have come to enquire about your sister's child?'

'No, my *olpiron*. I have come to give you good news of the sheep which have not suffered from the drought and carry a good crop of lambs. Your brother is taking them now to the area between Olbalbal and Simjan where it has rained and where there are many pools of water, and further on the new grass is growing. There will be trouble with lion and cheetah as all the animals are moving in that direction, but I have sent eight more *morans* to help and to stay with the flocks until the game goes on to *Serenget*. There is also plenty of dry-herd grazing beyond where it rained and tomorrow my dry herds go with many *morans* to escort them. If you wish your herds to go with mine, there will be grazing enough for all.'

'Why do you talk of my herds going with yours when you know mine are about to go elsewhere?' Olengesen asked, his face stern.

'Because,' Dangoya replied earnestly, 'when your *morans* reported on the area to which you wish to take them they said the grazing there was limited, lasting a short while only, by which time they hoped the rains would come and they could move on. The place where I am going has plenty of grazing for all the cattle and if the rain does not continue and the water dries up, we shall be one and a half days from the permanent water in the Sanjan river and there will be grass there too when the game has gone. Our only worry is protection of the stock from wild animals and for this I have arranged for an extra eighteen *morans* including myself.' Olengesen sat listening, saying nothing as Dangoya continued. 'The young *morans* will have opportunities to prove themselves against wild animals and may even have a chance to fight raiding parties. Your senior *moran* with the sheep will be able to train us in warfare and if your dry herds come too there will be more senior *morans* to guide us and we shall gain in knowledge.'

Olengesen made no comment except to tell Dangoya to fetch one of his *morans*, sitting deep in thought until Dangoya returned with Legetonyi.

'Go,' the older man told Legetonyi, 'and tell the party which is to move the dry herds that tomorrow they will go together with all Dangoya's cattle to the Sanjan. They shall hear from Dangoya himself all they need to know about the route.' He dismissed Legetonyi, then said, 'you are going away at first light tomorrow. Do you not wish to hear what your sister's husband had to say?'

'Indeed, I am most anxious to hear news of your visit.'

'The *laibon* is a very sick man and believes that either you or your sister has laid a curse on him. I have told him that if this is the case I will ask you to lift the curse.'

'I have put no curse on the *laibon*, but my sister may have done so. I shall see her and if she has, will ask her to remove it at once.'

'About the child,' Olengesen went on, 'no curse was laid upon it by anyone at the *laibon*'s *manyatta*. I think now you should leave the matter to your mother.' He was pensive, twirling his stick in the sand at his feet. 'When I returned home I received a message from the *laibon* Oldimbau saying that *Ngai* was very annoyed about the fighting between the clans, and the spitting of fire was to warn them to stop and make battle instead against the *Olmeg*, thus bringing riches to the Masai. A meeting of all the great *laibons* will be called soon at Ngong at which the action to be taken will be decided on and the greatest of all *laibons*, Mbatian, will be consulted. You will shortly be told how many head of cattle your *manyatta* will contribute and the *morans* who are appointed to escort Oldimbau will take these.

'The meeting will probably be held as soon as the rains are over, so as to enable the stock to travel the long distance to Ngong. Some of the *laibons* will be coming from far places such as Laikipia in the north and from the south beyond Ngasumet.' Olengesen looked at Dangoya from beneath his brows. 'You, Lengerebe and the girl Muriet may have to go to the meeting to tell of how you saw the fire and of Muriet's dream, but this is not yet certain as there are others too who saw what you saw. Go now and get your cattle ready.'

Dangoya went directly to his mother's house where he told her of his talk with Olengesen, knowing that she would deal with the matter not only of the deformed child, but also of the *laibon*'s fear of a curse.

Kilimben went there too, in search of Dangoya, as he had heard the cattle were to leave in the morning and felt he should go with them. 'Unless I, an elder, am there to give the orders you, with your junior status, will be overruled by Olengesen's senior *morans*. They will take control of both the grazing and the *morans*.' Kilimben guessed who the senior *morans* would be, the only two available, and had not much faith in either. In his usual blunt fashion he had approached the problem head-on. 'As I have said, I shall be going with my dry herds tomorrow and would like to know what you have seen on your journey to the Sanjan.'

Kilimben's last words gave Dangoya a chance to voice his opinion and give his instructions, which would be passed on by Kilimben as being his own. The elder then left the house to begin preparations for the cattle drive and to direct the senior *morans*, telling Dangoya to deal with the junior *morans*, *layonis* and girls as he would be too busy himself.

Singira laughed when he was out of earshot, but had to admit to Dangoya that he had indeed chosen well when he adopted Kilimben. 'He thinks of nothing but the stock and the *manyatta*. And we as a family are all his property too!'

That evening as Dangoya passed among the cattle he saw Muriet squatting beside a cow singing softly as she pulled on the long teats, the warm milk squirting neatly into a broad-topped *calabash*. She had not seen him, and he stood watching her for a moment.

Taller than average with a light skin indicating her Mbulu blood, her fine bones were well-covered yet gave an impression of slenderness. She had small breasts, the nipples dark against the paleness of the surrounding flesh with little beauty scars cut into the swelling roundness beneath, but it was her face which fascinated Dangoya. A wide mouth above a small chin, there were three tiny vertical scars adorning each cheek below fine slanted eyes, the lashes thick and furred, her look distant and aloof, with a secretive solitariness about her which confused and bewildered a man intent on earthy physical contact.

Now, as she stood bent over milking, her only adornments the trinkets in her ear lobes, the beaded headband circling her shaven skull and the crossed strands of beads running from her shoulders to round her breasts, Dangoya felt a strong attraction, a magnetism, emanating from this strange girl.

When word of her dream spread with all the talk about Lengai Mountain, Muriet had initially received a lot of attention from the *morans*, but added to the belief that she possessed prophetic powers, was an element of awe which commanded more respect from them than was usual for a girl of her age. A reputation too for coldness in the act of making love soon followed her, resulting more from her selectivity when choosing partners. Those she liked - Dangoya included - found her bed rewarding. She was overdue for circumcision, having menstruated for the past two full rainy seasons, and the fact that she had not become pregnant gave rise to doubts about her ability to reproduce. Although coitus interruptus was practiced among the young unmarried people, mistakes were expected to occur and caused surprise when they did not.

Muriet looked up and saw Dangoya watching her. They had drunk milk together and become *asanjas* soon after her arrival at Engaruka.

'You will go tomorrow with the dry herds to the Sanjan,' he told her.

'That is nice,' she replied quietly. 'Are you coming, my *asanja*, to my house tonight?'

'I am going there now,' Dangoya felt a congestion grow in his loins, a burning warmth which quickened his breathing.

'Wait there for me and I shall bring you food when I have finished this work.'

She turned back to her task and said no more, her indifference belied by the slight flush that rose from her neck, colouring her face, and it seemed to him that her hands trembled in unsure haste as she continued with the milking.

Dangoya loved Muriet that night with a punishing urgency, feeling almost as though he were raping her in his unreasoning desire to reach the inner spirit of her, yet she gave herself with warmth and willingness. He could not understand her - knew he never would - and allowed his mind at last to slide away from introspection.

'I shall not be able to stay long with the dry herds on the Sanjan,' she said, 'as I have been spoken for by Olengesen and must return for my circumcision.'

Dangoya grunted in reply, his hand on the silky roundness of her rump.

Muriet lifted her head to look at him. 'Before I come back to the *manyatta* I shall be with child by you.' Her eyes were dark in the feeble light from the fire.

Dangoya laughed. 'How could you know whose child it would be?'

'I shall know,' she said. 'It will be your son.'

'You are talking nonsense,' and he pinched her gently. If she did indeed fall pregnant during the trip to the Sanjan it would not be through his carelessness, although tonight he had been swept along on such a flood of excitement he had almost not withdrawn in time. Lying thinking about her last remark, remembering what he had heard of her predictions, it did seem as though events occurred as she said they would and it made him uneasy, but once again he brushed the unsettling thoughts from his head and fell asleep.

At first light the *manyatta* bustled with activity as the *layonis* and *nditos* loaded the donkeys with their requirements for the long stay on the Sanjan. The *morans* separated the cattle, selecting only the dry cows and those nearly dry, the steers and young weaned stock, and the cows heavy in calf, leaving the lactating cows with suckling calves, the old and sick animals, and those few oxen which would be needed for ceremonial slaughter.

Herded slowly to the first water point, the stock waited, drinking their fill in preparation for the long day's trek without water. They were joined by the pack animals when the move began in earnest. Some two thousand head of cattle and donkeys flowing forward in a mass of hooves and horns, billows of choking dust rising about the surging animals, the sun hot on the heads of the escorting *morans*.

Dangoya and Lengerebe, ordered to lead the herds as they knew the way, went to the front, and as they walked Dangoya found his thoughts

151

centred on Muriet and what she had said the night before. He tried to think of other matters, but could not get her out of his mind. He knew her reputation amongst the *morans* - that they thought her unloving and cold, turning down most approaches - yet he had experienced nothing but avid response each time he had lain with her. Last night she had encouraged him to take her three times and he had to admit she was as good, if not better, than any other woman he had known. Her remarks about having his son - how could she know? How could she know she would even have a child? Most girls of her age had already had children or been aborted to avoid the shame of bearing a child before circumcision, which pointed to Muriet's infertility. Yet she seemed so sure of herself.

Dangoya broke the silence. '*Bagishu*! I spent last night alone with Muriet and she told me she has been spoken for by Olengesen and that she will soon go back to the *manyatta* to be circumcised.'

'That is true, *Bagishu*. My mother has made the arrangements for the ceremony.'

'Whether she has a ceremony or not, is not what I am thinking about,' Dangoya said. 'She told me that she would be pregnant before she left the Sanjan, and the way she said it she seemed to have no doubts. Do you think she can have a child? Is she a witch and can she truly see into the future? If she falls pregnant as she says she will, we shall have to think again about what she said the night Lengai was on fire.'

Lengerebe replied thoughtfully, 'I have for a long time believed her to be strange and the *morans* feel it too, standing in awe of her. She told my mother she would bear a child before the next rains start, a child by the *moran* of her own choosing, and when my mother asked how she knew this she replied only that she knew and would say no more.'

By noon the heat was intense and the first hold up occurred when a young heifer unexpectedly calved down, the *morans* having to take it in turns to carry the calf, slinging it across their shoulders, a pair of feet held in each hand. The pack party were given two *morans* and told to go ahead with Lengerebe to the first night's stopping place while the main body lumbered on. The heat and closeness in the air slowing the progress of both men and animals. Cloud began to build up in the east and when the sun was hidden the air became cooler, so the animals moved at a brisker pace and very soon caught up with the heavily laden donkeys.

At nightfall the herds were reasonably well settled with fires dotted around them and the *morans* and *layonis* dispersed between the various fires. Thunder could be heard and lightning seen in the north. The thirsty animals smelled the rain, becoming very restless. Game streamed past moving towards the rain, and prides of lion followed, adding to the unease of the cattle.

Two attempts were made on the stock by lion and a *layoni* successfully speared a lioness as she stalked an ox. A couple of the *morans* were not too pleased at this as they themselves should have been there, but had left the boy on his own while they sought out the girls. As these young men were of Dangoya's choosing, he was not very kind to them with his tongue and insisted that they approach the cattle owners for a reward of two heifers to present to the *layoni*.

It was a sleepless night for all and with the first weak light of dawn Kilimben found Dangoya and told him the cattle were too unsettled to try to hold them back any longer. 'The *morans* must help load the donkeys and we shall proceed with the herd immediately. Get out in front and start them moving.'

A fair distance was covered before sunrise when without warning a couple of black-maned lion attacked the rear of the herd, killing a donkey and very nearly stampeding the cattle. Lesirwa together with another young *moran* killed one of the lion, but not before Lesirwa had received a nasty mauling with a lacerated arm and three long tears down his back. As he lay winded on the ground and the other *moran* finished off the killer, Muriet picked up Lesirwa's spear and with no hesitation chased off the second lion, before turning back to help the bleeding *moran*. The other girls and boys were putting as much distance as possible between themselves and the scene of the killing, but Muriet's remarkable act was witnessed by a number of the *morans* who said very little at the time although their respect for the girl was greatly increased.

Lesirwa lay in a daze, pain and shock filling his body as careful hands cleaned his wounds with urine and slapped fresh cow dung on them. His companion in the killing busied himself with skinning the lion, taking sufficient skin for head-dresses for them both, while the other *morans* ran on to join the herd. After a little while Lesirwa had recovered enough to be able to walk and although he was in great pain, managed to proceed at a fair pace.

Some time before catching up with the herd, they came across a young *moran* skinning a lion and when they asked who had killed it, he grinned and proudly said, 'I did!'

Lesirwa contrived a weak smile. 'Look what we got too,' he said, and pointed to the wet lion skin on his companion's shoulder. 'This is more exciting than sitting in an *olpul* all day!'

Dangoya, leading the herds at the front, had enough problems of his own to contend with. He knew they were having trouble in the rear with lion, but could not leave his position to go and investigate. At least the cattle had not stampeded, and on reaching rising ground, he was able to look back and see the vast phalanx of animals moving in an orderly fashion. Then he spotted Lengerebe and Kilimben to one side of the herd approaching fast from the rear. When they were near enough he called out, asking for news.

'One donkey killed, no cattle. But other things have happened which Lengerebe will tell you about,' Kilimben shouted. He seemed out of breath, Dangoya thought, and studied him closely as he came up.

'I shall take the lead while you go back,' Kilimben said, walking on past to the front of the herds. The junior *morans* were Dangoya's responsibility entirely and although Kilimben's beloved son staggered injured in the rear, it was not the father's place to attend to him.

As they walked back quickly, the cattle flowing past, Lengerebe told Dangoya what had happened. 'Lesirwa has killed his first lion but is badly hurt - you can see how grieved the old man is. And you will never believe what Muriet did! She took a spear and went straight for the other lion! It was so frightened, it is running still!'

Dangoya laughed in amazement at this news, but his face fell at the thought of Lesirwa. 'Come,' he said, 'we should hurry to see him.'

Dangoya eyed the cattle, noting how well they looked and the speed with which they travelled. 'There seems to have been plenty of rain since we were here several days ago. If the water in that river ahead is running well I think we should move into those old *manyattas* on the other side. The grazing there was good and we could stay a while until Lesirwa recovers, letting the game go on past us. Later we can follow the game and join the sheep. If I can persuade Kilimben, do you think it a good plan?'

'*Ebaye*,' said Lengerebe, 'I do.'

They were amongst the donkeys and stragglers and saw Lesirwa who was making a brave effort to keep up, smiling faintly as he approached his *laigwanan.*

'I hear you had to give your spear to an *ndito* to protect you!' Dangoya said as he shook the young *moran*'s hand, and everyone laughed. 'Come. I shall support you and we will move to the front out of the dust.' Taking Lesirwa's good arm he lifted it around his neck, holding the *moran* firmly about the waist with his other hand.

Slowly they made their way forward, Dangoya encouraging the youth at every step. When they reached Kilimben at the front of the moving herds, Dangoya said to the elder, 'My father, I have brought my brother Lesirwa to help me in the lead and to take him away from the dust of the herd. I have left Lengerebe in his place and come now for your instructions.'

Kilimben looked impassively at his son, the only sign of affection and concern being the swift touch of his hand on Lesirwa's shoulder. He turned to Dangoya. 'Tell me of the country ahead.'

'There is a river not far from here which I think will be running where there are a number of old *manyattas* surrounded by grazing as good as any we found on our first visit. It is one day with cattle from the Sanjan and about the same distance from the sheep which I was told would be grazing in this direction. I think the flocks will need more *morans* to help as they will be in the path of the game moving between Ngorongoro and Malambo.'

'When shall we reach this river you talk about?'

'When the sun is overhead. It is not far now.'

'Good. We will take the cattle across and use the grazing there, living in the *manyattas*. I shall go now to give instructions to the *morans*.'

One by one the lead cattle smelled water and broke into a trot and without enough people in the front ranks to control them they became a wild, rushing mob, the stronger animals breaking through the thin human barrier and careering headlong towards the river. Their stampede was slowed when they reached thick wet black-cotton soil, sinking in the mud to their hocks, but finding little pools of water at which to drink. Others coming from the rear pushed their way through and in the chaos one of Lengerebe's bell oxen broke a leg and was forced down into the sucking mud, its struggles thrusting it deeper until it suffocated in the black swampy soil.

No one saw the ox die as all the Masai were busy rounding up the cattle and driving them across the river, and by the time the herds had been checked and one found to be missing it was late.

When reasonable calm had been restored Muriet ran to find Dangoya to ask if he had seen Lesirwa. No one, she said, had seen him since the start of the stampede, so all attention was directed at once to finding the lost *moran*. Dangoya was about to go back to search for him when Kilimben ordered him to stay with the herds, sending Lengerebe and Loito instead.

They found the young warrior halfway between the river and where Dangoya had of necessity abandoned him to run· after the cattle. He was upright, but only just; his courage and determination taking fearful toll of his last-remaining strength, too utterly exhausted to speak when the others reached him. Loito prepared to help him along, brushing off the swarming flies that fed on his wounds. Then looking in the direction at which Lesirwa speechlessly pointed, he saw some distance away the half-submerged steer, and two crouching hyena slinking up to the carcass.

'I shall take this *moran* over the river,' Loito said to Lengerebe. 'You start skinning the ox and I will send the donkeys for the meat.'

Lengerebe yelled at the hyena to frighten them off while Loito proceeded slowly and painfully with Lesirwa. At the river he washed the wounds and helped the *moran* to drink, then led him up the slope towards the *manyattas*. Muriet saw them and came running to help, and together they half-carried Lesirwa into one of the huts, Loito leaving immediately to organise the fetching of the meat.

It began to rain hard and the light was fading as the donkey party left to re-cross the river. The cattle were being sorted out and driven into the enclosures around the abandoned *manyattas*. There was not a hut that did not leak, and Muriet struggled on her own to hang a hide from the roof above Lesirwa to keep his corner dry. She had started a small fire with a few sticks and pieces of dry cow dung, putting a pot of water on to heat, and as she waited, mixed mutton fat with ground-up roots which she shook out from a little skin bag. When the water was warm, she gently washed Lesirwa's wounds and smeared the oily paste on them, talking softly all the while, then leaving the *moran* to sleep, called Nairasha, and together they set about making the hut habitable.

From time to time people called at the hut to enquire after Lesirwa, but Muriet would let no one in saying, 'He is all right. Let him rest.' However, when Dangoya came she allowed him in, but gave instructions that he was not to talk. 'Then go and tell his father where he is. And when the meat is brought find a fatty piece for him, and some liver or the spleen. In the morning I shall want fresh blood for him to drink.'

'Should not I send for a *laibon*? One who knows how to treat such wounds?'

'You may send for a *laibon* if you wish, but I tell you a *laibon* can do no more for his sickness than I can.'

It was a wet miserable night although the rain had eased to a drizzle, and as Dangoya went out into the dark and down to the river he could hear the voices of the *morans* as shifts were arranged to stand guard through the night. The gates of the *manyattas* had rotted and fallen away, and with the area thick with predators no one would have much sleep. From far across the river he heard the sounds of the donkeys returning and walked through the ankle-deep water to go to meet them. As he got nearer he called to let the *morans* know it was he who approached and one of them shouted back, 'Watch out for the *narobong gotonye* hyena! There is a clan of them trying to get to the loaded donkeys. One has already gone off with a spear in his side, and we have had some lion following us too, but we think they have left.'

Lengerebe started to yodel and the others took it up half-heartedly.

'Save your noise!' Dangoya called. 'The girls are all too tired, and I doubt if any of you could raise your manhood on this cold wet night, nor are there any gates to be opened.'

A damp uncomfortable night was endured, cold too as very little firewood was to be found in the vicinity of the *manyattas*, but at last the new day dawned in bright sunshine and spirits rose as *morans*, girls and *layonis* set about their tasks. A number of cows had calved down on the journey; not unexpected when such large numbers were sorted before a move, heavily pregnant heifers in particular slipping through to the dry herd, their condition unnoticed. The girls milked only the best milkers and those that had newly calved.

After the cattle had left the enclosures the girls collected fresh dung to repair the huts, smearing the dung over the cracks, fixing the dilapidated doors and sweeping out each hut with little brooms of bound twigs. Those *morans* not herding with the cattle repaired the thorn fences and gates, walking miles to fetch sufficient brushwood.

Firewood became very short, so an added chore for the girls was to collect and store dry dung to supplement the available wood. They complained too that they had no olive-wood strips for cleaning and freshening their *calabashes* as those they had brought from Engaruka were finished.

For the first few days life was full and busy for everyone with no time for teasing or love-making. The *morans* protected the grazing herds and the *manyattas* at night, some forming escort parties for the *nditos* when they went out foraging for firewood. A large body of *morans* was sent to help bring in the sheep, the herdsmen with the flocks having had a strenuous time moving against the migrating game with its attendant lion, cheetah and hyena. By the third day the sheep had settled in nearby camps with a good crop of new lambs and most of the game had vanished to the *Serenget*, allowing relaxation for all as they attended to their routine chores.

Muriet was very pleased with herself as her patient was well on the way to recovery and able to move about unaided. His wounds healed fast and before long he joined the sheep, bearing his scars with understandable pride. Muriet had other reasons too for feeling elated, having the undivided attention of Dangoya with whom she lay most nights, holding him tightly to her, not allowing him to roll away before each final joy. Her persistence showed results and by the second full moon she had fallen pregnant, and arrangements had to be made to take her back to Engaruka for her immediate circumcision.

Kilimben decided that Dangoya should go with Muriet as he wanted word taken back that he himself would bring his second son Suyanga and Loito's young brother for their circumcisions together with two other boys from Olengesen's *manyatta*. Dangoya would have to see that arrangements were put in hand for the ceremony, the sponsors of each boy advised, honey beer brewed in good time and the Ndorobo circumciser informed of the day.

Dangoya left quite happily. He knew the stock was in good hands and the grazing improved daily. The sheep had finished lambing and now followed the new grass across the plains, the need for numerous *morans* was not now so pressing as the danger of attack had almost passed. The *morans* themselves had had a good and exciting time, with several having proved their courage; now they enjoyed the long peaceful days, visiting other *manyattas* and some going off to new areas.

Singira was delighted when they arrived at Engaruka and told her of

Muriet's pregnancy. Being fond of the girl she had worried about her failure to conceive, especially as she was to become the third wife of so important a man as Olengesen. Conferring with Lengerebe's mother, Muriet's foster-parent, the circumcision was arranged and performed by Singira herself two days later. Olengesen was perhaps more relieved than happy when he heard the news and did not say very much, knowing full well that the child was not his own.

As it would be a little while before the *layonis* arrived for their circumcision, Dangoya used the time to go to Gelai to see Naidu's *laibon* husband. His mother had assured him that Naidu had put no curse on the man, and Dangoya was advised by Olengesen to inform the *laibon* as soon as possible. There had been a long enough delay already, Olengesen told him, the *laibon* now being very ill and he should go as quickly as he could in case the *laibon* died before he could reach him. That could bode ill for Dangoya, with the chance of a curse being laid on him in revenge.

Travelling fast Dangoya was back from Gelai in two days and reported his visit to Olengesen.

'The *laibon* is very sick, but listened to what I had to say.' Dangoya dismissed the matter abruptly and continued. 'All along the way I saw cattle dying from the drought. Little rain has fallen there to the east of Gelai Mountain, only a few showers which were not sufficient to fill the pools or to start the grass growing.' He spat in contempt. The *morans* are all at the *moran manyatta* and there is no one to take the cattle to better grazing. This is why I will not leave my herds and go to the warrior *manyatta* until I can be certain they are cared for while I am away.'

'You are right,' Olengesen said, 'but remember you have already proved yourself. These others have perhaps not yet done so.'

'They do not have to go to the *moran manyatta* to prove themselves! They can prove themselves while they help the elders with the cattle at a time like this!' Dangoya's voice rose with conviction. 'Have I not proved myself many times over? Did I have to go to the *moran manyatta* for this? Have not the *mbarnotis* from your own *manyatta* proved themselves more on this move to the plains - and their Fire Stick is not yet broken - than their older brothers of the previous *olpiron* have done in all their time at the *moran manyatta*?'

Olengesen shook his head. 'My pupil, you say dangerous words for a young man.'

'I do not say the *moran manyatta* is not good for the young *morans*. What I am saying is that it is not the only place for training our warriors, and should not be used as an excuse to avoid the real work of the Masai - that of taking care of our cattle and sheep, and increasing our wealth!'

'You may be right, but you must not say these things,' Olengesen admonished him.

'I have to say them,' Dangoya stated flatly. 'It swells my heart in pain to see those once-good cattle dying of hunger when they could be fat like ours, and increasing in number if the *morans* were there to take care of their stock.

'*Morans* are like the rhino who, when he sees a man, will charge with his eyes shut, sometimes in the wrong direction. If the man steps aside the rhino goes past, leaving his rump for the warrior's spear. If the rhino could think, he would not charge but walk away.' Dangoya felt there was no more he could say. He could not change the children of *Ngai* anymore than the *laibons* could bring rain in the dry season.

Olengesen appreciated his talks with Dangoya. The young man had a wise head, but Olengesen liked to have time to weigh up everything which had been said, and on this day he had much to occupy his mind. 'Go now and tell your mother of your journey to Gelai,' and Dangoya was dismissed with a wave of his stick.

Within a few days Dangoya had rejoined the herds on the plains and the routine life continued as before. The rains had set in well after the poor beginning and the stock thrived on the rich grazing. The sheep had had an exceptionally good season and Dangoya could not remember when so many lambs had been born to survive the rigours of the first few months. He made frequent visits to the sheep camps, pleased beyond measure with Lesirwa who fulfilled his duties so ably. They now addressed each other as 'Bagateng' as Dangoya had given him an ox in friendship, and his affection for Lesirwa took second place only to the brotherhood he felt for Lengerebe.

On returning one day to the *manyatta* beside the river Dangoya received the news that he and Lengerebe were required to attend the *laibon* Oldimbau. They were to present themselves at his *manyatta* together with an ox and four fat sheep.

Chapter 10

Mbatian

The mighty crater of Ngorongoro lay at their feet, its encircling walls thick with dark forest, and a lush green floor below, wide and flat, pools and streams and swamps glinting in the clear sunlight, the herds of cattle and game mere dots, the whole a microcosm of some dreamer's paradise, as though *Ngai* - who was the Rain - had himself carved the great bowl from the dry rugged earth and set therein the sweetest grasses, the coolest water, the shadiest trees, in the protection of the high steep walls.

Panting and out of breath, his ears popping and heart pounding from the altitude, Dangoya stood and gazed in wonder at the strange world beneath. He had heard of this place often, the Kisongo clan being in virtual possession during the dry season, but never could he have imagined its vast reality, the serenity and the enclosing safety of the crater.

Sinking to the ground beside Lengerebe, Dangoya stretched his tired legs, calves aching and muscles knotted with the unaccustomed climb, his breath slowly quietening in the rare, high air, although his head continued to throb with a persistent pressure. He lay back to think again about their coming meeting with Oldimbau, senior *laibon* of the whole area stretching from Dulen through Tarengire, Ngasumet, Lengkito, Malambo, Soitayaiyo, and Seronera.

To the south the senior *laibon* Olehau held fief and to the north the great Mbatian. Mbatian was Chief *Laibon* of all Masailand, his achievements in witchcraft widespread throughout the land.

Out on the plains near the Sanjan when he had first received the message to appear before Oldimbau, Dangoya was sure the summons could only be in connection with the eruption of Lengai as Olengesen had warned him his presence might be required, but Lengerebe's anxiety at being called was acute. Dangoya had told him the little he knew, but Lengerebe's apprehension was not entirely stilled.

'After all, we know Lengai has been throwing fire for many years – the elders have told us so. It is true whenever *Ngai* speaks something terrible happens, but what can we do about it?'

'*Bagishu*,' Dangoya replied, 'you have said we can do nothing about Lengai. We can also do nothing about Oldimbau until we know what it is he wants of us. We must go to the *laibon* as fast as we can and listen to what he has to say.'

Selecting their contributions to the *laibon*, gritting their teeth as they chose not too good an ox from the herd and four young wethers from the flock, they set out driving the animals before them.

On approaching Olbalbal they had seen flock after flock of sheep, more than either had ever seen in such close proximity, and when they learned that almost the entire flocks owned by the Kisongo were in the area, brought there because of the drought, they had both decided it was a region to be avoided in the future. They were told by a herdsman that after moving their sheep to the Sanjan so many flocks had been brought in that the water dried up before the rain had had any real effect on the supply, with great numbers of sheep dying and battles fought amongst the Kisongo *morans* over the diminishing water. The surviving sheep were weak and in poor condition, fit now only to follow the new grass.

The *morans* had spent the night in one of the sheep camps, meeting with some surprise one of the Kisongo who had been in the raiding party they had dispatched with such lethal efficiency. Both sides had stiffened on recognition, Dangoya's nerves taut to begin with, then relaxing as he sensed good fellowship in the exchanged greetings. The Kisongo *moran* said he too had been called to Oldimbau's *manyatta* and would accompany them the next day.

'I have been ordered to present three sheep, so with three of us to take our offerings the journey will be easier. I know too the best paths.'

That night around the fire the story of the battle with the five Kisongo had been bandied about in good humour and Dangoya was asked what medicine he had used to kill the two *morans*, but seeing the survivor of the raid looking uncomfortable, Dangoya made light of the affair, feeling a tinge of remorse for the poor fellow who perhaps felt not only shame but also sorrow for his lost comrades.

Following the walk from Olbalbal, the *morans* had had a hard and continuous climb up the outside ridge of the Ngorongoro, the incline at times nearly perpendicular, making the task of driving the animals extremely difficult, but their new companion took the slope with ease, his lungs attuned to the altitude, outshining the others as he chivvied the stupid sheep, chasing them on and up through the forest while Dangoya and Lengerebe brought up the rear with the ox.

They lay now resting on the lip of the crater, too exhausted to move, while the Kisongo saw to the animals, tethering them to nearby trees before he too sat down to rest.

Oldimbau's *manyatta* was at Lerai on the western edge of the crater, and the three *morans* arrived shortly before the *laibon*'s cattle were brought in for the night. They made themselves known, handed over the ox and the sheep and were directed to a *manyatta* close by to wait until Oldimbau was ready to receive them. For five idle days they sat about talking, eating and sleeping, until eventually they were sent for.

Outside his *manyatta* Oldimbau sat surrounded by his followers under a cluster of big yellow thorn trees. A meeting was in progress, the *morans* were told, and they were sent to sit at a distance with others also waiting to be called. They joined the group and sat down, all eyes on the elders at the conference and ears straining to catch what was being said, but nothing reached them across the intervening space, the wind taking care to fling the speaker's words to the plains below.

Wafts of fresh beer, stale too, came their way, and they could see Oldimbau, his *laibons*, *laigwanans* and elders quite clearly. Oldimbau was not as old as Dangoya had expected; a tall man, well-covered yet not fat, wearing an *ngelan* of blue monkey skins which reached to his ankles. He sat on a three-legged stool, in his right hand a wildebeest-tail fly switch with a beautifully beaded handle, with more beads in the belt around his waist. A broadsword hung on his left and an ivory-handled *knobkerrie* was thrust through the belt on his right. Beside him on the ground stood a tall thin-necked *calabash* of beer from which he took copious draughts and, although he tried to listen to what was said, he was obviously drunk for he kept falling asleep, jerking himself awake to stop his headlong fall to the ground.

The lesser *laibons* and elders also passed *calabashes* of beer amongst themselves and some were very drunk, subsiding to the ground in heaps and waking perhaps hours later, ready to join in the deliberations with all the dignity they could muster. Dangoya could see a number of elders whom he knew, and presumed that some business was being done by those with good heads for liquor. Every so often a *moran* would be called to fetch more beer or meat, and for the first two days that was the only activity performed by the *morans*.

Each day when Oldimbau grew tired and could no longer stay awake, he stopped the meeting which, thought Dangoya, at least released the *morans* from their boredom and allowed them to visit various *olpuls* in the area. The elders continued to drink and sleep under the trees until nightfall when the cattle came in, then those who were capable followed the stock into the *manyatta*, the sober helping the drunk to their huts where they carried on drinking and eating through the night.

On the third day some of the *morans* were called to address the elders, among them Dangoya. As he approached an older introduced him as '*Laigwanan* of the Loitayo *morans* of the Chagga raid, Dangoya of the One Eye,' and went on to list his many feats. Dangoya went forward to shake Oldimbau's hand then stepped back ten paces and sat down.

Oldimbau scrutinised him carefully, then called to the assembly of elders. '*Abaya*! You have all heard of this *moran*'s achievements. Is he worthy to speak before us?'

'*Ebaye*!' shouted the elders.

'Tell us what you saw the night *Oldonyo* Lengai spoke with fire,' commanded Oldimbau, and Dangoya related the happenings of that time. He told also of Muriet's dream and how she seemed to possess powers of prophecy.

The *laibon* asked several questions concerning the burning mountain, and wished to know Muriet's exact words, then dismissed Dangoya with instructions to return to his *manyatta*. Lengerebe had to wait another two days before being called for questioning, but finally the *morans* were free to leave Lerai, having received no indication at all of whether or not any conclusions had been reached at the meeting.

They both knew and accepted the fact that it was a matter which would now concern the *laibons* and elders alone, and that it would not be wise to discuss it between them, although they might quite well be called upon to take part in any action decided on. However, their friendship was a close one, cemented by shared experiences and confidences, and on the journey back to the plains Dangoya suddenly stopped in his tracks.

'*Bagishu*, do you like to talk about the meeting?'

Lengerebe too had stopped, frowning as he studied Dangoya's face. 'Yes, but first I want to know if this *laibon* Oldimbau gives you strength in your head.'

'No! He makes my whole body feel wet like the dung of the cow that has eaten fresh green grass! Never could I take him a problem of my own. I would rather go all the way to Olbosimoru and give my cattle to the *laibon* Sendeu.'

'I do not know how he spoke to you, but he was nearly asleep or drunk when he talked to me. He fell over three times and had to be put back on his stool.' Lengerebe spat, the contempt tight in his voice. 'I say he did not hear one word I said, and the elders were the same. Some had been asleep for the past two days when I was called. I can only hope that this matter will go before the great *laibon* Mbatian.'

'You know, *Bagishu*,' Dangoya said thoughtfully, 'I told him about Muriet. Now I worry that she may find trouble, although I do not think he heard much of what I said.' His head lifted in anger. 'You saw the sheep dying off at Olbalbal! Why did he not bring rain for his own people? I am told he took many sheep and cattle from them and promised rain, yet we had the rain long before they did. He must have made much wealth too from this last meeting, but I cannot see him taking away the bad curses *Ngai* has put on us.' Dangoya started to walk forward, then suddenly hailed and turned to face Lengerebe. 'We have spoken on a matter which does not concern us. We must now keep our hearts and our tongues to ourselves.' He put out a hand to touch Lengerebe's shoulder. 'Come *Bagishu*. Let us go.'

The rains came to an end and preparations began to move the stock back to Engaruka. There was talk too that the *olpiron* would soon be broken, putting a stop to any further circumcisions, and that the oldest group of *morans* which included Olengesen would take part in the *orgesher*, the ceremony in which they became elders. Dangoya hoped his *olpiron* and instructor would be made a *laigwanan* of the elders, his good sense and social standing making him a very likely candidate. Dangoya's age-group would similarly be elevated, being given for the first time a name by which it would be known forever and entitled to go to war under the command of the next oldest age-group.

Reports were received that Lengai was once again active, not spitting fire but boiling within and making angry rumbling noises which, the people said, showed *Ngai*'s displeasure and annoyance at his warnings going unheeded. On dark cloudy nights the reflection from the burning lava in the crater glowed on the clouds above, not as frightening as before but quite as awesome.

With the cattle safely back at Engaruka, Dangoya and the young *morans* of the area were making ready for their departure to the *moran manyatta* when he and Lengerebe were ordered to escort Oldimbau, Olehau and other lesser *laibons*, together with numerous elders and offerings of stock to Ngong for a meeting with the greatest of all *laibons*, Mbatian. The order upset Dangoya's plans, but he was pleased that at long last the question of Lengai was to be taken before Mbatian.

Five changes of the moon passed before Olehau arrived with a large force of men and some cattle on their way through to Ngong. The individuals travelling in the group would collect more of their animals from various *manyattas* as they moved north - a Masai's wealth was always distributed about the country, a form of insurance against drought and disease. To Dangoya's impatience there was still no sign of Oldimbau, but three days later the *laibon*'s contingent appeared without him. Oldimbau, they said, was too ill to travel. More likely too drunk, Dangoya thought privately. However, the *laibon*'s half-brother, a respected witchdoctor in his own right, had come in his place.

As there were enough *morans* in the escort, with more joining the party en-route, Dangoya, Lengerebe and three others decided to go to Ngong by way of Olgosorok where they would collect their contributions of stock from amongst their herds in that region. After a lot of thought,

Dangoya also resolved to take Muriet in case Mbatian required her for questioning, although she had not been ordered to attend. He would leave her at Kajiado, close enough to Ngong if he had to fetch her.

Dangoya's little group, as they pressed on north, were joined by a number of *morans* eager for action and excitement and to be in such illustrious company, so that by the time they reached Kajiado they were twenty strong, with thirty-two head of cattle. Muriet was left in a relative's *manyatta* and the *morans* carried on across the dry stony plain towards the ridge of rounded hills which was Ngong.

Numerous camps had been set up in the area of Mbatian's *manyatta* and a teeming throng of people swarmed about, with hundreds of animals brought in tribute. The first of Mbatian's meetings had been concluded and Dangoya learnt that the great man was now seeing individuals, and at times shutting himself away to make his magic in secret.

Dangoya was one of those to be called and he gave his story with care, forgetting no detail. The great Mbatian listened intently, his keen intelligent eyes never leaving Dangoya's face, taking in everything the young *moran* said. When Dangoya had finished, Mbatian asked where Muriet was and questioned him about the girl and her history. Dangoya was unable to tell more than the little he knew, that she had grown up as a slave in Lengerebe's family and then been adopted, that she was spoken for by Olengesen and that she was pregnant.

Mbatian sat deep in thought for a while, then asked about the Kisongo raid, his eyes lighting up and a faint smile creasing his lips as he heard the story. 'Go now and do not rest until you have brought the *siangiki* Muriet before me,' and he dismissed Dangoya with a wave of his fly whisk, turning then to his attendant *laibons*, intent on learning more about this young *laigwanan* with one eye.

Muriet sat before the great *laibon* with lowered eyes, her rounded belly and swelling breasts proof of her growing pregnancy, her beauty scars dark against the pale skin. The men stared at her, appreciation in the oldest eyes and little flickers of something more than approval on the faces of the younger. Mbatian studied her in silence for a long moment, and in the quiet under the trees Muriet felt a fear trickle through her body and her breathing quickened.

'Tell us your story,' Mbatian said gently. With relief at the compassion in his voice Muriet looked up, and one of the elders let out a faint gasp at the strangeness and beauty of her face.

Slowly Muriet began to speak, relating how her dreams occurred, and when she had finished Mbatian ordered everyone to leave him alone with the girl. From a distance the men turned to watch him talk in earnest with her and saw him eventually send her away. He called then for his son Sendeu who was commanded to tell the *laibons* and elders that they and their followers were to keep away from Mbatian's *manyatta* for three full days and nights, after which the senior *laibons* were to return to hear his words. No fires were to be lit so that Mbatian would be able to see the glow from *Oldonyo* Lengai clearly when God spoke to him with his tongue of flame.

For three nights the people stood watch and gazed in the direction of Lengai Mountain in the south, but nothing was seen. Muriet, however, whispered to Dangoya that from Mbatian's *manyatta* three bursts of bright fire had been seen in reply to his three questions to *Ngai*. When Dangoya asked what questions had been put, she said she did not know.

On the morning of the fourth day the senior *laibons* were told that *Ngai* had answered Mbatian's questions. They were told too that Muriet was to be taken to him once again and that each of the clans was to produce cattle totalling over one hundred and fifty head for his herds. There would then be a meeting at which everyone would hear what he had learnt from *Ngai*.

Mbatian received Muriet in private and their words remained a secret never divulged by either, but the *laibon*'s instructions to Dangoya were issued in a clear voice heard by all. He was told to escort Muriet to her *manyatta* at Engaruka with all possible care, and there to wait beside her until her marriage. He was to give her the utmost protection, taking as many *morans* of his own-age group as he thought fit, and girls to help her on the journey, so that she did not lose the child she was carrying.

'You are to travel at her speed. If she complains of tiredness, rest. She must receive only her own treatment should she ail, given under her own instructions. Her wishes must be fulfilled, and any communication she desires with anyone may be passed on only through you, Dangoya of the One Eye.' Mbatian eyed Dangoya sternly and admonished him further. 'No senior *moran* or elder will accompany your party, and you alone are responsible for her safety and welfare until she leaves her *manyatta* and goes to her future husband. He then will take over responsibility for her care.'

Dangoya received the instructions with mixed feelings. He was honoured that the great *laibon* should give him such a task, but it seemed to him that the strictures laid down were contrary to tribal custom and practice in every respect. He could not still his uneasiness by requesting reasons without appearing to doubt the *laibon*'s powers. At the back of his mind, however, was the thought that he might have been chosen as protector of Muriet to guard her from opposing *laibons* intent on harming the child through the girl.

Shrugging off his fears, Dangoya went to confer with Lengerebe, and between them they assembled a formidable band of young *morans* and girls, leaving the *manyatta* at Ngong shortly after midday.

The journey home was slow although Muriet was in good health and bloomed in the glow of approaching motherhood. Occasionally, when they were alone, she offered little bits of information relating to her interviews with Mbatian, such as that the child she bore was to be born within sight of Lengai, and that it would be born with great powers if the Masai people did not default in carrying out Mbatian's instructions. Dangoya listened, but could not comprehend these strange things, preferring to enjoy Muriet rather than delve into the unknown. Each night she lay with him, loving him with a soft and endless serenity he was to remember all his life. It was as though they floated to Engaruka on a cool highland wind, above the heat and tribulations of the long, hard walk across the plains, the power of *Ngai* lifting them above all danger.

Olengesen, having travelled back to Engaruka at twice the speed of Dangoya's *morans*, was there waiting for them, all the arrangements for the reception of Muriet complete, and after handing the girl over to Lengerebe's mother with a guard of seven *morans* around the hut, Dangoya was called to one side by Olengesen and followed his instructor out to the tree which grew between the *manyattas*.

Pointing at a large root with his herding stick the older man said, 'Sit there,' and placed himself on a fallen log opposite Dangoya. 'I have many things to say to you. You have done well by following the great *laibon*'s commands, and I shall now tell you what he said at the meeting after you left.' Olengesen shifted his weight on the log, narrowing his eyes as he stared out over the tree-dotted plain. 'It is nothing new for *Ngai* to warn us when we do wrong. In Mbatian's lifetime this is the second occasion on which *Ngai* has spoken with rage and fire. The first time his father was warned that the *morans* were not ready to go to war, but the *morans* would not listen and we all know how they were defeated and humbled. Now *Ngai* has spoken again as he is not pleased with the way the *morans* fight between the clans. And not only that!' Olengesen banged his stick on the ground. 'The *morans* are killing the other clans' relatives such as the wild animals which roam the plains and those in the forest. Those animals are the cattle of the Ndorobo people!

'The *morans* kill other creatures too; the python, the warthog, the leopard. All these are relatives of the clans and should only be destroyed when they break the rules of *Ngai*, as when the lion eats the stock of his Masai brother, or if the *morans* have to prove themselves. Then and then only may they break *Ngai*'s commands.'

'It is true what Mbatian says, my teacher, but how to restrain the *moran* when he requires feathers for a new head-dress? The excitement is in his blood when an ostrich stretches his wings.'

Olengesen ignored Dangoya's comment. 'It is said that some *morans* have done business with the Arabs, exchanging lion fat and elephant teeth for wire, blankets, beads, and many other things. All this must stop! The *morans* must prepare for war and be ready to conquer the *Olmeg* and bring back riches to their people, for there is going to be a great drought and much wealth will be lost through starvation and disease. The *morans* must make the Masai rich so we can withstand heavy losses, but they must not go to war until the *laibons* have ordered it. It will be the last big war of the Masai nation, and the girl Muriet, soon to be my wife, will bear a son destined to be a great *laibon* – if he survives. It will depend on the behaviour of the *morans*. If the child dies, the Masai people will suffer new sicknesses, never before seen, and many will perish.' Olengesen frowned, his expression withdrawn, haunted. 'We will become like the *Olmeg* and be ruled by others who will take us over, as we have taken over the Ndorobo and the Sonjo.'

Dangoya said nothing, digesting the fearful import of Olengesen's words. The older man rose, laying his hand on Dangoya's shoulder. 'You must take your *morans* and return to the warrior *manyatta* after I remove Muriet from your care. I shall soon attend the *orgesher* and have been chosen leader of the elders for all our area.' He smiled bleakly at Dangoya and walked to his *manyatta*.

Dangoya had not been long at the *moran manyatta* at Namanga when word reached him that Ngenia had given birth to a stillborn girl, but that she herself was well. As he was not yet an elder, Ngenia lived with Singira and it was from his mother that he also learnt the reason for the child's death, news which recalled for him vividly his last conversation with Olengesen.

A *layoni* from another clan had killed a cobra outside Singira's house as it was slithering in to attend Ngenia during childbirth - and the cobra was related to the Loitayo clan. Olengesen was dealing with the matter, he was told, and the father of the boy would be made to pay dearly with cattle to the *laibon* for his son's crime against *Ngai*. Dangoya felt sad for Ngenia, but quickly became resigned to the death of the baby. He had many things on his mind at the time and soon forgot the event in the midst of other more pressing matters.

Although he still commanded great respect among the *morans*, Dangoya had fallen from favour in the eyes of many as he adamantly refused to take over the leadership of his age-group in the *manyatta*, preferring to lead only his chosen warriors, a body amounting to less than thirty, but all tried and tested men. The *morans* trained under their *laigwanans* and waited for the call from Mbatian, enjoying their trials of strength and the company of the girls, but growing a little impatient and eager to pursue more exciting occupations.

Tales of white men were brought in daily to the *manyatta*, most to their credit, but one story related by a returning *moran*, his arms bearing a blanket, some white cotton cloth and blue dye for colouring shields, was not at all complimentary to the foreigners and it disturbed Dangoya as he had built up a mental picture of the white men as strong, brave warriors with exceptional powers, more so even than the Masai. He would not at first believe the tale, that two of these strange, pale men had been seen bathing and found to be nothing more than uncircumcised *layonis* with dark hair surrounding their *njabos* and *ndereges*! He was shocked and disappointed, but decided he would have to see for himself.

For a long time he had been considering a raid into the Pare mountains with the hope of making some sort of contact with the white people. The *morans* had been at Namanga for many moons, yet still the *laibons* would not let them go to war and they became very bored and impatient, with not even the thrill of short raids to procure meat for their *olpuls* from neighbouring clans. That had been forbidden, but there had been a few long distance strikes on other tribes which had not been well executed and Dangoya's party had not been invited to take part.

The latest news of the white men therefore gave Dangoya the realisation that it was time to take his *morans* off. They would go direct to Larusa, find out what they could of the white men, and continue south east along the great Ruvu river until they found some *Olmeg* tribe to raid. He consulted the *laibon*, but was told not to leave until the rains had started.

'This will bring the cattle out to graze on the plains and your *morans* will be able to fight away from the heavily defended home areas,' the *laibon* said, which Dangoya thought fairly good advice, but resolved to leave immediately anyway, and wait at a *manyatta* somewhere along the route for the rains to start.

Clad in full war dress to impress the white men when they met, shields bright with the new blue paint, feathers fluttering and spears silver-sharp from honing on river stones, the *morans* led by Dangoya set off across the Engasurai and reached a *manyatta* at *Ngare Nairobi* where they stayed for some time, filling in the wait for the rains to break. There they learned that four *morans* from the south had not obeyed the *laibons'* instructions and had traded with the Arabs, bringing back beautiful articles to their *manyatta*, but now succumbing to a mysterious sickness, and it was said that *Ngai* was punishing them for their disobedience.

At the next *manyatta*, Dangoya elected to spend a night or two as he came across an elder who had actually spent some time with two of the white men. This was too good an opportunity to miss and Dangoya was all ears as he sat and listened to the man.

'It is quite true,' the elder said, 'that they are *layonis* waiting still to be circumcised. And when they come to water after a day or two's walking, they remove leather coverings from their feet which are tied on with long strips of very thin hide which goes in and out of many little holes. Truly their women can sew! You have never seen such leather-work. Then under these coverings, clinging close to their feet, are more coverings of soft stuff and there are some holes in them too through which you can see their white, white skin.'

All this information was so fascinating that Dangoya urged the man to go on.

'Then they undo a belt which has a wire thing holding the ends together, and they fiddle with little round stones down the middle from their navels to their *njabos*, and the front part of the *ngitati* which the *Olmeg* call trousers comes apart. They take out first one leg then the other and you can see their *njabos* quite clearly - that they are uncircumcised! After that they do something with more little stones on their chests, and pull another *ngitati* off over their heads. On the belt is a small gun, a bit bigger than your hand, which lies in its own scabbard, and they both put their guns on a rock near the river...' He paused, shaking his head in wonder and amusement. 'The first time I saw them get into the water I could not believe it, they were so white - like milk - all over! Both had hair on their *njabos* and under their arms, and on their faces. The shorter one had very black hair on his head, on his chest too and his shoulders. The other had brown hair, but not so much, and with these eyes of mine I saw they were uncircumcised.' He stopped again in contemplation at the amazing sights he had seen, tutting under his breath.

'Go on!' said Dangoya. 'What did they do in the water? What did they get in there for?'

'I think to cool themselves. The black haired one got in first and covered himself with white froth which smelt horrible - like nothing I have ever smelt before. Then he washed all the froth off and gave the other one the little red stone, and he too put froth on his body while the first one took his place beside the guns on the rock. When they were dry, they put on their *ngitatis*.'

'Where did you go with them?'

'To Oltukai,' the elder replied.

'And were these *layonis* not afraid? Or were there many of you to protect them from the *morans*?'

'They were not afraid!' the man said. 'They do not know fear! They were wise and brave, and our party consisted only of myself and another elder with two *Olmeg* to carry the white men's possessions. When we reached Sinya we were faced by a large body of *morans* who threatened us, and the *Olmeg* porters dropped their loads and started to run. We two elders were ordered by the *morans* to move away from the white men, which we were about to do when the shorter of the white men shouted to the one *Olmeg* who understood our language, and both *Olmeg* came back. Then speaking the words of the white men, the *Olmeg* called to the *morans* that the strangers came in peace and wished to be friends, and if the *morans* did not let us pass or send their *laigwanan* to talk in peace, the white men would make women of the *morans* in front of the elders.'

'The leader of the *morans* shouted to us to turn and go back to where we came from or we would all be food for the hyena before the moon rose. At this the white men spoke together, then the taller one began to walk towards the *morans*, and he kept on walking followed by the rest of us, and we walked right through the *morans* who fell back on either side. They have strong medicine, these white people!' The elder leaned forward to Dangoya. 'These same *morans* followed us all the way to Oltukai! And there they slaughtered a fat ox for us to eat!' He looked ruminatively at Dangoya and said, 'If you are thinking of taking your *morans* to fight these people, even though your warriors are of proven ability, I tell you now you will feed the hyena, my son.'

'No, my father! I have no desire to fight them! I want only to learn more about them and their magic.'

'How do you hope to approach them? Have you anyone who can take you to them?'

'Only a thief and coward named Sawati,' replied Dangoya.

'You are too late to see Sawati. He is dead, the *narabong gotonye*, from his sickness the Arabs have brought our people. The white men say it is like the *lodwa* in cattle, what they call *rinderpest*. It will spread through our nation and kill many.'

'How many white men are there in Chagga country?'

'I do not know, but there are quite a few.' The elder thought for a moment then said, 'If I took you to them, would you agree to lead them around *Oldonyo Naibor* to Lengkito and Mondul and back?'

Dangoya's heart thumped, but he replied carefully, 'I could do that but first I would want to talk with them. There are many things I want to know. Why do you ask such a favour of me, my father?'

'They asked me to find a man like you, and you are the first one I have met who could take them on such a journey.'

'What will they give you for doing this?'

'I do not know,' the man shrugged. 'They said they would tell me when I had found the person.'

'I shall think about this,' Dangoya said, 'and talk with my *morans*.'

The next morning Dangoya led his men away from the *manyatta* to discuss the proposition put by the elder, but all the *morans* could talk about was the number of people smitten by the Arab disease, 'It is spreading from the south and also from the north east where the land ends and the Big Water begins,' one of them said.

Dangoya's concern grew as he listened, realising a sickness of such magnitude could cause him to alter his plans, but after mulling the matter over he suggested that they go with the elder to meet the white men. Some of the *morans* showed no interest at all, while others wanted to know what the rewards would be, but a few like Dangoya were intrigued by the new strange men.

The meeting dragged on and eventually Dangoya said, 'Listen to me, you *morans*.' He repeated in detail what the elder had told him and having caught their interest went on. 'To the north we are told our brothers are dying of this sickness. If your cattle are healthy and you hear there is *lodwa* disease in an area, do you take your stock there? No, you do not. And when you are walking about the country and see a bush move, do you not go to investigate?'

The *morans* were quiet, listening. 'Has not the *laibon* told us we are not to go on our raid until the rains have started? I say to you we can do one of two things in the time before the rains begin. We can go with this elder to find out whether these white people are really men or not and see their medicine with our own eyes, and by doing so will avoid the places of sickness. Or we can go back to Namanga.' He waited, seeing indecision on some faces. 'I am going to see the white men, and those who want to come with me can do so. We shall leave tomorrow with the elder at first light!' and Dangoya stalked back to the *manyatta*.

Chapter 11

The Scourge

The Germans advanced into the *morans' olpul* with heavy tread, their boots huge and clumsy looking, their clothes seeming to rustle and squeak, so much leather and thickness everywhere. They came with the contact man sent by the elder to bring the foreigners, and with eleven *Olmeg* who looked about them nervously, seeing the formidable party of *morans* resplendent in their war attire.

Dangoya held his breath, his fascinated gaze going from the boots to the unusual eyes and back again to the boots. His eye ran up and down both men, seeing for himself the little stones down the front of their clothing, noting the wide belts they wore and the holstered revolvers on their hips. How straight the hair on their heads was he thought, yet their faces were covered in thick, curly beards, and the eyes so pale, one with blue, the other with green.

The elder moved to greet them then turned to call Dangoya, saying through the interpreter, 'This is *Laigwanan* Dangoya of the One Eye.'

Dangoya stepped forward, so close he could smell the strangeness of the men, and shook their hands in customary limp fashion, scarcely hearing the buzz of conversation which sprang up as tensions eased. Gingerly he put out a hand to feel the clothing of the white man nearest him and as though to convince himself these beings were real, he touched then pinched the flesh of a hairy forearm, and feeling the warmth between his fingers knew this was indeed a man.

The rest of Dangoya's party began to press forward, curious and eager to explore with their hands, crowding close on the two Europeans who became slightly apprehensive and called to the interpreter to tell the *morans* to keep their distance, to stand clear of them and their *Olmeg* escort.

'We will talk with the leader and one other,' they shouted, and gradually the *morans* backed away and sat round their fire. The Germans, Dangoya and Lengerebe, together with the elder and the interpreter made another little group, while the *Olmeg* squatted uneasily on the periphery of the gathering.

Throughout the day the discussions went on, questions and answers flying back and forth, the Europeans being as interested in Dangoya as he was in them. There was so much Dangoya wanted to know that he was reluctant to end the talks, but at last one of the Germans brought the conversation to a halt and stated the purpose of their visit, which was to obtain an escort of *morans* to take them into Masai country to meet some of the great *laigwanans* and *laibons*. The elder interrupted to say Dangoya was one of the greatest of the young leaders and would be prepared to take them deep into Masailand – for a consideration.

On being asked what the payment would be, the elder said, 'Two hundred head of cattle!'

The black haired German slowly shook his head and replied that they had no cattle but would pay with blankets, beads and wire.

'Tell them,' Dangoya said, 'They will have to pay with their magic fire-throwers and they will have to teach us the magic.'

The Germans conferred together and agreed that when the rains were over Dangoya and his *morans* would escort them into Masai country for the payment of five guns, blankets and beads. Dangoya accepted the offer gravely, concealing his excitement and pleasure, then realising that soon these men would be gone and that he might not have another opportunity for some time, put out his hand to feel their hair, something he had been longing to do all day. It was so straight and silky, softer even than the belly hair of a newborn calf, and he marvelled that they should grow hair like that on their heads while their beards were rough and curly. The two Germans smiled and stood up to leave, calling over one of the *Olmeg* with presents of blankets for Dangoya, Lengerebe and the elder, and distributing beads and matches to the other *morans*. The matches caused great excitement and the Masai were warned not to waste them as once used their magic was finished.

In the hubbub of their noisy departure one of the *morans* spotted an *Olmeg*, a burly Chagga with thick shoulders, wiping his knife on a tuft of grass before putting it in its sheath.

'Give it to me!' the *moran* said, childlike in his eagerness to possess something new.

'No!' the man said and closed his hand defensively over the knife.

The Masai grabbed his belt and a scuffle ensued, the *moran* landing hard on his bottom. Immediately other *morans* surged forward, their excitement rising as the *Olmeg*, all of whom were armed, made threatening gestures. Quickly the tall German strode into the centre of the disturbance, shouting at the *Olmeg* to remove themselves which they did, backing off with angry glares at the *morans*. The Masai started to follow, urged on by the instigator of the fracas who had worked himself up into such a state that he was beginning to throw a fit, his eyes rolling and little specks of foam appearing on his lips. Lengerebe flung his arms around him in restraint and Dangoya, seeing two more *morans* also throwing fits, called for help to overpower them too. Putting on his lion's mane headdress and picking up his shield, Dangoya shouted to Lengerebe and one other to remain behind and mustering his forces together marched them away at a slow pace so that those in convulsions could be helped to keep up. When they were well out of sight of the camp he instructed Oleserya to continue the march for a while before returning to the *olpul*.

Hurrying back Dangoya found the Germans ready to leave, waiting only for him to appear before they set off for Machame.

'There are two things I wish to ask before you go,' Dangoya said through the interpreter, 'and the first is when will you *layonis* be circumcised?'

The Germans looked at each other and laughed. Then one said, 'Never. Customs are different in our country.'

'*Usho!*' Dangoya said, astonished. 'You cannot remain a *layoni* all your life! The girls will not want you! '

As his remark was translated there were roars of laughter from the *Olmeg* and the recent tension and animosity were swept away, with Dangoya taking the amusement at his expense with great good nature.

'The other thing I want is to see proof of your magic guns,' he said.

'What proof?' asked one of the Germans.

'Can the gun kill a man behind my shield?'

'Stand your shield up against that tree and I will show you. Where do you want the bullet to enter?'

Dangoya pointed to the centre of the shield, but the German shook his head, saying the grip behind would be shattered. However, Dangoya insisted that that was where he wanted the bullet to strike because it was the strongest part. The shield was given to one of the porters to place against a tree a hundred paces from where they stood and the German took aim.

There was a loud report for which the Masai were quite unprepared, putting their hands over their ears and shouting, '*Usho!*' But when they had finished exclaiming about the noise and saw that the shield stood upright as before, they began to laugh. Asked why they were laughing by the puzzled foreigners, they said because it was obvious the stories they had heard about the magic guns were lies.

'Go, see if they are lies,' and the interpreter pointed at the shield.

Lengerebe walked over to the tree and as he got nearer the shield, stopped and looked at it carefully.

'It is holed!' he shouted, and as he turned it over and saw the fragmented grip where the bullet had gone through the thick hide, he yelled, '*Bagishu!* It has finished the shield, this thing!'

Long after the white men had gone and the *morans* had all returned to the *olpul*, they sat discussing the magical weapon and the things they had seen and heard that day, but it was the power of the gun which impressed them most, even those who had not witnessed the exercise, but who had heard the report from a distance. Lengerebe could give a fair imitation of the noise, and this kept the *morans* entertained for several hours.

The next night heavy rain fell and plans were made to move south east to the Pare mountains in anticipation of finding some sizeable herds to raid, but the sudden arrival of the *moran* who had escorted the elder back to his *manyatta* wiped all thoughts of cattle raiding from their minds.

He brought bad news, he said. The Arab disease had reached the *moran manyatta* at Namanga, killing many and leaving numerous sick including Dangoya's sister Nairasha.

'Those who recover are left with terrible scars, but it is said that very few have survived. The large Purko *moran manyatta* at Lengesim has also been struck and there is talk of abandoning both these *manyattas*. People have already fled from the Kisongo *manyatta* at Lolkisale and others down in the south.'

The *morans* listened in dismay, urging the young man to repeat everything he had heard, their initial unbelief giving way to stark realisation of the horror that had come upon their people.

'What do the *laigwanans* say?' asked Dangoya. 'Has anyone consulted the *laibons*?'

'Mbatian has repeated that *Ngai* is angry as the *morans* have not listened to his warnings and will suffer.'

For several hours the disastrous news was discussed and eventually it was agreed that Dangoya and Oleserya should go immediately to consult the *laibons* near Sanya, but when they arrived they found that all the *laibons* of the area were attending the *orgesher* ceremony at *Oldonyo* Moruok where the senior *morans* were to become elders. Not knowing for a moment what to do, Dangoya determined to press on alone to see if he could try to contact Olengesen who would most certainly be at the ceremony, sending Oleserya back to inform the others.

Dangoya had great difficulty getting a message through to Olengesen, the area being closely guarded to maintain secrecy, but at last after two days his *olpiron* came hurrying out to speak to him. Without hesitation Olengesen advised their immediate return to Engaruka and told Dangoya he must abandon both his proposed raid into Pare country and the journey with the Europeans.

'The disease has not touched our people at Engaruka, of that I am quite sure as I received word from there within the past few days.' Olengesen paused, then added, 'I have news too of my wife Muriet. She has given birth to a son who thrives, and of that I am very pleased. Our hope lies in this infant and his continued good health.'

'That is indeed good news.' Thoughts of Muriet welled up within Dangoya and he remembered the nights of the Sanjan, her legs tight around his waist as new life flowed into her body, refusing his withdrawal. His son! Jolting himself back to the present he shook his instructor's hand and left to return to his *morans*.

The *morans* were unanimous in their decision to go first to the *moran manyatta* at Namanga before moving on to their home areas. Many had left their mothers, *asanjas* and other relatives at Namanga, and all were anxious to see how they had fared. No time was wasted and they left within a few hours of Dangoya's return from seeing Olengesen.

It rained continuously, which raised hopes that the evil spirits causing the sickness would be washed away, but when the *morans* reached Namanga the situation was far worse than they had expected. Thirty two people had died and been fed to the hyena, while scores had suffered the disfiguring disease and now lay recovering, a few attempting in their weakened state to tend those less fortunate. Many had already fled the *manyatta* and the numbers of untouched *morans*, girls and older women could be counted on two hands.

Dangoya found Nairasha weak but on her feet; her face, arms and legs covered with hard dry scabs which left, as they fell away, red raw pockmarks, pitiful in their awfulness. She burst into tears at sight of Dangoya, and as he comforted her at a distance - unable to embrace her because of her unshaven state - the bile rose in his throat with revulsion at the horror of this disease which had destroyed the young soft skin of his sister's face.

Holding her by the hand, what little strength she had mustered in order to greet him melting away in her weakened legs, he swallowed the bitterness in his mouth. 'As soon as you are strong we shall leave this place and go to our mother. Cry no more. I am here to take care of you.'

Sending Lengerebe to assess the state of those belonging to his *manyatta* and that of Olengesen, Dangoya led Nairasha to her hut and sat beside her bed, her hands clutching his in fear that he should leave her, his fingers feeling the rough dry scabs.

Lengerebe returned shortly, his face bleak as he reported the deaths of two *morans* from Olengesen's *manyatta* and that a girl and another *moran*, also Olengesen's people, had had the sickness but were now recovering.

'Although the *moran* is still hot with fever, his sores yellow with pus and his body so weak he cannot lift his head, the others are well, or seem to be. One of the older women is on her bed but says she is not sick. *Bagishu*! It is terrible, this thing that takes our people!'

Dangoya looked down at the poor scarred face of his sister, her streaming tears thwarted in their run by the thick ugly scabs. 'As soon as the *moran* is able to stand on his feet, we leave! Arrange with the *morans* to feed and care for the sick ones. We will stay here no longer than we must.'

Impatient as he was to leave Namanga, Dangoya could not desert the sick *moran* who lay like a helpless child, his strength so slow to return, but at the end of a week he was able to sit up and Dangoya ordered an immediate departure from the stench of sickness and death that lay over the *manyatta* in the close fetid air.

With two young men half-carrying the *moran*, the people of Engaruka left for home, driving their small herd of animals before them. The rain had eased and the first four days of their journey were covered over dry ground, but they walked slowly, assisting the weak and stopping often to rest. On the fifth day Lengerebe fell silent and it was only towards evening that Dangoya eyed his friend with concern.

'It is nothing,' Lengerebe said. 'My head hurts a little with the heat, but my betrothed Nairasha shall comfort me tonight.' He tried to smile, but his pretence was short-lived and he admitted to Dangoya that he felt sick and feverish, nausea filling his throat when he drank a little water.

They stopped that night at a small abandoned *manyatta* with six huts in varying stages of collapse, the bulk of Kitumbeine Mountain rising behind them, and Nairasha led Lengerebe into one of the huts where she made a rough bed for him of hides. Dangoya lay beside him through the night, feeling often his friend's hot head, sure in his heart as he stared into the darkness about him that Lengerebe would die. As the hours slowly passed Lengerebe's condition worsened, and by morning his fever raged and he became incoherent.

'Is this the same Arab sickness?' Dangoya asked his sister, but he knew before she nodded her head in reply that she could only confirm his worst forebodings.

Nairasha began to cry, so weak herself and now this added sorrow to be borne.

Feebly she lifted a *calabash* and with small scabbed hands sprinkled water on Lengerebe's burning forehead. 'I shall stay with him,' she said. 'He cannot be moved, so you must carry on with the others.'

'Never shall I leave him!' Dangoya shouted, and with a heavy sick feeling in his belly got to his feet and strode outside to bring together the rest of the party. 'Listen to my words,' he called when everyone came out from the huts. 'We have with us people who are recovering from the Arab sickness. My sister says that Lengerebe also has the same disease, and is now too ill to move. It would seem that this is like the *lodwa* in cattle which is passed on from one herd to another if the herds graze in the same place, or drink from the same water, or even sleep in the same *manyatta*. I have been told that our *manyattas* at Engaruka are free of the disease.' He halted, his eye running over the faces in front of him. 'At Engaruka is a very important child who must not be taken with this sickness, so we must safeguard all who live there.' There were murmurs from the little crowd standing in the clean morning sunshine about him.

'Look around you!' Dangoya raised his arms. 'We are in this *manyatta* which needs only some dung to make the houses dry and comfortable for the sick. There is water nearby and plenty of wood, and we have our cattle for milk and meat. Now that the sickness has started most of us can expect to fall ill. Some will feed the hyena, others will recover, and when we are all clean and well we can go to our *manyattas* as people who have not brought death to their clan.' He looked directly at the *morans*. 'What is the difference if we die here or in battle?' Not a man moved. 'None! There is no difference! I and my family will stay here until this is all over, but I ask those who do not wish to stay, on the commands of the Great Mbatian, not to take this sickness to the newborn son of our *laigwanan* Olengesen. All of you have heard that the child will be a great *laibon*, so will know the importance of what I ask. Now, would those who wish to leave move their cattle out of the *manyatta* first? I shall help you.'

Dangoya walked to the crude gate they had made with branches the night before. Behind him he heard a *knobkerrie* strike the ground and Legetonyi's voice broke the silence. 'Wait!' he cried, 'I have something to say!' He turned to face the others. 'You have all heard what our *laigwanan* Dangoya has said, and I agree with him on everything but one. Did we not, all of us, leave our *manyattas* to go to Namanga together? And does that not make us all of the same family? I say let there be no talk about who should do this or that. We have our leader whom we have made *laigwanan* not once but many times! *Nena age*. That is all.'

'*Ebaye!*' someone shouted, and others joined in agreement, and talking amongst themselves the little band of people began to go about their work of making the *manyatta* habitable.

Within a few days the *manyatta* looked as though they had always lived in it. The thorn enclosure was repaired and strong makeshift gates put in place. Leaking roofs were soon sealed, keeping out the showers that fell from time to time although the rains were scanty. An aging cow, breaking its leg when negotiating the steep bank of the river, was slaughtered and Dangoya carried some of the raw liver to Nairasha's hut for Lengerebe to eat.

For two days the fever had wracked his body and he appeared to be sinking fast, his face and extremities covered in small watery blisters. Nairasha shook her head when she saw the meat and put her face in her hands.

'It is no good, you bringing him food. He cannot eat, or even talk. I think he will be dead before the next sun rises,' she whispered, her anguish beyond tears.

'No!' Dangoya cried. 'You cannot let him die! Anyone can die but not the one who was happy to die himself to save me! No! No! He must not die!' And the tears started to course down Dangoya's cheek, his face crumpling like that of a child as he sobbed for Lengerebe. 'If he dies, I shall die with him!' and Dangoya knelt beside the restless, sweating *moran*, taking the hot hands between his own and holding them to his wet face.

Gradually his tears dried and he shook himself angrily. Here he was making an utter fool of himself before his sister, crying like a woman over a broken *calabash*. Everyone knew he had a great respect and liking for Lengerebe, but not even he had realised until now how deep were his feelings for the young *moran*, his ally of many dangerous moments, his friend too in laughter and shared thoughts. Getting quickly to his feet he left the hut.

All through the day, and the next, Dangoya moved dumbly about his duties, dreading each visit to the hut where Lengerebe struggled in his fight against death. In the evening he carried food to Nairasha, the girl now so weak and exhausted with her vigil that he had to lift the food to her mouth, encouraging her to eat. Lengerebe lay in a coma, the restlessness of his delirium now still, the dotted pustules yellow with thick pus, his breathing so faint that Dangoya kept thinking him dead, putting out a hand every now and then to feel the feeble heartbeat. Nairasha lay beside Lengerebe through the night, crawling to the fire at intervals to add pieces of dried cow dung to the embers, while Dangoya slept fitfully where he sat, his knees drawn up and his head cradled in his arms.

Towards dawn Nairasha woke him and his first conscious thought was of the smell of death, so thick and putrid was the air in the hut, but Nairasha's voice was elated.

'The sores have broken! Now I think he will live! It has been like this with the others, when the pus flows and smells, the worst is over.' She began to cry in her happiness and relief. 'See how he moves a little, and the heat has left his body. By tonight he will be eating!' She swayed in her weariness and Dangoya, feeling a joy which matched her own, forced her gently down on to the bed of hides.

'Now you must sleep. I shall arrange the milking and fetch more water, but I will be here beside you both.'

Nairasha slept soundly until midday when she woke to hear Lengerebe call for water and saw Dangoya hold a *calabash* to his lips. That evening Lengerebe was able to drink a little blood mixed with milk, his first nourishment since falling ill, and when he lay back giving them both a weak smile Nairasha busied herself with smearing sheep fat on his sores. Dangoya could only grin at his friend, remembering with some shame his flood of tears, grateful that no one but Nairasha had seen them.

The cow had been eaten and for some days they had had no meat, so Dangoya debated with Lesirwa about which animal they should slaughter next.

'Why kill our wealth?' Lesirwa queried. There are so many tame buffalo right here in the forest above us.'

'That is good talk!' agreed Dangoya, looking up towards the slopes of Kitumbeine where buffalo were dotted on an open shoulder of the mountain. Calling to two *morans* to bring their spears the young men set off on their hunt. Dangoya returned shortly, leaving the others to skin the buffalo which had been killed, and called to the girls to harness their donkeys and go to fetch meat.

'Lesirwa has killed a heifer buffalo in calf with one single spear thrust,' he shouted gaily, and went in search of Lengerebe to take him to the kill to eat raw, hot liver and spleen.

'That will be the best medicine for you, to give you strength!'

Lengerebe, barely able to totter around, cheerfully complied and with one arm round Dangoya's shoulders was led off up the slope.

Around the fire that evening, the buffalo meat roasting over the coals, the *morans* boasted of how Lesirwa, stalking the buffalo, had approached from behind a bush and thrust his spear into its shoulder, then standing back and waiting for it to charge had neatly side-stepped the onward rush as though it was an ox he had speared, and how he had retrieved his spear from the still-living buffalo as it lay thrashing on the ground.

Lesirwa had taken part in several acts of bravery and had helped kill a lion, but this single-handed slaying of the buffalo had been so coolly, so well executed, that the *moran*'s admiration shone in their eyes and rang in their voices as they applauded him.

The smallpox struck again the next day, felling two of the *morans*, with Lesirwa going down the day after. Dangoya watched over him anxiously through the fever and the appearance of the spots, sitting beside his bed to wet his cracked lips with water, but he never recovered or regained consciousness. His vigorous young life slipped away and with a choking sorrow Dangoya touched the boy for the last time.

'My poor brother, how short-lived was your fame. Now I cry again like a woman.'

Lengerebe's hand fell on his shoulder. 'He is dead, your adopted brother?'

'Yes, he is dead! All my brothers are dead or dying! And how shall I tell Kilimben, his father!'

For four days after Lesirwa's death Dangoya ate nothing, said nothing, but sat alone in his grief, feeling in some way that he was to blame for the boy's passing. Like an older brother of the same blood he had felt responsible for Lesirwa and had taken special pride in his growing prestige amongst the *morans*. At night he slept on his own in the forest above the *manyatta*, but when he saw how Lengerebe too was affected by Lesirwa's death he chided himself for his selfishness and sat in silence beside his friend whose initial fast recovery was slowed by his depression, and when Lengerebe developed a cough and ran a temperature Dangoya was jolted from his introspection and putting all thoughts of Lesirwa behind him tended to Lengerebe's needs and did not leave his side until he was well.

Death among the *morans* was not normally accompanied by great sorrowing. It was an ever-present fact of life, but Lesirwa's slow dying had left a gloom over the entire party and it was many days before the pall lifted. After the first buffalo the *manyatta* was never short of meat as the *morans* needed only to climb the slope to kill another. When the rains ended they would stay with the kill, turning the occasion into an *olpul* and sending meat back to the *manyatta* for the women and the sick. The *manyatta* site was beautiful, with water close at hand and plenty of good sweet grazing for the stock. In the forest they found fruit and honey, and firewood for the taking where passing elephant had paused to feed, pulling down branches and stripping them of bark.

Their prolonged stay in the sheltered valley on Kitumbeine could have been a pleasant if not a happy time, but it was neither. Whenever they thought the disease was past a new victim would be claimed, and very few escaped. Dangoya was one of the lucky ones and helped layout four of his *morans* for the hyena. Two girls and an elderly woman also died, and many who survived the sickness were long recovering, their faces badly scarred and their resistance low so they succumbed to pneumonia.

Impatiently Dangoya took continual stock of their position and at last, after two full moons had passed with no one falling sick, he decided it was safe to make contact with the outside world and instructed the *morans* to bring any travellers they saw to the *manyatta*. Hitherto, any passer by had been warned not to approach too close, and in the few instances when someone had been encountered the shouted news they had received had never been of special concern to them, telling only of the ravages throughout Masailand, but never any word of Engaruka. Within a few days they would be ready to move on home and waited now for the last of the convalescents to build up their strength.

Five Purko *morans*, two of whom were unknown to Dangoya, appeared one evening on their way through from Narosura to Loiborserrit and were persuaded to stay at the *manyatta*. They brought bad news, but Dangoya soon discounted the veracity of much of what they had to say when he learnt he was himself believed to have perished in the epidemic. The visitors reported deaths in all quarters of the country, and their own people the Purko had been badly affected not only by the disease and in battles against the clans in the north, but also by poor rains. In some instances as many as three *manyattas* had had to be combined, so great were the losses of human life.

'All this has been brought upon us,' said one of the Purko, 'because the *morans* did not listen to the words of our great *laibon* and now that the boy child of Muriet, wife of *laigwanan* Olengesen, has died we are truly finished.'

Dangoya and Lengerebe jerked to attention, their heads turning immediately to the man.

'You must not say such things unless you know them to be true,' said Lengerebe firmly.

'Of the child's death I am sure,' the *moran* replied. 'The mother was ill too and very nearly died. Many in *laigwanan* Olengesen's *manyatta* have died, and we heard he himself was very sick.'

'How did you receive all this news,' Dangoya said, 'when you have come from far in the north and we ourselves are only two day's walk from Engaruka, yet have not heard it? And when did you hear it?'

'We were told three new moons ago by a group of elders and *morans* who were sent by Oldimbau's younger brother to report to Mbatian that Oldimbau had died of the sickness. Some say his brother put a curse on him and he choked to death with drink.' The Purko looked uneasily at Dangoya and said, 'We shall call at Engaruka and bring you more recent news when we return this way.'

'I shall come with you.' Dangoya felt sickened by the conversation. He had all along imagined his people at Engaruka to be safe. Now he knew not what he would find. His mother, Ngenia, his family, all dead?

'I am coming too, *Bagishu*,' Lengerebe said. 'The others can follow in their own time.'

Chapter 12

The Survivors

As they traversed the plain below Gelai Mountain it became obvious how poor the rains had been in that area with short dry grass growing valiantly amongst the rocks and wind-whipped sand. Dangoya's apprehension grew as he realised the difficulties Kilimben would be experiencing, trying to keep the home-based herds alive. He trusted Kilimben's judgement implicitly and was certain the dry herds would be grazing wherever he had been able to find good grass, but with the entire country rife with smallpox and the imminent threat to their cattle of the dreaded *rinderpest*, Dangoya knew he could not expect to find matters as they should be. Everyone might be dead, elders, *morans* and *layonis*, and the cattle roaming untended.

The *manyattas* at Engaruka came into sight and with overwhelming relief Dangoya saw smoke from the cooking fires and a few figures moving about the enclosures, but his fear remained and neither he nor Lengerebe spoke as they entered the gates and went first to Dangoya's mother's house. Standing outside Singira's door they hesitated, anxious for what the next moment would reveal, but to Dangoya's intense joy he heard his mother's voice, tired perhaps and older sounding, yet nevertheless the same commanding, optimistic tones belonging only to Singira.

'Why do you stand outside?' she called. 'Come in my sons!'

Carefully placing their spears on the roof of the hut they bent to enter, unsure of how their own voices would sound, not trusting themselves to speak.

'So you have come back,' she said fiercely, holding Dangoya in her arms, her pupils large in the dim light. 'Why have you stayed away so long? And what has happened to my daughter Nairasha?'

'She is at Kitumbeine and you shall see her soon. She was ill but is better.' Dangoya's voice was husky and he coughed to clear his throat. 'Now tell me first everything that has happened here, then we shall tell you our news.'

'My *morans*, you must drink before I say anything,' Singira said, picking up a *calabash* of milk, and she watched as they drank thirstily, seeing their thinness and the deep etched lines about their eyes. Then with shock she realised Dangoya's skin was quite clear of pockmarks. 'You did not have the sickness?' she cried, then as suddenly noticed Lengerebe's scars and began to weep.

Dangoya took her hand in his. 'I have not been sick, and you must not cry. Now tell me everything from the time Olengesen came back from the *orgesher*.'

'You must prepare yourself for very bad news.' She lifted her head and looked at him directly.

'Tell me!'

Slowly and carefully she told him of those who had died. His sister Naidu, his wife Ngenia, his little brother, Kilimben's wife and Muriet's baby son. 'There have been so many deaths here at Engaruka alone. And of your married sister at Piyaya, I have heard nothing. A great number of people have had the sickness but have survived, most with changed faces although a few seem not to be badly scarred.' She turned then to Lengerebe. 'You have heard enough bad news from me. You must hear the rest from your own mother.'

'And what of Olengesen?' Dangoya interrupted. 'What news of him?' His thoughts were in a turmoil, his anguish for Ngenia and Naidu tightening his chest.

'He has been very ill and would be in the belly of a hyena now if it had not been for Muriet and me who looked after him without cease until we were ourselves ready to die.'

'And the cattle?'

'Of the cattle the news is bad too.' His mother sighed. 'We have lost a lot because of the drought and Kilimben has taken those that could walk to search for grazing. To add to our troubles we have heard that the *lodwa* sickness has broken out in the herds at Dulen.'

'I must go to see Olengesen. I have to tell him his *moran* Lesirwa is dead.' He told Singira then of what he had found at the *moran manyatta* at Namanga and the reasons for their long stay at Kitumbeine through many moons until the smallpox had passed.

Her eyes searching both their faces, seeing only honesty, knowing them incapable of dissembling, Singira said, 'You did right, my sons, but no one will believe you, the fools!' She turned away in exasperation. 'Go now and see your *laigwanan*. He is still very weak, but will be pleased to talk with you. He lies in Muriet's house.'

His mind confused, feeling nothing but dejection, Dangoya walked across to Olengesen's *manyatta* and left Lengerebe to visit his mother. It was late and a few straggling animals were being driven in by a small *layoni*, his face puckered, legs like sticks beneath his *ngelan*.

Muriet was outside her house, blending a mixture of fat and mildewed dung on the flat side of a big stone. She was very thin and her head was thick with matted hair. A few pockmarks dotted her face, but she seemed quite well and her eyes brightened when she saw him, rising at once to greet him.

'What are you making?' he asked.

'Medicine,' she replied, smiling at him.

'Why use such old dung? That is many days old.'

'Fresh cow dung cannot heal as well as this.' She stood looking at him and he felt a surge of longing well up in him, an ineffable desire for comfort in her arms.

'I shall talk first with the *laigwanan*, and he stepped inside the hut carrying the vision of Muriet's dark eyes in his mind.

191

Olengesen lay gaunt and wasted, his once big frame fragile like that of an old man, but there was some resilience in his spirit and his voice was strong. 'You have come! I thought you dead!' He sat up, leaning his weight on one elbow. 'You have brought me good news?'

'No, my *laigwanan*. There is no good news for our tribe in these terrible days.'

'Yes there is! Seeing you alive and home to help with our troubles - that to me is good news. You have seen your mother?'

'Yes, and I have heard all of what has happened here.'

'Then tell me where you have been and what you have done.'

When Dangoya had related everything to Olengesen, the older man sighed and said, 'I lie here like a feeble child. I need your help, my *olpiron*, so tell me what you think we should do.'

'I have not thought. I have only listened to words and my head becomes confused.'

'Then go and rest, and talk with me in the morning.' Dangoya left the hut, the evening air hot and still with the rain that would not fall.

'Where are you Muriet?' he called.

'I am here,' she replied from amongst the cows, her hands busy as she milked. She had taken off her skirt which was not unusual at that time of the year with the weather so warm, and Dangoya stood talking to her. When she had finished milking the cow she straightened and turned to face him, the *calabash* held carefully in her hands. He saw at once that she had a thick growth of pubic hair, so much hair that she must have fallen sick many moons before. Surely, he told himself, she was quite better? She was thin it was true, but otherwise seemed to be in good health.

'Are you not recovered from the Arab sickness?' he asked.

'Yes, I am very well.' She lowered her eyes and even in the failing light he could see the faint flush of blood rising in her face. It was a thing of great fascination to Dangoya, this tendency to blush which only the pale-skinned Muriet seemed to possess amongst all the girls he knew. 'Are you staying here for a while? '

'Yes!' His voice sounded thick in his throat.

'Then tomorrow I shall shave and move my sick husband to the house of one of his other wives.' She looked directly at him then, her head back. 'And you must not leave Engaruka until I am once again carrying your child!'

A quick anger flared up in Dangoya. 'How can you talk of such things at a time like this? Half our people dead and our very livelihood in danger from want of grazing!'

'This, my brave *moran*, is the time we should talk, and then act! If our child had lived we should have been saved the disaster that has struck our people. And you cannot say that is untrue, as Mbatian himself told you. So we must make another child who will be a great *laibon*.'

Dangoya hesitated, bewildered and uncertain, a tiny fear at the strangeness of this girl infecting him. Then suddenly he remembered the nights he had lain with her, the very flesh and blood of her jolting him back to reality.

'How will you make sure the child is mine?' Dangoya's uneasiness left him as quickly as it had come.

'Have I not left all this hair to keep the men away from me while I waited for your return?'

'How did you know I would return?' he asked, smiling down at her.

'I knew, my *asanja*. I knew!'

Dangoya stared at the girl, wanting to take her in his arms, but knowing she was untouchable in her unshaven state. 'I shall talk with you tomorrow,' he said curtly and stalked off.

Looking for Lengerebe he passed a number of girls and women at their milking, all of them naked in the heat of the evening. One was his *asanja* of a long time past who had been with him at the *olpul* before he left for Namanga. She was now married with a child and he stopped to speak to her, asking if she had anyone visiting her that night. She replied that she had not and that he could do so, but would receive no more than food and a bed. She tossed her head and turned away from him, and Dangoya shrugged and moved on.

Lengerebe was in Singira's hut and Dangoya, seeing his spear at the door, called as custom directed for permission to enter.

'Come in, his mother said. 'Your *Bagishu* is here and we are waiting for you.'

As soon as he saw Dangoya, Lengerebe blurted out, '*Bagishu*, I speak in the presence of your mother as she is wise and may guide us to take the best path. Bareto and Pushati have been here in our absence and have spoken many untrue things about you!'

'What are these words they have spoken?' Dangoya asked. 'I have heard nothing.'

'That you ran away from the field of battle when you were hit in the eye by a Chagga and pretended to be dead, hiding in the forest like a coward.' Lengerebe's eyes flashed in anger. They said too that the Loitayo and Kisongo *moran manyattas* at Namanga and Lolkisale asked you to be their leading *laigwanan*, and in both you refused because you were frightened they would discover your cowardice. They said you led a group of *morans* to talk with the white men, and when trouble started you ran away with your men as you were scared of the Europeans' guns. But these things are nothing to what they said next, *Bagishu*! They said you did not then go back to the *moran manyatta* but took your cattle and a few followers and went into hiding as you were ashamed to face your people! Does it not hurt you that these *narobong gotonye* say these things?' Lengerebe was very agitated.

'Let them say what they wish!' Dangoya said coldly. 'Everyone knows the truth, and when our present troubles are over I shall find and thrash that son of a pig Pushati in his own *manyatta*, and shall challenge Bareto not to use the *seki*.'

Singira spoke for the first time, her voice quiet. 'People do believe these lies, my son, as you will quickly discover when you leave this house. There are but a few who have not abused me because of this talk, and there is nothing now you can do about Bareto as he is dead.'

'I have only now left Muriet's house and seen *laigwanan* Olengesen. He was pleased to see me and I have told him all. He has asked me to go back in the morning. And Muriet has invited me to visit her tomorrow.' He remembered suddenly the other girl's snub.

'But she cannot!' Singira was shocked. 'She is unshaved!'

Dangoya smiled at her. 'She will be shaved tomorrow.'

'That,' said his mother, 'is the best talk I have heard in many days!'

'Come,' Dangoya said to Lengerebe, 'let us go and see how many times we are rejected by the *nditos* before we are accepted.'

They wandered between the huts and when from one they heard noisy laughter and talk, girls' voices in birdlike counterpoint to the deep tones of the *morans*, they entered. There was a hush, and all eyes turned on them.

Dangoya looked about him in the dim light, recognising one by one most of the young people there. 'Have you *nditos* no manners? Do you not greet your *morans* when you see them? Either that, or incite your *asanjas* to challenge us cowards who ran away from the *Olmeg* and the white *layonis*!' Bent over as he was in the low hut it was difficult to attain a commanding position, and yet Dangoya succeeded, the *morans* and girls struck dumb. 'We have no *seki* branch, but we have our spears outside!' His voice was taut with menace.

A *moran* rose as best he could and Dangoya realised with some surprise that it was Suyanga, second son of Kilimben, grown to manhood since last he saw him and so like Lesirwa in appearance it was almost uncanny.

This forgotten adopted brother broke the silence in the hut. 'Then I must be the third coward,' he shouted, 'for I would rather run with you than stand and fight with the rest!'

The air was charged with tension, then suddenly all the *morans* leaned forward or got to their feet, moving towards Dangoya as a wave, shaking his hand, smiles showing white in the murky, smoke-filled hut. The girls too clustered about Dangoya and Lengerebe, presenting their heads in greeting, but nothing was said about the defamatory remarks made by Bareto and Pushati.

Talk dropped to its normal level until a visiting *moran* from a nearby *manyatta* spoke up, sensing the inner curiosity felt by them all. 'Why do you not tell us the true story of what kept you away so long?'

'We have told you,' Lengerebe said, 'we were at Kitumbeine. And the rest are still there. '

'But why did you not come back sooner?'

Impatient with this unnecessary talk, Dangoya snapped at the *moran*. '*Usho*! How many times do you have to hear, or were the *nditos* caressing your *njabo* when first Lengerebe told you?'

Someone laughed, and Dangoya took the opportunity to talk of other matters. Lengerebe had made it clear he intended spending the night with one of his *asanjas*, so Dangoya enquired if a certain young married woman would be free. Learning that she had no visitors he went to her house where she made him welcome and certainly did not refuse him, yet for all that Dangoya noticed an underlying lack of enthusiasm which he quickly shrugged off. He was sure this general antipathy towards him would wear away in time.

In the morning Lengerebe and Dangoya conferred together, discussing their reception by the *morans* the night before.

'I think we should forget all this harmful talk,' Lengerebe said. 'There are more important things to do.'

'I agree, and our cattle and sheep must come first in our planning. Let us go now to see Olengesen.'

The *laigwanan* had been assisted out into the cool of the big tree between the *manyattas* and sat with his back against the trunk, several elders with him. The two *morans* approached to within a respectful distance then stopped, waiting to be invited to join the elders. At the end of the formal greetings Olengesen went over the happenings of the last two seasons and concluded with an account of his discussion with Dangoya the previous evening, and the manner in which both young men had behaved with the *morans*. News had spread fast through the *manyattas* that neither would stand any nonsense and were prepared to challenge any *morans* of their age-group who might be unwise enough to make a wrong move.

'We have heard your answers to the accusations made against you,' one of the elders said. 'What now do you intend to do about these?'

Dangoya stood up - thereby showing his defiance - and said, 'My elders, I speak with respect, and I thank you for allowing me to speak. I say to you elders I shall not deny anything Bareto has said as he cannot come out of the belly of the hyena to challenge me. I was not present when these accusations were made. So I say to you, go ask the *morans* who were with me on the occasion of all these happenings, if you do not know the truth. I shall not look for Pushati, that cowardly son of a warthog, because I know he will not move anywhere without the *seki*, but I will say in front of you, my elders, that if he - alone or with any number of his *moran* friends - wishes to challenge me, the *seki* will not be called on. And the *morans* on my side will not exceed his in number. Send that message to him!' The elders exchanged glances and waited. Dangoya continued, looking straight at Olengesen. 'It is true, my *laigwanan*, that you told me at *Oldonyo* Moruak that I would be best advised to come home and this was my intention when I left you, going direct to the *moran manyatta* to fetch my people and cattle, and we left Namanga to come here. You know our reasons for staying at Kitumbeine and I shall not repeat them. I have said all, and will speak no more of Bareto or Pushati.

'You told me yesterday I was to speak of what I would do now, and these are my plans. Lengerebe will go to Kitumbeine in the morning, taking with him some of the older women and small children, and any elder that will go. There is plenty of meat and milk there as the grazing is good, with water close by. I shall not move any cattle there because of the *lodwa* which has been reported from many places. Lengerebe will return here, bringing most of the *morans*, while I shall go with Suyanga to find Kilimben, then on to the sheep at Piyaya, and to search for grazing and water. I shall come back with news.' Dangoya looked about him at the elders surrounding Olengesen. 'If any of you, my elders, wish to oppose my plans, speak now.'

'You have spoken my words,' Olengesen said. 'Go now and find food and rest.'

The elders murmured their agreement and the *morans* returned to the *manyatta*, going first to Muriet's hut where she gave them food. She was freshly shaved, her head clean and shiny, and had adorned herself with trinkets. Her skirt, newly coloured with red ochre, swung from her too-thin hips, not fitting as well as before. Her hut too had been refurbished, and the appalling smell of sickness was gone, swept away by her broom of freshly cut wild sage.

'I shall come to you this evening,' Dangoya told her, and he and Lengerebe went out to see the milking herd.

They had no difficulty finding the small herd on the bare and dusty plain below Engaruka. Dangoya grew tight-lipped as they approached the senior *moran* in charge, noting the wretched condition of the animals, ribs prominent and coats dry. Only a matter of time, Dangoya thought, and this herd would start dying off. Suyanga and another young *moran*, together with two *layonis*, accompanied the cattle - more herdsmen than would have been necessary under all ordinary circumstances - so Dangoya assumed they were having trouble with predators too.

Everyone gathered to talk, but Dangoya was quick to notice that the two young *morans* expressed no opinions about the cattle although significant looks passed between them. The senior *moran* was a relative of Olengesen's and appeared not unfriendly towards Dangoya and Lengerebe, but seemed to them both to be slightly simple. A few cows straggled behind the others and Dangoya took the opportunity to be alone with Suyanga by offering to go with him to round them up while Lengerebe held the older man in conversation. When out of earshot, Dangoya questioned Suyanga who told him that since being ill with the Arab sickness the man had not been right in the head.

'He was very sick and nearly died, and has been like this ever since.'

'But can he not see there is no grass here for the cattle?' Dangoya was angry.

'We have tried to take the herd up to the forest, but he says there is *oldigana* disease there in the sour grazing,' Suyanga explained. 'We cannot tell him what to do!'

'I shall talk to the *laigwanan* about this. In the morning I am going to find your father with the dry herd. Will you come with me?'

'Yes!' Suyanga seemed pleased. 'I shall arrange for someone to take my place with this herd.'

Dangoya knew he would have to see Olengesen alone and that he would have to rely on his mother to arrange a meeting; and he pondered the worrisome issue of the grazing on the way back to the *manyattas*.

Singira sang to herself as she prepared to clean her *calabashes*. Into the fire in front of her she put several strips of olive wood and waited until one was well alight.

Quickly inserting the burning strip into the first *calabash*, she covered the opening with her hand and shook it so that the charcoal rubbed off on to the inner lining. She repeated this two or three times, satisfied at last that the smoky scent of the olive wood had penetrated the *calabash*, knowing that milk would keep fresh in it for up to five days.

She looked up and saw Dangoya, and knew from his face that he was disturbed.

'I wish you to arrange for me to see Olengesen here later,' he said, and went back to the gate to wait for the cattle to come in.

Dangoya was shocked by what he had seen that day, and as he studied the cows passing through the gate he wondered how it could be possible to squeeze milk from any. Just then his mother walked by singing for the first of her cows, reduced once more to this daily work since they had lost so many girls.

'Go to my house and wait,' she said and disappeared among the cattle.

He walked slowly to her hut, entered and sat down, smiling when he saw Naidu's children there. The little boy, slightly scarred, was sturdy as he toddled about, playing with a stick. The girl, her deformity worse now as she grew older, came towards him and bent her small head. He placed his hand on her shiny crown in greeting and she looked up and tried to smile, dribbling as she did so, the teeth like sharp little tusks jutting from the flesh beneath her lower lip. Her skin was quite clear.

'Were you not sick?' he asked, but she made no reply.

Olengesen appeared in the doorway, weak still and unsteady on his feet. 'You have words for my ears alone?'

'Yes, my *laigwanan*, but I do not wish to show disrespect to my seniors.'

'Speak,' Olengesen ordered. 'My lips will be closed when I leave this house.'

Dangoya took a deep breath, looked at his *laigwanan* and began. 'You have been sick a long time and have not had the strength to visit the herds since Kilimben left with the dry stock.' Olengesen was silent, his eyes hard, and Dangoya went on in some trepidation. 'I respect the senior *moran* who takes out the cattle, but I see he is not completely recovered from his sickness. Half the cattle will soon die of starvation and when the *lodwa* comes - as it must - they will all die, as those which could live through the drought will not have the strength to fight the disease.

'There is good grazing in the *oldigana* area of the forest. The older animals have survived *oldigana* before and although many of the younger ones will get the sickness, many of them will recover and become strong, producing more milk and blood for the few of us who are left. A great number of the cattle will die of *oldigana* it is true, but those that do survive will never starve again. You, my *laigwanan*, are the only one who can order this.'

Outside the hut the little girl laughed and they could hear the baby banging his stick on the ground. Olengesen cleared his throat and spat, his eyes tired and depressed. 'How do you want me to do this?' he asked.

'I am not telling you what to do, my *laigwanan*. If you feel what I have said is correct, send that senior *moran* away on a task and make the elders of your *manyatta* do some work until the *morans* arrive and can take over. And tell them the cattle must go into the forest.'

Olengesen made no immediate reply, but sat staring into space. Then he said, 'I hear no singing, the milking must be finished. Tell your mother to come in.'

Dangoya went to fetch Singira, and when she came in carrying the fresh milk, she offered some to the older man and he drank. 'Have you guests tonight?' Olengesen asked her. 'Only you.' Singira smiled.

He acknowledged her reply gravely and said, 'Listen well and speak if you have anything to say.' He faced Dangoya. 'How can I order the elders to work when the most I can do myself is walk from my *manyatta* to here!'

Dangoya answered carefully, very aware of his mother, her eyes intent on his face. 'Before you were taken by the sickness you would sometimes go and herd your cattle when there were not enough younger *morans* to do so. And you would be doing that now if you were not sick. We all have troubles at present, and it is for everyone to work until these troubles are over. Mother Dangoya here has finished her working life and been given the freedom of the *manyatta*, with the same status and rights as an elder, yet she is working harder now than when she was a young *siangiki*. Kilimben too! He is an elder of standing now, a member of our family, but he does not sit around the *manyatta* waiting for beer to be brewed! I say that if the day did come that we became poor and had no cattle, those elders would leave and go like the vultures to seek another carcass!'

Singira drew in her breath sharply. 'My son blasphemes, but he speaks the truth.'

Olengesen said nothing, weighing Dangoya's words in his mind, knowing he must tighten his grip on his people once more. Eventually he looked up. 'Go now,' he said to Dangoya, 'and let me rest. And tell my wives I shall be sleeping here. You did well to speak to me.'

Dangoya left his *manyatta*, a young boy closing the gate behind him, and walked across the bare dusty ground through the still hot air of evening to Olengesen's *manyatta*. The little wicket gate was open and he shut it firmly and went straight to Muriet's hut. She was waiting for him and he told her to go quickly to Olengesen's other wives, to inform them the *laigwanan* would not be returning that night. He thrust his spear into the ground beside the door and entered, and in a few minutes Muriet was back, bending down to tend the fire. She wore only a skirt and had oiled her body, the faint light from the fire shining on her skin and the curve of her long back.

She turned to look at him. 'You are late.' Then standing up she removed her skirt, tucking it away at the far end of her bed.

With a sudden thumping in his chest he saw the newly shaved mound of her pubis, the flat belly, the hip bones too prominent and the buttocks less rounded since the days of health and food in plenty.

'Have you eaten?' she asked.

'I have not come for food,' Dangoya said, his voice level, but the rising excitement within him apparent to the girl who laughed breathlessly and sat down on her bed, her knees unexpectedly weak.

'What is wrong?' she teased. 'Have all the girls rebuffed you? Come to my bed and I shall not refuse you.' She became serious, matching his mood, her eyes dark on his face as he moved to sit beside her. 'There is nothing you cannot have from me, because I know what is true about you.' She leaned against him, her breast soft on his ribs and his arm, moving herself gently back and forth, caressing him with the warm touch of her flesh. 'When the two *morans* came here and spoke badly of you I was sick and did not see them, but if I had, I should have spat on them and they would have had to fight the *morans* of this *manyatta* or leave in disgrace!' She had closed her eyes, but now opened them to look at him. 'You are not hearing my words!' she exclaimed in surprise.

Dangoya was aflame with desire for her, a desire he had never before felt with such deep urgency, and her voice washed over his consciousness in a blur of soft sound. He was astonished at the effect she had upon him, at the wonder of her. 'You have bewitched me!' he said thickly, a tiny spark within him believing it to be true.

Muriet moved her hands down his chest and over the hard muscles of his stomach, and cupped the heat of him in her palm. 'Oh my *asanja*, my lover,' she whispered, 'in these two *nderege* sleep all my children,' and twining her arms about him leaned back and pulled him to her.

They lay uncovered on the bed, for the night was warm and the only ventilation was through the breaches in the crude doorway and the small smoke-hole in the wall. Too hot to sleep they talked, recalling all that had happened over the last two seasons since they had seen each other, Muriet listening, making pointed comments, not afraid to express her opinion. She is like my mother, Dangoya thought.

Her hand crept between his thighs, feeling the small softness of him. '*Aish!*' she laughed. 'It is dead! You and it are both the same; when something gets into your head, nothing can stop you getting what you want - like when you killed those *morans*. Yet when you have had your way, no one would believe you able of catching a bird for an *mbarnoti* head-dress! And this,' she squeezed gently, 'a short time ago was like a cobra about to attack a lion, but now it has had what it wanted and is like a leech.'

He laughed. 'We were speaking of serious matters and you have interrupted me.

'Well, tell me more about the white men. Have you heard whether they have found some other *morans* to bring them to our country?'

'I do not know. But having no guide will not stop them. When they wish it, they will come. They are brave and possess strong powers. When our people and cattle are no longer dying, I shall see the white men again.'

'And now?' Muriet said quietly. 'What are you going to do now?'

'I shall visit the dry herd and then go on to the sheep,' Dangoya said. 'Then I shall come back here.'

'You will come to me then! I shall not give the hospitality of my bed to anyone until I am with child by you,' and Muriet wound her arms and legs around Dangoya to love him again.

Chapter 13

The Parasites

They found the dry herd below Empakai, the cattle making do on virtually no grazing, browsing rather on low scattered bushes, but water appeared to be plentiful with both rivers in the vicinity running.

Kilimben was with the herd himself, unlike the elders at Engaruka who sat about the *manyatta* in idleness, and Suyanga's keen eyes picked him out from a distance, the older man's gaunt figure firm as a tree as he stood watch, motionless in the glare, the only movement the flapping of his skin clothing in the harsh, unrelenting wind. With a paralysing chill Dangoya knew he could not tell Kilimben of his son Lesirwa's death and sent Suyanga forward to break the news to his father.

Kilimben had seen the two young *morans* approach, and when Suyanga began to move towards him alone he recognised his younger son and a small foreboding tightened his chest, making his heart beat faster. Suyanga walked more quickly, sensing in the stillness of his father that he must already know that the news of the death of his son had been carried to him on the hot winds of the plains.

With mouth dry the boy neared his father, Kilimben's eyes steady as he watched the big frame of Suyanga almost running towards him.

'My father! My brother Lesirwa is dead!'

With shock Kilimben received the news. He said nothing, nor moved, his face set as he stared at Suyanga. Then for one instant his body slumped before he turned away to recover his composure. He faced Suyanga again, his cheeks wet with tears, then, passing his hands over his eyes, he wiped away his sorrow and held Suyanga to him briefly.

'Is that our *laigwanan* of the One Eye with you? Go tell him to come here.' Kilimben pushed Suyanga away gently.

'He has been hurt by my brother's death worse than any, and grieves still. Let him come on his own.' Suyanga turned to watch Dangoya as he slowly walked towards them.

Through the soft noises of the plains, the wind a never-ending soughing, Dangoya moved to join the others and as he walked he began to shake, his head whirling in chaotic turmoil as though he was about to throw a fit. The shaking became uncontrollable and Suyanga reached out quickly, catching Dangoya in his arms and setting him down on the ground. Calling to a *layoni* to bring water, Kilimben sank to his haunches beside Dangoya, taking his hands in his own, saying nothing until the boy ran up with a *calabash*. Raising Dangoya's head, Kilimben put the water to his lips and after a little while he sat up, his thoughts once more in order.

'Take my place with the cattle,' Kilimben told Suyanga. 'It is time for them to drink.' He stayed beside Dangoya to talk of all that had happened since last they had seen each other.

'I am pleased you have come,' Kilimben said. 'You can now help me to think.' He waved an arm in the direction of the herd as it moved towards the river. 'You see those cattle of ours. None have yet died of starvation, but they will not last much longer without good grass. And there is *lodwa* sickness in one of the Kisongo herds below us, and in the game animals on the plains.' He pointed to a *manyatta* some distance away with his herding stick. 'Three head have died there in the past few days. There is no grazing anywhere down on the plains. The only grass is up in the forest where the *oldigana* disease will kill off many animals. If all these cattle were ours, I would take them to the forest tomorrow, but we are the keepers of the wealth of the Engaruka *manyattas* and I cannot do it.'

'My father,' Dangoya said, 'I believe I speak with the tongue of Olengesen. These cattle have lost their fat and all are weak. The lesser witchdoctors have taken our stock, but have not stopped the Arab sickness amongst our people, nor brought the rain, and now we have the *lodwa*. This is our punishment for not listening to the great Mbatian. Many in our herds will perish. Is it not better then that we save a few? A few that will in the future be able to graze in the forests when others die on the plains?'

They had discussed before the limited advantage of forest grazing. Weaker animals would certainly succumb to East Coast Fever, but the majority would gain life-long immunity. Whereas the scourge of *rinderpest* could wipe out entire herds, to leave the animals in its path would be madness.

'Tomorrow,' said Dangoya, 'Suyanga and I will help you take the cattle into the forest where we can move towards and join the wet herd, which I am sure Olengesen will send there. The two of us will then go on to the sheep. Have you heard if the flocks have left Olbalbal?'

'They must still be there.' Kilimben got to his feet. 'Let us go to the *manyatta* for some food.'

The cattle were about to enter the enclosure when one of the *layonis* ran up to Kilimben to report that two animals were sick.

'How do you know they are sick?' he asked the boy.

'Because they do not eat, are very hot and cannot keep up with the others. Both have diarrhoea which smells different and unpleasant.'

Dangoya and Kilimben threaded their way through the herd to inspect the sick animals and found one was a large ox and the other a young bulling heifer, neither in unreasonable condition yet now very obviously stricken with *rinderpest*. Kilimben ordered the immediate slaughter of the steer for meat, but decided to leave the heifer to take its chance.

The next day the herd was moved into the forest, with the *morans* taking over an empty *manyatta* nearby. Dangoya and Suyanga went on to the sheep, travelling throughout the day and half the night before stopping to rest at moonset when the going became difficult. There were not only buffalo which they almost fell over before seeing, but also the area was thick with large clumps of wild sisal, and to be scratched by the nasty poisonous thorns on the tips of the long leaves could be very painful. With the lightening of the dawn sky they carried on, but before reaching the sheep camp they were charged by rhino three times which Suyanga found exhilarating, Dangoya choosing to regard the encounters with more seriousness and caution.

The news given them by the *moran* at the camp was cheerful, with the sheep in good condition and the crop of lambs fair. The flocks of another *manyatta* shared the grazing which although not good was sufficient for the time being, and water was still plentiful. Only two people, a girl and a *moran*, had been ill, but both would soon be fit enough to continue with their duties.

'But we are very short of *morans*, 'the herdsman said, 'As the plains game - the wildebeest, zebra and eland - move away, so we are left with the dangers of the predators'.

The *morans* with the sheep, he told them, were four young men of Dangoya's age-group, and to help them they had only three *layonis* and five girls. Dangoya could well understand their concern, and resolved to send reinforcements as soon as he could. With a flash of private anger and frustration, he remembered the elders sitting in comfort at Engaruka. What he would not give to bring them to Olbalbal and insist on them earning their keep.

'Have you any meat?' he asked, his hunger gnawing at his belly.

'Only part of a ewe killed by a hyena while lambing,' the *moran* replied.

'Slaughter a fat wether for us. We have had no food, and without food we cannot think well.'

Two of the children were sent out to the nearest flock and brought back a young sheep with a heavy fat tail which was immediately butchered, some parts of the intestines and fat being eaten raw, while the other cuts were put on the fire. The rich succulent aroma of roasting mutton which Dangoya had not smelt for over a year brought back memories of his childhood on the *Serenget* and the girl Masaiko. How did she fare now, he wondered. Had the sickness killed her too?

Turning the skewer to cook the meat evenly, Dangoya found the smell overpowering and too much for his empty stomach, and he began to slice off pieces of half-cooked meat, dipping them into the ash for a salty flavour. Suyanga too was ravenous and out of choice had one of the girls bring him some raw tripe which he shook vigorously to remove bits of partly digested grass. He slapped it down on the coals, turned it once, and ate it with gusto. Speechless with the joy of eating, their chins greasy, the young men grinned at each other as they filled their bellies until the skin was taut and they could eat no more.

'Now,' said Dangoya, 'I feel better. Let us go to see the sheep.'

Suyanga nudged him, pointing to where the *moran* sat sleeping in the shade of a tree. 'I have been told that the *morans* out with the sheep have been talking with Bareto's sympathisers. Let me visit them alone first, to give them the chance of saving themselves from having to fall on the *seki*.' He had lowered his voice so none could hear.

Dangoya sat for a moment thinking, then said quietly, 'You are right, my brother. We cannot afford to let our feelings get the better of us at a time like this. Go, and stay with the sheep. I shall join you later.'

He made himself comfortable, watching idly as the few girls in the camp busied themselves cleaning the skin of the sheep. One was a mere child, far too young he thought to be out here with the flocks. She must be the orphan his mother had told him about, whom he was to take back when he returned to Engaruka to help with Naidu's children. He called the little girl over to him and asked her name.

'My name is Siama,' she replied.

'And are you not to go with me to Engaruka?'

She nodded her head, acknowledging the fact, then Dangoya saw tears spring up in her great dark eyes. Quickly he leaned forward and placed his hand on her head.

'You must not be frightened, or sad. If you really do not want to go, you may stay here. But I know Mother Dangoya would be disappointed as she is looking forward to having you as another daughter.' He smiled and patted her cheek. 'Now go and fetch me water to drink.'

The child ran to bring a *calabash*, smiling as she handed it to him, and he drank and said, 'Because you brought it, it is the sweetest water I have drunk since I eased my thirst in the cold water on the Great White Mountain.'

Her smile widened and Dangoya noticed for the first time how beautiful her eyes were, with an ever-present laugh in the slant and length of her lashes, and he thought of how she would lead the *morans* a dance when she was a little older.

He got to his feet and took from the fire a leg of mutton, now well cooked, sticking his knife through the tendons.

'Where are you taking that? 'The *moran* was suddenly awake.

'To the herders.'

'It will not be eaten,' the young man grinned. 'They are sick of mutton. We have not had anything but mutton for many moons.'

'Are there no buffalo or eland amongst all this game?'

'There were plenty of eland before they moved away, but they were too fast for our spears and with no Ndorobo here to hunt them with their bows and arrows, we were unable to enjoy any eland meat.' The *moran* spat into the dust and gestured towards the river. There are some buffalo which come to water every day when the sun begins to drop from its highest point, but there are not enough *morans* to take them on.'

Dangoya grunted in reply, put the mutton back in a cooler part of the fire, and went off to the sheep, a feeling of great contentment filling his body as he belched once or twice and picked his teeth clean with a sliver of grass.

The *morans* stood guard on the flock, one at each point of the compass, leaning on their spears, one foot on the ground with the other against the side of the supporting leg. All were motionless, but as Dangoya approached, four heads turned in his direction to watch him as he walked around the grazing sheep. A couple of *layonis* moved about the perimeter and Suyanga strolled among the sheep examining them with a critical pastoralist's eye.

As Dangoya came to each *moran* in turn he was greeted politely but with reserve. 'The sheep look good,' he told them. 'Considering the bad year we have had they are in very fair condition and some are carrying big fat tails.' He wandered over to Suyanga. 'Come, let us find these *morans* some food,' and they walked nonchalantly away towards the river.

In a wallow to one side of the main flow they found three old bull buffalo dreaming and twitching in the heat, clearly in permanent residence during the long hot hours, feeding only in the cool of morning and at night.

'We could kill one of these easily enough,' Suyanga whispered.

'Yes, but think of how tough and smelly the meat would be. Rather let us wait until the herd comes to drink. '

The *morans* settled themselves on a large rock downwind of the wallow and well-screened by reeds, and very soon heard the approaching buffalo as they stamped and crashed their way to the water, the stronger males butting the females and smaller animals away in their insistent dominance to reach the river first. The old bulls were roughly evicted from the mud wallow and retreated with bellowing indignity up the further bank, where they stood and glared myopically at the splendid young usurpers who rolled and shoved and shook their great bossed heads.

A young heifer, picking her way through the rock and scrub of the river bank, chose the lower, downwind part, and the *morans* tensed as they watched her progress towards them. Suyanga scarcely breathed, so great was his excitement and anticipation, and the fear of perhaps making a wrong move.

In the softest of whispers Dangoya said, 'Wait until it is no more than a spear length away and in a good position for a heart throw.'

The animal lumbered by, just out of range, her intent to chase off a skittish young bull. Then she turned and once more came towards the hidden *morans*. Suddenly she was close - closer than a spear length, but presenting the boned mass of her head. She sniffed delicately and in an instant caught the smell of the hunters. She turned in an unbelievably fast, lightning movement, hurling her immense body round and away, but the spears flew with deadly speed and accuracy in that same second to lodge deep in her side. In agonised rage the buffalo rounded on the danger and charged, but got no further than the bastion of the rock where she stormed and roared, and butted her head in futile impotence, then took herself off to die.

The heifer's bellows of pain and fury alerted the herd which departed from the river in mighty crashing retreat, the stricken animal attempting in her dying moments to follow, but she fell in a thunder of drumming hooves and threshing legs to lie still at last.

Suyanga released his breath in a long hissing sound, his jubilation and the thrill of what he had helped to achieve almost more than he could bear.

'Come,' said Dangoya, clapping the boy on the back, 'now there is work to be done.'

Running quickly to where the buffalo lay, they withdrew their spears and straightened the shafts, then carried the weapons to the water where they washed them clean of blood. 'Start on the skinning,' Dangoya ordered. 'I shall go to tell the others to come and help.'

'*Ebaye!*' Suyanga's face was alight with excitement, his teeth flashing white as he laughed and talked, his knife ready in his hand.

It was not far to the sheep and when he was within earshot Dangoya called out casually to the *morans* to go and help cut up the buffalo they had killed. For a moment no one answered, then all four began to converge on him. One of the *morans*, striding up, thrust his face almost into Dangoya's and shouted, 'You lie!'

Dangoya pointed to the river where already vultures were swinging down from the sky and retorted, 'They also must be lying! Go and see for yourselves. One of you can stay with me to guard the sheep and leave one of the *layonis* too. The other boy can run to the camp to tell the girls to bring their *calabashes* for the blood.'

The *morans* found Suyanga happily skinning the buffalo and he greeted them with pointed jibes and much boasting. To begin with they were slightly uncertain, but his good humour was so infectious that soon all the *morans* joined in the skinning and cutting up of the animal. Then the girls arrived, chattering and exclaiming, to collect the blood, and everyone clamoured for details of the killing.

'Oh, my *morans*!' Suyanga said. 'If anyone values his life, do not take any chances with my *laigwanan*. Remember! When angered he has the bravery of a lion and the cunning of a leopard; nor does he have any nerves; but always you will hear only truth from his lips!' He looked down at his bloody hands, then added, 'And yet I have seen him cry like a child at mention of my brother's death.'

The *morans* were silent, then one of them cleared his throat and spat noisily. 'I do not now believe one word of what my mother's brother Bareto spoke! After hearing you and seeing what I have seen this day, I shall tell the *laigwanan* of my feelings,' and he returned angrily to the job in hand.

The *morans* had not quite finished cutting up the meat when they spotted a pride of lion sitting in the bushes a little way off eyeing the carcass, the smell of which had drawn them to the kill. Now they waited for the men to move away. Working more quickly the *morans* divided the meat into convenient loads, leaving behind enough to appease the lion. They also took sufficient hide for two shields - one of which would be for Suyanga - and for making sandals.

By nightfall they were back in the camp. The fire was built up and stakes driven into the ground to support the meat over the embers. The girls ran about excitedly, helping to settle the sheep in the enclosure, fetching more wood and being so brave as to tease Dangoya and Suyanga. Little Siama hid from no one her adoration of the heroes of the day and waited upon them tirelessly, sitting close beside them when there was no more she could do. A mood of great conviviality swept over the *morans* and the day's killing of the buffalo was relived and discussed endlessly as the young people gorged themselves on the tender meat, their boredom with the monotonous diet of mutton forgotten.

Two *morans* from the neighbouring sheep camp had come visiting and decided to spend the night when they saw the buffalo meat and were offered generous portions to take away in the morning. One of them invited Dangoya to return to their camp to refute Bareto's allegations before their clansmen, but all Dangoya would say was that he could not speak against a dead man.

At this Bareto's nephew struck the earth with his stick. 'Listen to me!' he cried. 'I have today seen and heard what these two *morans* have done, and the manner in which they have done it. This is not the doing of cowards!' He turned to face the visitors, his voice insistent and with anger in his eyes. 'Go tell your *morans* that I say I am ashamed of my uncle. By associating with a known coward like Pushati, and by lying about the achievements of the greatest *laigwanan* of our age-group, truly he has brought disgrace to my family.'

The *morans* shouted in agreement and looked expectantly at Dangoya. 'I say thank you for your words, but let us throwaway no more time on this matter.'

They waited, certain he would continue, but Dangoya glanced down at the girl beside him and said, 'Go, Siama, and fetch the piece of buffalo hide we have set apart for making sandals.' She brought the wet skin and crouched close as he made small holes round the edge with the point of his knife. 'Now take this and put it away where the hyena cannot steal it, and in the morning peg it out in the sun. We will cut out the sandals later tomorrow before the skin gets too dry and hard for cutting.'

'When are we going to Mother Dangoya?' Siama asked.

'Go, put that away, then come back and I shall tell you.'

The girl disappeared from within the circle of light thrown by the fire and the *morans* began to talk again, no one daring to re-open the subject of Bareto. In a little while Siama returned and sat beside Dangoya, waiting until he had finished speaking then softly touching him on the knee. 'When are we going?'

Dangoya quickly looked down at her. 'We will cut out the sandals tomorrow and let them dry for another day. Then we can put on the straps the next day. After that, if the sandals are ready, we will leave.'

'Who else will be going with us?'

Dangoya laughed. 'You ask too many questions! I do not know yet.'

'Will you tell me when you do know?'

'Yes,' he answered. 'Now I am going to ask you a question! Whose *asanja* are you?'

'Yours!' and she threw back her head and laughed.

Dangoya pretended to look shocked. 'But you have not yet invited me to drink milk with you.'

'I will when I am bigger,' said Siama, and looked impudently at the grinning *morans* around the fire. Encouraged, she faced Dangoya again and said, 'How did you kill the buffalo?'

'Go and ask that *moran*,' Dangoya pointed to Suyanga. 'He killed it.' And the girl went to badger Suyanga, ignoring the older *ndito* who sat caressing him.

Comfortable and content, the *morans* sat about the dying fire, some nearly asleep, others having taken the girls off to lie in the dark of the camp. Dangoya had dozed but was now awake and talking in low tones to one of the visiting *morans*, when suddenly, from halfway along the thorn fence came the cry of a *layoni* and the crashing of a large body through the barrier. All the sheep rose and ran bleating to the other side of the enclosure.

'What is it?' yelled Dangoya.

'A hyena!' shouted the *layoni*. 'He has not got anything except my spear, but has made a big hole in the fence. There are lion also outside the other gate!'

The *layoni*'s first alarm had been enough to rouse everyone. The *morans* quickly repaired the breach in the fence, and with shouts and burning brands frightened off the lions who kept clear until just before dawn when they became very active, moving up on the camp with roaring audacity. Most of the *morans* had been able to snatch some sleep during the night, but now all were kept on their toes as they held the lion at bay, again using smoke from their brands and hurling insults at the persistent beasts. With sun-up the pride sauntered off in pursuit of easier prey, and the *layoni* found his spear with a broken shaft stuck in the thorn bush of the enclosure where the departing hyena had charged through in its flight. The boy cursed and sat down to repair his spear.

Dangoya was thoughtful as he watched the sheep being driven out to graze. Up until now the shepherds had done very well, but he knew they would soon be unable to cope with the increasing calls made on them by the predators. Discussing the situation at length with the *morans*, he decided to leave immediately for Engaruka to organise reinforcements, sending at least four more *morans* and a couple of *layonis* to help guard the flocks. Suyanga, he said, would remain with them, and he would take only the girl Siama.

Their rate of progress governed by the shorter legs of the child, Dangoya and Siama nevertheless covered the distance to Engaruka in three days. They spent two nights on the open sloping wastes above the immense plains, each time tucked away in some sheltered place - the first night in a small gully, the second at the base of an acacia tree. The girl became very tired but did not complain, and Dangoya felt a growing attachment towards her, certain too that his mother would find in her a happy companion to fill Naidu's place.

They saw the vultures from a long way off, and as they neared the *manyattas* the stench of rotting carcasses filled their nostrils. Some of the dead animals were partly eaten, the bodies of others still intact, and of these a few had been skinned then left. Neither the Masai nor the scavengers could cope with the gruesome bounty of death. As he looked about him and understood the implications of what he saw, Dangoya felt an acute disappointment, a bitter resentment for what Olengesen had failed to do.

On leaving Engaruka to visit the dry herd and then the sheep, he had been certain that Olengesen would once more pick up the reins of command and move the wet herd into the forest. With little sustenance the wretched animals had fallen to *rinderpest*.

The only good news to greet Dangoya was that seven *morans* and four girls had arrived in his absence from the haven of Kitumbeine, and of these he intended sending four *morans* at once to help with the sheep. Not only were the cattle dying at an alarming rate of nearly ten a day, but the smallpox continued to take its toll, two more people having died and several others laid low, their chances of recovery as yet uncertain. To add to the miserable tale, his mother told him that another two elders had come from distant *manyattas*, thinking perhaps that at Engaruka life might be easier, with beer and food more plentiful than in the areas from which they had departed. They were not even old men, Singira said, but young middle-aged, and sat about doing no work.

'Olengesen himself has today gone out to herd the cattle, although he is very weak and seems unable to regain his strength. The elders say they are already tired and want to rest.'

On hearing this Dangoya felt an enormous rage, his anger at the elders and the futility of their existence leaving him speechless.

'Do not upset yourself, my son,' Singira tried to calm him. 'I think Olengesen is waiting for your return before he takes any action against the elders.'

'But why wait for me? I cannot do anything about the elders!'

'He will tell you. I shall meet him when he comes home and he will come to see you here. Go now to Muriet while I tend Siama.' She smiled at him. 'I am glad you have brought her to me. Nairasha can have a change in her duties and go to the sheep with the *morans* from Kitumbeine.'

Dangoya rested for a while in Muriet's hut, preoccupied as she talked to him, and waited impatiently for the day to end. When he heard the cattle approaching the *manyatta* he went back to his mother's house.

Olengesen entered slowly and sat heavily on the bed, then lifting his head, greeted Dangoya. 'I am glad you are here, my *olpiron*.' A small flicker of shame showed in his eyes and Dangoya felt a burst of compassion for the weary, sick man. After hearing the news of the dry herd and the sheep, Olengesen thought for a while then said, 'With the extra *morans* the sheep will have good care, and Kilimben will manage in the forest.' He looked across at Dangoya. 'But what are we to do about these cattle, and the sick people?' His voice cracked slightly and Dangoya caught the plea for help, saw the indecision in his face. 'The elders do not like to work and there are too few people to look after the cattle. I know I was wrong to delay sending the herd to the forest, but I am not yet well after the sickness. I want you to tell me what to do.'

'I know, my *laigwanan*, that you are ill and tired.' Beneath the sympathy in Dangoya's reply was a steely resolve and he held the older man's eyes as he went on. 'The cattle that can walk must go tomorrow to join the dry herd in the forest. There is only one man who can give orders to those who are not too old to work, and that is you. You must be the leader of our people again! Call a meeting and tell us all what we are to do. Order the elders and the senior *morans* to take the cattle to the forest, and tell us at the meeting that there will be no more beer brewed or *olpuls* held until the people and cattle of Engaruka have stopped dying.' Dangoya paused to draw breath, then added, 'Anyone not doing what you say must take his cattle and family away. We do not want them here!'

Olengesen felt his blood quicken. 'Those are difficult words to say, my *moran*, but I shall say them. They have been said before and they shall now be said by me, for what was I chosen to be the *laigwanan* of our people? Go tell the *morans* and elders of all age-groups who are well enough and young enough to walk to the trees by my *manyatta*, that their *laigwanan* wishes to meet with them before the cattle go out to graze in the morning!'

With an overwhelming relief Dangoya heard the strength return to Olengesen's voice, and saw a vigour in his eyes that had been absent for so long. Getting quickly to his feet he took the older man's hand in his. 'I go now, my *laigwanan*, to carry out your orders.'

Chapter 14

The Return to Favour

Beneath the big tree between the *manyattas* Olengesen sat waiting in the clear morning light, the singing of the women as they milked their poor thin cows gentle on the still air. The elders and *morans* approached to take their places, not mingling but sitting in two separate groups and Olengesen eyed each man in turn as he would his cattle, knowing immediately that someone was missing. It was an elder, a distant relative who had not bothered to appear at the meeting and one of the others was sent to fetch him. The gathering was silent as they waited, some sitting in indifference, but most were curious to hear what their chief had to say.

The tardy elder ambled out of the *manyatta* gate and with a great show of weariness at being disturbed from his sleep, took a seat among his peers. Dangoya watched Olengesen carefully and was delighted when the *laigwanan* sat straighter on his log, spat accurately at the feet of the recalcitrant man and spoke in a clear strong voice.

'What reasons do you give for not attending the meeting I have called?'

The elder returned Olengesen's look with an insolent stare then replied, 'Is this not my own *manyatta*? And do I not do what I like in my own *manyatta*?'

An old man cackled and several of the elders smiled, but the *morans* showed disapproval on their hard young faces.

'I speak as *laigwanan* of these *manyattas*,' Olengesen said, his words slow and precise, his eyes never leaving his relative's face. 'You have said before all these people that you shall do what you wish in your own *manyatta*.' He paused and spat again. 'From this day this *manyatta* is no longer yours. Take your wife, your children and your cattle and go elsewhere to make your *manyatta*!'

The elder's mouth fell open in astonishment, his protests cut short by Olengesen. 'I have spoken,' he said curtly and ignored the few murmurs of objection which welled up amongst the elders. The path from my *manyatta* is wide and long.'

'*Ebaye! Ebaye!*' the *morans* shouted. 'We hear you, our *laigwanan*.'

'So listen well to what I say next.' Olengesen had risen and now stood over his people. 'From this day forward all will share in the duties of the *manyatta*, and the elders will work beside the *morans* and the *layonis* herding the cattle and sheep. We have been struck down by disease in our people and in our herds, and until the good days return everyone will work to rebuild our wealth. There will be no *olpuls* and no beer brewed until our stock thrives once more!'

Dangoya's eye ran over the faces of the elders, seeing surprise and in some cases shock. He noted too how furtively they looked among themselves for mutual support before joining in with grins and shouts of approval. Half listening as Olengesen outlined his plans to move the cattle into the forest, Dangoya wondered how long the elders' new-found enthusiasm would last.

Some would leave, to find a more idle life elsewhere, but if Olengesen could retain his firm hold, the next rains should bring a renewal in vigour, not only to the cattle but the people too. It took time to sort out which animals should go up into the forest and to allocate duties to the *morans* and elders. A few milking cows were to be left at Engaruka with those cattle too weak or sick to travel. Some elders too were to remain, and most of the women and children, to care for the victims of the smallpox. Dangoya himself was ready to go to join Kilimben, with Nairasha and the *morans* who were to help with the sheep accompanying him part of the way, and he went to Muriet's house to eat before leaving.

His head ached with the hubbub of the morning and his stomach had a peculiar emptiness which he put down to hunger, but after eating he felt no better. He rose to go but felt dizzy and sank back on the bed. When Muriet returned to the hut after helping with the loading of the donkeys, she found him lying inert and feverish.

'Are you not going to the dry herd? Your *morans* are waiting for you and the donkeys loaded, with your sister eager to be on the way.'

'I am sickening,' Dangoya said. 'Tell the others to go and I will follow when I am better.' He turned his head away and Muriet's hand flew to her mouth in horror.

Dangoya lay for the rest of the day without moving. By nightfall his temperature was high, confirming Muriet's worst fears. She and his mother smoothed cool, fresh dung on the back of his neck and over his shoulders to reduce his body heat, sitting beside him through the night and wetting his lips with water when he called out that he was thirsty; but his fever raged and consumed his mind and body although he clung tenaciously to consciousness, aware throughout of the presence of the two women.

He was ill for a very long time and when Muriet showed signs of distress herself, admitting to Singira that she was pregnant, his mother had him carried to her house. There he began his long fight back to health, and when he was recovered sufficiently to talk a little, Singira sat by him giving him scraps of news as people came and went from the *manyattas*.

Cattle losses from both *rinderpest* and East Coast Fever had been high, but the *rinderpest* had burnt itself out. Now the only deaths were from East Coast Fever which felled the younger stock in the forest grazing.

'We have something to be cheerful about, however,' Singira said. There has been no more Arab sickness anywhere for two full changes of the moon, and although we have lost more than half our cattle, we are luckier than most. I heard today that in some *manyattas* the herds are now so small through sickness and drought that there is not enough milk or blood to feed the few people who survived, and their *morans* are planning raids to replenish their stock, although they have been advised against such action for the time being.'

'What of the herd at Kitumbeine?'

There they had only the *lodwa* in the cattle, but as you know the herd was never a big one. Like all *manyattas* where there is still enough food, it has been overcrowded with starving relatives who lost all their cattle and sheep. At least the extra people there have relieved the *morans* of their duties and all have gone to join warrior groups, as have most of the *morans* from here.'

Dangoya lay thinking about what his mother had said. He had fallen ill before completely re-establishing his reputation as a great warrior and leader of his age-group, and now in his weakened state to imagine that he could join and lead a band of *morans* was out of the question.

Singira looked down at him, sensing his mood, and she smiled with her usual resilient optimism. 'I shall make you strong again. You were the smallest, weakest child ever born to a woman, and look how strong I made you!'

As soon as he was able, Dangoya took himself off to the sheep knowing the herders would need extra help when the rains came and the flocks were returned to the Empakai - *Oldonyo* Lengai area. Olengesen was quite recovered and in complete control of the *manyattas* and the elders, of whom there was now a preponderance, so many of the *morans* having joined warrior groups. He ordered new *manyattas* to be built below the original site at Engaruka, and that the old enclosures and huts be burnt. He thought long about the *manyatta* at Kitumbeine which had proved its worth, sustaining the herds and people through a time of long drought, so he decided it should be retained, but also with a new *manyatta* to replace the old. The herds there could be added to in time and it could become a valuable adjunct to the *manyattas* at Engaruka.

While Dangoya was with the sheep, news of raids both successful and otherwise filtered through almost daily and he could only think wryly of his misfortune, being unable to participate with others of his age-group. Good rains fell and they continued and set in, bringing life back to the country, raids on other tribes became less frequent. Few raided cattle had been brought in to Engaruka and as Dangoya was indirectly blamed for this lack, by the time the sheep reached Lengai, his popularity was at its lowest ebb and he decided to consult Olengesen.

The cattle were doing well and the numbers slowly increasing. For all their great losses, the *manyattas* of Olengesen and Dangoya were still amongst the biggest in that part of Masailand, not least due to Dangoya's good management and foresight. This fact was recognised by the cattle owners among them, but the majority of the elders bore him a grudge. They had so rightly, guessed that he had been responsible for their enforced labour and for the cessation of their drinking orgies, but he shrugged their opinions off. With good times ahead, they would soon forget him and drown their animosity in beer.

Olengesen's advice to Dangoya was to round up as many of his former followers as possible and execute a raid - well planned - into country not before penetrated by Masai. 'With one sweep you will be a hero again,' his instructor said, eyeing him speculatively. 'You should leave now and not return until you have achieved this. But before you go you must think about a new wife, and I shall speak for you.'

'I had not thought about it,' Dangoya said. 'Have you anyone in mind?'

'Speak to your mother,' and Olengesen dismissed him with a wave of the hand.

There had obviously been a little connivance between Olengesen and Singira for when Dangoya brought up the subject of marriage, she replied immediately that she knew of a most suitable girl.

'A distant relative of Olengesen's belonging to the Purko clan has a very young daughter. A bond uniting our two families would please him greatly.'

She smiled at him then added casually, 'You have heard of Muriet's new son? She and the baby have been moved to Kitumbeine.'

'No, I did not know. I shall visit her when I leave here.'

The only *morans* to volunteer to go with Dangoya were Loito and Suyanga; and Legetonyi promised to join them when he had recovered from an arrow wound in his thigh, received on one of the raids. They spent a few days at Kitumbeine and there recruited another *moran*. Dangoya enjoyed seeing Muriet again, now quite convinced that she did indeed have powers to see into the future, although the baby seemed to him to look like all babies and not exactly like him as she so often said.

'Can you not see, my *asanja*, how like you he is? He has two eyes, it is true, and his *njabo* is not twisted, but in every respect he is your son.'

He would have liked to have discussed his own future with Muriet, but hesitated to ask as it would have meant admitting to her his fears. She offered no information which might have been useful to him except to say that the white men, now appearing in greater numbers in various parts of Masailand, would prove too strong for the Masai, as they had with the other tribes. 'Did you know,' she said, 'that there are two tribes of white men? The ones in the north are relations of the man Ndomson (Thomson) who long ago travelled through our country. They are called Ngeresa (English) by the *Olmeg*. The men you saw are the Olgeremani (German).'

Dangoya was disappointed that more *morans* did not ask to join him, but he consoled himself that this was not due entirely to his waning popularity. Only three of the *morans* there had been with him before and were in any case tired of raiding. Most of his former comrades had gone to other *laigwanans* at the warrior *manyatta* or, like Lengerebe, returned to their home areas. Lengerebe's father had died and the family at Lengkito had sent for him to help move to Oltukai.

Leaving Kitumbeine and heading east, Dangoya bore these factors in mind, but was nevertheless disturbed by the decided hostility shown him by *morans* in several *manyattas*, particularly as not a few were men he had known well in the past. It was with some trepidation, therefore, that he and his small party arrived at Oltukai. Lengerebe, however, seemed genuinely pleased to see him and ordered an ox killed in his honour.

The leadership of the *manyatta* had been assumed by Lengerebe's uncle, a greatly respected elder and a rich man in his own right, owning some of the largest herds in the region of *Oldonyo Naibor*. He called a meeting for Dangoya's benefit at which he made a long speech extolling the young warrior's achievements. 'But,' he said, 'lies and insults are still being spread about you by Pushati. Our son Lengerebe tells us that you have done nothing to refute these accusations for fear of causing war between your clan and mine as Lengerebe's name is included in the lies. Pushati is with a warrior group not a day's march from here! We have *morans* who would join you, making your band equal in number to his. We also have senior *morans* to go with you to see that all is fair and just, and I shall send the senior *moran laigwanan* to explain any misunderstandings.' He halted, pointing at Lengerebe. 'We, the elders and *morans* of these *manyattas* will not stand by and have this our son of the Purko clan slandered, when we know the stories are untrue. Either you must both confront Pushati or go hide your shame with the Ndorobo of the forests!'

It was a challenge neither Dangoya nor Lengerebe could ignore. 'We request your permission to talk amongst ourselves first,' Dangoya said, and he with his three men, Lengerebe and a few of the *manyatta morans*, left the chief to confer together.

They were not long, and appeared again before the *laigwanan* who said, 'You have finished your meeting?'

'We leave today,' replied Dangoya, 'with any of our age-group who wish to go with us.'

Several old eyes gleamed while the elders shouted their approval, and Dangoya's heart lifted as the *morans* crowded round him, eager for battle and the excitement of the next day.

Unheralded, Dangoya and Lengerebe walked straight into the encampment ahead of their *morans* and the mediators. Half-lying on the ground, Pushati was taken completely by surprise as Dangoya stood over him, his spear angled at his chest.

'Do not move or this spear will go right through you!' Dangoya felt a rare hate, a loathing, as he looked into the face of his old enemy.

'Who is your leader?' Lengerebe called.

'I am *laigwanan* of this group,' replied a thickset *moran*.

'We have come here,' Lengerebe said, addressing the man directly, 'without any *seki* bush, and we challenge you as worthy *morans* to leave the *seki* for cowards. That son of a pig, lying there in his own cowardly sweat, either denounces himself as a liar in the presence of all these *morans*, or he fights either one of us. He has one other choice: he and a *moran* of his choosing can fight me and Dangoya, but failing to fight we *morans* and yours will go to war!'

In the frozen intensity of the hush that followed, Dangoya caught a movement in the corner of his eye and a *moran*, one of Pushati's friends, lunged forward - a withered stalk from a *seki* bush in one hand.

His brain whirling and his chest tight, Dangoya wavered above the prone figure on the ground. To plunge his spear into the evil heart of Pushati overrode all feelings of sense, and he felt his grip tighten as his arm rose higher, ready to drive the weapon home. Lengerebe's eyes widened in horror, then abruptly closed in relief as Dangoya rammed the spear into the earth beside Pushati's head.

Pushati, a grey pallor to his face, rose shakily to his feet and as age-old custom demanded held out his hand, but Dangoya turned away, refusing to touch him, although he shook the hand of his leader. A fury of thwarted anger consumed Dangoya and wave after wave of convulsions coursed through his body, froth flecking his contorted lips. As he staggered, arms threshing, Suyanga - perhaps the only one strong enough - enclosed him in his powerful arms and held him until the fit was over.

The senior *morans* from Lengerebe's *manyatta* had witnessed the entire scene and now demanded a meeting where both sides could state their case. The *laigwanan* of Pushati's party, impressed with the manner of Dangoya's challenge, agreed and said that Pushati and any who sided with him were to find another warrior group once the meeting had been held the next day. In the meantime he offered the strangers the hospitality of his camp and a steer was slaughtered.

Pushati slipped away during the night and was not heard of or seen again, and it was believed he had passed into country far to the north. Accounts of what had happened in the encampment spread like a bush fire and wherever Dangoya went he was greeted as a hero and accorded great respect. In a *manyatta* holding a fertility dance for women he was expected to contribute a heifer - a sure sign of his leadership. On all sides *morans* pleaded to be included in his group, but as before he declined to lead a big party, preferring a small quick-moving band of tried and tested warriors. He had cleared his name and the necessity for making a raid receded. Now too came news that the Fire Stick was to be mended which would mean his elevation to the ranks of the senior *morans*, but until that time he was free to do as he pleased.

The cloud had cleared from the summit of *Oldonyo Naibor* and the great dome shone white and clean in the soft light of evening, the mass of the mountain sweeping down darkly to the plains below.

'Have you heard any more of the white men?' Dangoya asked Lengerebe.

'They are everywhere now! I am told they are growing gardens just as the *Olmeg* do, on the other side of *Oldonyo Naibor* which they call Kilimanjaro.'

'And they have started making an iron snake which begins at the Great Water and will reach Larusa. It is like the one the other white tribe have made in the north.'

'An iron snake? What would they want to do that for?' Dangoya laughed, then remembering suddenly how he had scoffed too at the guns of the Europeans, became thoughtful. 'Perhaps they have a reason.' The fascination he had always felt for the white men returned in force and he questioned Lengerebe, eager for more information. 'Surely they do not scratch the ground to grow their crops, like the *Olmeg*?' A man who worked with his hands deserved no respect.

'Oh no. They make the *Olmeg* work for them, also on the iron snake.

And when the *Olmeg* do not obey, they beat them with whips of rhino hide!'

'That I must see!' Dangoya chuckled, then began to laugh and all the *morans* joined in, their laughter clear and free like that of children, some hugging themselves, rolling on the ground. Tears streaming down his face, Loito pranced and minced before them. 'Beat me! Beat me, great white uncircumcised master,' he cried until he too collapsed helplessly.

This caused further mirth until Lengerebe hushed them and said, 'We should not laugh so long. Those *Olmeg* are being taught to use the magic spears that spit fire, and now they are becoming very brave and cheeky.'

'You say the white men are everywhere, *Bagishu*, but is *Oldonyo Naibor* the only place they make gardens?'

'I think so, but the great *laigwanan* of the Kisongo at Mondul has made agreements with them to move about Kisongo country, so perhaps they will grow crops there also. And they trade there too like the Arabs.' Lengerebe ticked off on his fingers the goods bartered by the whites. Beads, wire, knives, cotton cloth, blankets, matches, maize meal - for the women to eat, he said with some scorn - and sugar. All these in exchange for hides, wild animal skins, cattle, sheep and donkeys.

'*Bagishu*, we must go again to find these people. Remember they promised us guns if we helped them. And we must see the iron snake! Tomorrow we will go.'

Most of the *morans* had never seen a white man before and were eager and very excited when they came across a lone European on the Ngasurai. He was accompanied by a number of *Olmeg* dressed as he was, with small flat kepis, flaps down the backs of their necks. All carried rifles and the white man had a revolver on his belt. Other *Olmeg* followed, but they were not in uniform and carried loads on their heads.

The *morans* stood and gaped until the European waved, using a few words of Masai in greeting. That seemed to be the limit of his vocabulary and an interpreter took over, asking where they were going and how far to the next water.

'Surface water is at least half a day's walk from here,' Lengerebe replied. 'But over there where the grass is green, water lies under the ground for the *Olmeg* to dig out.'

On hearing this the German ordered his men to set up camp and others to go dig for water. The *morans* watched with interest as a tent was erected, then poked about inquisitively amongst the porters' loads, exclaiming over items such as pots and pans, and the white man's pipe which he lit and puffed on furiously for their benefit.

The German observed Dangoya covertly and when he was settled by the fire called him over to offer him a mug of coffee. It required an explanation from the interpreter, but after a few tentative sips Dangoya smiled and said it was good. His approval brought the *morans* crowding around, asking what the drink was.

'Try it!' Dangoya held out the mug, and some did drink while others refused to touch it.

'You must be *Laigwanan* Dangoya of the One Eye,' the German said.

Quickly Lengerebe answered for him. 'You are addressing him.'

'We have heard of you and your feats of bravery.' The German put a match to his pipe. 'There is a man of my tribe called Sindoff at Mondul who wishes to travel to Loita to visit the great witchdoctor Sendeu. Would you take him?'

'If you know where Loita is, why do you ask me to take him there?'

The German was patient. 'We have only heard of the place, we have not been there.'

'I would think about it,' Dangoya replied, 'if you gave me one of your guns.'

'I cannot do that as the guns belong to our Great Chief, but the man Sindoff would reward you, perhaps with a gun, perhaps with other gifts.'

'I will think about it. Give me more of your black water.' Dangoya sat, the tin mug in his hand, watching the *Olmeg* about the camp. 'Why do the ones with guns do no work like the others?' he asked.

'They are warriors and their work is to carry their guns and fight if needed.'

'Only Masai are warriors and do no work.' Dangoya's retort was quick. 'All *Olmeg* must work like women and donkeys!'

The German was amused. 'You should go to Mondul, my friend. You would see many things to amaze you, even warriors using their hands to build houses.'

Dangoya stared into the pale alien face as the white man explained the setting up of an administrative post at Mondul. They come here, Dangoya thought, a few white men, and with no loss of blood, no fighting, install their leader in our midst. Truly they possess great magical powers.

'If you will let me hold your gun, I will go to Mondul to see this friend of yours.

'I shall do more than that. I will show you how to fire it in the morning,' the German said. 'It should be easy to teach you, with only one eye.' Seeing Dangoya's surprise he continued. 'We have difficulty teaching these people,' and he waved towards the soldiers, 'because they cannot close one eye and look down the barrel with the other.'

Inwardly excited, Dangoya grunted. 'They are *Olmeg*,' he said scornfully, 'they know no better.'

At a *manyatta* lying in the hills above Mondul, Dangoya and his men rested for two days. There they met again their old friend Olembere who said he knew the German Sindoff and would take them to meet him. He also professed a knowledge of Swahili, but in the event could manage only a few words. He did however introduce them to tea - a dirty greasy brew which delighted them, and which they all thought far better than the coffee they had tasted on the Ngasurai.

Here too they were given firsthand information on the female of this strange white species. 'She had long straight white hair, tied in a tail down her back. And her breasts! They were as big as buttocks! We were all astonished. Her body was completely covered, right down to her feet and when the girls and women of the *manyatta* tried to lift the coverings to see what was underneath, this white woman became quite cross. They were nice people, however, and very friendly, but the smell of them is not good. People say it is the white froth they wash themselves with. I heard one *ndito* say she would not have a white man in her bed because of the smell.'

The little settlement of Mondul amazed them, especially the buildings, and when they were led into an Arab shop, crudely constructed from poles and daub with a flat roof, they gazed up at the rough ceiling in wonder. It was the first time any of them had stood upright inside a building. Outside the owner was busy loading donkeys with hides for barter and he waved the Masai off impatiently, so they meandered up a pathway to where a big building was under construction.

The work was supervised by a white man and Olembere told them it was to be the meeting place for the white chief. 'See the whip the man carries. If the *Olmeg* do not work well, he beats them.'

The *morans* laughed, pleased to hear the story they had been told was true.

'Where is Sindoff?' the German was asked through an interpreter.

'He has gone to Larusa, but will be back. For what purpose do you wish to see him?'

Lengerebe stepped forward. 'This is *Laigwanan* Dangoya of the One Eye whom the white man at Ngasurai has asked to lead Sindoff to the *laibon* Sendeu through the forest and into the great hole of Ngorongoro, where the rivers run into the big water of *Magadi*.'

The German said, 'Go back to your *manyatta*. If you return here tomorrow or the next day, Bwana Sindoff will be here.'

'That is good,' replied Dangoya. 'Now where is the tea?'

'Tea!' the German retorted. 'Can you not see I am working? I do not have tea at work.'

'Then take me to where you do have tea,' Dangoya said simply.

'When Bwana Sindoff comes he will give you tea.' The German was becoming exasperated.

Just then one of the workers dropped his load of raw bricks which broke and the European ordered him brought forward and administered two strokes with his whip to the bare back of the unfortunate *Olmeg*.

The *morans* thought it a great joke and asked the German to do it again. He looked crossly at them. 'Well, do it to the others,' the Masai called, but he was not amused and told them if they did not mind their own business, they would get the whip themselves.

Quick as a flash, Dangoya was beside him. 'And you will get this!' he said, thrusting forward his spear. Again the *morans* laughed, enjoying themselves immensely, and the German had the good sense to join in their merriment.

After waiting a while to see if another whipping would be performed for their entertainment, with no success, the *morans* grew bored and wandered back to the shop. News of the arrival of the famous Dangoya had spread amongst the *Olmeg* and many nervous glances darted his way. Some of these men, from various tribes, had settled around Mondul under the protection of the Germans and others had been brought in as porters. They had mixed feelings about the sudden appearance of Dangoya, some saying he would bring in his warriors to wipe out the few white men and themselves, and others believing he was there to make a treaty with the Germans.

It was not surprising therefore, when he strolled arrogantly into the shop and asked for the first thing he saw, that he should not be refused. It was a saucepan, and the Arab handed it to him without a word. But when he then began to ask for other things, expecting to be refused, the Arab made no bones about it and shook his head. Dangoya tried to exchange the saucepan for a blanket and when, from the corner of his eye, the Arab saw Loito grin, he realised the *morans* were playing with him. He did however bring tea when asked, and the Masai eventually left the shop in high spirits, carrying away the saucepan with great glee.

Back at the *manyatta* they could talk of nothing else but about what they had seen - the goods in the shop, the buildings, the cart they had watched being drawn by oxen - and could barely wait for the morning.

Sindoff was at the building site, a big hairy man, older than the other Germans they had seen. He greeted them with a few words of Masai and told them through his interpreter that he wished to travel in their country to see the great *laibon* and to look for a suitable place in which to build a house and a *manyatta* for his stock.

'I have many things to barter and will trade them for cattle and sheep. I have some *Olmeg* whom I have trained as soldiers and will require some Masai too, for herding the cattle. Would the *Laigwanan* Dangoya be able to arrange this?'

Standing on one leg and leaning on his spear, Dangoya ignored Sindoff's question and asked, as he had done the day before, 'Where is the tea?'

Sindoff smiled in his beard but the interpreter broke in. 'Answer the Bwana Sindoff!' He was very brave with the big German standing beside him.

'Tell him,' said Dangoya, 'we want tea now, or we go.'

Sindoff understood Dangoya's reply before the interpreter had time to translate and with a broad gesture invited them all to follow him to the house further up the hill. There he told them to wait under a tree while he went to the house and spoke to a woman in the doorway, then walking over to where they lolled in the shade said that the tea would come soon.

'Is that Sindoff's woman?' one of the *morans* asked the interpreter.

'No,' the *Olmeg* answered. 'She is the wife of the white *laigwanan*.'

Sindoff seemed to understand what they were talking about and asked why they were interested in the woman.

'Is she sick?' Lengerebe enquired.

'No, why do you ask?'

'Because she has not shaved her head.'

'White women do not shave. For them it is a sign of great beauty, to have thick long hair.'

The *morans* could see the point of this, but then Loito asked, 'Well, how do the men know when they are fit for intercourse?'

'They have intercourse only with their husbands.'

The *morans* found Sindoff's answer very amusing and the whole question of white womanhood fascinating. They wanted then to know why they wore so many clothes and if the woman, beneath all that covering, was the same as a Masai woman.

Here the interpreter put an end to the conversation by saying that the Europeans did not discuss these things, and that if anyone tried any nonsense with their womenfolk they would be shot.

Just then the woman appeared with the tea and Dangoya gave her the customary greeting reserved for women. '*Tagwenya siangik*,' he said politely.

'*Eego*' she replied, which was the correct response for a woman to make to a man. The *morans* were delighted and the woman laughed with them at her success. She handed them mugs of tea and they drank with noisy relish.

'How many cattle would I have to give for this woman?' Dangoya asked, emboldened by the friendly attitude of the Germans.

Glancing quickly at the woman, relieved that she knew no more Masai than the few words of greeting, Sindoff said, 'Oh, this one would cost many, many cattle as she is so nice and fat.'

'Truly she is that', said Lengerebe as he fingered her long fair hair. 'Tell me, Sindoff, have all your women these big breasts like Chagga women?'

'Some do and some do not.' Sindoff spoke to the woman and she collected the mugs and returned to the house. 'Now,' he said, 'can we talk about our business?'

'You must tell me again what it is you want.' Dangoya knew he was being annoying, but Sindoff patiently repeated his requirements. Dangoya astutely noted the man's forbearance - they had trifled with him over the tea too, yet he was obviously not a man to be easily provoked.

'Everything you wish can be achieved, but what will we receive in return?'

Palms up, Sindoff spread out his hands in front of him. 'What do you want?'

'Guns,' said Dangoya.

Chapter 15

The New Magic

Standing among the rocks on the river bed, the water icy about their feet, the *morans* looked up in astonishment at the railway bridge. 'Where,' said Dangoya, 'did they get all this metal? And how did they hang it up there?' He fell silent and Olembere, unable to answer his questions, could only say, 'Wait until you see the strange thing that slides along the iron snake. So big it is, and with such noise!'

Leading them up the steep sides of the little ravine on to the flat, he showed them the rails curving away to left and right; and each in turn banged the lines with his spear, their wonder at the quantity and hardness of the metal reducing them to silence.

A growing sound to the east lifted all heads and Olembere became quite agitated, imploring them to stand back or be killed. With beating hearts they obeyed and stood clear, but it was only a small inspection trolley which came swiftly around the curve, propelled by two *Olmeg* while a white man sat serenely on the bench. The railway workers, each with one leg firmly rooted on the trolley, pushed with their free legs, and this sight swept away the *morans'* awe and all five collapsed in laughter.

'These white men are true *laibons*,' said Dangoya as they watched the trolley disappear. 'This is not the work of ordinary men but shows the power of the great witchdoctors.'

'Wait,' Olembere boasted, 'until the big one comes!'

'How many *Olmeg* push that one?'

'None! It goes with a man putting wood into a fire.'

'*Aish!*' retorted Suyanga. 'That I do not believe.'

But when the train came, the *morans* were momentarily struck dumb by the size and noise of it before racing off behind when told it would stop at a place nearby called Moshi. However, at the station they were refused entry by soldiers on guard who threatened them with guns. Inside the goods yard was an ox wagon, much bigger than the one they had seen at Mondul, and they watched as men loaded it from the train.

'Where are the cattle to pull it?' they called across the fence.

A wiry Chagga looked over at them and replied in halting Masai. 'They graze now, but will be tied to the wagon when we are ready.'

They continued to pester him with questions and were told how the wagons delivered goods brought up from the coast to places like New Larusa where an administrative centre was being built - a 'Boma' the Germans called it in Swahili.

'A Boma is a big house where the white chief lives and holds his meetings, and beats or imprisons people who do not do their work properly, or who run away from their work. Also people who get drunk, and those that steal property or "heller" from each other or from the Europeans.'

'What is "heller"?' Lengerebe asked.

'It's smaller than this,' the Chagga said, and pulled a rupee from where it had been tucked in his garments. He walked closer to the fence to show them. 'This is what the white men give in exchange for cattle or other stock, or skins. Or if a man works for them he is given these which he can then take to the Arabs to barter for goods.'

'And a Masai will give cattle for those little bits of metal' Dangoya could hardly believe his ears. 'How many for a sheep?'

'A good fat sheep would get one of these, but if it was old and thin, or very young, it would be worth only a few hellers.'

The *morans* digested this incomprehensible information and Dangoya's gaze wandered across the yard to where a group of prisoners were digging under the guard of two soldiers. 'Are those men given these pieces of metal for working?'

'No,' the Chagga said. 'They are prisoners and receive only food - and the whip if they do not work well.'

'We have been told that the white man does not have slaves and will not allow the Arabs to take any or the *Olmeg* chiefs to sell slaves to the Arabs, but what are these but slaves?' Dangoya snorted derisively.

'They are not slaves,' the Chagga said firmly. 'When they have finished their time and paid for their wrong-doing, they are released.'

'What happens if they refuse to work, or run away?'

The Chagga looked at Dangoya sharply. 'The guards will shoot them.'

'Then they are slaves.' Dangoya turned on his heel and the other *morans* followed him, but not before Loito had asked for the man's rupee. He refused and waved them away, returning to his fellows beside the wagon.

At the gateway to the little station they were almost bowled over by a rickshaw which came rolling out, an *Olmeg* in the shafts and another running along as he pushed from the back. Beneath the white cloth canopy sat a European couple, the woman fanning herself with a small handkerchief. The *morans* were delighted to see further evidence of the *Olmeg* being made to look ridiculous and laughed out loud as the rickshaw moved along the path. The Europeans must have been interested in the *morans* for presently the rickshaw returned and stopped beside them. Neither party knew what to say but just stared, then all began to laugh and the white pair waved as they moved off with their puffing rickshaw men.

The *morans* slept that night in a *manyatta* nearby, their heads full of the things they had seen that day. The others wanted to go back to Moshi to see more of the big wood-burning engines, but Dangoya reminded them that they had a long way to go to reach Mondul in time to take Sindoff on his travels. He had struck a bargain with the big German who had promised not only guns and ammunition, but also blankets, beads, cloth and tea. The one stipulation he had made was that Dangoya's part of the transaction should be completed before anything was handed over. Dangoya had agreed to this and a day arranged for the commencement of the journey.

On their way to Mondul they caught up with a wagon drawn by oxen, its wheels creaking and bouncing over the rough ground as it made its slow progress towards New Larusa. As the *morans* approached the wagon, an armed tribesman warned them off, telling them to keep their distance, but they ignored his threats and the man fired. Fortunately no one was hit and the *morans* unashamedly showed their bare bottoms to the *Olmeg* as they ran off, their laughter lost in the wide expanse of the flat, grassy plain, and their shouts of '*narobong gotonye*' only faintly heard by the nervous wagoners.

The *morans* sat panting and amused behind a tall anthill. 'We could raid those oxen tonight!' Loito's eyes sparkled at the thought of action.

'We could, but they can only belong to the white men. That wagon may be Sindoff's and we could be recognised and lose our opportunity of getting the guns.' Dangoya was determined nothing should come between him and possession of his own firearm.

'Yes! Let us get the guns first then come back and frighten these *Olmeg*.'

Loito paused, then became thoughtful. 'But we must learn how to use them properly, not like that fool who could only make a noise with his like a farting donkey. I wonder if the white men have given the *Olmeg* the correct medicine?' He began to laugh again. 'It's a good thing there were only *Olmeg* to see us run away, and they were probably uncircumcised.'

Skirting the track taken by the wagon, they neared Meru, its great jagged crater rim stark against the blue of the sky. Beneath the mountain lay the new Larusa which the Masai overlords had found to be better country for the growing of tobacco by their slaves, and where the Germans were setting up an outpost.

On the slope of one of the foothills the *morans* saw a flock of sheep, and noticing Dangoya's interest in these, Lengerebe said, 'I have not eaten mutton for a long time. Let us take one, but you of the One Eye must keep hidden or you will be recognised.

Conceding this point Dangoya proceeded on his own to an arranged meeting place and was soon joined by the other four carrying a large dead sheep which was almost more than one man could manage.

'Go forward and I shall watch the rear,' said Dangoya.

'No need,' panted Lengerebe. 'No one saw us take it. They were all far too interested in their girls to notice us.'

They continued deep into the forest, twice dropping the sheep to dive into or under trees to escape charging rhino, but eventually reached a place beside a stream where they quickly made a fire, using the new European matches to light the little bits of kindling which they collected in the fading light of day.

Content and well fed, they sat beside the fire talking about the events of the past few days.

'I do not think,' Dangoya mused, 'that the white men have given the *Olmeg* the good magic that they use with their guns. You remember, *Bagishu*,' he said to Lengerebe, 'that hole in my shield, and that day the white man let me fire his gun and then he used it to kill an eland? The gun the *Olmeg* used today had not the same power otherwise one of us would be in the belly of the hyena now.'

'You are right,' Olembere said. 'I have been told that only the *Olmeg* dressed as the white men with little flat head-dresses and bindings on their legs have the proper magic, and then it takes a long time to teach them.'

Dangoya frowned. 'If what you say is true we must make Sindoff show us correctly before we accept the guns. I will speak to him before we take him on this journey.'

'Did you hear what happened to the Chagga?' Olembere asked. 'Their *laigwanan* gave the white men pieces of land and people to help plant their coffee trees and build houses, all in exchange for guns. And when the Chagga had acquired many guns they told the Europeans to go away and leave their belongings behind, but the white men refused. So the Chagga *laigwanan* told his people to burn down the houses and kill the intruders with their new magic spears.

'When the white chief heard this he sent his *Olmeg* warriors to fetch the Chagga *laigwanan* and personally whipped him many, many times on his backside and called all the Chagga to witness the punishment of their leader.

When the *laigwanan* had recovered from his beating he gathered together all his men who had guns and they attacked the Europeans and their few *Olmeg*, but the magic of the white men was too strong and a great number of Chagga were killed and the rest chased away. The *laigwanan* was caught, and his lesser leaders too, and all were strung up from a tree by their necks until they had stopped kicking. The Chagga people were forced to watch the hanging and not allowed to remove the bodies for two whole days. Then the Chagga were disarmed and made to work in the white men's gardens.'

'Where did you hear that story?' Dangoya asked. Olembere gestured with his hands. 'It is well-known in these parts.'

'I heard it too.' Suyanga leaned forward eagerly, 'when I was at the Kisongo *manyatta*.'

Lengerebe spat contemptuously into the fire. 'What else could you expect from mother-fucking Chaggas!'

'I agree,' said Dangoya, 'but we must be wise when we get our guns as we may have the good fortune and opportunity to use them against other tribes like the Mangati and Nyamwesi, or even the Kipsigis in the north - and they are not like some, who live in holes in the ground like warthog! We have a lot to learn from the Europeans. Now we are soon to be senior *morans* and no longer have to prove ourselves at the *moran manyatta*, I shall seek to learn what I can.'

The caravan of laden donkeys set off from Mondul, the *morans* striding ahead with Sindoff in their midst, his interpreter a very short-legged man having difficulty in matching their pace. Behind, keeping watch on the donkeys, came a body of twenty armed *Olmeg* dressed in a variety of cast-off army uniforms, their eyes moving ceaselessly from right to left with an occasional glance to the rear, ever fearful of sudden attack or treachery on the part of the *morans* leading them through this unknown stretch of country.

They fed well, with Sindoff shooting game for the pot; and each night camped at waterholes or beside streams. If a *manyatta* was near, the *morans* would sleep there, but otherwise they made themselves comfortable by the camp fire. Sindoff slept in his tent and to the amusement of Masai and *Olmeg* alike, stripped each evening and, if beside a river, immersed himself in the water, or if at a waterhole would splash and wash away the dust using a little tin bucket. To the *morans*' gratification it was noticed that he was circumcised, and they all felt far better about accompanying him and accorded him the respect due to an equal. Their one regret was that they did not see him lose his temper and use his hide whip on any of his men.

Bartering took place at all the *manyattas* they came across, and slowly a herd of cattle was collected which the *morans* helped to herd. Sheep were unobtainable at that time of the year as the flocks were away grazing in the traditional dry-weather areas, but Dangoya assured Sindoff they would be able to find flocks as they neared Ngorongoro.

They passed through Semingor and on to Engaruka where Sindoff was introduced to Olengesen and offered the hospitality of the *manyattas*. Gifts were exchanged and Dangoya ordered the slaughter of an ox. He organised the erection of an enclosure for Sindoff's cattle, and the herd was taken out daily with the Masai stock, leaving Sindoff and his party free to visit other areas to seek more animals. Olengesen had given permission for the German to move about in the region, on condition that he was at all times accompanied by the *morans*.

When offering Sindoff hospitality no difficulties were envisaged as all knew he was no *layoni* and obviously of a different clan, but he politely resisted efforts to make him sleep in the *manyattas* and resolutely spent each night alone in his own tent beside his cattle. This caused some disappointment amongst the girls and young women as they were eager to find out, and discuss at length, the sexual prowess of the stranger.

The next few weeks were spent in neighbouring areas, bartering for stock and returning every night to Engaruka. Sindoff talked constantly with Dangoya on these short trips, particularly about the place he would find in which to build a permanent house and there to live as one of them. Dangoya had known of this from the start, yet it was a concept still so new that he could not quite decide whether he liked it or not, and relegated it to the back of his mind, telling himself that at the end of it all he would have a gun.

With a gun he would be all-powerful, as were these Germans; with its magic he would kill a buffalo at two hundred paces and chase away the most fearsome Kipsigis. He was obsessed by the sleekness of the metal and the symmetry of the barrel, but no matter how hard he pleaded with Sindoff he was never allowed to do more than stroke one of the many rifles carried by the party. Sindoff played on his fixation, saying, 'When I have settled in my own *manyatta* and you and your *morans* have helped me build up my herd, then you will be rewarded.'

As their language difficulties slowly vanished, with Sindoff becoming fairly fluent in Masai and Dangoya and the *morans* picking up enough Swahili to talk with the *Olmeg*, Dangoya puzzled over the German. He never discovered if he had a wife, or not, but Sindoff did say his brother would join him later when his *manyatta* was ready.

'Why,' asked Dangoya, 'do you not spend any nights with our women? Several girls have told me they would drink milk with you.'

'Then tell them to invite me, and perhaps I shall drink with some of them.'

'Which ones?'

'Any of the girls in these *manyattas* at Engaruka. I will tell you which ones I like and you can arrange it.' He added after a moment, 'Would a girl come to my tent?'

'If you wished it, she would,' said Dangoya, 'provided she is not circumcised of course. An *ndito* will go anywhere for a *moran* she likes, but a circumcised woman with her own house may not leave it to spend time with a *moran* elsewhere.' Dangoya became quite earnest, anxious to assure Sindoff that all possible care would be taken to provide him with a pleasurable companion.

'When we get back tonight you must choose an *ndito* and take her to your tent after drinking milk with her. A girl may not lie with anyone of the same clan - but you are German.'

Sindoff, not wishing either to upset Dangoya or jeopardise his future in the country by becoming involved in tribal matters, gently replied that he would think about it when the work on hand was finished. His good intentions, however, weakened that evening when he saw a girl who attracted him, and from that time on various girls visited him regularly in his tent at night.

On one of their day-long trips, Dangoya led Sindoff to the source of the other *Ngare Nairobi* river near the lip of the Ngorongoro Crater, but it was the crater itself which held Sindoff spellbound. His greying hair long and shaggy about his face, a spark of youth leaping in his eyes, he gazed at the splendour before him. His heart pounding, his breathing quickened with the altitude and the sheer joy of having found what he had been looking for, Sindoff was unable to say a word and sank to the ground, motionless and awed, to stare at the wonder of the world spread out at his feet.

He roused himself at last and gripping Dangoya's arm said urgently, 'This is the place! Down there I shall build my *manyatta* and my house!'

'I cannot take you there,' Dangoya replied reluctantly. 'This area does not come under the leadership of Olengesen and you would have to ask the permission of the Kisongo *laigwanan* at Lerai.'

'Well, go and ask him and make all the arrangements!' Sindoff's tone became arrogant and peremptory, broking no further argument.

Dangoya's temper flared, sensitive to the man's changed attitude. 'I am neither your servant nor your slave! Only when we have received payment for what we have already done, will we do any further work for you.' The German had risen, towering over the *moran*, an angry flush in his cheeks, but Dangoya stood firm. 'We have brought you all this way from Mondul, and given you our protection. Now you speak to me as if I were one of your *Olmeg* load-carriers. You have not begun to teach us the magic of your guns. We get the guns today when we go back to my *manyatta* or we will take all that is owed us by force and you will be left on your own!'

The two men glared at each other and when Sindoff saw Dangoya's grip tighten on his spear, he dropped his hand from the holster on his belt.

Now Dangoya took command and ordered an immediate return to Engaruka. They marched in silence and that evening Sindoff refused to discuss the matter, shutting himself in his tent and leaving his men to sit in nervous anxiety throughout the night beside their camp fire. There was no movement in either of the *manyattas* and an uneasy calm lay over the quiet barricaded enclosures.

In the morning Sindoff ordered his men to load the donkeys and release his cattle from their pen, and going to Dangoya's gate called to him to come and talk.

'We leave now,' Sindoff shouted, 'and when I am settled at Ngorongoro you may come to claim your due.' Dangoya made no reply, his face expressionless, stony, as the German continued. 'But if any of you attempt to follow with evil intent, we shall shoot!' He turned away and commanded his caravan to move on.

'We could kill them now!' whispered Loito. 'Look how frightened those *Olmeg* are.'

'No!' Dangoya cut in. 'Let them go. We are too few, and an attack will need to be planned. We will take our payment later.'

Dangoya moved fast in the next day and a half, eager to confront Sindoff before he reached the Kisongo *laigwanan*'s *manyatta* at Lerai. Runners had been sent to three neighbouring *manyattas* and reinforcements totalling twelve *morans* had been enlisted. Travelling very fast towards Ngorongoro, the German's tracks plain to see, they came upon them in late afternoon as the *Olmeg* were setting up camp. Leaving his main body hidden, Dangoya approached Sindoff quite openly, flanked by Lengerebe, Loito and Suyanga, all of whom Sindoff knew well.

'We have come for our payment,' Dangoya called pleasantly. 'We completed our side of the bargain and are now due our guns and the other things you promised us.'

Sindoff was no fool and precisely five minutes before the *morans* stepped to within two hundred yards of his camp his lookout, perched high in a tree, had sent back a warning messenger, so he knew a sizeable force had come to attack him. 'Get back,' he cried, 'or you will be shot! I told you to come when my *manyatta* was built and not before!'

'You have broken your word,' Dangoya shouted, not believing Sindoff's threat, but the German drew his revolver and fired above their heads. With a cold tremor of fear Dangoya swung away and ran, followed by the other three.

The hidden *morans*, hearing the shot, broke cover and swooped on the camp, but before they had a chance to attack with their spears, the *Olmeg* had opened fire with their rifles. In a frieze of shocked, arrested movement, the *morans* saw two of their number fall, great holes of bloody bone and matter flowing down their straight brown backs. Seeing their indecision, Sindoff halted the fire and when Dangoya shouted for them to flee, they obeyed and ran swiftly from the scene.

When all was once more quiet, Sindoff walked over to where the dead *morans* lay, a feeling of great sadness sweeping over him, and a tiny nagging alarm. He stared down at the naked, lean young bodies, distorted now in death. 'You poor reckless fools,' he said, and scuffed the fallen leaves that littered the ground about their heads with his boot.

Dangoya brooded over his defeat, consumed by a frustrated anger which he communicated only to Lengerebe. The other *morans* had gone their separate ways, the incident not forgotten but philosophically assigned to the past, their sights aimed at new exciting events in the future, their tale of the rout near Ngorongoro embellished to the point where not one but ten white men had fired with guns the size of cannon.

The rains came, changing the dry, parched land, giving colour to the pale yellows and browns, bringing in the many shades of green and brightening the watered plains and hills with wild flowers in splashes of vivid red and blue. The herds followed the grass and the clansmen tended their wealth, content with the goodness of *Ngai*; and when the last showers had fallen and the grass lost its sweetness, they retreated to their dry-season grazing where the cattle would be sustained but not fattened, there to wait for the next rains. Then with the first cold winds of the dry season, when a man shivered in the bright sunlight and sought the shelter of a tree or the warmth of the protected side of an anthill, Dangoya said one day to Lengerebe, 'walk with me, my friend,' and they strolled on past the *layonis* guarding the cattle.

'You may have heard,' Dangoya said carefully, 'that the Europeans are looking for men to train as warriors, to use their guns.'

'Yes, I have heard.' He could tell nothing from Dangoya's still profile.

'If we, you and I together, went to New Larusa and offered ourselves as warriors, then the white men would teach us how to fire the guns.'

'That is true.' Lengerebe knew now what was coming next.

'We are not stupid, you and I, and when we had learnt everything we would each have a gun.'

Lengerebe began to laugh. '*Bagishu*, we shall go to New Larusa whenever you say! And we shall wear those funny head-dresses and wind our legs around with stuff.'

Although he grinned, Dangoya said, 'I am serious. We leave in two day's time.'

At the District Office, built like a fort, the recruiting officer looked in some surprise at the two *morans* before him. Their hair, thick, matted and plastered with red ochre, sat like helmets on their heads, pigtails tied to stick frames hanging low on their necks. They stood each on one leg, nonchalantly leaning on their spears, and said through the interpreter that they wished to be warriors of the Great Chief Kaiser from over the Big Water.

Behind the officer stood a very young lieutenant, still pink and fresh to Africa, whose eyes boggled slightly at the bareness of the *morans*, and when Lengerebe caught this look he casually swung his *ngelan* over his shoulder, leaving himself completely exposed. 'Look how big his eyes become – seeing my *njabo*, *Bagishu*. Now he can see what *morans* we are!'

'Stop that!' the interpreter said sharply. 'You must show these *laigwanans* great respect.'

'His *njabo* must have a foreskin that reaches to his knees, and when he pulls it back the smell is enough to make the hyena vomit.'

Dangoya grinned at Lengerebe's remark.

'What are they talking about?' the .recruiting officer asked.

'Sir, they enquire about how soon they can start their training.' The interpreter shot them a quelling glare.

'Good,' the officer said, 'it shows they must feel keen.' He looked at the two *morans* who gazed back at him indolently. 'Though I must say they do not look very keen. We should not really take the one who has lost his eye, but I imagine he will come in useful for tracking.' He gestured to the interpreter. 'Tell them now about the army.'

'If you wish to become soldiers you will have to learn many things. You will eat the food you are given which will not be milk and blood as you are used to, but maize meal and other foods. Your heads will be shaved and you will wash with soap and water, and wear the clothes of the army. You will learn Kiswahili and obey orders from *Olmeg* soldiers who are senior to you. If called upon to go to places other than Masai country, you will have to do so, and may even have to fight Masai people if necessary.' He paused, half expecting some response, but when there was none he continued.

'If a soldier disobeys orders he may be whipped or even shot. You will live with men of other tribes and be treated exactly like them - what you Masai call *Olmeg*.' Again the interpreter waited, knowing the Masai scorn for all other tribes, but they seemed to accept the idea with equanimity. 'When you have finished your training you will be issued with guns and given rupees every month.' Now at last he saw a spark of interest.

'You are not lying about the guns and the rupees?' Dangoya asked.

'No, I am not lying. You may go and think about it, and if you still want to be German soldiers come back tomorrow and the officers will take you.'

'We do not want to come back tomorrow,' Dangoya replied, 'we are here today and are ready to do everything you say, but if we go - we will not come back.'

This exchange was repeated to the officer who thought for a moment then said, through the interpreter, 'You say you are a *laigwanan* of your age-group?'

'Yes, I am.'

'Why then do you not return to your home and bring back with you all your *morans*. You can then join forces with my men and go raiding for cattle which we can then share between us.'

Dangoya replied with some disdain. 'I have many cattle and do not require more. I would in any case prefer to go raiding on my own and would never share the stock taken.' He spat eloquently. 'We are here to learn how to use your guns and to fight in your army, otherwise we shall return to our *manyattas*.'

'What about your *morans*? Why have they not come with you?'

'They will come, once we have the gun and can use it with your powers.'

The officer looked hard at both *morans*, then turning to the interpreter said, 'They will do. I shall enlist them today.'

242

To begin with Dangoya and Lengerebe, intrigued by all they saw and learnt, their obsession to use a firearm uppermost in their minds, took the hard life and discipline in their stride and settled down to the rigours of being part of an organised force. They became fluent in Kiswahili and both excelled in rifle drill. It was then, after ten months training when their proficiency in marksmanship satisfied not only themselves but their officers too, that they both began to find the way of life and the discipline extremely irksome and applied for leave. They did not intend to return.

Leave was granted on condition that they brought back recruits from amongst the *morans*, and both were promised promotion, but permission to take their rifles with them was flatly refused. All they could do was pretend to agree to bring as many *morans* as they could and be in the barracks on the date specified.

They had learnt the white man's magic and although they had been unlucky about obtaining guns, somehow they would lay their hands on them. Part of their objective had been achieved and they set off for home in high humour, thoughts of family and friends lengthening their strides as they passed over the plains in the heat of the approaching rain.

Chapter 16

The Enemy

The *manyattas* of Olengesen and Dangoya had moved to Lobo on the northern edge of *Serenget*, an area of vast flat plain broken by rocky outcrops where little hyrax sunned themselves on the great slabs of stone, quickly disappearing when their domain was invaded by sleepy, indolent families of lion who used their vantage points to survey the herds of grazing game.

For one full season the two returned *morans* basked in their new-found notoriety, discarding their European clothes and regaling the others with tales of their experiences, their fame enhanced from time to time by news that the Germans were looking for them, which in no way bothered either of them. Cut off as they were from the south where the Germans were very active, and from the north where the British listened anxiously to the rumblings of war in Europe, they continued to lead their normal lives, tending their large herds of cattle and making periodic visits to other areas.

Further afield than usual at Lengkito, not far from where the *moran manyatta* had been and where they had spent their happy training days as new *morans*, both men were recognised by an army patrol. Placed under arrest they were marched to New Larusa and given twenty five strokes with a rhino whip, then sent off to Moshi. There they were made to work as prisoners with a building gang, and their hands, muscles and minds - unaccustomed to any manual labour - created new agonies which they had neither the forbearance nor the discipline to withstand. However, as a not unsympathetic corporal told them, they were indeed lucky not to have been shot as deserters, for the army was eager for recruits and men such as they who had completed their training might quite well be given the opportunity of rejoining the German forces. It was this possible chance which helped them survive the hard work of the construction gang and having been exemplary prisoners they were at last freed and sent back to New Larusa and the ranks of the army.

'*Aish!*' said Lengerebe. 'That was a bad day for us at Lengkito. If you had two eyes they would not have recognised us.'

'That is true my friend, but it is of no use to cry now. The Germans say if there is war and the British win, we shall lose our cattle and be slaves.' Dangoya frowned. 'Better this - to fight for the Germans.'

With this previous experience standing them in good stead, Dangoya and Lengerebe quickly settled to the discipline and ordered life of the army, rapidly outshining the other recruits, and were eventually sent on active service with their new platoon under a Lieutenant Hendik. This young German was well liked by his troops, having a reputation for being fair but strict, and a friendship of sorts sprang up between him and Dangoya when the *moran* agreed to teach him to speak Masai.

At Mondul Dangoya was promoted to corporal and given the task of training new Masai recruits for the first three months after enlistment before being sent on to New Larusa, or Arusha as it became known. War was declared and Lieutenant Hendik was transferred together with the Mondul contingent, leaving behind only Dangoya and half a dozen new soldiers, with Lengerebe to assist him. Another German officer arrived with twenty men from the Mbulu tribe and a new platoon was formed, the little force together with wives and assorted camp followers moving first to Sonjo then to Olgosorok, which was to be known as Loliondo, close to the newly drawn border between British and German territory.

Among the Mbulu was a Sergeant Quatlema who was hostile towards the Masai under his command, going out of his way to make them appear stupid. This was made easy for him as all the Mbulu men were soldiers of at least a year's service, with a degree of sophistication which left the naturally gregarious and boastful Masai with nothing to say for themselves. The Mbulu soldiers had travelled fairly extensively and spoke loftily of the sights they had seen, from the Big Water in the east to the inland sea in the north. To make matters worse the Masai recruits could not yet understand Kiswahili and were inclined to take orders only from Dangoya or Lengerebe, rather than from the sergeant. The German lieutenant had been joined by a senior non-commissioned officer, a Sergeant Zeiss, and these two Europeans gave Dangoya no opportunity to approach them directly with the problems faced by the Masai troops.

Out on patrol one day Sergeant Quatlema with one of his tribesmen and two raw Masai recruits stopped at a *manyatta* for the night. On hearing that the British had passed through a matter of a few days before, paying well for the ox they had requested, the sergeant demanded a goat for which he refused to pay, then that drink and women be produced for his men. When the Masai soldiers refused to arrange for these comforts, they were placed under arrest and marched back to Loliondo where they were subjected to twenty four strokes for disobeying orders. They were given no chance to state their case and dissatisfaction among the Masai grew, spreading quickly to nearby *manyattas* where the news that the *Olmeg* in the German army, aided and abetted by the Germans themselves, were abusing and maltreating the Masai troops.

Dangoya knew the situation could now only deteriorate and his fears were confirmed when Quatlema, together with a friend, wandered off duty into a *manyatta* and ordered the company of two girls. Incensed, a group of *morans* set upon them and it was only the fortunate arrival of Dangoya and Lengerebe which averted bloodshed and worse. Fighting beside the

Mbulu at the risk of their own lives they managed to extricate themselves, Lengerebe knocking unconscious a *moran* about to spear the sergeant.

The incident had brought the matter to a head and the Germans found they had no other recourse than to investigate the whole affair. The lieutenant congratulated Dangoya and Lengerebe for their loyalty and quick action and was about to despatch them both to bring in the offending *morans*, when word came that a large British force was advancing on Loliondo.

All tribal differences were swept away as the army prepared to halt the enemy, other units arriving from the west to reinforce the position at Loliondo. Reports of the British movements were received two or three times a day and it became clear that their intention was to march on Sonjo, passing to the east of Loliondo unless harassed. Dangoya and his Masai soldiers under the command of Sergeant Zeiss were detailed to set up an ambush on a well-worn cattle and game track with a view to turning the enemy advance westwards through the Loliondo forest and thus into the arms of the main German force. This they succeeded in doing without loss, but killing and wounding a number of the British troops, and having swiftly removed themselves from the scene, they doubled back and joined the main contingent.

Elated, adrenalin running high through their veins, Dangoya and the Masai soldiers enjoyed their first success. It was the type of guerrilla warfare they all understood and this initial encounter encouraged and gave them tremendous confidence, earning the approval of the German officers who found themselves surprisingly impressed with the dash and bravery shown by the young *morans*.

For two full days the British made no move, but on the third morning began their advance down the valley. German snipers started firing at midday and by late afternoon had pinned the enemy down, their casualties seemingly heavy. The German commander had achieved his objective and ordered his main force to retire, leaving Dangoya with six men to hold the British down during their retreat. The withdrawal had barely begun when firing from the rear was heard and Sergeant Zeiss crawled up beside Dangoya to tell him they were surrounded and that their platoon lieutenant had been killed.

'I will send you a few extra men to keep this position, but do not fire unless the enemy show themselves clearly. In the meantime think of how we can get out of this when it becomes dark.'

Zeiss crept away and Dangoya took a quick look at his men. The machine-gunner, his shoulder smashed in the last few minutes, lay behind the cover of a rock and Dangoya motioned to Lengerebe to take over and operate the gun.

'Do not fire, *Bagishu*, and give away the gun's position unless they get too close.'

Just before dark a bayonet charge was launched by the British and would have succeeded had Lengerebe not held his fire until the enemy were close upon him in the confines of the narrow valley. The target loomed large in his sights and he began firing, mowing down the advancing troops in a bloody swathe, their screams and shouts clear through the clatter of the gun.

As the British hesitated and reformed in retreat, Sergeant Zeiss appeared again beside Dangoya. 'Now!' said the Sergeant, 'While the light goes fast and in the confusion we must leave. The machine-gun will cover our retreat. Every man must go barefoot, every man.'

The German withdrawal was led by Dangoya with Zeiss bringing up the rear. They filtered through the encircling British and in silence moved through the lower forest of Loliondo towards Waso. Shots still rang out as the British fired at shadows, and Dangoya was not too certain that he had not heard Lengerebe's machine-gun on single fire, but he dismissed this as being unlikely.

The German commander and his officers were very pleased with the manner in which they had extricated themselves from a nasty predicament without attracting attention from the enemy, nor were their casualties high. They had stopped to assess their numbers and to congratulate each other, and Zeiss, unexpectedly hearing the scornful snort of Quatlema beside him, knew he, too, realised it was Dangoya's skill which had brought them safely out of range of the enemy.

At that moment Dangoya himself walked up to Zeiss. 'Lengerebe, his machine-gun and the ammunition carriers have not appeared.' He knew it was no good asking for permission to go back to look for Lengerebe, so he tried another tack. 'That gun saved our lives today and it would be foolish to leave it behind. I volunteer to go and fetch it.'

He sensed the two men's doubt when neither answered and quickly added, 'I shall take a man who is half Ndorobo with me. He is so secret a tracker he can walk between the legs of an elephant and not be noticed.'

'All right,' Sergeant Zeiss agreed. 'But we cannot wait for you. You will have to make your own way to the ford on the Waso. I shall leave some porters there in the morning to help you if you have been successful.'

Dangoya and the young *moran* whose mother had been an Ndorobo, stripped and handed over their guns and equipment to the rest of the party. Silently, they disappeared into the forest, making for the scene of the day's battle. Moving with stealth they neared the enemy, their inbred bushcraft guiding them through the difficult terrain with precision and delicacy, and Dangoya sent the *moran* ahead to pinpoint the exact positions of the British sentries. He was back within a short time.

'Lengerebe is dead,' he whispered, 'But the gun is still there. The sentries on this side appear to be asleep and most of the force has moved off across the valley.'

Dangoya received the news with numbing shock, unable to truly believe until he had seen and touched his friend's body. Together he and the *moran* slipped through the dark night and reached the machine-gun, the barrel now as cold as the man who lay beside it. Silently Dangoya cursed the British and swore he would make them pay for this death, even if it killed him to do so. The two ammunition carriers were also dead, and not twenty feet from the gun lay the bodies of the British troops, cut down as they swarmed in attack.

Back from scouting higher up the hill, the young *moran* reported that he could account for all their missing men except for one, who might quite well have got away on his own. 'Two are still alive but unable to walk. We will have to leave them,' he said.

With frightening clarity Dangoya remembered how he too could have been left for dead so long ago, yet Lengerebe had dragged and carried him to safety.

'No! We will take them one by one as far as we can, then hide them until we can return with the porters.'

But when, in the pitch black of the night with even the faint starlight reduced by cloud, he touched the first wounded man, his hands passing quickly over the body feeling the wet coils of the man's guts strewn on the ground at his side, he knew it was hopeless to think of moving him.

The other man was still conscious, the wound in his shoulder oozing blood.

'Can you walk a little if we help you?' Dangoya whispered.

The answer was faint, and Dangoya and the *moran* got the soldier to his feet, one on either side. Half-carrying him, they led him away from the carnage of the battle, settling him as comfortably as they could in a thicket while they went back to bring out the machine-gun.

By dawn, exhausted and hungry, both the wounded man and the gun having been brought as far as the ford, Dangoya and the *moran* sat recovering their breath while the porters moved on toward Waso with their burdens. Now with time to think, the shock of Lengerebe's death hit Dangoya hard and with his head bent on his folded arms, knees pulled up, he allowed himself a few tears for his dead friend.

The Masai troops had acquitted themselves so well during the battle at Loliondo that they found the men of other tribes amongst the soldiers treating them with a new respect. Sergeant Quatlema, in particular, was quick to extend the hand of friendship to Dangoya, realising only too well how the fast-reacting Masai had been instrumental in leading them from defeat. Nor had he forgotten the debacle in the *manyatta*.

Bivouacked for many days at Waso after the main German force had left, news of what the British were doing was uncertain. The new lieutenant assigned to the platoon sent out parties to bring in cattle from neighbouring *manyattas* and this, more than any other thing, brought together the various tribesmen in a common distaste for their overlords. Not only was the slaughter of cattle indiscriminate - it was unpaid for. On the surreptitious advice of Dangoya the Masai civilians began to move away from the area, driving before them their precious herds of stock, speaking with disdain of the Germans as the *lameyu* - the disease. This meant the army having to go further afield to search for meat and if word of Dangoya's actions had reached the German officers, he would have been shot.

After ten days they received a report that the British had reached Sonjo, and that fighting was taking place at Ikoma to the north west of *Serenget*. As the nearest German settlement was at Ngorongoro, in the crater, the decision was made to march there as quickly as possible. As soon as Dangoya heard of the impending move, he sent warning to the *manyattas* there that the *lameyu* was on its way, and this was sufficient for the *laigwanans* to remove their people and herds from the greedy clutches of the German army, for now they were not only slaughtering animals but destroying what they could not use, fearful of leaving food in any form for the enemy.

As the Masai stock vanished the Germans resorted to shooting game, but stocks of maize meal, sugar and tea were running short. This was no disaster for the Masai troops who were quite happy to live on meat alone, but the *Olmeg* soldiers and porters found their enforced diet insufficient for their needs, used as they were to filling their bellies with great quantities of meal.

Dangoya, born and bred in the area, was continually consulted as they went south. He would be sent too to make contact with Masai espied from a distance, in ones or twos as they passed by on their own business. Because of his one eye Dangoya was always recognised and the Masai would talk with him, but if they observed other German soldiers approaching they would take to their heels, for the Germans had also gained a reputation for rounding up tribesmen for forced labour. Dangoya became adept at inventing reasons for not bringing in the lone Masai travellers - they had come from a *manyatta* struck down by disease, or were lame and halt - and according to his reports the herds of Masailand were disappearing fast because of *rinderpest* and other dreaded sicknesses.

At Olalaa there were two *manyattas* belonging to Dangoya's foster-father, father of his old enemy Pushati, with most of the people there related too to Bareto. Dangoya therefore deliberately sent no warning of the army's approach and both *manyattas* were quickly surrounded. Dangoya thought too it was time the Masai soldiers had some fresh milk and female company to cheer them up as the camp followers, mostly married women, declined to be generous with their favours. So Dangoya joined in the selection of two good beasts for slaughter with military thoroughness, being of course recognised and received in hostile silence.

Making camp beside the river, the Germans sent for the *laigwanan* Dangoya's foster-father - and another elder. They were told to give orders to their people to produce fresh milk both morning and evening, and that the cattle were not to be released for grazing in the morning without permission from the officers. Failing this they would both be shot.

Strangely, hearing these harsh commands, Dangoya felt a sudden pity for the two old men and later approached Sergeant Zeiss, asking him to arrange the freeing of the elders and to see that no further stock was slaughtered on the grounds that this was his father's *manyatta*.

'I will guarantee that none of these animals falls into the hands of the enemy,' he promised, and Zeiss after looking at him hard said he would speak to the lieutenant.

The elders were paraded before the officer and told they would be released and that no more cattle would be taken because their son Dangoya, a good German soldier, had said these *manyattas* were friendly towards the Germans and could be relied upon to keep their stock well away from the British. The elders thanked the lieutenant politely and were later advised by Dangoya to give two more oxen to the army to carry away with them on their journey to Ngorongoro. 'In this way you will get rid of us more quickly and be left in peace. '

That evening milk was brought in *calabashes* to the army camp and the Masai soldiers were given permission to sleep in the *manyattas*. The old *laigwanan* sent for Dangoya and offered him honey beer.

'I have waited long,' he said, 'to show you my friendship and to give you my apology for the behaviour of my relatives. When you are finished with this fighting for the white men and come home, I shall hold a meeting at which a public confession will be made, exposing the wrongs that have been done to you by members of my family.'

'My father speaks good words to me.' Dangoya noticed how thin and wrinkled the *laigwanan* had become and thought fleetingly of his mother. Then with a sudden surge of longing he remembered Muriet too and the yearning became an ache in his belly, localising, drawn to a more physical desire. So it was with a rueful regret that he thought again of Muriet in the morning when his needs had been soothed and washed away by a girl from the *manyatta*.

Dangoya and the other *moran* soldiers had noticed that a large number of the girls, women and some of the elders too wore their hair long, and they wondered what sickness could have afflicted them for all looked healthy. With disquiet they heard it was *olmerega* - syphilis - a disease prevalent in the south among the Arabs and in the north among the Indian railway workers.

'Nothing is the same these days,' the *laigwanan* complained. 'We seem still to suffer the anger of *Ngai*.'

'It may be *Ngai*'s intent to punish us,' agreed Dangoya, 'but also there is much movement of people from one country to the next, and we have allowed too many strangers to pass among us.'

Within three days they reached Ngorongoro and Dangoya was immediately recognised by Sindoff, the big man moving impulsively towards him, hand outstretched and all past grievances forgotten. Sindoff knew the Masai people too well to think Dangoya would harbour a grudge against him and he was right, for Dangoya grinned and clapped him on the back.

'When are you going to pay me my debt?' As far as Dangoya was concerned, what has been was over and done with and he gave it no further thought. 'I can shoot better than you now,' he said, and Sindoff threw back his big unruly head and laughed, calling out in German to the European officers, letting them in on the joke.

Orders to escort Sindoff and all his cattle to Mbulu awaited them at Ngorongoro, a considerable task as his herds now numbered about fifteen hundred head. The animals were far larger than the Masai stock due to upgrading with imported bulls, but had lost much of their inbred hardiness and resistance to local diseases. At first Dangoya and the other Masai were very impressed by the cattle which seemed so big boned and fat, with good-sized udders showing on the cows, but once on the move they proved to be poor performers, lagging behind, going lame and some collapsing with fatigue and unable to make the long distances between watering points.

No one was allowed to touch any of the animals that died, nor were any slaughtered for food; and when at Endabesh the soldiers were ordered to acquire eight head from the Barabaig tribe by force, Dangoya could not help but think how unfair were the methods of the army. However, as he had learnt so well to do, he kept his mouth shut and did as he was told. Sindoff's cattle continued to succumb to disease and exhaustion, and by the time they reached Mbulu the animals were dying off like flies.

There was a small body of troops at Mbulu under an officer and a German sergeant, with men drawn from the Nyeramba, Ufiomi and Mbulu tribes and two Wanyamwezi instructors. Most were newly enlisted men and none had seen any action with the exception of the officers. Together with the contingent from the north, the force was formed into one unit of two sections, each under the command of a German sergeant. Dangoya was promoted to sergeant under Zeiss while Quatlema moved to the other section.

A fort had been built at Mbulu, very like the one at Arusha, which housed the Administration offices as well as the private quarters of the

German administrator. There were half a dozen or so white civilians in the area too, either settlers or traders, all of whom came under military jurisdiction and could be called upon to take up arms when required. One of these, a Greek trader, always moved conveniently into the bush at the first signs of military activity, re-appearing when the dust of battle had subsided and joining whichever side had won supremacy and held power at Mbulu at the time.

Being of equal rank, Dangoya and Quatlema fell into a friendship of convenience and shared experience, speaking Mbulu to each other which Dangoya picked up with ease. As none of the Masai troops took their women with them on their moves with the army, Quatlema obliged Dangoya by producing a girl for him, his own full sister. Like most Mbulu women she was exceedingly good looking, with small, fine features, slender-boned and pale-skinned. In so many ways she reminded Dangoya of Muriet, and from their first meeting he had lost his heart to her.

To formalise the arrangement so as to allow the girl to live with Dangoya in the barracks, an Mbulu marriage ceremony took place with drink and food, and an agreement on Dangoya's part to pay an agreed number of cattle to Quatlema's father as soon as the war was over. Dangoya was led by his new brother-in-law to the girl's hut where she lay on the bridal bed, beads from around her neck lying on her breasts, and with a beautiful skirt of soft, pale calfskin almost entirely covered with tiny beads sewn on in intricate designs. Quatlema leaned over to untie the leather fastenings, exposing the slim, nubile body of his sister and Dangoya caught his breath at the loveliness of the girl, feeling an arousal such as he had only felt with Muriet.

Forcing the girl's legs apart, holding them in that position, Quatlema turned to Dangoya and asked as Mbulu custom dictated, 'Are you satisfied with your purchase?'

'Yes!' cried Dangoya impatiently, and waited for Quatlema to leave.

The British attacked Mbulu late one afternoon and the German army was forced to evacuate under cover of darkness. Within two days the enemy mounted a follow-up campaign, heading for Basoto in which direction they believed the Germans to have fled. By one of those bizarre freaks of war, it was Sindoff - still moving south with his depleted herd - who lost his all. On hearing that the British were behind him and thinking he was the object of their hot pursuit, he drove the miserable remnants of his herd, with patriotic zeal, over a precipice and into the depths of one of the ferrous-reddened Basoto lakes, giving rise later to the legend that it was the blood of the cattle which had turned the water permanently red. To the Barabaig tribesmen in the area the lake became forever taboo and the story of the big German was enshrined in their tribal history.

While the British thundered on towards the south, the German unit from Mbulu went into the forest at Murai, worked their way back to the north then re-formed to the east of Mbulu before swooping down on the handful of men left by the British to recapture the fort. They were, however, completely cut off from the rest of the German army far to the south, but due to the British custom of not laying waste an evacuated territory, food was plentiful and the unit spent a peaceful time recruiting and training new soldiers. This pleasant existence ended abruptly when the British once more attacked the station and the German troops fled as before into the forest, there to wait until the British reduced their garrison, before attempting a come-back.

A new element arose to increase the unit's isolation. The local population, sick of the constant interruptions to the order of their daily lives, began to feel a greater sympathy for the British whom they found to be less strict and demanding than the Germans. Several Mbulu soldiers deserted during the long uncomfortable nights, fleeing from what they could only see as a lost cause.

A shortage of food added to their problems as careless raiding forays might lead to their discovery, so they were continually on the move. Dangoya grew disgusted by the raids on the local people, and the destruction of their granaries when all that could be carried was first removed, sneaking away to new hiding places along the wall of the Rift Valley. The burning of good grazing land, the pastoralist in Dangoya found totally abhorrent, along with the senseless killing of stock - all carried out to prevent the British laying their hands on any form of sustenance - turned his stomach. He resolved that he would, somehow, leave this unrewarding life behind.

One day while out seeking food for his men in the Dongobesh area, Dangoya came across Quatlema on a similar exercise. They spoke about the unfriendliness of the people although they were Mbulu and Quatlema's own tribe. Many had already fled the region, seeking peace to the south and west.

'You must be thinking the way I am thinking, my brother,' said

Dangoya. 'May I speak without my words being spread by the winds?'

'You are my true brother! Have you not married my sister, and have you not saved my life? Speak what you will and my tongue will be as though it had been cut off when we leave here.'

Dangoya hesitated, uncertain, then blurted out his thoughts of desertion. 'I am now a senior *moran* and it is time I went home to take over the leadership of my *manyatta*.'

To his relief Quatlema said he too had ideas of deserting. 'But it would not be easy for me. My home is too near the fort at Mbulu. The Germans would soon find me and I should be shot as other deserters were after the last reoccupation.' He scratched his head and frowned. 'Do you believe these tales that the Germans are beaten, that the main army has already fled over the Big Water?'

'I do not know what to believe!' Dangoya was impatient. 'I tell you, my brother, you could come with me to Masailand. We can take some of your family and my wife - your sister - will look after the women.'

'You cannot take my sister with you.' Quatlema's flat denial hit Dangoya like a whiplash. 'You have not paid for her!'

'The bride-price for her shall be the beginnings of your new herd in Masailand!'

'No,' Quatlema's voice rose in anger. 'My sister cannot leave Mbulu. And as you have not paid for her, she is not your wife!'

Quatlema's sudden change of attitude beyond all the bounds of reason shattered Dangoya's composure and his temper flared. Had the Mbulu not been quick enough to see it coming, he would have been struck by Dangoya's rifle. The men parted without another word and went to oversee their troops.

That evening when both parties camped together, Dangoya sounded out two of the Masai from Quatlema's section - the only Masai in that section still remaining, and both young men Dangoya had known since they were boys. They said they were tired of the army and wanted to go home, and agreed to desert with him. A meeting was arranged for two days' time close to Mbulu where Dangoya's wife had been left with her family after the German withdrawal.

Dangoya had no intention of going without his wife, and that night as he tried to sleep, thinking of her, he knew he could not give her up. He could not remove her by force, although he was certain she would go wherever he wished to take her. Her brother, her family and friends would never permit her departure without a fight, so he might have to rely on the *morans* for assistance.

The two sections went their respective ways the next morning, and the following day Quatlema found the two *morans* missing, and a Munyamwezi corporal gone too. He was not anxious about the corporal, although he pretended great concern, for he had sent the man himself to make a report to the Lieutenant, informing him that Dangoya intended deserting. The Munyamwezi, however, had other plans. He had always held Dangoya in high regard and now travelled with the two Masai to the meeting place at Endegikot.

The night was dark and overcast with a persistent drizzle which made the path slippery, and by dawn Dangoya had not made as much progress as he had hoped towards Mbulu. He was cold, wet and exhausted, and all he desired was a warm hut and something to eat, but the country was bare of human habitation and he could expect to see no one until he reached Tlawi. Game was plentiful, but he dared not use the gun to shoot; then he suddenly remembered he was no longer in the army and need account to no one for the ammunition used. Choosing his prey with care, he downed an impala and having carried the carcass to a rocky outcrop, he made a fire which thoroughly warmed his body as he skinned the animal. After eating pieces of half-cooked liver and leaving the rest of the meat to cook slowly over the embers, he drew up his knees, cradled his head in his arms, and quickly fell asleep.

He woke to a cold sensation of fear and a low growling and snapping as three hyena tussled over the remains of the impala. A fourth stood eyeing him, its grotesque, smelly body far too close, its malevolent stare horrifying to the man sitting vulnerable and not fully awake. Sliding his arm out to his rifle, his eye never leaving the hyena for one instant, he saw the other three alerted by his movement and all four inched closer. It was clear from their intent expressions and the raised hackles running the length of their backs, that they meant business and would not be shooed away. He knew only too well that there were few animals more frightening than a hyena when roused, and that his position was precarious. Unless he acted fast and with precision, these obscene killers of the bush would tear him apart in seconds, mangling his flesh and crushing his bones to nothing.

257

Not waiting to lift the rifle more than an inch or two from the ground, Dangoya fired. The bullet whined amongst the rocks, but in the flurry of the hyenas' startled departure he was able to take aim and drop one. That was sufficient warning for the remaining three which slouched away to take cover in the bush at the base of the outcrop.

The incident had been enough to remind Dangoya that he was not yet safe in Masailand and should not be moving about on his own in strange country where both animals and circumstances were different. The rain had stopped and with full daylight he was able to walk fast, sweating as the clouds dispersed and the sun shone hotly on his back. As he passed Lake Tlawi, the water cool and fresh, he thought how good it would be to move the lake to *Serenget*, or Lobo, or anywhere in Masailand where the grass was sweet but where there was never sufficient water.

At the far end of the lake he saw a few head of small Mbulu cattle and he approached with caution, but on seeing only three herdsmen he walked up to them boldly and asked for news of the fort at Mbulu. The British were still in control, they told him; and when he enquired how they liked the enemy, could see at once their reluctance to answer a soldier in German uniform.

'You can speak to me,' he said, 'I am deserting the army and going home.'

His words made them a little more forthcoming and he heard the usual story of the British being preferred as they took only what they needed and paid always in full.

'But it is confusing,' the oldest of the men said, 'because the British troops come from other tribes far to the north, yet the German army consists mainly of our own people. We wish they would all go away and fight somewhere else.'

Another man spoke. 'You would be unwise to go any further in those clothes. Many men have deserted and gone home, but if the Germans find them they are shot, so let us give you something else to wear.'

Speaking their language, Dangoya had successfully passed himself off as one of them, come to collect his bride before leaving for home, and now as he accompanied them as they drove their cattle along, he gave private thanks to his short-lived friendship with Quatlema.

The Mbulus' house was built into the side of a hill, the entrance looking like a small landslide, and apart from the bare ground of the path leading into it, scuffed by the hooves of the stock as they came and went, nothing in the vicinity had been disturbed and the camouflage was perfect. The Mbulu tribe had been forced, together with their cattle, to live underground by the Barabaig and the Masai whose continual raids made thorn enclosures impossible to protect. Had the Mbulu herdsmen known Dangoya was a Masai, he would not have been helped.

Now dressed in a long robe of skins, his rifle and ammunition hidden beneath the folds, he set off for Mbulu and reached the house of his wife's family as darkness fell. His welcome seemed genuine enough and the girl herself was very happy to see him again, pressing food and drink on him with loving attention. When he had eaten, the members of the girl's family left them alone, but they had barely departed when she moved close to him and in whispers told him she knew he was going away.

'I know, because my brother has sent word of your intentions and has made arrangements to stop me going with you.' She shuddered and hid her face in his shoulder so he had to lift her chin to hear her next words. 'He has also sent a message to the British, to inform them you are here to fight them. He wants you killed!' Her voice broke and her eyes filled with tears. 'You must go now before they find you!' She clung to him as she sobbed, and as Dangoya tried to comfort her his mind swung to survival and what his next move should be.

'You must go,' she repeated. 'You can come to fetch me later when they no longer seek you. Not only me, but also the child I am carrying.'

Suddenly at the door there was a request for entry and to Dangoya's surprise his two *morans* and the Munyamwezi corporal came in.

'You must move from this house at once,' the corporal said. The British are out looking for you now and we risked much to come and warn you.'

'This place is well hidden,' Dangoya said calmly. 'To strangers it is no different from a cave. I intend to sleep here tonight and leave in the morning.' He had complete contempt for the fighting ability of the British troops and refused to give way. With some anxiety the others left to find sleeping places in an adjoining house.

That night, close to the girl he had grown to love, Dangoya slept fitfully; dreams of Lengerebe, his mother and the great laughing Lesirwa invaded his short moments of sleep so he became impatient for the morning, for action, for the walk home and the new plans that would have to be laid.

At first light the four men passed as shadows from Mbulu, the whitewashed fort gleaming palely far to the south as they set their faces for home. An elation filled Dangoya, a longing for the sights and smells of his own country to spend his days with his herds, to drink again the blood of his steers and the sweet milk of his cows; to see the *morans* pick up their spears and go to battle with laughter high in their throats, no terrible pillaging, burning and destruction as the white men conducted their wars, no crying when the fight was lost, no shame felt if a better man won. He yearned too for the boys and girls of his *manyatta*, their heads bent to receive the touch of greeting; the singing of the women with their cows and the considered scrutiny of the elders as they sent the cattle out in the mornings, following at their own slow pace to spend their days in the shade of a tree. And he thought of the long days on the plains guiding the cattle to the good grass, leading them to water, the drive on to fresh pastures, and the ceaseless movement of nomadic life across the endless savannas.

'Halt or we shoot!' a voice rang out.

With jarring shock Dangoya saw the enemy uniforms and the raised guns, and he trembled with an uncontrollable anger and frustration.

'We shall never stop!' he yelled and lunged forward, desperate to reach the safety of a tree on the path ahead.

'Your guns cannot touch us, you useless sons of pigs! Come on!' he urged his men. 'Fight them back! Fight the *narobong gotonye!*'

Dangoya ran as a man possessed, the bullets thick and fast about him. Three more paces to go, he thought, and I shall have cover.

Then his brain exploded and he fell headlong, the warrior son of the Loitayo clan, lying slain on the alien soil of the Mbulu tribe, the scars of the vultures of long ago erased forever by the explosion in his head of that fatal bullet.

Nena age

Printed in Great Britain
by Amazon